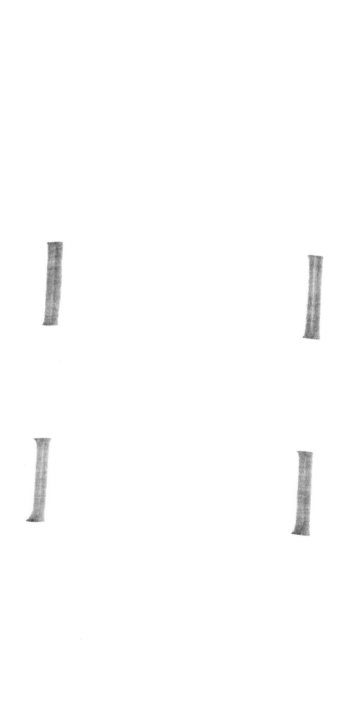

THE ONE-EYED MAN

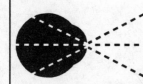

This Large Print Book carries the
Seal of Approval of N.A.V.H.

THE ONE-EYED MAN

RON CURRIE

THORNDIKE PRESS
A part of Gale, a Cengage Company

A Cengage Company

Farmington Hills, Mich • San Francisco • New York • Waterville, Maine
Meriden, Conn • Mason, Ohio • Chicago

LIBRARY OF CONGRESS CATALOGING-IN-PUBLICATION DATA

Names: Currie, Ron, 1975– author.
Title: The one-eyed man / by Ron Currie.
Description: Large print edition. | Waterville, Maine : Thorndike Press, a part of Gale, Cengage Learning, 2017. | Series: Thorndike Press large print Bill's bookshelf
Identifiers: LCCN 2017014177| ISBN 9781432841393 (hardcover) | ISBN 1432841394 (hardcover)
Subjects: LCSH: Large type books. | BISAC: FICTION / Literary. | FICTION / Satire. | FICTION / Family Life. | GSAFD: Satire.
Classification: LCC PS3603.U774 O54 2017b | DDC 813/.6—dc23
LC record available at https://lccn.loc.gov/2017014177

Published in 2017 by arrangement with Viking, an imprint of Penguin Publishing Group, a division of Penguin Random House, LLC

Printed in the United States of America
1 2 3 4 5 6 7 21 20 19 18 17

To my fellow Americans

The influences of the senses has in most men overpowered the mind to the degree that the walls of time and space have come to look solid, real and insurmountable; and to speak with levity of these limits is, in the world, the sign of insanity.

— RALPH WALDO EMERSON

In the land of the blind, the one-eyed man is king.

— ERASMUS

1
DON'T WALK

That morning, in an effort to restore some normalcy to my weekend, I left the house and strolled to the coffee shop for a Grande Americano, just like a regular, irrational person.

At the end of my street the cross signal read DON'T WALK, so I stopped on the curb and pushed the large silver button several times even though I was fully aware that it took only one compression to activate the signal. The coffee shop, a single-story cut stone building with one large plate glass window, sat on the corner directly across from me. It was busy, as midmornings on Sunday tended to be. People rushed in and out like they were looting the place. They pushed strollers and dragged dogs by the leash and carried great rolls of newsprint under their arms. I watched them come and go, glancing up now and again at the crossing signal, which still read DON'T WALK.

While waiting for the crossing signal, I received a text message from Tony. It said that Alice didn't want me at their house anymore. I felt a twinge of regret, like the mild fleeting sadness I'd experienced the previous night when hearing a story about Christians slaughtered like beef cattle at a Kenyan mall. But at the same time I understood why Alice didn't want me around. After all, I'd vandalized her home. It was Sunday, so they likely had to wait another twenty-four hours for someone to come and fix the window, and in the meantime Tony probably had to tape a piece of cardboard over the hole to keep the cold out. Not a great scene. Our punk rock days, insofar as we'd had any, were well behind us. We were supposed to be weaning babies and fertilizing lawns and building equity — those yardsticks of nascent maturity — not breaking windows for the sake of doing so. I made a mental note to send Tony a check to cover the replacement.

The signal continued to insist that I not cross the street.

I shifted my weight from one foot to the other and back again. I checked my watch and saw that two hours had passed since I'd first left the house. The coffee shop was somewhat less busy now, but even though

I'd gotten out of bed that morning intending to behave just like anyone else, I couldn't bring myself to cross against the signal. People in cars stopped, stared at me expectantly, then shot goggle-eyed looks of exasperation when I waved them through.

Contrails stitched the sky overhead, some tight and linear, other, older ones dissipating into bulbous puffs in the stratosphere. My mind, compensating perhaps for the ongoing physical stillness, wandered about. Somewhere in the world, surely, at that moment, someone was inflicting unimaginable pain on a dog. Somewhere else — perhaps even quite nearby — a stranger hurried through a silent, fraught ethical calculus while deciding whether to make up the difference on the grocery bill of a poor person in front of him. Elsewhere, no doubt, a man was inserting a finger into his own rectum as he masturbated. As I stood there on the street corner, a mere two lanes of intermittent traffic away from my coffee, people were roasting alive in fires, learning to crochet and speak rudimentary Spanish, planning weddings and murders. The Earth continued to plunge through the universe at an inconceivable speed, and upon it I waited in vain for the crossing signal to change, tongue cleaving to the roof of my mouth as

11

I dehydrated slowly, thighs stiffening with the cold, a modest awe at the vagaries of creation blossoming in me, as it did most days, these days.

A few hours later the streetlamps flickered on, casting circles of bilious yellow across the pavement. Headlights from passing cars strobed my torso and face. The picture window in the coffee shop's façade glowed a warm, beckoning orange, and people sat at tables before mugs that steamed like scale-model nuclear power plants. They slouched on their tailbones with their legs splayed in front of them, relaxed and comfortable. They watched videos on their tablets and turned the pages of analog books with studied contemplativeness. Gradually, as the evening drew on, in ones and twos they all departed, and by and by the girl behind the counter readied the shop for closing.

Hands in my pockets, I watched as the girl came to the front door and threw the dead bolt, then emptied all the coffee urns into the sink and rinsed them with water from the tap. She upended the chairs and set them on tabletops and gave the floor a perfunctory mopping. She counted out her register and jammed a bunch of bills into a burlap cash bag, hurrying, hurrying. Maybe

12

she had a date to get ready for, or maybe she was meeting friends. Perhaps she was just tired of work and had no plans more pressing than to not be at the coffee shop any longer, but whatever the reason there was a real urgency to her movements.

I shivered. I looked at my watch, then again at the crossing signal. Despairing of my coffee, thinking I should finally turn back toward home, I glanced one last time at the picture window, and that was the moment when the man emerged from the bathroom and pointed a gleaming obsidian pistol at the girl who had served me my Americano all these years.

For a moment they just stood there, the girl frozen in disbelief, the man trying to figure out what came next, like an actor waiting for his line. Then the man yelled at the girl, and motioned with the gun in a threatening way. I couldn't hear what he was saying, of course, being across the street and on the other side of a thick pane of glass, but I could guess at the gist of it. He wanted money, certainly. Maybe he wanted something in addition to money, as well. One read about such things, from time to time.

I reached for my phone. The crossing signal continued to glow red: DON'T WALK.

The girl took the cash bag off the counter and held it out to the man. Before her arm was fully extended, he snatched the bag away and yelled at her again. At this the girl clapped her hands over her ears and bent at the waist, trying to disappear, trying to will herself to time travel, or disintegrate, or to become any of the versions of herself that she had ever been or would ever be, anything but this version of her who thirty seconds prior had perhaps been daydreaming about a glass of Pinot Grigio and was now wondering if she would live to see another sunrise.

The girl's mouth hung open, ragged with terror.

"9-1-1, please state the nature of your emergency," a woman said into my ear.

"The nature of it?" I thought for a moment. "The nature of it is . . . frightening. Quite dangerous, I think. Involves a firearm."

"Sir, do you have an emergency you want to report?"

"Thank you for rephrasing," I said. "That's much easier to answer. Yes, there is a man holding a barista up at gunpoint."

"And where are you, sir?"

"I'm standing across the street," I said.

"*Which* street, sir?"

"Appleton. Across from Hilltop Coffee."

"A man is robbing Hilltop Coffee on Appleton Street?" the woman said.

"That's correct."

The man motioned toward the cash register, and the girl moved past him, careful to keep as far from the gun as possible. She came around the counter and punched a few keys, but fear made her clumsy, and the register refused to open. After a few moments she began to pound on the keypad with the heel of her hand, pleading with the machine to perform its only function and save her life.

"Officers are on their way, sir," the woman said to me. "Can you tell me what's happening now?"

When the girl failed again to open the register, the man became impatient and pressed the barrel of the gun to a spot just below her hairline. He did this very gently. He could have been pressing his lips to her forehead, rather than a .38, he was so gentle about it. And that was when the girl let out a scream that I could both see and, very faintly, hear.

She thought it was over, just then.

"I think I have to do something," I told the woman on the phone.

"Sir, do not interfere," the woman said.

15

"Officers are on their way. Tell me what's happening."

I put the phone back in my pocket.

DON'T WALK.

I checked for traffic in both directions, then hustled across the street, veering out of the crosswalk as I approached the coffee shop. I stopped in front of the picture window. This close I could see that the man and the girl were both trembling. I was too, at this point. I had no plan, no weapon, no black belt in Krav Maga. The door was locked, the picture window thick enough that I would have needed a hammer to break it. And then what? Crawl over stalagmites of glass while the man unloaded his gun at me?

The expression on the girl's face was what one would expect: ghastly, pathetic. But bearable to witness. Looking at the man, however, I could feel the blood flush from my cheeks. He wore a murderous sneer from the nose down, capped by the wide wondering eyes of a child. An impossible, nauseating expression. His fingers gripped the butt of the gun so tightly that his knuckles strained the skin white, and the crotch of his jeans bulged with an erection.

It was plain that the man no longer cared about the register, no longer cared, in fact,

16

about the money in the cash bag, already his to take and run with. Whatever was human in him, whatever his upper consciousness consisted of, had evaporated. I recognized, without even the slightest doubt, that he was only moments from doing something terrible and irrevocable.

I could think of nothing else, so I raised a hand and rapped on the picture window, thrice.

2
AN ODD SATURDAY, PRESAGING AN ODDER SUNDAY

The previous afternoon, at Tony's house, I'd just used the toilet and was washing up. Rude sunlight burst through the window, stenciling a brilliant yellow rectangle on the floor in front of the toilet. Downstairs in the living room Tony and Art were watching football and drinking a limited-edition seasonal mead that had been fermented at a repurposed auto body shop only three blocks away.

As recently as five years before, if you'd walked these streets after dark you stood a decent chance of having your skull caved in by a feldspar-wielding hood on crystal meth. Now two-bedroom houses were going for half a million dollars. The sound of the neighborhood waking up was the chirrup of one hundred late-model Subarus being unlocked at the same time. There was a community garden, and a boutique corner grocer where you could spend the monthly income of a family from Ghana on a single root vegetable. Young men sporting wispy mustaches sat around pumping accordions and plucking banjos. Body odor was wielded as both siren call and political statement. Every dog in the neighborhood — and there were many — had a full wardrobe of seasonally appropriate jackets, sweaters, and paw booties.

These were the things on my mind as I scrubbed my hands. Then, for whatever reason — boredom with the familiar tropes of gentrification, perhaps — I decided to scrutinize the label on the bottle of soap I'd just used.

The first thing I noticed was that the stuff was not, according to the manufacturer, actually soap. It was, rather, "liquid hand wash." Even more perplexingly, it had been "formulated with cleansing agents." This language stopped me cold. I stood there with the water running over my hands and tried to understand how "formulated with cleansing agents" could be interpreted as something other than a euphemism for "made with soap." I tried to give this liquid hand wash the benefit of the doubt and convince myself that there really was something special about it, something that made it infinitely better than a crappy old bottle of regular soap and justified such breathless language. But every time I read that line — "formulated with cleansing agents" — all I could see was the plain-English translation.

And I realized slowly, as I stood there hunched over the sink, that it was making me crazy.

Why this bottle of liquid hand wash, of all the nonsense I'd encountered in nearly forty years on the planet, was the thing that suddenly sent me over the edge, I cannot say. I will simply report what I know: that there in Tony's bathroom I was visited by the hammer-stroke certainty that the culture I counted myself a part of, the culture that had weaned and reared me, had become proudly, willfully, and completely divorced from fact.

I went downstairs, carrying the bottle of liquid hand wash. In the living room the guys were camped out around the flatscreen. Tony had his eyes on the game — Alabama versus Texas A&M — while Art sat mashing the screen of his phone like he was engaged in some sort of speed-typing competition, the loser of which faced the indignity of being shredded by rabid beagles.

"Did you buy this?" I asked Tony.

He looked at me, then at the bottle in my

hand. "What is it?"

"I thought it was soap. But it's liquid hand wash."

Tony's gaze went back to the television. "Yeah. So?"

"So did you buy it?"

"Maybe. Probably."

Art looked up from his phone. "Why are you holding a bottle of soap?" he asked me.

Alabama's offense was driving, making eight- and nine-yard gains on every play.

"That's just it," I said. "It's not soap."

"It's not soap," Tony corroborated, keeping his eyes on the game.

"What is it," Art asked, "if not soap?"

"Liquid hand wash," I told him.

"It has moisturizers," Tony said. "Doesn't dry your hands like soap."

"It doesn't say anything about moisturizers," I said, scanning the label once more. "It just says 'formulated with cleansing agents.' "

"Cleansing agents?" Art asked.

"Correct," I told him.

"That sounds an awful lot like soap, to me," Art said.

"My point exactly," I said.

"Guys," Tony said, pointing at the television. "Watching football."

Looking down at his phone again, Art

grunted. "Contaminated chicken," he said.

"How's that?" Tony asked.

"Contaminated chicken," Art said. "I just got an email. 'The USDA is about to finalize a dangerous rule for how chickens in the United States are inspected.' "

"Dangerous?" Tony said.

"It says 'dangerous,' " Art told him. "There's a petition."

"Forward it to me," Tony said.

"I'm just trying to understand," I said to Tony.

"You're always just trying to understand," Tony said, still not looking up from the television. "And never quite getting there."

"I mean I washed my hands, and this stuff behaved an awful lot like soap. It foamed up, and smelled sort of chemically floral, and my skin was free of dirt and oil afterward."

No one responded.

"I just need to figure this out," I said.

"You need to have a mead and relax," Art said.

"How much does this stuff *cost*?" I asked Tony. "I mean, compared to a bottle of actual soap?"

"Third and goal," Tony said, pointing at the television. "Sit down. Chill out."

"I need you to take this seriously," I told him.

On the sofa, Art made a noise somewhere between a chuckle and a snort. "Bathroom wipes are clogging up sewer systems all over the country."

"Shit," Tony said. "I use those. They're supposed to be flushable."

"Funny you mention that," Art said. "It says here that no regulatory body governs claims of flushability. That you could put a 'flushable' label on a sleeping bag, but that doesn't make it so."

"Lying bastards," Tony said.

"And get this: apparently there's a way for the sewer district to tell exactly which house the wipes came from. Some pretty serious public shaming going on. Also, in some instances, civil charges."

"Are you serious?" Tony said. "Alice will divorce me."

"Doesn't she use them, too?" Art asked.

"Nah, they're mine," Tony said. "A man's gotta have his own little things, you know?"

I opened my mouth to say something else about the liquid hand wash formulated with cleansing agents, but Tony silenced me with one raised finger as Alabama's quarterback lofted a pass. It drifted down into the arms of his receiver, who did a balletic job of sneaking a toe inbounds before the ball's trajectory carried him out of the back of the end zone.

Tony bolted up from his easy chair. "That's the spread!" he hollered.

This outburst brought Aggie, Tony's Goldendoodle, running from the kitchen. She nudged Tony's hand with her nose, seeking reassurance, as dogs will, that his agitation did not mean her world was coming to an end.

"That dog," Art said, "looks like an Ewok."

"She's hypoallergenic," Tony said, watching slow-motion multiangle replays of the touchdown. "No fur, just hair."

"A gay Ewok," Art said.

Why did I choose that moment to hurl the bottle of liquid hand wash through the window behind the sofa? I didn't know then, and I don't know now. It certainly wasn't because I disagreed with Art — the dog did, in fact, look like a gay Ewok.

At the sound of glass shattering, Art dropped his phone and threw his arms over his head in a panicked warding gesture. The dog bolted back into the kitchen, tail firmly tucked.

Tony stared at me. "What the fuck, K.?" he said.

24

"I'm sorry," I said. "I just need you to engage me about this thing. This hand wash/soap thing. It's really bothering me."

"No shit," Art said. "Why would you throw a bottle of soap at me, if nothing was bothering you?"

"I didn't throw it at you," I told him. "I threw it at the window. That you happened to be sitting in front of the window I chose to throw it at is totally coincidental."

"Cool, so I'm just going to pick this coincidental glass out of my hair," Art said, reaching up with both hands.

"And it's not soap," I told him. "It's liquid hand wash."

"What's the fucking difference?" Art asked.

"That's it," I said. "That's it exactly. What *is* the difference?"

"When I say 'what's the fucking difference,' " Art said, "what I mean is, 'who fucking cares?' "

"Well, I do," I said. "I mean, look at me. I'm shaking. I feel a little sick, too, actually."

"Do me a favor and don't puke in my living room," Tony said. "Alice is going to freak out as it is. First the bathroom wipes, and now this."

The dog poked her snout through the

doorway, trepidatious yet hopeful that the worst of the disturbance had passed.

"Listen, Tony, I'll pay for the window," I said.

"You're fucking right you will."

"But can I have the bottle of liquid hand wash?"

"What *for*?" he said, then stopped, closed his eyes, and waved his hands in the air as if to erase the words he'd just spoken. "Wait, you know what — never mind. I don't care. Yes, you can have the goddamn bottle of goddamn soap."

"You mind grabbing that for me?" I asked Art, nodding toward the sill where the liquid hand wash had come to rest.

He fished the bottle out and handed it over.

"Okay," I said, looking around. "So I'm going to go."

"Good idea," Tony said.

We all stayed there for a second longer, looking at each other, the dog included.

"Anytime you're ready," Tony said.

There were plenty of places in town where Tony could have purchased the liquid hand wash formulated with cleansing agents, but Total Foods seemed the most likely. So I got on the highway, the most direct route across town to the Total Foods plaza.

Some might think it kismet that the moment I merged with traffic was also the moment when the blue pickup truck happened along and settled into the cruising lane in front of me. But by that point in my life, I no longer engaged in this kind of magical thinking. That I ended up behind the truck was completely random, the not-so-improbable result of the fact that I lived in a place where rural meets aspiring urban, hillbilly meets hipster, Bud Light meets brunch.

The truck was a 1980s vintage Ford, tailgate honeycombed with rust and rear bumper not a bumper at all, but rather a slab of aftermarket steel that presumably had replaced the original bumper when it rotted away. It bore a single sticker, centered above the trailer hitch: WHOSE NEXT, the sticker read, in star-spangled font, and beneath that: DON'T TREAD ON AMERICA.

I cruised behind this truck for a while, considering. Then I started flashing my headlights and honking my horn. After about a mile of this, the truck finally veered to the breakdown lane. I eased in behind it and put my car in park.

The driver of the truck unfolded himself from the cab and looked at me, arms out,

27

palms up, face decidedly sour. He was big, well north of six feet, and wide of both shoulder and hip. Long stringy hair dangled from underneath his baseball cap like tangles of dirty cobwebs.

I got out of the car and walked toward the man. He met me halfway, and we stood gazing at each other where the front of my vehicle met the rear of his. He had a look in his eyes that was not good.

"I wanted to ask about your bumper sticker, there," I said to him.

He looked at his truck, then back at me. "That's what you were going crazy about?"

"I wouldn't refer to it as 'crazy.' But yes."

The man stared. "Jesus. What about it?"

"I'm having difficulty understanding what it means, exactly," I said.

"What don't you understand?" he said. "Who's next. Like when you're fighting. 'Who wants what this guy just got?' "

"What which guy just got?" I asked.

The man hesitated, and a slight smile played on his lips. "You're gonna make me say it?"

"I'm not trying to make you do anything," I told him. "I just don't know who the guy is that you're talking about. And that's setting aside, for the moment, the fact that your sticker uses the possessive form of 'who' rather than the contraction of 'who is.' "

The man squinted, evidently his way of asking for clarification.

"If you're trying to say 'who is next' — which is clearly what you're trying to say — it's 'w-h-o-apostrophe-s,' not 'w-h-o-s-e.' "

"Like anyone gives a shit, genius."

"Fair point," I said. "It's true that very few people care about the difference between an adjective and a conjunction anymore. But again, setting that aside. Who is the person who had this terrible thing done to him that you're now threatening to do to other people?"

The man looked out at the passing traffic. "Now I don't even know what you're talking about."

"Okay," I said. "Let me start over. You put that sticker on your truck. My understanding of how bumper stickers work — and I've never had a bumper sticker on any of my vehicles, so forgive me if I'm way off here — is that a person agrees strongly enough with the sentiment expressed on the sticker that he feels it is a good and accurate way to represent himself to the world. Is it fair to say that about your relationship to this bumper sticker?"

"Sure," the man said. "If you want to

sound like a stuck-up douche bag about it."

"Right," I said. "So if you agree with the sentiment on the sticker so thoroughly that you're eager to put it on your truck, then explaining that sentiment to a third party — in this case, me — should not be difficult. In theory."

"Still not clear on what you're asking me, bub."

I thought for a moment. "How about this," I said. " 'Who's next' implies that someone came before. Who was that person? Who got the beating that your bumper sticker now threatens to visit upon someone else?"

Understanding dawned on the man's face. "The fucking towelheads," he said. "Who else?"

"Which towelheads?"

He stared at me.

"I'm asking sincerely," I said.

"Osama and his whole fucking crew, man."

"And they're the ones treading on America?" I asked.

"Them and the rest," the man said.

"So, *all* the towelheads?"

"Fucking right."

"But what are they doing to us, exactly?"

"You mean besides 9/11?"

"Aside from that."

"Ain't that enough?"

"Surely. But your grievance seems to be ongoing. So I imagine the offense is ongoing as well."

"They're all 'Death to America' all the time. Burning flags and shit. They hate us because we're free."

"Why would they hate us for being free? That's like hating us for breathing, or eating Twinkies."

"They hate us for being free because they're not free."

"So they don't like us because we have something they aspire to?"

"Yeah," the man said. Then he glanced again at the traffic whizzing by and said, "Are we really standing on the side of the road talking about this right now?"

"We are," I told him, "and I'll be happy to let you go in a moment. But have you considered that there are probably more than a handful of reasons why the towel-heads hate us, and none of those has anything to do with anyone's relative freedom?"

"Let me tell you something, bub —"

"Israel and Palestine, for starters," I said. "Iran, 1953."

"Who the hell is talking about *Iran,* you simple son of a bitch?"

31

"I'm just saying, there are other, more likely reasons."

"I don't really spend a whole lot of time thinking about it, if you want the God's honest."

"Don't you think you ought to, though?" I asked him. "I mean, if you're going to drive around with that bumper sticker on your truck?"

"I *think*," the man said, "that you ought to mind your goddamn business."

"Of course," I said. "Except I would argue that you made it my business by broadcasting your beliefs about towelheads."

The man leaned toward me. "It's a fucking *bumper sticker.* I forgot it was even there until you started going crazy behind me. It don't mean anything."

"But of course it means something," I said. "It means you're a racist. It also means that complete ignorance of a subject does not preclude your having strong opinions about it."

The man slitted his eyes and took one heavy, menacing step forward.

"Which, in fairness, makes you not unlike many other Americans," I said.

He jutted his belly up against my chest, knocking me back half a step.

"I really hope," I told him, "that you're

not about to do what I think you're about to do."

The knob over my left eye, having sprung up instantly under the man's knuckles, had turned a grotesque blue-black by the time I reached the Total Foods parking lot. My brainpan throbbed, and I felt more than a little sick to my stomach, but I had arrived, however belatedly, so I grabbed the liquid hand wash and went in.

The Total Foods entrance was choked with heaps of pumpkins: pumpkins on the floor, pumpkins on small wooden stands and apple crates, pumpkins stacked precariously on one another. A few steps inside, amidst the obscene plenitude of the produce section, a group of people had gathered around a long banquet table. A sign to the right of the table read GET EXCITED ABOUT GOURDS, and near the sign a man in a Total Foods apron with tattooed arms stood stuffing baby pumpkins with a mixture of brown rice, lentils, and mushrooms. He had on a Bluetooth headset, and talked into it at length about the brown rice, lentil, and mushroom mixture, his voice amplified by a small wireless speaker on the table. A tray of pumpkin lasagna, already mangled by the throng, rested next to the speaker, along with a large steel bowl of crunchy pumpkin salad.

The crowd ate these various permutations of pumpkin off of tiny compostable plates. They turned to each other and nodded and said indecipherable but enthusiastic things around mouthfuls of food. The air smelled of garlic and scorched vegetable matter and, ambiently, armpit.

"You okay?" a guy next to me asked. He was very short, barely above midget stature, and had a startlingly perfect pompadour fade. It looked more like carbon fiber than hair, looked, in fact, as though it had been manufactured under great heat and pressure somewhere far away from his head — Pennsylvania, maybe. He wore thick-framed black glasses and an expression of real concern.

"I think so," I told him. "Why?"

"Well for starters, your face is jacked up," he said.

"It's been a strange day, even by my standards," I told him. "But I think I'm alright."

"Cool," he said. "Try the lasagna, and you'll be even more alright."

But even if I'd been interested in trying the lasagna, there was no way, really, as the crowd around the table was seven deep and packed as tight as a Roman phalanx. Instead, I watched from a distance as the man in the apron topped the stuffed baby pumpkins with a sprinkle of parsley, then moved on to a bowl of pumpkin bar batter.

"Excuse me," I called to him.

He looked up from his mixing. "Yes?" he said. "There's a question? We're happy to answer questions. Any question at all that you have about pumpkins. That's what we're here for."

"Great," I said, "because my question is about pumpkins. Listen, I don't mean to be a noodge, but I'm wondering about the sign you have over there."

"What about it, man?"

"Well it says that we should get excited about gourds. But then here you are working exclusively with pumpkins. Which are not gourds, I don't think."

The Total Foods guy smiled as he continued to stir his batter. "Actually, that's a really good point," he said. "The interesting thing is that there's no consensus regarding the difference between pumpkins, gourds, and squashes. Although in terms of common usage, the general rule of thumb is: cook a squash, carve a pumpkin, and look at a gourd."

"But you're cooking a pumpkin," I said.

"Right. Because, really, any of the plants in the *Cucurbita* family can be called a gourd. And for our purposes, here today, a *pumpkin* is a gourd. Ergo, get excited about gourds."

"But why not just say 'Get excited about pumpkins,' and avoid any confusion?" I asked.

The guy was still smiling. "Well then you'd lose the alliteration."

"What alliteration? 'Get' and 'gourd'?"

"You got it, buddy."

"Again, I'm sorry to nitpick," I said, "but 'get' and 'gourd' are a bit far apart in that phrase to really count as alliteration."

People turned toward me, their faces scrunched up with displeasure even as they continued chewing. The Total Foods guy, apparently having reached the limits of his knowledge of poetics, just stared.

I turned to walk away, but before I got out of earshot I heard someone say that they thought Republicans shopped at Sam's Club. This caused a great and knowing laughter among the crowd at the banquet table. They were still tittering when I reached the end of the produce area and turned left past the wines to enter the Total Foods Premium Body Care section.

It was, in a word, mammoth. Two sets of

shelves, each taller than me, stretched one hundred feet or so in length. My eyes flitted over innumerable products, searching in vain for a bottle to match the liquid hand wash formulated with cleansing agents. What I found instead were daily facial cleansers and gentle skin cleansers, bioactive facial washes made with eight (unidentified) berries, Exfoliating Walnut and Apple Wood Face Scrub, six varieties of Authentic African Black Soap, a pyramid of Neem and Turmeric Handcrafted Cleansing Bars, and a dozen bottles of Apricot Milk Wash with Probiotics. Not to mention the Sea Buckthorn with Ester-C Rejuvenating Facial Cleanser, the Organic Vetiver Cedar Triple Milled Soap, and something called Chamomile and Soap Bark Cleansing Cream, which seemed, if one could believe the label, to somehow be soap, cleanser, and cream at once.

All this, while Rome burned.

The scope of the problem, and thus the scope of my dilemma, was much greater than I had anticipated. In search of an answer to the riddle of the liquid hand wash formulated with cleansing agents, I'd instead stumbled into a thicket of yet more riddles. I began to tremble, there in the Premium Body Care section. I began to sweat. I felt dizzy, though whether from anxiety or concussion was unclear. I even started to talk to myself a bit, the sort of comforting nonsense noises one makes to soothe a fussy baby.

After a few moments I closed my eyes, blocking out the sight of all that skin care. I took several shuddering breaths, in through the nose, out through the mouth. Thus semicomposed, I strode head-down out of the aisle in search of a Total Foods employee.

I found one in the next aisle, a woman in her midtwenties bent over a large cardboard box marked "Stuffed Shells." Inside the cardboard box were other, smaller boxes, and each of these was marked "Stuffed Shells" as well.

I couldn't help myself.

"Shouldn't those be called 'Stuffing Shells'?" I asked. "Or 'Shells for Stuffing'?"

The woman looked up from her work. "What do you mean?" she said.

I wiped sweat from my forehead with a shaking hand. "Well, they're not stuffed yet. They won't be stuffed until someone takes them home and stuffs them. As of this moment they're just uncooked pasta sitting in a box. Same as all the other pasta here."

The woman stood up; at her full height,

the top of her head came only to my ster-num. Her dark red hair sagged in a loose, off-center ponytail, and her face was asym-metrical in the way one sometimes sees with fashion models, which is to say she looked like nothing so much as an extremely pretty extraterrestrial. She put her hands on her hips and gazed down at the boxes. "I can see your point," she said, smiling. "That's funny."

"Thank you," I said.

"For what?"

"For seeing my point," I told her.

The woman took a good look at me for the first time, and her smile faded. "You okay?" she asked.

"Can I ask what your name is?" I said.

"Claire."

"I'm not entirely okay, Claire, no. But don't worry. I'm not dangerous or any-thing."

"Alright," she said, eyeing me a moment longer. "Then what can I help you with?"

Claire followed me around the corner to the Premium Body Care section.

"Everything's organized by type, not manufacturer," she said, examining the bottle of liquid hand wash formulated with cleansing agents. "So all we have to do is look for the hand cleansers, and . . . hey

39

presto. Here it is."

"That's the stuff?"

"That's the stuff," she said.

"What's the price on that?"

"Let's see." She dropped into a crouch and peered at the price tag affixed to the shelf. "Eighteen ninety-nine."

"Eighteen ninety-nine."

"Correctamundo."

"For eight ounces of hand wash."

"Would seem so."

"You wash with it."

"Yes," Claire said.

"And it's for hands only," I said.

"That's how it's labeled."

"Okay. I'm able to accept that I should never, under any circumstances, wash anything but my hands with this. But I need to know why."

Claire stood up again and glanced around as if searching out eavesdroppers. She leaned in, and I caught a whiff of metabolized alcohol, like the smell of a bottle redemption center, on her breath. "They say it has to do with pH and how soap is alkaline and dries your skin and all that, but I think it's mostly bullshit," she said. "I mean, in the winter my hands get a lot drier than my face. So you'd think that your hands are the part of your body that need special treatment."

"Why are you whispering?" I asked her.

"Because we're in Total Foods."

"You have to whisper when you're in Total Foods?"

Claire looked at me. "Do you always take everything so literally?" she asked.

"I didn't used to," I said. "But I'm not quite myself today. Or maybe I'm more myself than I've ever been. It's hard to tell."

"Okay," Claire said. "Then I'll spell it out for you. I'm whispering because even to suggest it's okay to wash your face with soap would not go over well with the Total Foods crowd."

"And by 'not go over well' you mean . . ."

"Best-case? I get a lecture about the Total Foods ethic, and how my words and actions should always reflect that ethic."

"And worst-case?"

"I get shitcanned."

"For saying it's okay to wash your face with soap."

"For merely implying it," Claire said.

"Huh."

"Yup."

We were quiet for a moment.

"So how about the language on this bottle," I said, pointing at the liquid hand wash. "What exactly does 'formulated with cleansing agents' mean?"

"You want the Total Foods employee handbook answer, or the no-bullshit answer?"

I considered. "How about both?"

"Okay. Here's the former: 'This gentle hand wash is blended with premium ingredients formulated to provide a soothing hand-cleansing experience.' "

"And the latter?"

"It's soap. You wash your fucking hands with it."

I looked at her. "Claire," I said, "can I tell you how glad I am that I found you today?"

She smiled at me, a bit guarded, a bit perplexed, still, by my strange questions and facial contusion. For a moment I thought about how this Claire, model-pretty, with her burgundy ponytail and wry manner, might be someone I'd like to know better. But of course I was not young enough to entertain such thoughts for longer than a second or two, and so I broke the smiley silence between us by thanking her, and walked away.

When I got back in the car I saw Sarah's old cell phone, the one possession of hers I'd neglected to destroy, sitting in the cup holder. It had been in the car for months, which is why it had been spared the fate of her other belongings. I'd meant to take it in for recycling but instead had been driving around with it, forgetting about it, throwing it on the passenger seat to make room for a bottle of water or a Grande Americano. As I pulled out of the Total Foods parking lot I realized that now was my chance to finally be rid of the thing: across the throughway at the mall loomed the sign for our local Big Buy, a school bus–yellow beacon in the gathering dark.

I walked through the whoosh of automatic doors with the phone in hand. A second set of doors opened onto the main sales floor, where hundreds of electronic devices flashed and blared for an audience of a few dozen shoppers who paid little attention to their overtures. I wandered around looking for a place to drop the phone, figuring this to be a simple enough task. After a full lap of the store, though, after strolling past the video game section, the home theater section, the computer and tablet section, the DVD and Blu-ray section, and finally the weird anachronism of the music CD section, I was forced to admit defeat and headed for the exit.

But then, in the same entryway I'd passed through only a few minutes before, I now noticed a long, squat recycling bin. Along the top of the bin were six round holes, each fitted with a rubber gasket through which one could drop whatever it was one wanted to recycle. The first hole was labeled for toner cartridges, the second for laptop batteries, and the third for portable GPS units. Inexplicably, the fourth through sixth holes weren't labeled at all.

I stood there for a minute, still holding Sarah's phone, unsure what to do, wondering what those last three holes were for.

Then, above the bin, I spotted a sign: WE ALSO RECYCLE TELEVISIONS, COMPUTERS, FURNITURE, CELLULAR PHONES, CAMERAS, GAMING CONSOLES, HOME APPLIANCES, AND MORE. PLEASE SEE A SALES ASSOCIATE FOR DETAILS.

I went back inside through the automatic doors.

It made a certain kind of sense, I imagined, that the sales associate I needed to talk to about recycling a phone would be assigned to the phone section. There I found a girl in her early twenties, plump and pretty and brown haired, clad in the ubiquitous Big Buy polo shirt and khaki pants.

She looked pleasant enough. Hope rose.

"Can I help you?" the girl asked brightly as I approached. She either failed to notice, or was unfazed by, the fresh bruise on my face.

"I think so," I said. "I need to recycle this phone."

"Sure," she said. "There's a bin out in the entryway where you can drop it on your way out."

I looked at her for a moment. "Right," I said. "See, I was just there. That bin has slots for toner cartridges, batteries, and GPS units. And then up top it says that if I have a phone to recycle I should see a sales associate."

She cocked her head to the side, her smile widening. "It's fine," she said. "You can put phones in there, too."

I half turned toward the exit. "Okay," I said. "Because that's not what the sign —"

"It's fine," she reiterated.

I went back to the entryway and stood there for a couple of minutes. I read the labels and the sign again several times.

"See the thing is," I told the girl when I returned with the phone still in hand, "I understand that when you say '*You* can put phones in there too,' what you mean by *you* is one, or anyone, is allowed to put phones in the bin. Not *you* as in I, specifically, can put phones in the bin. Because *I* can't. When *I* go to the bin and it says if I want to

45

recycle a phone I should see a sales associate, I can't, given explicit instructions to the contrary, bring myself to just put the phone in there."

The girl's smile had disappeared. "Sir," she said, "you've seen a sales associate. *I* am a sales associate. And I'm telling you it's perfectly fine to put the phone in the bin."

We stared at each other. My hands began trembling again, and I could feel the muscles in my face twitching and bunching as they tried to narrow my eyes and draw my lips back from my teeth. I clasped my free hand over the one holding the phone.

"What I'm having difficulty with, see," I told the girl, trying to keep my tone even and personable, "is the labeling system. If it's okay to put all manner of things in the bin, then why label it at all? To have signage allowing a certain behavior is, by implication, *prohibitive* of other behaviors. I would not, for example, assume that because I can deposit a GPS device I can also deposit a pot-bellied pig. So if a sign reads 'insert toner cartridges here,' in the absence of another sign that says 'insert cell phones here,' one is forced to conclude that cell phones are not allowed. Do you understand what I'm saying?"

The girl's expression of impatience had

devolved into a wariness, the sort of furtive look a woman will cast at a dark figure in a parking garage when she's four strides from her car. She shook her head.

I tried again to comport my facial features. "It's actually very simple," I said. "This should not be tough to grasp. At all."

"Listen, let me find my manager," the girl said, backing away without taking her eyes off of me.

"Okay," I called after her.

The girl returned several minutes later, accompanied by a large man whose abdomen strained the fabric of his Big Buy polo shirt like water in a waterbed mattress. They stopped before me, a rank of two.

"Sir, you can feel free to deposit your phone in the recycling bin out front," the large man said to me.

"Okay," I said. "Could you maybe tell me which hole I should deposit it *in*?"

"It doesn't matter," the man said. "Whichever one you prefer."

I looked at them both. "Have you ever read Kafka?" I asked.

The girl stared at me, her eyes baleful in their frames of mascara, and said nothing.

"Is there maybe someone else I can talk to?" I asked.

The man held out his hand. "Just give me

47

the goddamn phone," he said.

Sarah had died in winter, about seven months previous. This was why when I pulled up to the house all the lights were still off. When I went inside it was cold because I'd turned the heat down earlier and Sarah was not there to turn it back up.

I'd had occasion, since leaving Tony's place that afternoon, to wonder why he hadn't been more upset with me for breaking his window. Why he hadn't just tossed me out the front door. Here, now, was the answer: because my wife had died only recently, which meant that no one really expected me to act like a normal human being and, further, granted me dispensation when I did behave inexplicably.

The cat wound around my ankles in the entryway. We'd had him since he was a kitten, and now he was five or six years old. Sarah had given him a name that I couldn't recall. For a month after she died I tried to remember the cat's name, asking friends if they had any idea, searching Sarah's social media legacy for pictures of the cat, all to no avail. Eventually I just started calling him Meowser, for reasons lost to me by this point.

Meowser followed me into the kitchen,

trying his best to trip me up as we went. He traced figure eights through my legs as I turned on the lights and placed the bottle of liquid hand wash formulated with cleansing agents on the table.

It was very quiet in the house. For company, I turned on the television that rested on a small stand next to the table. I'd put it there after Sarah died. She would never in the vast disk of eternity have allowed a TV in the dining area, or bedroom, or really anywhere other than the living room. She hated having a TV in the house at all. But now I was my own man, and I didn't need to compromise with anyone. I could screw a flat-screen into the ceiling over the bed, if I liked. I could install one in the wall opposite the toilet. Whatever I fancied.

On CNN a panel of four people, none of whom was Kenyan, or African, or even black, offered their considered opinions regarding a terrorist assault on a mall in Kenya. Scores of shoppers had been killed. Women had been blown up with hand grenades, and children ripped open by large-caliber bullets. The men responsible had reportedly ushered Muslims out of the mall, then opened fire on the people who remained. They wanted to kill everyone who wasn't Muslim simply for their non-

Muslimness. There were other reasons they wanted to kill people, too, according to a statement they'd released. They were sore, for example, about Kenyan troops occupying parts of Somalia. They also seemed just generally to not be fans of anyone whose view of God or the world or existence differed from theirs. There were a lot of things that upset them, it seemed, which made sense, since most people wouldn't murder children unless they were really mad about something.

I changed the channel to a late football game. The cat wound and wound between my legs. I realized in a distant way that I should probably sit down, make myself comfortable in my own home. I couldn't do it, though. Maybe because the heat had just kicked on and it was still quite cold. Maybe because my head was throbbing. Maybe because as usual I was hungry but had no appetite.

A therapist I talked to a few times after Sarah died had told me that hunger, along with anger, loneliness, and fatigue, has a much greater effect on our ability to relax and be well than we realize. He gave me an acronym, to remind me to watch out for those four things. HALT: Hungry, Angry, Lonely, Tired. Hunger fucks with your head, this person told me. He seemed uncomfortable with the tented-finger formality of conventional Freudian practice, so he talked how a regular guy talked, and peppered his speech with profanity. Hunger makes it impossible to be still, he told me, in either mind or body. If you're hungry you've got to eat. Fucking priority one. None of the other strategies to manage grief and be productive and act like a normal human will do a goddamn bit of good if you're starving yourself.

The therapist told me some other things, too, before I stopped showing up at his office. One of those other things was: If you blame yourself for someone's death but the cops disagree, then you're being a self-indulgent jerk, and you need to get over it.

He was very practical, this therapist. After a few sessions, though, I began to suspect that his regular guyness was a front, a manufactured therapeutic strategy, and that when he went home he put on women's clothing and slathered himself in peanut butter and danced around his living room while making noises somewhere between laughing and sobbing. I began to suspect, in other words, that he himself was not forthright in the way he expected me to be, in the way he insisted I must be for our work

51

together to bear fruit.

That was one of the reasons I stopped seeing the therapist. Another was because the love seat in his office was old and lumpy and had one sharp spring that poked me in the rear end no matter how I adjusted my position. That also influenced my decision not to return, if I'm being honest.

In any event, his advice about eating seemed sound. So with the Florida/South Carolina game blaring in the background, I made my way to the refrigerator and dug out a slightly rusted head of iceberg lettuce and a bottle of ranch dressing. I put the lettuce on the one plate in the house and put the dressing on the lettuce and put the whole thing on the dining table in front of the TV.

I ate the entire head of lettuce, but barely tasted a thing.

By the time I finished, the football game had given way to a nightly sports news program, and I realized I had no idea what the final score had been, or even who had won. I rose from the table, rinsed the one plate in the house, and climbed the stairs to the bedroom. Meowser wound and wound. I took off my shoes but didn't bother with the rest of my clothes, and was under the covers before I remembered I'd left the television on in the kitchen. It was just loud enough for me to hear the steady drone of the news anchors, but not loud enough to make out what they were saying. I lay there for a while, thinking perhaps I should get up and turn it off, as well as tend to minimal personal hygiene, but then Meowser draped himself across my ankles. I stayed flat on my back, long after it became uncomfortable and the urge to roll over struck, because I didn't want to disturb the cat.

I listened to the mumble of the television for a long time. The bedside lamp was on, but it sat just out of reach, so I let it burn. For hours I lay there, neither tense nor relaxed, my eyes trained on the ceiling. By and by, though, I must have fallen asleep, because the next thing I knew it was Sunday morning, a Sunday like any other, except that somewhere in our prosperous little city a man was preparing to rob my coffee shop, a man who thought he just wanted money when in fact what he really wanted, but was not yet ready to be honest with himself about, was to frighten and humiliate and kill a pretty dark-haired young woman.

I got out of bed, neck stiff, clothes spectacularly rumpled, thinking I should give Meowser his breakfast. But then a caffeine yen gripped me, and I put on shoes and went out for my Americano, thinking I'd be back in ten minutes, twenty at most, and that the cat could certainly wait that long for his marinated morsels.

3
Guns Don't Kill People . . .

Ten hours later, as I knocked on the coffee shop window, it was the cat I thought of. Although strictly speaking this was less a thought, I suppose, and more a spasm of indistinct anxiety over how long it would take someone, after I'd been shot dead, to discover Meowser crouched in a dark corner of the house, his innate friendliness supplanted by distrust of a world that had stolen his human companions and left him hungry and alone.

Or maybe I was being sentimental. After all, Meowser would've eaten me with good appetite if I died and no other food was available. There were documented cases of such.

In any event, it was the cat I thought of when the man simultaneously turned toward the sound of my knocking and pulled the trigger on his .38. I was pushed back hard, as though shoved rather than shot, and I fell to the pavement while shards of glass tinkled like sleet all around me. For a few moments I lay there, trying to understand what had happened, listening to the girl moan on the other side of the now-empty window frame. The sound came from her long and low, like the pealing of church bells, and it occurred to me, in a distant way, that if she had breath to cry that meant she was still alive. After a while I tried to get myself up off the sidewalk, but my left arm didn't seem to want to work, so I lay down again and waited, though for what I had little idea.

By and by the faces of two men blocked the night sky above me; one wore a baseball cap, the other was hatless and bald.

"Oh shit," the one in the cap said.

The bald man reached down toward me. "C'mon, let's get him out of this glass," he said.

Hands grasped and lifted, sending a jolt of pain through my shoulder, and I groaned in inarticulate protest. Pebbles of glass crunched under our feet as the men guided me to a bench in front of the shop. I could still hear the girl crying, quieter now, and also sirens in the distance echoing up the hill.

"Have a seat, buddy, ambulance'll be here

any minute," the bald man told me. I did as instructed, collapsing onto the bench with enough force to make my shoulder sing anew. The bald man looked at his palms, stained with a black wetness I did not immediately recognize as blood, and wiped them on the front of his jeans.

"Someone," I said, "should check on the girl."

"What girl?" the man in the cap asked.

"In the coffee shop," I said. "Just follow the sound of weeping."

"I'll go," the bald man said to the man in the cap. "Steve, stay here with him."

Steve and I watched as the bald man tried the door and, finding it locked, opted instead to climb through the open window frame. He hopped down and disappeared into the shop's interior. I half expected to hear another gunshot — or a series of them — but there was nothing but the sound of sirens, ever louder.

Steve looked at me again. "Jesus, you're bleedin' bad," he said.

I leaned back against the bench. "I think this is the part," I said, "where you're supposed to assure me I'll be okay."

Steve didn't respond. Instead he glanced down the street, in the direction of the approaching emergency vehicles, and said,

"Come *on,* hurry up already."

"Never a cop around when you need one," I said.

"I guess the hell not," Steve said.

"While we're on the subject of municipal ineptitude," I said. "The crossing signal."

Steve looked at me again, perplexed. "Hey," he said. "Stay with me, okay?"

"I'm sorry," I said. "What I meant was that crossing signal there, in front of us. It's broken. That's the whole reason I'm here in the first place."

Judging by his expression, Steve again failed to register what I meant.

"I should probably write a letter to the city," I told him.

The bald man appeared in the window frame again. "She's okay," he called to us. "Scared, but okay."

"That's good," I said.

Steve hooked a thumb in my direction. "He's not doing so hot," he said to the bald man. "Talking gibberish."

"I'm perfectly lucid," I said, rising to my feet by way of demonstration. "And I think I'd like to go. My cat needs to be fed, and this letter to the city is sort of writing itself right now. I'd like to get it down on paper before I forget."

"You see?" Steve said to the bald man.

"I'll find something to try and stop the bleeding," the bald man told Steve. He disappeared inside again.

The crossing signal on the opposite side of the street, interestingly enough, seemed to be functioning just fine — it displayed, in encouraging crystalline LED light, the outline of a man walking. So I walked, albeit a bit unsteadily.

Behind me I heard Steve call out. "Guy," he said, "where are you going, you fucking got *shot.*"

But I hadn't eaten all day, hadn't had a thing to drink all day, and I was cold and tired and the cat needed to be fed, and now that I was on my feet I just wanted to be home. So I ignored Steve's entreaties and crossed the street, still composing the letter of complaint in my head. I intended to use a fairly light, casual tone, while simultaneously making clear that, in my view, crossing signals were an important component of public safety and warranted the same prompt attention that would be afforded, say, a broken traffic light.

I'd covered maybe half the distance to my house when police strobes suddenly blazed all around, deflecting off of tree trunks and vinyl siding, chasing shadows around the neighborhood at the speed of light. Behind me a car screeched to a stop, and I heard two doors open.

"Stop right there!" someone yelled. I surmised, though I could not confirm visually, that for the second time that night a firearm was being pointed at me. "Hands, motherfucker! Let me see your hands!"

I raised my good arm overhead, extended the other as far out to my side as I could, and turned to face the blinding lumens of a roof-mounted spotlight.

"Down on the ground, now!" I was told.

And I obeyed this directive, however unintentionally, by passing out.

4
As Much as She Needs

Sarah died as she had lived, which is to say: furiously.

I'm referring here to the very last day of her life, during which she flailed through something called the agonal phase.

Depending on one's perspective, "agonal" is either an apt and evocative description of the phenomenon, or an inaccurate, perhaps even hyperbolic description of the phenomenon.

Apt because during this time the dying person often thrashes about, throws her head from side to side, makes strange animal noises, and generally behaves as if she were in tremendous discomfort.

Inaccurate and perhaps hyperbolic because neuroscientists agree that the agonal phase is a cognitive state resembling deep surgical sedation, and so despite all the gasping and moaning the person experiences no discomfort — let alone agony —

whatsoever.

On average it lasts for two minutes, give or take.

Sarah's, by contrast, went on all day and into the night.

This was by no means the only way in which she was exceptional.

"I know it seems awful," the hospice nurse said while I sat at Sarah's bedside and held her hand. "But I've done this many, many times, and she can't feel anything. She's miles away."

Every half minute or so, Sarah would heave for breath and squeeze my hand with a strength I'd never known her to possess. Each time it felt like the small bones in my hand might crack. I winced and held on despite the fact that Sarah could not feel or know anything, and thus could not care less whether I was holding her hand.

"I'm here," I told her over and over. "Okay, okay. Easy. I'm here, Sarah. I'm here."

As the first hour passed, the nurse expressed surprise that Sarah was still alive, and began uttering platitudes that had no basis in either medicine or human physiology.

"She's not ready to leave you yet," the nurse said. Also: "It's amazing sometimes how long people hold on, out of love."

When it was over, I learned that patients whose cancer migrates to the lungs, as Sarah's had, could sometimes struggle for hours before finally expiring. This seemed, for reasons both scientific and personal, a much more likely explanation for her protracted agonal period than any reluctance on her part to leave me.

But I nodded along, pretending to share the nurse's amazement at the power of love to forestall death. I held Sarah's hand and stroked her cheek and separated her lips as the nurse squirted morphine from a wide-gauge syringe. I read aloud: Tolstoy, bits of levity from Nora Ephron, Robert Lowell's visions of New England, where Sarah and I had grown up, met, fallen in love.

Though I made no phone calls, people arrived throughout the day, summoned by a force they could not name — and like the Magi, they bore gifts.

"We just felt like we should drop by," Alice said, proffering a baking pan full of manicotti. Behind her in the doorway stood Tony with a vase of flowers, strange blossoms in muted earth tones (months later, when Alice was out of earshot, he apologized for the grim arrangement, referring to it as "FTD's 'Sorry Your Wife Is Dying' bouquet").

After that, friends showed up every half hour or so. As the house filled, Alice took over the minor domestic duties — keeping coffee on, answering the door, policing those who neglected to remove their shoes — while I continued my hand-pulverizing vigil at Sarah's bedside. People took turns sitting in the only other chair in the room, on the opposite side of the bed. Hardly anyone spoke to me. No one except Alice ventured to take Sarah's right hand, even though every half minute or so she seized up like someone being hit with a defibrillator and waved that hand around in a sort of grotesque invitation. Most visitors, the first couple of times this happened after they took a seat, recoiled in spite of themselves. Maybe they were afraid of how Sarah's hand would feel — and they were right to be afraid, because her hand was hard and cold, like she was not a person but rather one of those antique dolls with the porcelain eyes that stare and stare. So they watched Sarah thrash and listened to her moan for as long as they could bear to do so, then stood and withdrew to the light and warmth of the kitchen.

Much as I might have wanted to, I certainly couldn't blame them for excusing themselves. Watching someone die isn't just unpleasant, it's also pretty dull. At least in the kitchen there was hot coffee and conversation, people eating casserole from paper plates, sharing hugs and gossip and opinions about sporting events. It became a sort of safe zone, like the designated spot in a children's game where one is immune from being made "it."

Eventually everyone served their time at Sarah's bedside, and I slept, my forehead pressed against the hard raised seam at the edge of the mattress. Evening had flowed like a black liquid into the corners of the room when Alice woke me and insisted that I take a mug of tea. I looked up, blinking and mute, and Alice gazed at me and used her free hand to touch an indentation the mattress had left in my forehead. Her thumb was hot from holding the mug, and for just an instant it burned me. Alice traced the line in my skin and cooed mournfully, her head tilted to the side and her eyes brimming, an empathic tenderness the likes of which she almost certainly had never shared with Tony, and suddenly I was relieved of thinking about Sarah and instead free to marvel at the ways in which human relationships defied neat categorization and constraint, how Alice and I, until now mindlessly chaste in our interactions, were here thrust by grief into a moment as physically and emotionally intimate as sex, and thus could have been rightly accused of violating the covenant of both our marriages — in front of my dying wife, no less. And I almost confessed to Alice then, almost told her that I was responsible for the fact that my Sarah was dying, and how the worst part of being guilty was having no one suspect you in the least. But then I noticed my hand ached as if someone had been pounding on it with a claw hammer, and this drew my attention away. I looked down, and Alice pulled her thumb away from my forehead, and the moment ended. Alice set the mug of tea on the nightstand and said, "Drink that, you." She left me there, flexing my hand and contemplating the bruises gathering on the meat between my thumb and forefinger, purple marks the exact size and shape of Sarah's fingertips.

Sarah continued to seize and sigh. Dinnertime slipped on toward full night and sleet began to scratch at the windows. By and by people rinsed their coffee cups, tossed their paper plates in the trash, and gathered their things to go. They drifted into the bedroom, regretful sounds issuing from their throats, eyes wet and helpless. They

squeezed my shoulder, kissed Sarah's forehead, took their leave. Soon the hospice
nurse had to go as well. She pressed eight
syringes of morphine into my hand and told
me to give Sarah "as much as she needs."

She held my gaze for a moment after she
said this. When she left, I put the syringes
in the nightstand.

Tony and Alice stayed on after everyone
else had departed. While Alice sat with
Sarah, Tony and I huddled outside under
the overhang on the top step and shared a
cigarette. It was early morning now, and the
sleet had changed over to a chill rain that
puddled on the ice coating the driveway.

"The nurse gave me enough morphine to
kill Sarah," I told Tony.

"What?"

I dragged on the cigarette, handed it over,
and repeated myself.

"But that's just so you have what you need
to get through the night, right?" Tony said.
"She doesn't actually want you to give her
an overdose."

"I think she does," I said. "Or at least she
wants me to have the option."

"But she didn't actually *say* 'Here's a
bunch of morphine, give your wife an
overdose.' "

" 'Give her as much as she needs' were

her exact words."

Tony gave the cigarette back to me and peered out into the darkness. "We're good enough friends that I can say what I'm thinking, right?"

"Sure," I said.

"Because it seems to me the nurse didn't mean anything but exactly what she said. I think you heard what you wanted to hear."

"Just so I understand," I said, "you're saying, in essence, that I want someone to tell me it's okay to kill my wife."

"Not in so many words, K.," Tony said. "Jesus. But that said? If it's me? With what's going on in there? I'd give it some serious thought, man. I really would."

I flicked the cigarette into the driveway, where it landed in a puddle and hissed out. "I think," I said, "that we should probably go back inside."

As the darkest part of the night went on and Sarah continued to thrash her covers, I kept remembering those syringes. At first the thought of them would flit through my mind for just an instant, usually in the moments when Sarah seized up and her eyes flew open, furious yet vacant, and she sucked at the air like a fish in the bottom of a boat. Alice kept her seat on the opposite side of the bed, her eyes closed and her lips moving silently, and Tony stood in the bedroom doorway looking stricken, every once in a while bowing his head and running a hand through his hair or kneading the muscles in the back of his neck.

Around three A.M. my cell phone buzzed. It was Peggy, Sarah's mother, calling from the road.

"Is she gone yet?" Peggy asked.

"How far away are you?" I asked.

"Three, four hours," she said. "I'm on goddamn ever-loving 84 in Hartford."

"She isn't gone yet," I told Peggy.

"And you know what I'm thinking, as I drive through Hartford?" Peggy asked. "I'm thinking there's very little wrong with the health-care system that couldn't be solved by dropping a smallish nuclear weapon on this town."

"Peggy," I said.

"They're fucking vampires," Peggy said.

"Okay." I rubbed at my eyes.

"How much longer?" Peggy asked.

"Until what?"

"How much longer," Peggy said slowly, "does my daughter have?"

"It's hard to say," I said. "She's hanging on pretty tight."

Then I told Peggy about the hospice nurse, and the syringes in the nightstand drawer. Several moments passed, during which the only sound between us was the sharp inhalations of Peggy smoking one of her Winston Lights.

"What are you waiting for?" she said finally.

"I'm sorry?" I said.

"Not me, I hope," she said.

"You think I should give Sarah the morphine?"

"I think it's your decision," Peggy said. "But if I have a vote."

I stood and walked out of the room, squeezing past Tony in the doorway. "I don't know if 'votes' are really what we're talking about," I said. "Maybe more like . . . I don't know, Peggy. I'm pretty exhausted, and my wife is dying at a rate that suddenly everyone but me seems to think is not fast enough."

Predictably, this inspired little overt sympathy, or even fellow feeling, in Peggy. "Is she uncomfortable?" she asked.

"She seems like it," I said. "But the nurse insists she can't feel anything. That she's basically comatose."

"What is she doing, exactly?"

"I'd rather not describe it in detail, Peggy," I said. "Suffice to say that most people would think yeah, that looks awful and someone should do something about it."

"So be practical," Peggy said. "For Christ's sake, K."

Understand, this did not seem at all strange, coming from her.

"Alright," I said. "Maybe I should just go grab a big rock and do the job right. Wouldn't want to take the chance that the morphine won't work."

"Don't be an asshole," Peggy said flatly.

"I think I will, actually," I said. "Considering that I'm the one whose wife is dying, I think I will be an asshole, if I feel like it."

"She's my daughter."

"Get here as soon as you can, Peggy," I said, and hung up.

The bedroom air was thick with the discomfort of those who have overheard an argument to which they are not a party, and neither Tony nor Alice looked in my direction as I came back in. Neither said anything when I took my seat again, gazed at my wife, opened the nightstand drawer, and pulled out one of the syringes. Neither said anything several moments later, when I pulled out the rest. They remained silent when I tossed the last empty syringe in the trash and crawled onto the bed next to Sarah, though Tony did come around the bed, remove the small grocery bag containing the syringes from the trash can, and leave the house for several minutes before returning empty-handed to watch as Sarah took a final, choking breath.

I never asked what he did with the bag, and he never told me.

None of this, incidentally, has anything to do with why I felt responsible for Sarah's death. That die was cast well before the night she died — before, in fact, either of us had any idea that she was sick.

5
FIFTEEN MINUTES

Hospitals aren't as bad as people make them out to be, so long as you're not in mind-erasing pain and have a private room and a nurse who's willing to let you eat your fill of ice cream. I'd hit the jackpot in all three regards. My pain was sufficiently blunted by a Dilaudid drip. I had a private room, owing ostensibly to the quality of my job's HMO plan, but moreover to my new status as a local hero. And I had the most solicitous nurse I'd ever met in my life, maybe the nicest person to ever grace the halls of an intensive care ward. She was shaped like a Bartlett pear, and treated me with a grandmotherly indulgence that was pleasant rather than oppressive.

I didn't have to ask for the ice cream. It just showed up, one three-ounce cup after another, its satiny sweetness rendered all the more delicious by the Dilaudid buzz. I tasted every bite in a way I hadn't tasted anything in a long time. The only problem was all they had were cups of Neapolitan, so I had to excavate the chocolate and vanilla from around the stripe of strawberry, which was not anything resembling easy with only one useful hand. But the nurse was far too kind for me to complain about such a trifling thing, so I made do.

I was in the ICU because the bullet had ricocheted off my collarbone and nicked my subclavian artery. By the time I hit the table in the emergency room I'd lost a quarter of the blood in my body, and I lost another quarter of it before they got the artery repaired.

"You were very lucky," both the surgeon and the nurse told me.

The pear-shaped nurse was more excited at my good fortune than anyone else. I just smiled and nodded, because she was so nice and I didn't want to do anything to disappoint her.

It was different with the surgeon.

"This doesn't feel lucky," I told him.

"I know it hurts," he said, meaning my broken collarbone, "but really, a quarter of an inch further down and you would have bled to death in the street."

"I guess my point," I said, "is that the man with the gun wasn't aiming at me, or really aiming at all — he just turned in my direction and pulled the trigger when I startled him. The bullet could have gone anywhere. That it ended up in my shoulder, given the odds, doesn't feel lucky. It feels bad-lucky."

"Mmm-hmmm," the surgeon said while he hen-pecked at a tablet computer.

"Lucky," I went on, "would have been something like, for example, he fires the gun and the bullet misses me altogether but hits the ATM across the street, causing it to malfunction and spit out thousands of dollars, which I then could have collected before the police showed up."

"Right," said the surgeon.

"*That* would have been lucky."

The surgeon typed some more. His fingertips made faint little padding noises on the tablet screen.

"I've never understood why when bad things happen people fall all over themselves to tell the victims how lucky they are," I said. " 'You're lucky they caught the cancer early and all they had to do was cut your colon out.' "

The surgeon finished typing and placed the tablet screen-up on his lap. "Do you have any other questions?" he asked brightly.

"I don't mean to sound ungrateful," I told him.

"Okay then," he said, standing to go. "I'll check in with you tomorrow afternoon."

Aside from the doctors and the matronly nurse, I had plenty of other visitors.

First came the police, two uniformed cops and one detective in pleated khakis and a red oxford with a badge clipped to his waistband. They arrived not long after surgery on my artery had concluded. It was now early evening, and I'd come out of sedation just enough to begin speaking something that resembled English. The detective asked the questions. The guys in uniform stood silent and stone-faced the entire time; for all I knew, they might have been the world's only mute cop partners. I'd never been interviewed by the police before, and had imagined that it would be a less pleasant experience. But I had enough narcotics in my system that thumbscrews would have seemed only moderately uncomfortable, and besides, the detective turned out to be almost as kind and solicitous as my nurse. He thanked me several times, for being at the coffee shop the night before, and for my willingness to talk so soon after such a harrowing experience. He said that he planned to recommend me, with vigorous insistence, for something called the

Citizen's Valor Award. He said, in parting, that he hoped his son grew up to be half as brave as I was. On his way out he put a hand on my good shoulder and gave it a squeeze.

Tony and Art showed up the next day, carrying a miniature wooden palette box with the words MAN CRATE stenciled on the side in a blocky, masculine font.

"It's like a gift basket," Tony said as he pried the lid off with a miniature novelty crowbar. "Only, you know, for a guy. Got some jerky in here, some corn nuts."

"I don't know if I'm allowed jerky or corn nuts," I said. "You'll have to clear it with the nurse. She's very nice."

"This was Alice's idea, by the way," Tony said. "I've been trying for years to figure how to get out of the doghouse with her. Turns out all you need to do is get shot."

"She's not mad at me anymore?" I asked.

"She's still mad," Tony said.

Art nodded confirmation of this fact.

"She's just more worried than mad, at the moment," Tony said. "But if you want to stay in her good graces, you're probably going to have to up the ante and die in the next couple days."

"I'm not a physician," I said, "but that seems unlikely, at this point."

"Then take it from me," Tony said, handing over a plastic sack of jerky, "enjoy the reprieve while it lasts."

Art helped himself to some trail mix. "So tell us," he said around a mouthful of peanuts and Craisins, "what in the actual fuck happened?"

I pushed a button to raise myself to a sitting position. "I got shot," I said.

"Clearly," Art said. "But how?"

"I intervened in a robbery," I said.

"K., we read the newspaper," Tony said. "What he's asking is, did you wade in there like a boss? Karate chop the guy in the neck?"

"I knocked on the window to get his attention," I said.

They stared.

"Then he shot me," I said. "It was pretty low on the heroism scale."

Tony shook his head. "Seriously, K.," he said, "the more time goes by, the more I think Alice is right."

"Right about what?"

"That you've lost your goddamn mind."

"What would you have done?" I said.

"Me?" Art asked.

"Either of you," I said.

"I would have hidden in the bushes like a little bitch," Art said. He tossed back another handful of trail mix.

"Perhaps you've heard of 9-1-1?" Tony said.

"Of course I've heard of 9-1-1," I said.

"Did you think to dial it?"

"Yes," I said.

"And then you just strolled over and knocked on the window," Tony said.

"I didn't really have many options," I said.

"You had the option to hide like a little bitch," Art said.

"That's true," I said.

"Well crazy or not, you're a better man than I am," Tony said. "Because I gotta be honest, I wouldn't have the stones to do what you did."

I motioned for Tony to hand me the cup of water on my bedside tray. "It had nothing to do with stones," I told him.

"I don't mean literal rocks, ya mook," Tony said. He lifted the cup and placed it in my good hand.

"I know," I said. "You mean testicles. As a metaphor for courage."

"Very good," Tony said.

"It would have been a different calculus for you," I told him. "You've got Alice. You've got the kids."

Tony tilted his head from side to side, not entirely convinced. "Still," he said.

"Besides which," I said, "I can tell you

79

that this wasn't courage. At least not the way I understand the word. It was more like being a robot. Or a golem."

I raised the cup to my lips. The water, having sat on the table for several hours, had gone utterly inert except for a slight chlorine bouquet.

"Plus," I said, handing the cup back to Tony, "there's that other thing."

Tony pointed an admonishing finger at me. "The thing of which we will not speak," he said.

"That thing," I confirmed.

"Which thing?" Art asked, digging around in the trail mix bag for the last few peanuts.

"The utterly batshit thing of which we will not speak," Tony said to him. "You're out of the loop. And trust me, you want to stay out of the loop."

"Actually, now that you mention it, I know about that thing," Art said, looking to Tony. "I knew about it before you did."

"Both of you," Tony said. "Zip it."

The girl from the coffee shop, whose name was Felicia, showed up a few hours after Tony and Art left. The extremely nice nurse announced her arrival, and then Felicia walked into my room slowly, hands clasped in front of her waist. For a few moments she stood just inside the doorway, staring at me. Tears brimmed in her big dark eyes, shimmering in the light from the overhead fluorescents. She was, to all outward appearances, unharmed by her encounter with the man who had semiaccidentally shot me. Behind Felicia stood a kid with satellite dish ears and a blond crew cut, presumably her boyfriend. The boyfriend held a bouquet of roses and daisies. Instead of a vase, the bouquet was jammed into a large mug painted to resemble a can of Campbell's chicken soup. FEEL BETTER SOON, the mug read.

"Hello," I said to Felicia.

"Hi," she said.

"Are you alright?" I asked.

Felicia didn't answer. Instead, she started to cry. She put her hands to her face — much as she had in the coffee shop when the man pointed the gun at her — and crossed the distance between the doorway and my bed with quick, shuffling steps. She threw herself against me, causing my shoulder to launch a flare of pain through the cool fog of narcotics. I put my good arm around her and kept quiet while her body hitched with sobs.

The boyfriend remained in the doorway, still holding the bouquet and shifting from foot to foot. I motioned with the hand slung over Felicia's back for him to put the flowers on the nightstand.

Felicia eventually cried herself out, and then, still clinging to me, she spoke in a voice so quiet I could barely hear it despite the proximity of her lips to my ear. "You saved my life," she said.

Until now I hadn't really thought about this, so I took a second to respond. "We don't know that for sure," I told her.

Felicia pushed herself up from the bed and looked at me. "He was going to kill me," she said. "I saw it on his face. I can't stop seeing it."

"Maybe after a while, if you're lucky, the memory will fade."

"Never," she said. "It'll never go away. I see his face, and then I see you falling."

"Still, even if he had shot you," I said, "it's not a foregone conclusion that you would have died."

The fingers of Felicia's left hand, which rested on my good shoulder, tightened slowly, bunching the thin cotton of my hospital johnny. "You saved my life. I want you to say it."

I thought for a moment. "I suppose," I said, "if I hadn't finally crossed the street and knocked on the window, it's at least likely you would have died."

"What do you mean, 'finally'?" Felicia asked.

"I'd been standing on the corner for hours, trying to get to the coffee shop for my Americano. You probably know me as the Americano guy."

She blinked several times. "Lots of people get Americanos."

"Doesn't matter," I said. "The point is, the cross signal was broken. It just kept saying DON'T WALK. So I didn't walk. Until I heard you scream. That sort of broke the spell."

She furrowed her brow. "You were out there all afternoon?"

"Yes. A good portion of the morning, as well."

"So wait. If not for the broken cross signal, you would have come and gone hours before I got held up."

I considered this. "I suppose so, yes," I said.

Felicia smiled warmly, and her fingers released the johnny. "It was fate. You were *meant* to be there," she said. "You're a hero."

The first reporter, a thin guy who looked like he'd graduated from college five or ten minutes before arriving at my hospital room, came in later that same afternoon. He worked for the local CBS affiliate, and looked the part: cheap shirt and tie, cheaper haircut. For a television personality he was, at first, surprisingly taciturn. His cameraman took ten minutes to set up, during which time the reporter said almost nothing to me and barely looked up from the screen of his smartphone. As soon as the camera began recording, though, the reporter transformed utterly. His face, previously stony and bloodless, came to startling life, filled with color and fellow feeling. His eyebrows undulated like caterpillars, and he leaned toward me as he spoke, punctuating his words with swipes of the silver pen in his right hand. While I talked, he listened with the intensity of a supplicant straining to hear the voice of God. He nodded vigorously at every other word out of my mouth. He had several set expressions that he could assume in an instant. There was The Pensive: eyes squinted in concentration, hand on chin, index finger nestled in the hollow beneath his bottom lip. There was The Aghast: hands clasped before his chest in a pantomime of nervous anticipation, mouth ajar and eyebrows raised so high they nearly collided with his hairline. There was The

Agreeable: nodding and smiling, his face cheerfully vacant, as though he were chatting with an ethnically balanced group of friends in a beer commercial.

Like most performances it seemed garish in person, but likely would be quite affecting once filtered through the cheesecloth of television.

"But so let's go back a moment," the reporter said, his pen slicing the air. "Because what I want to know is, at what point did you realize you were the one who had to save the girl? What was that moment like?"

"Well there was no moment when I realized I had to save her," I told him. "That wasn't how it went, really, at all."

The reporter seemed not to hear this. "Were you frightened but determined? Or were you perhaps angry that this was happening here in your safe, quiet neighborhood, where people should be able to go out at night without worrying that they'll be robbed?"

"Neither of those things," I said.

"So you were just blank, then. Pure id. Full of purpose."

"Um. Yes. That's probably more accurate."

"You saw what you needed to do, and you did it."

I considered. "Yes," I said finally. "That's fair."

"Amazing," the reporter said. "Just amazing. But so tell me, how did you happen to be there at the critical time?"

I pointed to the tray of food next to my bed, which the very nice nurse had brought in just before the interview started. "Do you mind if I eat a little? I haven't had much of an appetite for months, and suddenly I'm famished."

"It won't look great on TV," the reporter said. "But you're a hero, and you're convalescing. People won't begrudge you a little food."

"I'm really quite hungry."

The reporter gestured toward the tray: *go ahead.* "So. How you came to be there at the moment the girl was being robbed."

"Actually," I said, lifting a forkful of something that bore a vague resemblance to stroganoff, "I'd been there all afternoon."

"At the coffee shop? Wait one minute. My understanding was that you were outside."

"I was," I told him. "I'd been outside most of the day."

For a moment, genuine bewilderment pierced the reporter's tidy façade of professional interest. "I'm sorry. Can you explain?"

The stroganoff was cold and tasted like a mud puddle, so I set it down and reached for a small plate of strawberries. "I was on the other side of the street, waiting for the crossing signal to change."

"For the entire afternoon."

"It was broken," I explained.

He paused. "But why not, uh, just cross the street, once you realized it was broken?"

"You know," I said, "I've never liked strawberries out of season. They're too tart."

An innocuous enough thing for a person to say, you might think. But as soon as the words left my mouth, that shuddering panic I'd experienced days earlier at Tony's and Big Buy Total Foods descended again. Sweat sprung up on my brow, and I was suddenly sick with self-loathing. This feeling was immediately intolerable, in the same way I imagine being burned alive would be intolerable.

"Can you tell me," I asked the reporter, "how many people in the United States don't have enough to eat?"

He looked at me. "Are you alright?" he asked.

"Please," I said. "Just look it up, if you would? On that phone of yours?"

"Mike," the cameraman said, "what the hell, man. This is supposed to be a puff piece. Come *on*."

Ignoring him, the reporter stood and pulled the phone from his pocket. The cameraman sighed and rolled his eyes skyward. The very nice nurse poked her head in the doorway; I smiled and tried to look well so her tacit inquiry would end there.

"About thirty-three million," the reporter said. " 'Approximately thirty-three million Americans struggle to put food on the table' is the exact quote, here."

"What's the source?" I asked.

"The USDA," the reporter said. "Via NPR. Seems reputable enough."

"Okay," I said, and hammer-fisted myself in the face, hard enough to feel it through the Dilaudid.

"Whoa," the cameraman said. "Whoa, whoa."

"Did you get that?" the reporter asked. "Tell me you got that."

"I got it," the cameraman said. "Weirdest fucking thing I ever shot, man, but I got it."

"You're bleeding," the reporter said, pointing to my nose.

"I'm getting used to it," I said, dabbing at my upper lip with one finger. "It's been happening a lot lately."

For what might have been the first time in

his nascent career, the reporter then asked a question he seemed to genuinely want to know the answer to. "Why did you do that?"

"Because," I said, "complaining about strawberries being too tart while other people starve is about the worst thing I've ever done in my life. I deserve to be punched, for saying something like that. But I wouldn't want to ask anyone else to do it for me."

"Okay," the reporter said.

The cameraman laughed behind his hand.

"Are you in the habit of punching yourself in the face?" the reporter asked. "Is that how you got the bruise over your eye?"

"No," I told him. "That was some guy on the side of the interstate."

The reporter stared at me for a moment, then turned in his seat toward the cameraman. "Bobby," he said, "how much room does that thing have left on its memory card?"

"So you've come completely unhinged, then," Claire said from the doorway of my hospital room two mornings later.

"How do you know I wasn't unhinged before?" I asked.

She came around the foot of the bed, beautiful extraterrestrial eyes shining with good cheer. Her hair was down now, brighter red in the sunlight from the windows and curled slightly at the ends. "Oh, you obviously were," she said. "You freaked out about a bottle of soap, basically made an illegal arrest of some hillbilly, got into a semantic argument with a Big Buy clerk, and managed to get yourself shot, all in less than thirty-six hours."

"I take it you saw the Newschannel piece," I said.

"Also, you're a recent widower," Claire said. "Which, along with everything else, is pretty sexy."

"That's an odd thing to say."

"I'm joking," Claire said. "Being facetious. You know, facetious?"

"I know the concept. I also used to be able to detect it in conversation. Lately, not so much."

Claire sat on the edge of my bed, and as before I caught a sour whiff of last night's alcohol under the spice of some perfume. This close I could see her eyes, though cheerful, were shot through with angry red capillaries. "So you watched the piece, too?" she asked. "You big narcissist."

"All I do here is watch TV," I told her.

"It's getting a lot of attention, you know. Your little breakdown. They've interviewed me. The guy with the pickup truck who socked you. The Big Buy girl. Of course the girl from the coffee shop."

"I saw all that. Like I said, all I do here is watch TV."

"I'm flattered," Claire said, "to be in such exalted company."

"That's a joke?"

"Very good."

"But you did the interview," I said.

"Sure I did. And not just with Newschannel 9. I'm as big an attention whore as the next girl. Phone's been ringing off the hook."

"Mine too," I said.

"They still haven't found the guy who held up the coffee shop, by the way."

"I know," I said.

"Does that worry you?"

"Should it?"

"Maybe he'll try to find you so you can't identify him in court."

"I'm not sure this is the kind of criminal who hunts down and silences witnesses. He didn't seem that well organized."

The molded plastic phone on the nightstand purred for the eighth or ninth time that day. I picked up the handset. On the other end a man with a very low voice and syrupy diction said he wanted to put me on television. I told him I'd already been on television recently, and anyway I couldn't talk about it now, and hung up.

"Who was that?" Claire asked.

"Somebody named Theodore. He wants to give me a television show."

"Like a reality show?"

"I'm not sure. We didn't get that far. He wants to have lunch."

"You should say yes," Claire said.

"I know literally nothing about what he's proposing," I said.

"K.," she said, "do you realize how many people take pictures and videos of their lunch and their cats and their colostomy bags and put it online? It used to be just serial killers who needed that kind of attention. Now it's all of us."

"What does that have to do with whether or not I want to be on TV?"

"I'm just saying, these days even the most unremarkable life can be validated if enough people see a recording of it."

"Okay."

"The converse is true, as well," Claire said.

"And what's the converse?"

"That no matter how remarkable your life, it means nothing if it happens in private."

"I'm not sure I agree with that."

She smirked. "Whether you agree has no

bearing on whether it's true."

I decided to change the subject. "So how are things over at Total Foods?"

"Wouldn't know," Claire said. "I got fired."

"What? Why?"

"For speaking truth to power. About soap."

"Someone heard us?" I asked.

"You remember the old joke about why you should never tell secrets on a farm?"

"No," I said.

"Because the corn has ears, the potatoes have eyes, and the beanstalk."

"I'm afraid I don't get it," I said.

She rolled her eyes. "The same can be said of Total Foods. And you don't have to be in the produce section for the corn to hear you."

"I'm sorry you got fired," I said.

"Well please, don't go punching yourself in the face over it or anything."

"Hadn't occurred to me."

"In any event, that's part of why I came. I figured since I've suddenly got a lot of time on my hands, and you clearly need someone to look after you, I'd pop by."

"I strike you as someone in need of help?"

"Um, *yeah.*"

"What exactly did you have in mind?"

Claire gathered her hair into a ponytail and secured it with an elastic from her wrist, talking while her hands performed impressive contortions seemingly of their own volition. "I don't know," she said. "Live-in nanny. Business adviser. Human shield. Haven't really thought it through, just yet."

"Maybe I should help you get your job back."

"In this economy? Please. It was filled five minutes after I walked out. There are thousands of people in this town who would kill to stock overpriced cheese for ten dollars an hour."

"Still. Maybe I could talk to your boss. I seem to have new cachet, as a hero."

"He's not my boss anymore," Claire said. She smiled brightly and poked my good shoulder with one finger. "You are."

6
BETTER THAN FINE

Aside from the uncomfortable love seat and the sense that he expected a forthrightness that he himself did not traffic in, I also stopped seeing the foul-mouthed therapist because of an Albert Einstein biography.

As far as revelations go, the book arrived innocuously enough: wrapped in plain brown paper like pornography, with no return address. The note inside indicated that it was a bereavement gift from an old college friend, now a physicist at Stanford. Bobbing in the wake of Sarah's death, I had no particular interest in Einstein, or really anything other than drinking brown liquor and staring blankly at whatever happened into my field of vision, but I took the book to my back porch, along with a bottle of bourbon and a rocks glass from a set Sarah had purchased years ago for our first dinner party as newlyweds.

It was a clear dry afternoon in July. I sat

in the creaky Adirondack chair whose now-redundant twin rested in the dark of the basement. I poured some whiskey and looked out over the contents of our small backyard: the wildly tentacled rosebush, the fecund oval of mulch under the magnolia, the rainbow of pistils and petals in the flower bed that ran the length of the brick foundation, everything bursting and bright and violently alive.

I sat considering all this unruly optimism that had screamed out of the ground with neither help nor encouragement from me: Sarah's legacy, staunchly perennial though she herself was no longer so. The first sip of whiskey stung my lips. After a few minutes I looked down and reread the note from my old college friend, saying he'd heard about Sarah, and was sorry, and further that he regretted we hadn't seen one another in so long.

I set the letter aside and picked up the book. I turned it over in my hands, read the synopsis on the back, looked at the black-and-white photo of the author, cracked the spine.

Einstein lived a long and eventful life, but I am a fast reader, and the bottle of bourbon had only just been opened.

Toward the end of the book, Einstein's

colleague Besso, who was perhaps closer to him than any other person in his life, died. Einstein, ever decent, penned a letter of condolence to Besso's widow. He wrote: "In quitting this strange world he has once again preceded me by just a little. That means nothing. For physicists the distinction between past, present, and future is only an illusion, however persistent."

I read this passage half a dozen, a dozen, two dozen times. The sky blushed, then darkened, and with the sun's exit the air grew still and the branches of the magnolia ceased whispering. Soon the only sounds came from my roiling guts and the mosquitoes that alighted on my forearms to take their fill. I was stricken, elated, as confused as I'd ever been. When twilight finally blinked out, rendering the words on the page illegible, I looked up as if snapping to sudden consciousness, then switched on the porch light and read the passage some more.

What could Einstein have known that eliminated all grief over the death of his best friend? Was such revelation even possible? Or was this simply a bit of hyperbole Einstein wielded to leaven a widow's anguish?

That means nothing.

I knew very little about relativity, and I had never in my life needed so badly to understand something. I took the porch stairs two at a time and called my old college friend, using the number he'd provided in the note.

"Oh, I think Einstein was sincere," he told me, his voice hoarse with sleep. "He found comfort in what he'd proven. You can't dedicate that much time and brain space to a problem, solve it so unassailably, and not take to heart its implications."

"And so its implications, in this case, being that no one really dies?"

"Christ, K., what time is it?"

"One in the morning. Eastern Daylight."

"And you've had how much to drink, exactly?"

"I just really need to know about this," I told him.

My old college friend sighed. "I mean it's all theory, K.," he said. "In both the scientific and practical senses. So that's the huge caveat. There may come a day when we figure out how to apprehend time accurately with our hearts as well as our heads. But for now, we're stuck with the illusory. That car has two hundred thousand miles on it. That bologna has gone bad. That person is dead."

"Right," I said. "But the word 'illusory.' "

"I mean, I see where you're going with this," he said.

"I'm just trying to understand what it means."

"You should sober up," he said. "Get some sleep. This might not seem so seismic in the light of day."

"It's absolutely not possible," I told him, "for me to sleep right now."

He coughed, and I could hear him rub at his face on the other end of the line. "Is there someone I should call, K.?" he asked. "Someone who can come and be with you for a while?"

"I don't need company," I said. "I need to understand."

Another sigh. "Alright," he said. "Well if you really want to understand the persistence of grief, you need to dig down into Newton."

What I came to learn, reading through the rest of the night and into daybreak, was that Isaac Newton is the enemy of the bereaved — that in fact he could be held responsible for (to borrow my friend's words) the persistence of grief, if not the original concept. Time, to Newton, was absolute: it flowed linearly, and therefore when the present became the past it remained so forever. Once you chose a sweet roll for breakfast, that moment faded out of existence for the rest of eternity. And so it was with all things, up to and including death. But then Einstein proved beyond a doubt that Newton had been wrong, that in fact time is relative, malleable, altered by all manner of things, gravity and perception chief among them. It can be — and is — warped, bent, folded, reversed, sped up, or knotted like a shoelace.

What wonderful, startling news: Besso lived! But how, exactly, had this been news to me? I was a grown man, educated to an extent that in most of the world would have been considered obscene, yet the most important implications of relativity, proven a century before, were so obscure to me that one might have suspected the gears of a conspiracy had been churning to keep it that way. My head swam with questions. Why did we persist in teaching our children that gravity is a force? Why did we still consider the moments of our lives as comparatively inconsequential parts of a whole, rather than discrete, immutable universes unto themselves? Most important by far: why did we continue to grieve as though no one had corrected Newton's error? Why were there no flyers in funeral homes and oncology wards declaring on their covers, in bold caps: **NO ONE REALLY DIES**? Why so much noodling about death on daytime talk shows, but no discussion of its illusory nature? We still answered the phone and collapsed on the floor at grim words from the other end. We still threw ourselves, wailing, onto caskets, still shrieked and tore at our clothes, still sat alone in quiet houses drinking too much and staring at the walls.

But now, the more I read, the more I understood that Einstein's sanguinity at the death of Besso had been genuine. I realized how ridiculous it was to feel abandoned, or bereft, or alone. I switched from bourbon to coffee, smiling as water burbled through the percolator. My wife might have been absent, but she was not dead to me, any more than Besso had been to Einstein. And if she was not dead, then I could not be responsible for her death.

I stood at the kitchen window, mug in hand, as the sun began to crest the roof of the apartment building next door, sending spears of light through my corneas. My pupils contracted painfully, and I recoiled, returning to myself like a soul being yanked back into a body.

And I resolved, then and there, to no longer take part in the false propagation of mourning, and to never again trust, uncorroborated, the evidence of my senses.

But for now, first things first — since Sarah was not dead, was not a memory, then I had no obligation to keep her memory alive, to preserve the shrine of our house, to leave her things undisturbed as totems of my grief. The coffee, fresh and black, went down like molten steel. I gulped it, relishing the burn, then ran upstairs to the bedroom and began gathering things and placing them in a pile on the area rug next to the bed. I stripped great armfuls of Sarah's clothes from the racks in the closet and dropped them, complete with hangers, to the floor. Down went her jewelry boxes, various knickknacks, boots and shoes, a collection of matchbooks from places we'd vacationed. Down went mementos and decorative objects, framed photographs, a broken pocket watch that had been on Guadalcanal with her grandfather, a Victorian brooch that had belonged to her great-grandmother. When I'd finished clearing the bedroom of things that no longer served any purpose other than to inspire grim nostalgia, I spread Sarah's favorite childhood blanket on the floor, gathered everything into it, folded the edges over, and carried it downstairs and out the door into the front yard, where dew simmered on the grass and air conditioners had already taken up an electric chorus against the day's gathering heat.

I ran back inside, poured and slurped

another scalding mug of coffee, then set about clearing Sarah's things from the ground floor, where I was faced with more of the same: countless photographs, small ceramic figurines, a collection of jade elephants, glassware and silverware and china I had no use for, an entire cabinet of spices that ditto, a juicer and vegetable steamer and garlic press, decorative throw blankets, a rogue pair of Sarah's slippers that had made their way under the sofa during her illness. It's probably more expedient, now that I think about it, to mention what I kept rather than what I culled: one plate, one bowl, one glass, one fork, one knife, one spoon. One spatula, and one non-stick skillet. One medium saucepan. The salt and pepper shakers, the percolator and coffee grinder. A tiny flower Sarah had picked from the grass in Cape Cod and pressed into a book — spared only because I'd forgotten it was there. Half a gallon of 2 percent milk, most of a jar of peanut butter, an unopened bottle of hoisin sauce. A set of ceramic owl cookie jars, retained because I still used them to store cookies. Most of the furniture, except the Canadian rocker that only Sarah ever sat in, which I wrestled through three doorways and out onto the lawn.

By the time I'd finished, the ratio of belongings under the willow tree to inside the house was approximately three to one. I stood facing a miniature landfill, ten feet in diameter at its base, taller than me by an inch or two at its summit.

I drank coffee and considered what next. It wasn't as though I were going to hold a yard sale, and in the Prius it would have taken fifteen trips to the dump to get rid of everything.

If you're in need of what firefighters and professional arsonists call an accelerant, you can do much worse than 127-proof whiskey — though I would advise you to take care when setting it alight. Because when I dumped my last two bottles on the pile of Sarah's belongings and put a match to it, the flashover leapt at me like an apex predator, claiming all the hair on my right arm as well as most of my eyebrows. I fell back onto the grass, the scorched-dung smell of my own follicles wafting around me as a six-foot flame rose from the top of the pile. The lowest branches of the willow tree waved in the sudden updraft, their leaves beginning almost immediately to wilt and crisp, and a dozen startled chickadees lifted into the sky as one, chirping angrily as they arced away.

I got to my feet and recovered my coffee

mug from the grass. Here and there in the neighboring buildings figures drifted to the windows. Hands drew venetian blinds aside, and eyes stared. My neighbors had reason to rubberneck: in addition to the willow branches, which were now beginning to blacken, the power line feeding electricity to the house ran directly over the fire, and was starting to sag with the heat.

I ran to retrieve the garden hose from the side of the house. Cranking the spigot produced only a limp arc of water that wouldn't have been sufficient for putting out a hibachi grill. But it was all I had, so I dragged the hose to the front yard and, using my thumb to concentrate the stream, began spraying down the tree and the main fire in turns. Not surprisingly, this was of little use. One by one the willow leaves flashed into starbursts of flame, and then the twigs that held them began to catch. I managed to extinguish a few of these, but soon more tiny fires flared to life in the upper branches, above the range of the hose. These coalesced on the left side of the tree's crown, really crackling now, growing exponentially larger, reaching for the uppermost branches and the sky beyond.

By the time the fire engine showed up, accompanied by a police cruiser, the willow was properly ablaze, and the power line, its insulation melted away to reveal bare aluminum cords, had slumped down to rest in the burning pile of Sarah's belongings. Across the street people gathered in groups of three and four to watch as the firefighters dragged hoses up the driveway and through the gate in the fence.

"You," one said, pointing a gloved finger at me. "Out of here!"

I did as I was told, sidling past helmeted men and into the driveway, where I was met by a police officer with wraparound sunglasses and short blond hair.

"This your place?" she asked.

"It is," I said.

She put a hand on my forearm and stepped toward the road. "Come with me," she said.

I followed. We moved a few paces away from the fire truck so we could hear one another over the growl of the diesel engine.

The officer turned toward me and removed her sunglasses, revealing blue-gray eyes like a sled dog's. "You want to tell me what's going on?" she said.

"Just burning a few things," I said.

In the yard, two firefighters unleashed a torrent of water on the willow tree while several others looked on.

"I see that," the officer said. "What I want to know is why."

"I don't need them anymore," I said.

To me this seemed a simple enough explanation, but the officer continued to stare. After a few moments she turned her head to watch the firefighters work. "Usually when people don't need things anymore, they take them to the dump," she said.

"I understand," I said. "I'm sorry for not thinking this through. The best explanation I can offer is I was in a sort of ecstasy."

She looked at me again. "An *ecstasy,*" she repeated, her eyebrows bunched together.

"I'm prone to swoons of emotion, lately," I told her.

The tree fire succumbed quickly to the wilting force of one hundred gallons per minute, and the willow, now black as a charcoal briquette, wept streams of water onto the lawn. The firefighters withdrew from the yard, allowing the pile of Sarah's things to continue burning unchecked.

"By any chance, sir, was this *ecstasy* brought on by alcohol?" the officer asked.

"I don't think so," I said. "In fact, the moment it happened I stopped drinking."

"But you were drinking before."

"Yes," I said. "I'd been very sad."

"You guys just going to let that burn?" the

officer shouted to the firefighters.

"There's a live wire in there," one of them said. "Can't put water on it 'til the power company shows up."

"Perfect," the officer said under her breath. "Sir, I need you to come with me. You're going in my cruiser until I can figure out what to do with you."

As we walked toward the back of the patrol car, an electric buzzing started directly overhead, loud enough to make both me and the officer startle. Everyone on the street looked up in unison to where the transformer on the telephone pole at the end of my driveway had begun to spit and burn.

"Hey, get out of there," a firefighter hollered at us.

No sooner had the words left his mouth than the transformer exploded, a blinding blue flash like the death of a star. The officer and I hit the ground, our hands over our heads, as the gawkers on the other side of the street ran for cover. Sparks cascaded down, painful as bee stings where they alighted on my forearms.

"Goddammit!" the officer yelled. I stayed silent, reasoning that in light of the exploding transformer, nothing I could say was likely to improve my situation.

Firefighters pulled us to our feet and led us away from the telephone pole. When she'd gathered herself the officer pushed me against the trunk of her cruiser and secured my wrists so tightly they would bear seams for hours after the cuffs came off.

For a while after that, from the backseat of the cruiser I watched everyone else watching the fires — Sarah's things and, now, the telephone pole, which burned like an oversized candle. Eventually two cherry pickers from the power company arrived, yellow strobes flashing. With the electricity cut the firefighters dispatched both blazes quickly, and an odd sense of anticlimax presided — no deaths, no destruction worthy of anything other than a few column inches in the local newspaper. Firefighters wound hose and onlookers went back to wherever they had come from. The tree and the half-burned pile of Sarah's belongings sat there, sodden and charred, now about as interesting as fallen leaves or a bunch of cedar mulch.

It seemed almost certain that I would be spending some time in jail.

But in this matter I had a surprising advocate: Art, who showed up as if conjured and stood outside the cruiser talking with the officer. He cajoled and gesticulated. He crossed then uncrossed his arms. He listened intently, nodding his head. He pointed to me, then my property. He held his palms up and pleaded. After maybe five minutes of this, the officer, grim-faced, opened the cruiser door, pulled me out by the elbow, and spun me around to unlock the handcuffs.

"Against my better judgment," she said, "I'm only going to give you a summons. You're very lucky your friend showed up when he did, or you'd be getting booked right now."

"How did you know?" I asked Art.

"Always got the scanner on," he said. "I'm a world-class nosy Nellie."

"You will show up to court," the officer said to me, placing the handcuffs back on her belt. "You will be responsible for the damage to the utility pole."

"Yes, of course," I said, rubbing my wrists.

"You will most definitely have other fines and fees to pay, and you will pay them."

"All of that. Thank you, Officer."

"You will never set anything on fire again. Not so much as a tea light candle."

"Lesson learned, for sure," I said.

She stared at me a moment longer, then got into her cruiser to write up the summons.

"What did you say to her?" I asked Art.

"I told her," Art said, "that you were a recent widower, that you'd pretty much gone down the rabbit hole, and that given those circumstances it behooved her to cut you some slack."

"I don't need any special favors," I said.

Art laughed and clapped me on the back. "Broheim," he said, "if anyone in the history of the world ever needed special favors, it's you."

"Things are different now," I said.

Art ignored this. "What a fantastic mess, K.," he said, grinning at the scene in the yard. "Truly glorious. I mean seriously, man, what the fuck is this about?"

"The most amazing thing happened," I told him.

Later I set out for the public library, to learn everything I could about everything I could. Even in my sudden rapture, of course, I understood that no person could take in the entirety of human knowledge — but all the same, I intended to try. Every waking moment not spent at work or on the mundanities of existence, I read. I ignored mail, phone calls, the increasingly concerned overtures of friends. Like a competitive eater dispatching a mound of hot dogs, I devoured biographies, histories, science texts, whole sets of encyclopedias. I traversed the condensed *Oxford English Dictionary* in three days, all of Thomas Jefferson's writings in two, the important Greek texts in four. I felt the sloughing of my ignorance as a physical thing — a burden lifted, like a morbidly obese person shedding pounds steadily through sweat and privation — and yet understood that I still knew nothing. There was so much more. A whole literal universe. The library was so large, and yet so small.

When I called Peggy the next month to say I was flying back home for a visit, she responded in typically gruff fashion. I'd been in her daughter's life for two decades, and she'd come to treat me the same way she treated her children, Sarah included, which is to say with a mixture of affection and impatience — emphasis on the impatience.

"What possible reason could you have to come visit, K.?"

"I want to talk."

"You were just here two months ago for the funeral," Peggy said. "Besides, we're talking now."

"I'd rather tell you this in person."

"I'm going to be honest with you, hon," Peggy said. "This seems sort of rash and crazy and like maybe you're not dealing well with everything."

"Are you?" I asked.

"Am I what?"

"Dealing well. With everything."

Peggy sighed. "I've been trying to kill myself with cigarettes for forty years but still managed to outlive my daughter, K.," she said. "I'm drinking too much, not sleeping at all, and sometimes I'm so sad I want to rip my eyeballs out. Other than that, I'm doing great."

"That's just it," I said. "You didn't outlive Sarah. Not at all."

Peggy was the sort of woman who avoided entering public buildings because to do so would interfere with her smoking habit. She picked me up after the short flight, but I had to make my way outside baggage claim to find her at the curb, Winston Light smoldering between her fingers on the steering wheel. We drove along the throughways and side streets of my youth, past the high school Sarah and I both graduated from, the McDonald's where we both worked (badly in need of an update, its arches faded from golden to a washed-out yellow), and the cemetery where she was now buried.

Winter's grip on New England, ever tenacious, had not quite yet loosened, and the gutters and parking lots were lined with crusts of dirty snow. By the time we got to Peggy's house I smelled like I'd smoked a pack of cigarettes myself, and Peggy was already threatening to turn the car around and take me back to the airport.

I managed to make it inside, though, where Peggy poured us both a Rumford Martini, a cocktail peculiar to the place of my upbringing in the same way the blue-footed booby is peculiar to the Galápagos Islands. Equal parts coffee brandy and milk, with ice optional, the Rumford Martini was also known as Fat Ass in a Glass, which fact Peggy tacitly acknowledged by using skim milk instead of whole.

We sat opposite one another at the kitchen table. Between us, directly beneath the five-bulb combo ceiling fan/light fixture, rested a large glass ashtray with which you could have killed someone in any of half a dozen different ways. The ashtray was empty, and as clean as if it had just been purchased. Peggy never let butts sit in any of the dozen trays around the house. Burning cigarettes had a clean, pleasant scent, she claimed, while butts just festered and stunk up the place.

To my nose, burning cigarettes didn't smell any better than old ones. But if you were smart, you did not argue with Peggy about such things. About most things, in fact. As was being demonstrated now.

"You're like those little assholes who come to my door every three months with their backpacks and their name tags," she said through a scrim of smoke. "How someone who's only nineteen years old can be 'Elder' anything is beyond me. And never mind Jesus preaching to the frigging Aztecs. Give me a break."

"How do you know so much about it?" I asked.

"Sometimes I let them in," she said. "Gets slow around here in the winter."

"But there's nothing in what I'm saying that you have to take on faith, Peggy," I said. "It's all been proven. That's the difference."

"What you're saying," Peggy said, "makes even less sense than Jesus preaching to the Aztecs."

"Just because your mind experiences time linearly doesn't mean time is linear."

Peggy lit a new cigarette with the butt of her old one. She stubbed the butt out in the ashtray, picked the ashtray up, emptied it in the garbage can, rinsed it under the tap, dried it with a hand towel, and set it back on the table. By the time she was finished, the new cigarette between her lips had accumulated an inch of delicate gray barrel, which she dispatched into the ashtray with one deft tap.

"That cigarette," Peggy said, hooking a thumb toward the garbage can, "is gone. I smoked it to the filter, and now it's in the trash. Soon it will be at the dump, where it will rest with the coat hangers and dirty diapers and shopping bags for all eternity."

I shook my head. "It's just not true," I said.

Peggy pointed at me with the index and ring fingers of her cigarette hand. "Let me tell you something about Einstein," she said. "He knew he was full of shit."

"I'm sorry?"

She took a long drag, exhaling smoke as she talked. "He said it's possible to describe everything scientifically, but that there wouldn't be any point. You could think of a Beethoven symphony as a variation of wave pressure, but why would you, when you can just listen to it instead? In other words, K., *how our minds experience things* is the important part."

I sat there a moment, staring, trying to excavate a response.

"You're not the only one with a library

card, kid," Peggy said. She tapped her cigarette in the ashtray and gazed at the darkness beyond the kitchen window.

We were quiet for several moments. Then Peggy turned her eyes away from the night and looked at me in a way she never really had before. "My daughter is dead," she said. "What you're doing is hurtful and stupid and will only make things worse."

"You're wrong, Peggy," I said.

She shrugged. "Why should I expect you to listen now? You never have before. Neither of you ever did."

We sat there in silence. I lifted my glass, took a sip, and made a show of smacking my lips. "Good Rumford," I said. "Been awhile."

"Has it?" Peggy asked. "Or have you always been drinking one, since before you were born and after you died, across all space and time?"

That was pretty much all Peggy and I had to talk about, at that point. I cut my visit short by a day.

The implications of relativity were also the wellspring of my troubles with Alice, Tony's wife — and by extension Tony, and really everyone I knew, now that I'm on the subject.

After I got back from the trip to Peggy's I called Alice and asked her to join me for coffee. We met at the shop near my house and made small talk while we ordered, then went outside to a little courtyard scattered with wrought-iron chairs and tables. Once we'd sat down, Alice's face grew solemn. She took off her sunglasses and put her hand over mine on the table.

"How are you doing?" she asked, a strained, sympathetic smile on her face.

"I'm doing great," I told her.

"You don't have to be stoic on my account, K.," she said. "Sarah was my friend, and I miss her, but I'm here for you."

"Really," I said, "I'm fine, Allie. That's why I asked to meet, actually."

So I told Alice about that afternoon in the backyard, about Einstein and Besso and all the reading I'd done since, and I invited her to share the comfort in knowing how time and the universe actually functioned. At a certain point Alice started to cry, and I was glad because it seemed like she understood. When I finished talking she gathered her clutch and sunglasses, hugged me, said to take care of myself, and left me smiling in the bright morning sunlight.

Tony called that afternoon.

"Buddy," he said, "what the fuck?"

"What the fuck, what?"

"Einstein. Space-time. Alice is ready to have you committed. Or at least send you to one of those grief camps."

"Grief camps?"

"You know. Go off into the woods for a weekend. Talk about your loss. Release some butterflies to symbolize something or other."

"I don't need that, Tony."

"Nobody needs that."

"No, I mean I'm fine," I said. "Better than fine."

"That's what Alice tells me. She also tells me you seem crazed. Maybe manic."

"I thought she understood."

"She's too polite to say you upset her. So I will. I know it's hard, man, and I wish I could do something to help. But this is nuts."

"Okay," I said. "I get it."

"And I'm sure you understand that people worry when you start talking crazy shit like this. Like even under normal circumstances they worry. But especially now when Sarah just died."

I did understand this, and said so.

"Also, the fact that you almost burned down your house does not give the impression that you're mentally shipshape."

"The house was never in danger of burning," I said.

"*K.*"

"I'm just saying. To claim the house almost burned down is not an accurate description of what happened."

"And that couldn't be more beside the point," Tony said.

"Meaning what?"

"Meaning that after going on a drinking binge you took all your dead wife's belongings and set them on fire in your front yard. That is the salient fucking detail."

"It was hardly a binge," I said. "By the time I set the fire I hadn't had a drink for hours."

Tony sighed. "What is it with you, lately?" he asked.

"What do you mean?"

"I mean, when did you turn into Mr. Roboto? It's impossible to have a conversation with you anymore, you're so goddamn literal."

"I've gone through some changes," I said.

There was silence on the other end for a few moments. "I mean, believe whatever you need to to get through," Tony said finally. "Just don't go telling my wife it's okay her friend died because, you know, the speed of light and whatever."

"Roger that," I said.

Tony lowered his voice. "Tell me this, though, for my own sake. You don't really think Sarah is still alive, right?"

"Well, no. Not the way you mean it."

"How do you think I mean it?"

"Like lying-next-to-me-in-bed-at-night, drinking-coffee-over-the-morning-paper alive," I said.

"That's correct," Tony said.

"Then the answer to your question is no. It's just me and the cat."

"That's what I want to hear."

"I'm not crazy, Tony."

"Opinions vary," he said.

"But you should read about relativity. It really is amazing, if you can open yourself up to the truth of it."

"Maybe I will, bud," he said in a way that made clear he would not.

"Okay," I said.

"You good?" Tony asked.

"I'm good."

"Because I need to be able to tell Alice you're good, so she'll calm down."

"Fit as a fiddle," I assured him.

Another pause. "Okay, man. Basketball game Friday at Art's. I'm grabbing barbecue from that place down on Wharf Street. You in?"

"Count on it," I said, and because I was

not, in fact, crazy, or stupid, as I hung up the phone I resolved to stop talking about Einstein, as it had become clear that the reason people still believed time was absolute was because they needed to, and no amount of evidence to the contrary would free them from that willful ignorance. This was a resolution I wouldn't break for months, until the liquid hand wash incident set my personal world spinning on an entirely different axis altogether.

7

FIFTEEN MINUTES, EXTENDED

"You're the talent, K.," Theodore said. "We came to you, not the other way around. This is your project, and we trust, as we do with all our talent, that the show will be its best if you are allowed to make it whatever it needs to be."

There was a pause, during which it seemed evident Theodore expected some sort of response from me. "Okay," I told him.

"That said, we do have some ideas."

"Before we get into that," Claire said, "and I'm sorry to interrupt, but there's something I want to ask you."

"Of course," Theodore said.

"Does everyone call you Theodore?" Claire asked.

"Yes," Theodore said.

"Like, all the time?"

"Yes."

"Even your wife?"

"My dear, I am gayer than a pink suede sofa."

"Funny," Claire said. "You don't look it."

Theodore raised his meaty arms in a shrug. "I didn't ask to be W. H. Taft's twin brother. But who am I to quibble with the divine?"

"Okay," Claire said. "So no one in your life has ever called you Ted, or Teddy, or Theo."

"Not even once," Theodore told her.

"That's remarkable," Claire said.

"It really sort of is," I agreed.

"Excuse me," Theodore said, taking off his sunglasses for the first time despite the fact that we'd been indoors for twenty minutes, "but what is your relationship to K., again, my dear?"

"Manager," Claire said.

"Just 'manager'?"

"We're friends," I told him. "New friends. She has no managerial experience whatsoever, as far as I know."

Claire punched my good arm, hard enough to give me a mild charley horse.

"Any event, that's between the two of you, I suppose," Theodore said. "Though I like her, you know. Sharp tongued, pretty. She could make a good sidekick type."

"I'm sitting right here," Claire said,

"actively resenting being referred to in the third person."

Theodore made a distressed wheezing sound, and in short order seemed to stop breathing altogether. His face flushed, then cycled through rapidly deepening shades of red.

We stared, Claire and I.

After a few seconds Theodore finally drew a breath. "Don't be alarmed," he said, panting. "That's how I laugh. I'm obese and my lungs don't work properly. I haven't made a sound you would recognize as laughter since 2003."

I nodded.

"Alrighty then," Claire said.

"Which, coincidentally, was the year I won my first Emmy, as E.P. on *Funeral Home Confessions.*"

"Graceful segue into your bona fides," Claire said.

Theodore wheezed again. We waited, somewhat less alarmed this time.

"That's good," he said after recovering himself. "Maybe I should give *you* the show, my dear."

"Wait a minute," Claire said. "Did you say *Funeral Home Confessions*?"

"Yes," Theodore said.

"Someone actually made a show called

Funeral Home Confessions."

"It ran for four seasons," Theodore said. "I'm surprised, and perhaps a bit hurt, that you haven't heard of it."

The waiter arrived with our drinks: vodka martini for Claire, Murphy's stout for Theodore, Arnold Palmer for me.

Claire lifted the very full glass to her lips. "So, your ideas," she said to Theodore.

"Of course. Actually, it's less a set of specific ideas and more a general, mmm . . . *aesthetic."* Theodore paused to sip at his beer. "If you would indulge me in an analogy?"

"Why not," Claire said.

"I own a summer property on an island off the coast of Maine," he said. "This island has deer, but no coyotes. Do you know what happens when you have deer but no coyotes?"

"Lots and lots of deer?" Claire said.

"Lots and lots of destruction," Theodore said. "This property of mine, when I bought it, boasted voluminous flower beds, a vegetable garden spanning two acres, and a dozen dwarf apple trees. The flower beds were the principle and best landscaping feature. The apple trees dated back three generations, to when the land was part of a much larger orchard. The vegetable garden supplied our monthly barn dinners, which before the deer came were the highlights of the summer social calendar."

"Sounds very nice," I said.

"It was," Theodore said, wiping foam from his upper lip with a bar napkin. "When I bought the property, there had been several harsh winters in a row, and that kept the deer population down. But then two very mild winters occurred back-to-back, and when I arrived for my second summer on the island I found the property ravaged."

"Ravaged," Claire said.

"Completely," Theodore said. "Gardens torn asunder. Flowers gnawed off at the ground and not even *eaten,* most of them, but just strewn about. Wanton, pointless destruction. The apple trees, too. Low branches snapped off. Trunks worn raw by antlers. I was furious. *Furious.*"

"Didn't you have a caretaker?" I asked. "Someone to watch the place?"

"We had groundskeepers," Theodore said, "but they didn't live on the property, and these white-tailed hooligans did their work under cover of darkness. Besides, the groundskeepers' expertise was horticulture, not hunting."

"No more barn suppers for you," Claire said.

"Why do you think I was so angry?" Theodore swirled his beer around the rim of the glass. "So enter a gentleman named Rob Crockett. Like a lot of the island's year-round residents, Rob wears many hats. He is the propane delivery man, and also drives the municipal garbage truck twice a week. He's a skilled carpenter, a capable chess player, and, if a member of your crew is hungover or sick or dead, a top-rate deckhand on a lobster boat. Of course in this instance there were other skill sets for which I needed him. And no, that's not innuendo."

"In *your* endo," Claire said.

Theodore wheezed. "Don't I wish," he said. "But no. Sadly, Rob Crockett is straight as the day is long. Rob Crockett also is a crack shot, and has a healthy disdain for poaching laws. Really, laws in general. This made him useful to me."

"Rob Crockett, deer slayer?" Claire asked.

"Indeed," Theodore said. "And his M.O. was remarkably simple: he scattered rice bran all around the yard and set himself up on a hill with an old Gewehr 43 rifle that his grandfather found in a Nazi bunker in Aachen. Every night for two weeks I sat inside, drinking wine in the dark and waiting, waiting. I've never been so nervous in my life, wondering when the moment would come. Wincing, for hours on end."

"Not for nothing," I said, "but was it all that smart for Rob Crockett to be sitting on a hill basically aiming a rifle at you?"

"That was part of the excitement," Theodore said. "Such exquisite tension. I mean, he is an absolute madman. Would a deer's life end? Would mine? And *when*? That was the biggest thrill. Not knowing when."

Claire looked at me. I shrugged.

"So I waited," Theodore said. "Poured Pinot with a trembling hand. Sometimes I'd go to the window and pull the curtain aside to see if there were any elegant four-legged figures in the grass. At times I was sure I could see them, then immediately thought it my imagination. I would have turned on the exterior lights, but I didn't want to ruin the suspense."

Now Theodore closed his eyes, his jowls trembling with ecstatic reminiscence. "And then," he said, "when the report finally came, I would startle, sometimes spilling my wine, sometimes crying out. It's so quiet on the island — really, unless you've been there you can't appreciate the enormity of the silence — and a gunshot can feel like the world is coming to an end. The release, I don't mind telling you, was quasisexual. And as after sex, I almost immediately went to sleep with a smile on my face."

"Um," Claire said.

"What about the deer?" I asked.

"Dead," Theodore said, opening his eyes again. "Well, a dozen of them, anyway. Another ran off into the woods after being gut shot, and probably died. I offered to pay Rob Crockett, for his time, for his skill, and for the risk he was taking with the law. But all he wanted was to keep the carcasses. God knows what he did with them."

Theodore looked from me, to Claire, then back to me, his gaze obviously intended to convey something momentous. I had no idea what that thing might be, so I drank my Arnold Palmer and glanced around the dining room.

"You were saying before," Claire said, "this was supposed to be some sort of analogy?"

"It's not clear by now?" Theodore asked.

"Not to me, I'm afraid," Claire said.

They both looked in my direction. I shook my head.

"My goodness," Theodore said. "*You* are Rob Crockett, K."

"I am?"

"Of course."

"I don't follow," I said.

Theodore pushed his beer glass aside and

leaned forward, his elbows clomping the table. "K.," he said, "more than at any other time in our lives, the world is full of destructive deer. Idiots, ideologues, blind followers of bureaucratic protocol. People who believe with frothy-mouthed intensity in all manner of nonsense, despite the fact that this nonsense has been conclusively and repeatedly disproven. Those who would try to convince us they understand the nature of God. Those who hate and kill on His behalf. Those who confuse being willfully ignorant with being populist. Those who can't keep their mouths shut at the movie theater. Thieves, both petty and prominent. Chattering classes of all political affiliations. People living and dying within the comfortable, banal confines of online echo chambers. Serial self-affirmers. Those who believe traffic laws apply to everyone but them. Special snowflakes of every stripe. They have destroyed our discourse and stripped the gears of our republic. They are dragging us to hell."

Theodore paused, fixing me with a gaze, his eyebrows raised.

"Despite their myriad differences, there is one thing all these people agree on. This point of concurrence is itself the ultimate bit of nonsense, the inevitable endpoint of our fascist, bankrupt political correctness: an unblinking certainty that simply because they hold a belief, that belief is sacrosanct."

The waiter glided up to the table and asked if we wanted another drink. Theodore nodded, then leaned back in his chair, examining the nails on one of his hands.

"If a man tells you the sky is purple and 'cat' is spelled with a 'k,' " he said, "what do you say to him in response?"

"That he's wrong?" I said.

"Of course," Theodore said. "And that's what makes you different from everyone else. You're a beacon, K. You stand for the critically endangered ethic that we do not have to abide bullshit just because someone else happens to believe it."

The waiter returned with a fresh beer. Theodore didn't let it hit the table.

"I've been trying to make this show for years, but could never cast it," he said. "Of course there are plenty of people happy to play the contrarian, but that's not what I want. I want something *sincere*. Something that comes from the heart, the gut. And then, as though sent from heaven, you appeared."

"Laying it on pretty thick, Theodore," Claire said.

"But I am not buttering anyone's ass. Not

that I wouldn't *like* to butter your ass, K., in a more literal sense. But that's neither here nor there."

"I have only a faint sense of what you mean," I said. "Nevertheless, I'm glad that the literal buttering of my ass is not the topic at hand."

Theodore nodded. "I don't care in which direction you aim your rifle," he said. "I don't care if a few rounds go astray. Contrary to the shopworn colloquialism, there are no innocent bystanders. Not anymore. Everyone's guilty. Everyone's complicit. So you start with me, K. All that I just said. Tell me why I'm wrong. Kill my sacred cows."

"Your what, now?" I asked.

"My sacred cows."

"I'm a little confused," I said.

"About what?" Theodore asked.

"What happened to the deer?" I said.

"I'm sorry?"

"You were talking about deer, and now all of a sudden it's cows."

"You are familiar with the idiom 'sacred cow,' yes?"

"Of course."

"Well we're all deer, K., every last one of us. And the cows are our unreasonable beliefs."

"We're maybe mixing our metaphorical ruminants in a way that's difficult, for him," Claire said.

"That's the essential problem, yes," I said. "Too many ruminants."

"This is an example of why you're his manager, I presume?" Theodore asked.

"Manager," Claire said. "Translator. Like Rob Crockett, I wear a lot of hats."

"K.," Theodore said, "if you take this show, all I'm going to ask is that you do what you did with that girl at Big Buy. With that gentleman driving the pickup truck. I ask that you do what comes naturally, in other words. You're not polite. You don't mince or parse. You've demonstrated a constitutional inability to play nice. This is why we want you."

"I'm not trying to be a jerk," I told him.

"Which is what makes it so wonderful, so compelling," Theodore said. "You come by it honestly. Unlike most rabble-rousers and self-styled iconoclasts — your Rush Limbaughs, your Mother Teresas — you, K., are free of artifice or agenda. You simply *are*. Just as Rob Crockett simply is."

We were all quiet for a moment.

"So what do you say?" Theodore asked finally.

I considered, then looked over at Claire.

"She can have a job?" I asked.

"She can be in the show," Theodore said. "In fact, I insist on it."

"Okay," I said.

8
THE LITTLE THINGS

I got Sarah a bedside bell. At the time I thought it a way to spin horror into humor, an absurd bit of role-playing, me as her manservant, highly professional and dedicated, crisp in both uniform and manner, and she a pampered socialite who couldn't be bothered to rise from the sateen sheets and cumulus pillows of her four-poster. In keeping with this theme I decided I couldn't just buy any old steel handbell. It had to be fancy, though not necessarily ornate. So I spent the better part of a Saturday courting tetanus as I scoured the musty labyrinths of antique stores, salvage joints, and estate jewelers, until finally I found the closest approximation available of what I sought: a vintage dinner bell comprised of a single piece of sterling silver, with a wide shiny mouth and a handle carved with fleurs-de-lis.

I lifted the bell and gave a few experimental shakes; it chimed high and true, sounding more like crystal than silver, sounding, in fact, like the most gifted soprano in the Vienna Boys' Choir. It was a noise I would come to dread, then despise; it was a noise that on two occasions would reduce me to tears.

I talked the clerk down from $150, paid $120 cash, and walked out with the bell wrapped in baby blue tissue paper cinched by white ribbon around the handle.

"This is for you," I said to Sarah when I arrived home.

She sat in a recliner that for years only I had ever used, in an après-work, loosened-tie-and-highball kind of way; if we'd had children both they and we would have referred to it as "Dad's chair." Now, with Sarah faltering but not yet bedridden, she'd taken to spending long hours camped out on the velvet cushions, eyeballing daytime television's endless stream of commercials for disability law firms and feminine hygiene products. In effect, she'd taken possession of the recliner. I had little interest in it anymore, even on the rare occasion when I found it vacant. For that matter, I'd also stopped drinking highballs after work. Eventually I'd stop working altogether, when Sarah's illness took its long last turn toward the lethal homestretch and she required tending around the clock.

Now, though, I handed Sarah the package, and her eyes, which as she'd lost weight had grown until they seemed to occupy half of her face, flared with surprise and pleasure. She untied the ribbon, meeting my gaze several times as she did so, gracing me with the warmth of those eyes, the pupils wide as serving plates from oxycodone. She worked slowly, picking at the strips of tape with her thumbnail. I enjoyed the rustle of the paper under her fingers. She did not rip it, however slightly, even once.

When she'd folded the paper and set it beside her on the recliner, Sarah held the bell in both palms, considering.

"It's beautiful," she said.

"Why don't you give it a ring?" I said.

She looked at me again, then let her left hand fall away, gripping the bell by the handle with her right. It chimed, high and true: An icy F-sharp, or thereabouts. That, then, would become the note of our torment.

The thing is: on a long enough timeline, nobody suffers gracefully. Books and movies lie. When someone's dying they lash out, make demands like a postcolonial despot. This is unavoidable. I had no way of knowing it at the time, but that bell would become a cudgel. Which was hardly Sarah's fault. She didn't ask for the bell. She didn't ask to be dying, either.

"Why, though?" Sarah said to me, before all that.

"It's for you to let me know when you need something," I said. "A lot more elegant than hollering across the house, right?"

"Sure, I guess so," Sarah said. "It's really beautiful, anyway."

"You'll be like the queen of Sheba," I said. "And I'll be your attendant."

She rang the bell again. "You're a strange man, K.," she said.

"You knew that when you married me," I said.

"That's true," she said. "Can't start complaining now."

"Although I guess that to attend a queen in the ancient world I'd have to be a eunuch, right? I love you, but I'm not sure I'm ready to make that kind of commitment."

Sarah laughed, gave the bell another shake.

"What is it you desire, Your Highness?" I asked.

Sarah blushed with the ridiculousness of it — color flooding her wan face was, by then, just this side of miraculous — but she played along.

"My desire," she said, "is for an Orchard Peach–flavored Clearly Canadian. Half a degree above ice cold."

"Please forgive me, Your Excellency," I said, going to one knee and bowing my head in apology, "but I believe it has been many years since Clearly Canadian was available for retail sale, in our realm."

"What is this?" she asked, mock-outraged. "Are you refusing to honor my decree?"

"Never, exalted one," I said. "I'm simply suggesting that it may prove nigh impossible, even for a servant as dedicated as myself."

Sarah dropped the act. "Seriously though," she said, "I could really go for a Clearly Canadian."

And then, in the face of her sudden earnestness: Of course. How could I have forgotten?

You know how teenagers often will affect some benign idiosyncrasy to set themselves apart from their peers? Mine was a green-and-white polka dot silk shirt, an unfortunate sartorial mistake that I wore pretty much every day from sophomore year on. And Sarah? All through high school, even before we started dating, she carried a sea glass–blue bottle of Clearly Canadian everywhere she went. In classrooms. On field trips. At dances, and illicit parties where the other kids, myself included, were getting soused on Natural Light and Wild Irish Rose. Even at the House of Pancakes, where many of the girls in our class waited tables and where we spent school day afternoons nursing cups of coffee and smoking cigarettes, she would bring in her own bottle of Clearly Canadian.

I kissed her forehead, the skin hot and dry like a warming plate someone had forgotten to turn off. "Your wish," I said, "is my command."

It was, however, a command that proved difficult to obey, even in a hyperconnected global marketplace where one could order shark fin soup from Hong Kong on Monday and sit down to eat it Tuesday afternoon. Near as I could determine, Clearly Canadian, which when we were teenagers seemed to rival Coke and Pepsi in its ubiquity, had last been produced in the early years of the new millennium. And apparently soft drinks don't keep very long, because there were no old cases of Clearly Canadian available on eBay or Craigslist. Hours spent searching online yielded all manner of Clearly Canadian merchandise — beach towels, T-shirts, golf visors, even salt and pepper shakers crafted from the original bottles — but no soda. I missed, with agonizing closeness, a limited-edition run of the original Country Raspberry flavor, which sold out two weeks before I called, according to a nice woman at a specialty beverage distributor in Vancouver who apologized so profusely when she learned my circumstances that I ended up feeling worse for her than she possibly could have for me.

Meantime, the sterling silver bell chimed and chimed, pulling me away from the computer and telephone. I went to Sarah and counted out her pills, helped her to the bathroom, injected Coumadin into a pinch of her belly to ward off blood clots. I went to her with soup and ice chips and meal-replacement shakes formulated to keep octogenarians from dropping weight. I went to her with heating pads and hot water bottles, extra blankets, pen and paper. I went to her with everything she needed, never with the one thing she wanted.

One afternoon I went to Sarah empty-handed, with nothing to offer but the stupid mute warmth of a fellow mammal. This was an afternoon dusk in the deep freeze, a time of day and year when sorrow settles into and permeates everything even in the best of circumstances. I held Sarah while she watched snow fall outside the window and wept for her last winter on earth. I could not speak; I could barely even breathe. I was helpless, here in this room with my wife, but not so helpless, I hoped more and more desperately, to find that soda. It had to exist. The world was too big for it not to be out there somewhere, like the treasure of the Knights Templars, or those missing Fabergé eggs.

There is, of course, always a painful irony. In this case it's that over the next few months Sarah forgot all about her request for the soda. By then the cancer had crowbarred its way into her parietal lobe, and she began transposing words — "Did you leave the car in the groceries?" — and forgetting the difference between left and right, so Clearly Canadian was not the first thing on her mind. Eventually she took to sleeping nineteen, twenty hours a day. While she slept more and more, I continued to search, working the phones, whispering to store clerks and redemption chain CEOs, even the constituent service staffers of both our senator and congressman. I called the offices of the Clearly Canadian Food & Beverage Company over and over, finally getting something other than voicemail on the eighteenth try.

I explained my situation to the man.

"We'd love to help," he told me. "I hope you believe that. But it's not like we can just rattle off a single bottle. We're talking huge production facilities that have to be unshuttered. The original Clearly Canadian teardrop bottle is a custom job, and the molds would have to be made from scratch. It's just not possible. We sell baby food now, mostly, you understand."

"Baby food?" I said.

"That's correct."

"But then why are you still called Clearly Canadian?"

"There are only seven of us," he said. "We don't have the time or the money to change the corporation name, even if we wanted to. Which we don't, since it's the only thing of real value we've got left."

So that was it. I'd gone to the wellspring, such as it was, and come back with nothing. Which should have been okay, because Sarah was by now nearly nonverbal, could neither read nor write, could barely communicate at all, and likely wouldn't have cared a whit about some dumb soda even if she'd remembered her request. Orchard Peach Clearly Canadian could neither save nor redeem us. I knew this.

And yet.

What kept me up nights? What had me pacing barefoot at four in the morning, goose-bumped by the cold that seeped up through the floor from the basement, trying all the nonpharmaceutical relaxation aids late capitalism had to offer: melatonin, valerian, chamomile tea, aromatherapeutic balms, even, when nothing else helped, whole milk brought to a steam on the range top? What was it that sent me, eventually, to the liquor cabinet, even though with everything Sarah needed or might need (a brisk trip to the emergency room, for example) I had no business touching even an ounce of alcohol?

It wasn't her illness, I can tell you that. It wasn't the specter of her death. It wasn't her sadness or fear. It was not any of the things you might expect.

Deliverance happens, though, on occasion, and often the timing is such that our minds, which are programmed to establish pattern and meaning where neither exists, see this timing as something other than coincidence. We infer the fingerprint of the divine, or at least the benevolent intervention of some force or energy. Karma. Serendipity. Kismet. Back then, even I was not immune to this kind of thinking. So it was that right around the time I started to grow genuinely delirious with fatigue — miscounting Sarah's pills, dozing off while I administered her nebulizer treatments — I was all too ready to apprehend one phone call as the Universe smiling on us, however briefly.

The phone ringing, in and of itself, was not remarkable. We got a lot of calls during Sarah's illness — many more, in fact, than we ever had before. The silver bell was one of my masters, and the telephone the other. There were doctors to speak to, as well as in-home nurses, insurance representatives, hospice coordinators, far-flung friends. Also, of course, Peggy. She didn't sleep either, so we would talk late. Her sips of coffee brandy, and the muted pop and gasp as she dragged on a cigarette, transmitted to me by satellite, wire, and tower, became the soundtrack of my late nights and early mornings.

It wasn't the hospice this time, though, and it wasn't Peggy. It turned out to be the deeply sympathetic woman in Vancouver.

"Please tell me your wife is still alive," she said, her voice tight with anticipation of being answered in the negative.

"She is," I said. "She very much is."

"Oh thank God," the woman said. "Listen, I found you a whole case of Orchard Peach."

"You're kidding," I said.

"Oh, I would never," the woman said. "Not about this. I promise. I'm telling the truth."

"But where?"

"This is the part you'll have a hard time believing," she said.

"I'm already having a hard time believing," I said. "Don't get me wrong, I'm overjoyed. I just don't understand."

In the bedroom the sterling silver bell chimed, and for the first time ever I ignored it.

"Okay so here's the thing," the woman said. "There's this Saudi prince."

"There are a lot of Saudi princes," I said. "From what I understand."

"More than five thousand," the woman said. "That's one of the things I learned, in all this."

The bell chimed again.

"But so one of these Saudi princes went to school in America," the woman said.

"Again," I said, "many of them do, is my understanding."

"But this one, see," the woman said, "*this* one happened to be in college in the early 1990s, and he didn't drink alcohol, because he's a devout Muslim."

"I bet that's not true of a lot of Saudi

princes," I said.

"But he liked to be sociable, and so at parties he would always bring Clearly Canadian. When he learned they were going to stop producing it, he bought every bottle of the stuff he could find, so he'd have enough to last him a long time."

"And he bought so much that he still has some, all these years later," I said.

"He apparently still has quite a lot," the woman told me. "He's very strict about his consumption. One bottle a month."

"That's really something," I said.

"Which is why it's such a big deal for him to give you a whole case," the woman said. "He's actually a very kind man. Talked to me personally. Not what you'd expect, from a Saudi prince."

"What *would* you expect from a Saudi prince?" I asked.

The woman paused. "I'm not really sure," she said. "Just that he'd be sort of arrogant, I suppose."

"That's probably fair," I said.

The bell, louder this time.

"But so I told him your wife is very sick and I didn't know how much time she had left," the woman said. "Oh gosh, I apologize for putting it so bluntly."

"Don't worry," I said, though her words

had made me wince.

"And he offered to send it to you overnight. All the way from Saudi Arabia. Isn't that amazing?"

"It is," I said. "Genuinely amazing."

The case of Clearly Canadian arrived the next afternoon. To the delivery man it was just the latest in a Sisyphean series of packages that would end only with the hypothesis of his retirement, and though he paid no heed to the "Fragile" stickers on the box, I thanked him three times: once as he approached on the icy walkway, once while I signed, and once as he departed with no understanding of or interest in why I was so grateful.

I brought the package into the front hallway and ripped at the tape holding the top together. I still didn't really believe — despite the fact that there was no reason for me to think the deeply sympathetic woman was either a liar or a fool — that a case of Orchard Peach Clearly Canadian lay inside. I expected, right up until the moment I pulled the box flaps aside, that almost anything else would be revealed: a tangle of chinchilla carcasses, a pile of unripe bananas, any manner of inexplicably cruel practical jokes. But then I saw those peculiar blue bottles rank-and-file inside, padded carefully against breakage, and I breathed, finally, and looked to the ceiling as tears stung my eyes.

I didn't tell Sarah anything. I wanted it to be a surprise.

Two bottles went into the refrigerator, which I'd set to precisely 33 degrees, as per Sarah's original request that the soda be just this side of ice cold. I waited several hours, and then, the next time the bell pealed, I walked in with a bottle of Orchard Peach Clearly Canadian and one drinking glass from the set of crystal we'd been given for our wedding.

I have never in my life been what one would call euphoric, but in that moment I edged up against it.

Sarah's big sad eyes came open slowly, like a lizard's, as I entered the bedroom. She lay propped against a green husband pillow. There was almost nothing left of her. Her nightgown could have been draped over an empty bed, if not for the fact of her head poking out from the top.

"Hi," I said, smiling, waiting for her to recognize the improbability I held in my hand.

She blinked. "Hi," she said.

Nothing. I moved closer, holding the

bottle out in front of me to give her a good look.

"I rang. The bell," Sarah said. "Because I'm. Thirsty."

By this time, when she spoke she had to pause for breath several times in a single sentence.

"Well that's perfect," I said, "because look what I brought for you."

She leaned forward a bit, squinted. "What. Is it?" she asked.

I sat on the edge of the bed. "It's the soda you asked for."

"I didn't ask. For a soda," she said. "I didn't ask. For anything yet. You just. Came in here."

"No, I mean you asked for it a while back. Months ago. Remember? The day I gave you the bell?"

She furrowed her brow, willing the memory to surface. Like everything else, thought was a colossal effort for her now.

"I can't. Remember," she said finally, relaxing back onto the giant pillow with a sound like every cell in her body sighing.

I was obliged, of course, to reassure her it was fine that she had no idea what I was talking about. But after months of phone calls and vain searching, after the miracle of the Saudi prince, I needed this to matter to

151

her. I needed her to realize our good fortune, to understand my effort and worry. I was, in other words, making it very much about me. God as my witness, I could not, in that moment, have done otherwise.

"You were the queen of Sheba," I said. "And I was your devoted servant. You asked me to find you a bottle of Orchard Peach–flavored Clearly Canadian. And here it is."

I could see that, for all she understood, I might as well have been speaking Sanskrit.

"Sarah," I said, "it was your one true and fervent wish. Remember?"

She stared at me with those huge eyes, shook her head once, slowly.

We were quiet for a minute. I sat there still holding the bottle and glass like an idiot.

Sarah finally broke the silence. "Why," she said. "Are you. Crying?"

"It's okay," I said. I put the glass on the nightstand and swiped at my cheeks. "It's okay that you don't remember the conversation. But you must remember Clearly Canadian, right?"

She scrutinized the bottle again. At first there was nothing, and I felt the ropy tentacles of despair reach for me. But then sudden recognition struck Sarah, and she smiled weakly, gloriously, her ruined face half eyes and half teeth.

"I haven't. Had that. Since college," she said, sitting up a little again.

"That's because they stopped making it," I told her.

"I know. Where. Did you get it?"

"Saudi Arabia."

"Wha. What?"

"It's a very long story, love," I said. "Would you like some? Before it gets warm?"

"I would," she said. "Oh my. God, K. How?"

"Well, I love you," I said, still crying in spite of myself as I poured. "That's how."

Droplets alit on my hand as the soda effervesced. Foam climbed the sides of the glass rapidly, like a grade school science experiment, and I paused, waited for the soda to settle, then added a bit more. When I'd finished I placed the bottle on a spot on the nightstand where Sarah could admire it, popped a bendy straw into the glass, and gave it to her carefully, making certain her hands would support the weight before I let go.

Sarah eased back against the pillow, brought the straw to her mouth, and sipped. After a moment, she pulled the glass away and regarded it the same way one would an old friend who has behaved in a way altogether novel and dumbfounding.

She was merely disappointed. I, on the other hand, felt devastated beyond all reason.

Sarah looked up at me. "I. Remember now," she said, and I had no idea, still have no idea, if she was telling the truth, or if she just saw my stricken face and decided to lie. "I remember. The day. You gave me. The bell."

"That's good," I said. "That's good, Sarah, that you remember."

She raised the straw to her lips again, pretending that she enjoyed that familiar Orchard Peach flavor, that it was just as she remembered it, that all the poison we'd pumped into her body had not destroyed her ability to taste and, by extension, her ability to go back, with the help of a glass of soda, to a time when she was not here, and this was not happening.

9

A Thousand Dollars for a Kiss, Fifty Cents for Your Soul

When my shoulder had healed well enough for the doctors to clear me for travel, Claire and I flew to Los Angeles with Theodore. We went first class, courtesy of 20th Century Fox television, in seats the airline referred to as "suites." Each suite had its own entertainment system, with which you could choose from an extensive menu of television and films, music and video games. There were noise-canceling headphones and silk-lined sleep masks scented with lavender, a caviar and champagne appetizer upon boarding, and dry-aged rib chops for dinner. What was more, the flight attendants wouldn't leave us alone with the free cocktails. Claire got drunk and ate four bags of M&M's in addition to her meal; on approach to LAX she vomited a rainbow of whiskey, food dye, and carefully moldered meat into the aisle, and the flight attendant sopped this up with the same sanguine good cheer with which she'd executed all her other duties.

The next morning we took a town car to the Fox production lot to meet with a woman named Andrea Clewes. Andrea's face was all sharp, cruel angles, giving her the appearance of a very pretty concentration camp guard. She had waist-length black hair that gleamed like obsidian. By contrast, all the furniture in her office, including the desk, was stark white. She greeted the three of us at her office entrance and, after exchanging air kisses with Theodore, bade us sit down on several leather chairs that looked like they'd been constructed from giant marshmallows.

"*So* exciting to have you here," Andrea said, taking a seat herself behind the desk. "Before we discuss anything else, I want to ask how you'd like to offset your carbon emissions from the flight out."

"I'm sorry?" I said.

"It's a policy I implemented when I took over as president of production," Andrea said. "Anytime we fly someone here, we purchase carbon offsets, of your choice, to make up for the greenhouse gases produced by the flight. You can, for example, choose to protect a hectare of rain forest. Or buy shares in an algae bio-reactor."

"Ah," I said.

"There's some paperwork for you to fill out after our meeting, but I want you to be thinking about this now," Andrea continued. "It's very important to me, and to Fox."

"I'm not sure it should be," I said.

Andrea cocked her head, and a smile spread across her face like a crack in a glacier. "Excuse me?" she said.

"It's just that many smart people — meteorologists and oceanographers and climate scientists of every stripe, really — think these carbon offsets are pretty useless," I said. "Even a scam."

The icy smile disappeared. "Mr. K., do I seem like the kind of woman who would blithely send her banking information to a Nigerian con artist?" she asked. "We use a company called Carbon Monkey. They're quite reputable."

"Yes, I read about them recently. They were purchased by TD Wells Morgan," I said. "And it's just 'K.' No 'mister.'"

Andrea stared. Theodore pulled a handful of wasabi peas from a bowl on the coffee table and used them to stifle a giggle.

"Why do you suppose," I asked, "that a massive multinational investment bank would be interested in a small, purportedly green operation called Carbon Monkey?"

157

Claire, still hurting from the excesses of the prior evening, finally spoke up. "Because the enviroguilt of wealthy white liberals is hugely profitable?"

"That would be my guess," I said.

"Just ask the brass at Total Foods," Claire said.

"I *shop* at Total Foods," Andrea said, turning her gaze to Claire.

"Then you're a chump," Claire said. "Even if you can afford the markup."

Andrea stared, and Claire stared back without blinking, her hair blazing red against the white seat back.

"I mean, for all the good carbon offsets do, you might as well offer to have stars named after us instead," I told Andrea.

Theodore began to cough horribly, spewing bits of wasabi peas across the glass tabletop. He leaned forward over his legs and hacked onto the white carpet while Claire pounded him between the shoulder blades with a closed fist. He continued to struggle for breath long after the last of the peas had been ejected, and for a moment I thought he might have transitioned from choking into some sort of cardiac event. Eventually, though, he sat back and heaved several long, ragged breaths.

"You good?" Andrea asked him, not seeming the least bit concerned about the answer.

"I am good," Theodore huffed.

"Do you need anything? I can ask Grace to bring in some still water."

Theodore coughed a few more times, though he was composed enough at this point to do so into his hand. "I'm fine, my dear, really. But thank you."

"Good," Andrea said. She leaned back with her arms crossed so tightly that her wrists blanched as white as her chair. "Then maybe you can tell me what the fuck is going on, here."

"What do you mean?"

"I *mean,*" Andrea said, "that it is not a good idea for people to call the producer they hope to green-light their show a chump."

"*Co*producer, my dear."

"You really want to split hairs about titles right now, Theodore? Because that's not a good idea, either."

"I'm simply wedded to the notion of clarity."

"So?"

"So, what?"

"Explain," Andrea said.

"You shouldn't take it personally," Theodore said.

"Really, you shouldn't," I said. "I'm not

malicious. It's just sort of a reflex for me, since my wife died."

"Please," Andrea said, "I don't care if your wife was drawn and quartered. You'll get no sympathy from me."

"I'm not hoping for sympathy," I said. "I'm just trying to make clear it's not personal."

"Well don't bother, Gump."

"Hey lady," Claire said. "You know what? Feel free to take what I said super personally. Anyone who shops at Total Foods is an ass. Of course they just fired me, so I have a bias."

"That's it," Andrea said. "Get out."

"My dear," Theodore said.

"Out. Theodore, you know I love you, but this is bullshit. You should be embarrassed."

"This is the show, darling," Theodore said.

"I understand the *concept,* Theodore," Andrea said. "I speak English, which is the language you used to pitch me the fucking show. I hardly need to have its working parts demonstrated at my expense."

"No, you don't understand," Theodore said. He reached to his breast pocket and pulled at the button, revealing a small lens attached to a thin black cable. "Smile for the birdie, my dear."

Andrea's eyes narrowed. "You're *filming* this?"

It was news to me, as well. I looked at Claire. She shook her head.

Theodore popped another wasabi pea into his mouth. It was impossible to know if his composure in the face of Andrea's growing ire was genuine, or just a part of the calculated risk he evidently was taking with her.

"I'm tired of everyone on reality TV vamping for the cameras," Theodore said. "Things have gotten so stale that it's nearly killed the form altogether. My own projects bore me, Andrea. I've made six shows since *Pimp House,* and I've gained over one hundred and fifty pounds in that same period of time. This is not a coincidence. I'm eating for three: myself, Shame, and Boredom."

"*Pimp House*?" I whispered to Claire.

Her hangover having apparently reached existential-crisis levels, Claire now sat forward with her head in her hands. "Exactly what it sounds like," she said without looking up. "Six pimps, living in a house. It wasn't bad."

"People have become too self-aware to make good television," Theodore continued. He cast his eyes to the ceiling, gesticulating with one fat hand as he spoke. "A genera-

161

tion's worth of reality programming has, ironically, made it impossible to capture anything real. Everyone is a professional now. Everyone feels the eye come open and rest upon them the moment they get out of bed: traffic cameras, surveillance satellites, security CCTV, and, goodness, the phones, the phones, the phones. Everyone knows the tropes by heart. They hit their marks without even thinking about it, overact every minute of every day. And we're to blame, Andrea, because we're the ones who convinced people that life is just one massive episode of reality TV.

"Consider what just happened here with us. How would your reaction have been different if you'd known we were filming?"

Andrea bared her teeth. "I wouldn't have *let you* film it," she said.

"Of course. But let's say you had. Your reaction would have been measured. Calm. You would have played along, steered the conversation in a direction that made you seem easygoing, witty, better-than. But what we got instead — because you didn't know it was being recorded — was real incredulity. Real confusion."

"I wasn't confused. I was pissed."

"Real *rage*," Theodore said, shaking both his fists overhead.

"I'm *still* pissed, Theodore," Andrea said.

"But you're no longer insisting we get out of your office, are you, my dear?"

Andrea pointed toward me and Claire. "Lucky for you," she said, "those two have been quiet for a minute."

"We need to go all the way back to the beginning, Andrea," Theodore said. "*Candid Camera. This Is Your Life.* Some of the best reality television in history was made by people hidden in vans, around street corners, behind one-way glass. Why is that? Because the success of our business has always been tied to voyeurism. Real, watching-from-the-bedroom-closet-while-your-wife-fucks-another-man voyeurism. And not because it titillates us to be hidden. No. That's too base. We want to be hidden because we know, deep in our hearts, that to observe openly is to alter. And what we're all really after — what we're hardwired to want — is the unaltered. The genuine, the sincere, the pure. No matter how ugly."

"The uglier the better," Andrea said.

"So on this show, no camera crews or writers," Theodore said. "No anything. We prep the shot if we can; if not, we send these two in cold with cameras and mics and see what happens. But there's never any reveal.

163

We go in, we come out, and our subjects are never, ever the wiser. We're going to put the 'real' back in 'reality,' my dear."

"I like it, Theodore, as I told you earlier," Andrea said. "But what about security? Mr. K.'s mouth managed to get him beaten up and shot in less than forty-eight hours."

"Actually, it wasn't my mouth that got me shot," I said. "I didn't say a word that time."

"They'll sign the necessary waivers," Theodore said. "Whatever you want."

"We'll sign what now?" Claire asked.

"It's not liability I'm concerned about," Andrea said.

"Of course it is, my dear."

"Well yes," Andrea said, "it is my responsibility, as president of production, to not expose the studio to avoidable legal risk. But as a human being, I am worried about their safety."

"Andrea, let's be frank. You'd string your grandmother from a palmetto tree by her toenails if it meant you could get a couple extra points during sweeps."

"You know," I said, "the methodology used for Nielsen ratings is so flawed that the numbers might as well be completely made up."

"Not now, K.," Theodore said.

"I'm just saying, it's no way to make business decisions involving millions of dollars."

"Tell that to the guy whose show I'm canceling at lunch," Andrea said.

She and Theodore shared a knowing laugh, and then we were all quiet a moment, except for Claire, who groaned faintly behind her hands.

"So unless I miss my mark, Andrea," Theodore said finally, "there's really only one other matter of business."

"And what's that?"

"We'll need you to sign this release," Theodore said, smiling. He reached into his jacket and produced a thin sheaf of papers. "It authorizes us to use the footage recorded today for a new television show that will debut on Fox in the spring."

Andrea looked at the paperwork for a moment, then leaned back in her chair and smiled. "Deal," she said. "So long as you fill out your carbon offset forms."

After a celebratory dinner of vodka-cured salmon, watermelon salad, and filet mignon in wine sauce at a place called Nic's Beverly Hills, Theodore excused himself to "seek companionship," the particular nature of which could apparently be found only in Los Angeles. Before departing, he gave us both new sets of eyeglasses — pink cat-eye

frames for Claire, sober Buddy Holly specs
for me.

We sat side by side at the Nic's bar, which
had been constructed from a massive custom LEGO set.

"So tell me about Sarah," Claire said.

"You don't really want to talk about that,
do you?" I asked.

"Why not?" she said.

"It's my understanding," I said, "that
when embarking on a new romantic relationship, discussing one's ex is considered
taboo."

"Well, that's true, generally," Claire said.
She fiddled with the glasses Theodore had
given her, which were not just glasses but
also a high-resolution video camera and
microphone combo.

"Any talk of cats is also verboten, from
what I gather," I said.

"Do you have cats?"

"Just one," I said. "Now that I think about
it, the admonition against discussing cats
only really applies to women. Lest they
should be perceived as crazy cat ladies."

"Yet another double standard," Claire
said.

"Did you want to talk about my cat?" I
asked.

Claire turned her head to look at me

directly. "Why not," she said after a moment.

"Well the 'why not' would be because the cat actually belonged to my ex. Which brings us full circle."

"I'm not sure Sarah qualifies as an ex, K."

"For the purposes of this conversation, though, she does. Right? If we are in the embryonic stage of a new relationship?"

"Oh for Pete's sake." Claire lifted her beer and drained it, then motioned to the bartender for another. "Just tell me about your wife already," she said.

"She was very pretty," I said. "Like you."

"She looked like me?"

"Oh, not in the least. Sarah was much taller, for one thing. Her hair was short and black, not long and red. Also, hers was sort of a classic beauty, whereas yours is so exotic you almost, at times, don't look quite human."

"Thanks. I think."

"I mean that as a compliment."

Claire waved a hand. "You must miss her," she said.

I considered this while adjusting my own glasses, trying to find a more comfortable position for them that apparently didn't exist, or at least wouldn't exist until I became accustomed to the fact of them on my face.

"Not in the way you mean it," I said finally.

"And how do I mean it?"

"The same way most everybody does: Sarah is dead, never to be seen again, never to be heard from again, ashes to ashes, dust to dust, undifferentiated bits of carbon to undifferentiated bits of carbon, forever and ever, amen."

The bartender sidled over with a fresh beer for Claire, deftly laying a fresh cocktail napkin under the glass just as it hit the bar. Claire waited until he walked away again, then said, "Were you raised Catholic?"

"I wasn't raised anything," I said.

"Secular household?"

"Depended on the year," I said.

Claire smiled, nonplussed. "Are you always this opaque?"

"Opinions vary. Sarah probably would have said yes."

"Finally," Claire said. "We're talking about your wife."

"We can talk about whatever you like."

Claire swirled a fingertip through the head on her beer. "Okay, let's backtrack and try again," she said. "You told me you don't miss Sarah the way the rest of us miss dead people. Care to elaborate?"

"I would. But it's my policy not to, anymore."

"You're worried about it being in the show."

"Not at all," I said. "I've just decided it's like any other conviction the majority of people consider insane: best kept to oneself."

"You don't need to worry on my account," Claire said. "Since I was four I've believed that the inside of a carrot is poisonous. I nibble around the outside to this day."

"How do you know where to stop?"

"There's a little circle inside. You can see it. That's the border between healthy beta carotene and hot screaming death." She craned her neck and sipped from the top of her new beer without lifting it off the bar. "What do you think about that?"

"I think that what you're talking about is known as an irrational idea," I said. "Whereas what I'm talking about is completely rational. In fact, it's the only rational way to look at death, really."

"Okay," Claire said. "Then it shouldn't be a problem to spit it out."

"You're going to keep after me about this, aren't you?"

"Pestering," Claire said. "It's what I do."

"Alright," I said. "Let me answer your question with a question. What do you know about general relativity?"

"Not much. Cat trapped in a box, Geiger counter, flask of poison . . ."

"That's Schrödinger's cat," I said.

"I'm fucking with you, K.," Claire said. "Relativity. Speed of light. Time travel. All that shit."

"Correct."

"Got it. But what does that have to do with your wife?"

"Well, everything, really," I said. "In fact, it's the primary reason we're sitting here in Beverly Hills drinking twelve-dollar beers with spy glasses on our faces. Believe it or not."

"I believe almost anything," Claire said. "The inside of a carrot is poisonous, for example."

"Then would you believe that relativity indicates no one — including my wife — ever really dies?"

"That's news to me," Claire said. "And I took AP physics in high school."

"I could give you the broad strokes," I said.

"I've got nowhere else to be."

So I told her about the Einstein biography, the letter to Besso's widow, the fire, how the more I read and understood, the more the concept of death as absolute had crumbled like old mortar. Claire polished off her beer while she listened.

When I was finished, Claire put her chin in her hand and said, "This is by far the most interesting conversation I've ever had with someone about their ex."

"Thank you," I said.

"It also makes quite clear that you're mentally ill. As if we needed further proof."

"Says the woman who thinks carrots are as lethal as cyanide."

"But I *know* that's crazy, see. Deep in my brain, I know and acknowledge that's crazy. And so do you, with this stuff. Whether you can admit it to yourself or not."

"I've learned something essential about life and death. This is not delusional. My senses are the delusion. Sarah's last breath — that was a delusion."

"Fiddlesticks."

"Did you just say 'fiddlesticks'?" I asked.

"This is just you grieving in an extremely elaborate and unconventional way. You've fooled yourself into believing you're a slave to literalness. You pretend not to understand metaphor, but you actually understand it just fine. You pretend you can't cross the street unless the signal says it's okay, but when someone's life depends on it you jaywalk just like a normal person."

"All I can tell you," I said, "is that before

I read that book, I had the same two certainties as everyone else: death and taxes. And then suddenly, I was down to just taxes. After that, every assumption became suspect, no matter how self-evident."

"Like you can never use hand soap on your face, for example."

"I just need things to be true," I told her. "Actual. Clear. I need to be able to say, Yes, that is unequivocally so. Or unequivocally not so. Either way works for me."

Claire gazed at her reflection in the mirror behind the bar. "If I were a genie," she said after a minute, "I would tell you to wish for anything else. A billion dollars. Anilingus from a supermodel. The ability to communicate with fish."

"I don't think I want anilingus from anyone."

"The point is you probably think you're asking for very little, but you're actually asking for a hell of a lot."

"Why?"

"Because, K. Clarity? Certainty? Only children and Republicans expect life to be that simple."

We were quiet for a minute. Then Claire said, "So is this what we're supposed to be doing?"

"What do you mean?"

"Just sitting around shooting the shit? This is the show?"

"We're supposed to talk to other people, I think. There are events coming up, too. My award ceremony for the incident at the coffee shop, for example."

"Ah, of course."

"But mostly I think Theodore wants it to be spontaneous. Reality shows film hundreds of hours to put together just one thirty-minute episode."

"So I should stop worrying about being boring."

"They'll edit it out," I said. "Besides which, if you're worried about being boring, that means you're thinking about being on a show, which is exactly what Theodore wants to avoid. If I understood him correctly."

"Well of course I'm thinking about being on a show, K. Aren't you?"

"Not really."

"But you suffer from like late-onset autism. Those of us with functioning egos care when someone points a camera at us. We care a lot. Maybe more than we care about anything else."

"Anything else?"

"And let's not forget that this is just a pilot. That harpy Andrea could pull the plug

173

before we really get started."

"Even so," I said, "you'll still walk away with more money than you would have made in several years at Total Foods."

Claire studied my face. "Is that why you're doing this?" she asked.

"What do you mean?"

"I mean are you doing the show to make up for me getting fired."

"That's not the most precise way to describe it," I said.

"You really don't care about this at all, do you?"

"Care about what?"

"Being loved and hated by perfect strangers. Your name on the lips of millions of people you'll never meet. Getting paid just to hang out at clubs in Atlantic City and Vegas. Endorsement deals. A million Twitter followers."

"I'm not on Twitter," I said.

"You should be. Clothing lines. Shoe lines. Makeup lines. Ghostwritten tell-alls. TV drama guest appearances, possibly parlayed into regular acting gigs if you're any good, an Emmy nomination if your agent is any good. Speaking engagements. Waived parking tickets. I could go on."

"You've given this a lot of thought."

"You bet I have."

I considered. "If you mean do I derive self-worth or emotional satisfaction from the idea, the answer is no. I'm indifferent to it."

"So you're doing this for my sake."

"Yes," I said. "That is fair to say."

Claire gazed at me a moment longer, then turned and motioned to the bartender again. He came promptly, wiping his hands on a towel folded over his belt.

"Two shots of your best whiskey," she told him. "And another beer for me."

"It's two hundred dollars an ounce," the bartender said.

"Money is no object," Claire said. "We're celebrating here."

We waited for the bartender to return with fresh drinks. When he set the glasses in front of us Claire raised hers and nodded for me to do the same.

"You feeling better?" I asked.

"Don't judge," Claire said. "Everything preceding this I consider hair of the dog. I'm only just now starting to drink in earnest."

"Certainly not judging," I said. "Just surprises me, considering how bad you felt earlier."

We clinked glasses and drank.

"Do you drink much?" Claire asked, setting her glass back on the bar.

"Not really," I said. "I went through a period right after Sarah died when I was drinking a lot, by my standards. But that didn't last long."

"By your standards," Claire said.

"Half a bottle of bourbon a day," I said. "More or less."

Claire waved this away as an amount beneath contempt. "Want another?"

I hesitated.

"Come on," Claire said. "It's Andrea's dime."

"Alright," I said. "One more. Then I should sleep."

She signaled to the bartender.

At that moment Theodore walked back into the bar with a young Hispanic woman wearing large plastic dragonfly wings and a full-length red sequin dress. Given the woman's near-dwarfish stature, in this case "full-length" meant about four and a half feet.

"K. and Claire!" Theodore boomed, opening his thick arms to hug us simultaneously. "My new superstars. This is Arnulfo, a.k.a. La Hada Fabulosa."

Arnulfo executed a prim curtsy.

"My Spanish isn't what it could be," I said. "What does 'La Hada Fabulosa' translate to?"

"The Fabulous Fairy," Arnulfo said in accentless English.

"I take it you didn't choose that name for yourself."

"You take it wrong, *cabrón.*"

"We've got some whiskey coming," Claire said. "You want to join?"

"I would love one," Theodore said. "But none for Arnulfo, please. He's so wee, and I need him on top of his game later. In a manner of speaking."

"Don't you think you should let the lady decide for himself?" Claire asked.

"That is a fair point, I suppose," Theodore said. He turned to Arnulfo. "You are a woman of the twenty-first century, after all. I'm sorry to have been so presumptuous. Would you like a glass of whiskey?"

"Jesus Christ, no," Arnulfo said. "I'd rather gargle horse piss."

"Careful what you wish for, my dear," Theodore said.

"You're disgusting," Arnulfo said.

"And you love it," Theodore said.

"Where you from, Arnulfo?" Claire asked.

"Fairyland."

"Yeah, but I mean when you're off duty."

"Originally? Hoboken," Arnulfo said.

"And what do they drink in Hoboken?"

"Everything, up to and including Sterno," Arnulfo said. "But I'll settle for some white rum."

"My dear," Theodore said, "please be sure not to addle yourself."

"Relax. I've got half a dozen poppers in my clutch," Arnulfo said. "Let's hang out with your friends. It's early."

The bartender dropped off our whiskeys, and Claire asked him for one more, as well as a glass of Flor de Caña for Arnulfo. When the extra drinks hit the bar, Theodore raised his glass for a toast.

"To the genuine," he said.

We all drank.

"And speaking of the genuine," Theodore said, "it's interesting that you brought up Arnulfo's origins, my dears, because he and I were talking earlier tonight, and I think it might be good for all of us to go to Hoboken and visit his family."

"We didn't talk about *that*," Arnulfo said.

"Specifically, his father," Theodore said. "The last time Arnulfo saw him, the old man gave him a beating with a garden spade."

"I don't know what you have in mind," Arnulfo said, "but whatever it is, I want nothing to do with it. There's a reason I haven't been back there in twelve years."

"A garden spade?" I asked.

"One of those small ones," Arnulfo said, spreading his hands two feet apart to demonstrate.

"Still," I said.

"Arnulfo's father is a real *hombre varonil* in the Dominican tradition," Theodore said. "Which is to say that he is a homophobe of the very first order. I think I'd like to see you have a conversation with him, K. I think I'd like to record it, in fact. Very much."

"He beat you with a garden spade because you're gay?" I asked Arnulfo.

"Not exactly," Arnulfo said. "I mean, that was part of it. But also because I have a smart mouth and dress like a woman and can't play baseball worth a shit."

"But primarily because you're gay," I said.

"Honestly, I think it's the bustiers and feather boas that really get to him, even more than me sucking cock," Arnulfo said. "Having to hear about it all the time from his shithead friends at the bodega. That said, though, if someone had bothered to charge him with a hate crime the ACLU would have had a field day."

"So let's confront him, my dear," Theodore said. "Make him sorry for the torment he put you through."

"Why would I want to see that *puta*?" Arnulfo asked. "For all I know he's dead by now, anyway."

Theodore placed his glass on the bar and grasped Arnulfo's hands. "My dear," he said, "what if I told you that we could repay all the humiliation, all the pain, all the anguish, that man caused you in one fell swoop? Don't forget, I *saw* what he did to you, Arnulfo. I paid to have your teeth fixed."

Arnulfo shook his head. "He's a monster," he said. "I don't want to even look at him again."

"But you must! You can show him the brave, beautiful, fabulous man you have become. And we will be there with you."

"This is for your new show?" Arnulfo asked.

"We don't have to use it for the show, if you don't want to," Theodore said. "We'll visit your father, and if you think it goes terribly and want to forget it ever happened, we'll pretend it never happened, and no one, not even I, will ever view the footage. It will be destroyed. You have my solemn promise."

"Theodore," Arnulfo said.

"When have I ever broken a promise to you, my dear?"

"Never."

"And how many promises have I made?"

Arnulfo turned his eyes, dramatically framed with purple eye shadow, toward the ceiling. "A few," he conceded after a moment.

"Then why wouldn't you trust me now, my dear?"

"I don't know, *Papi . . .*"

Theodore turned from Arnulfo to me and Claire. "I'll work on him," he said. "The two of you should plan to fly to New York tomorrow, next day latest. And now I believe it's time for Arnulfo and I to take our leave. Speaking of which, have you yet decoded the exact nature of your relationship? Still going with 'manager and client'?"

"I've been wondering the same thing," Claire said.

"Word to the wise," Theodore said. "If you engage in any activities you don't want to appear on national television, take those glasses off. I'm decent enough to advise you thus, but not decent enough to pass on tasty footage if you serve it to me on a platter."

"Didn't you just tell Arnulfo you'd erase anything he didn't want seen?" I asked.

Theodore smiled and put a hand on my shoulder. "My dear," he said, "I love Arnulfo more than life itself. You, on the other hand, are at this point little more than a bare acquaintance."

Claire didn't want to remove her glasses.

"Do you mind if I leave them on?" she asked me.

"Theodore advised us not to wear them," I said.

In the dark, her hands found their way to my belt and began aggressive negotiations with the buckle.

"That's not what I asked," Claire said. "I asked if you care if I keep mine on."

"I guess I don't," I said.

Her lips brushed against the skin of my throat. "That's good," she said. "Because it's one way to make sure Andrea doesn't cancel us."

"They'll probably have to edit this out," I said.

"Be quiet, Gramps," she said, and so I was.

10
OEDIPUS THE GAY COWBOY

It turned out Arnulfo's father, Eduardo, was still drawing breath, though by the time we clomped up the six flights of stairs to his apartment in Hoboken his state of being was not one that could accurately be described as "alive." He was shriveled as a dead housefly, his skin mottled gray-green and alarmingly liver spotted, and though only in his late fifties he appeared, to even the most generous assessment, octogenarian. The grim vise of some lung ailment had grasped him, and his eyes were lit up with the panic of one who is drowning slowly from the inside. Despite this, he still smoked, and did so almost as incessantly as my mother-in-law. Then there was the matter of his oxygen tank, a small green torpedo that, combined with the open flame from his lighter, threatened to kill him with somewhat more expedience than the cigarettes. His hands were hooked into arthritic claws capped with long yellowed nails, and he could barely cross the width of his tiny living room without collapsing. But his son's hope — that Eduardo had died in his absence — was, at least upon our arrival, a vain one.

And what's the surprise in that, really? Experience told me nasty people like Eduardo often clung to life with remarkable doggedness, as though their hatred were so intense that it became its own animating force, and would not allow them to depart the world they loathed. Or maybe, in the case of Eduardo, he didn't hate the whole world, but just his son, and that alone was enough to keep him breathing. Because later, when Arnulfo came in, the low-grade panic in his father's eyes flared into something else, something hot and malign and, yes, for him, trapped in his old expiring bag of bones, invigorating. I doubt the man had felt so alive since he'd taken one last whack at his son with that garden spade.

First, though, it was Claire and I who showed up at his apartment, bespectacled and huffing a bit from the slog up the stairwell. I carried a giant check in my hands, written out for one hundred thousand dollars, and Claire held a bouquet of multihued balloons that bobbed cheerfully at the ends of their strings.

After we caught our breath I rapped on the steel-plated door, which raised a horrible racket in the empty hallway, the hollow sound of a place unlived in, left to the bugs and dust. We waited a full minute, exchanged glances. I knocked again, and again there was no response, but then, just as I raised my fist to knock a third time, I heard shoes scuffing carpet on the other side of the door. A series of locks tumbled open, and there stood Eduardo, handle of his oxygen tank cart in one hand, a Merit Gold smoldering in the other. For all the formidable things we'd heard about him, he was barely taller than his Lilliputian son, though to be fair he'd probably lost an inch or more to the slouch of illness.

"The fuck is this," he said, "Publishers Clearing House?"

"No," I said.

"May we come in?" Claire asked.

"Not until you tell me what's going on."

"We're here to give you one hundred thousand dollars," I said, turning the giant check around so he could read it.

"Which should be reason enough to let us in, don't you think?" Claire said.

"*Damita,* I could die in my sleep tonight," Eduardo said. "Money don't mean as much to me as you think."

"You could die a lot sooner, you keep smoking with that oxygen on," Claire said.

"Who asked you?"

"No one," Claire said. "I have a habit of speaking even when not given permission to do so. I know it's unseemly, in a lady."

Eduardo stared at her for a moment, his eyes rheumy and malevolent. Then he took two steps back into the apartment and said, "Come on, if you're coming. Don't let the cat out."

The cat in question, an orange tabby with a pendulous furry flap of a belly, darted in front of Eduardo as he made his way back into the living room. He unleashed a stream of obscenities at the beast for nearly tripping him, and we followed in the wake of this tirade.

"So what's the catch?" Eduardo said as he plunked down in a worn recliner and arranged the oxygen tank beside him. "I ain't never been lucky. So there must be a catch."

"Do you mind if we sit?" I asked.

"Sit the fuck down, already. What do you think this is, a state dinner?"

We all took a seat. The fat orange tabby leapt into Eduardo's lap, and he stroked its back and whispered profane endearments. The cat arched into a parabola and kneaded the leg of Eduardo's pants.

"You asked about the catch," I said.

Eduardo looked up. "I knew it."

"Simple," I said. "Reconcile with your son, and the one hundred thousand dollars is yours."

Eduardo's hand faltered at the base of the cat's tail. "My son," he said.

"Correct."

"Arnulfo."

"Yes," I said.

He scoffed. "That little fuck wouldn't dare show his face here."

"On the contrary," I said. "He's going to be at your front door in approximately six minutes."

"You're shitting me."

"We shit you not, sir," Claire said.

Eduardo looked from Claire to me, then back to Claire. "What the fuck is this?" he said finally.

"We just told you," Claire said.

"May I ask you a question?" I said.

Eduardo, still glancing back and forth between us and trying to decide whether he thought we were for real, didn't answer.

"Why do you hate your son?" I said. "I mean, I'm sure the reasons are myriad and complex, as they tend to be with family. But if you could maybe give a synopsis. Or else just tell me the one thing about him you hate the most."

"He's a filthy little faggot whose mouth is only good for two things: smarting off and chugging dick."

Claire glanced at me, eyebrows raised. She still held the balloons.

"That simple enough for you?" Eduardo asked.

"I assume that when you say 'filthy,' " I said, "you're not referring to his hygiene, which to me seems at least above average. Excellent, even."

"I'm referring to him letting people put their *bicho* in his ass."

"And *bicho* means 'penis'?"

"It means 'dick,' you dick."

"Okay," I said, "I just wanted to establish that your use of the word 'filthy' is a value judgment, rather than an assessment of Arnulfo's actual cleanliness."

Eduardo turned to Claire. "He always this dense?" he asked.

Claire held out one hand and tilted it back and forth. *"Más o menos,"* she said.

"It's not that I'm dense," I said. "It's that you're communicating imprecisely. And I'd appreciate it if you didn't blame me for your shortcomings."

"You can't do what Arnulfo does and be

188

clean, *cabrón.*"

"Actually, it's my understanding that most gay men are meticulous about keeping themselves and their households clean. But that's neither here nor there, because really, what you mean is that the sex acts your son engages in are not literally dirty, but rather unnatural and therefore deserving of scorn and condemnation."

Eduardo snuffed his cigarette out in a beanbag ashtray and lit a new one. "You think it's natural for two guys to suck each other off?" he asked.

"Perfectly so," I said.

"You ain't alone, these days," Eduardo said.

"But unlike most of those other people, my feelings about homosexuality are not informed by emotion, or ideology, or dogma. All I'm interested in are facts. And it's an objective fact that homosexuality is natural."

"You have anything to drink around here?" Claire asked.

Eduardo stared at her for a moment, then hooked a thumb back toward the kitchen. "Beer in the fridge," he said.

Claire stood up and disappeared into the kitchen, the balloons bouncing off the ceiling behind her.

189

"According to Arnulfo you're an insect enthusiast," I said.

For the first time since we'd entered the apartment the fear of death fled from Eduardo's eyes. Deep seams around his mouth, carved by decades of smoking, disappeared as if sandblasted, and I caught a glimpse of what he'd looked like as a young man: darkly handsome, imperious. "He told you that?"

I nodded. "He did. He said that if you hadn't been such a drunk, entomology could have been a profession instead of just a hobby."

Eduardo shrugged. "Not much point talking about 'if,' " he said.

Claire returned with a bottle of beer in her nonballoon hand.

"Actually," I told him, "that's what Arnulfo said, too. He told me that wishing you hadn't been a drunk was as pointless as wishing the Earth didn't revolve around the sun."

The seams returned to Eduardo's face, and the shadow to his brow.

"Do you regret drinking so much?" I asked.

"What do you mean, 'regret'?" he said.

"You don't know the word?" I asked.

"Of course I know the word, asshole," he

said. "I just don't regret anything. A man doesn't regret."

"Only liars and psychopaths claim to have no regrets," Claire said. "And you may be a hateful bastard, but you're no psycho."

Eduardo laughed and adjusted the cannulas in his nostrils. "I can't decide," he said to me, "if I like her a lot, or don't like her at all."

"I get that sometimes," Claire said. She swigged from the bottle of Heineken.

"Arnulfo told me you were particularly fond of beetles," I said to Eduardo.

"So?" he said.

"He said you had a collection of beetles that would be the envy of any natural history museum. In fact, he said the only thing you ever did together when he was a child was kill and mount beetles."

Eduardo nodded as he dragged on his cigarette. "That was before he went queer."

"He said he still loves the smell of the nail polish remover you used in the killing jar."

"If you're trying to make me all emotional, ain't going to happen."

"I bring it up because, for a man who was otherwise a brutal narcissist, it's a surprising pastime," I said. "Contemplative. Precise. Requires an outwardly directed interest and focus."

"I was better with bugs than I was with people, probably."

"That sounds like regret, to me," Claire said.

"You gonna regret coming here, you keep it up."

"Way ahead of you," Claire said, and drank again from her beer.

"Do you happen to have a specimen of *Tribolium castaneum*?" I asked Eduardo. "Common name flour beetle?"

"I know the Latin," Eduardo said. He glared at me and stubbed his cigarette out in the ashtray. "Flour beetles are only three millimeters. Almost too small to mount. I never had the equipment."

"In any event," I said, "you might be interested to know about the sexual habits of the flour beetle," I said.

Eduardo looked at Claire. "Honey, you want to fetch me one of them?"

"I don't fetch, babycakes," Claire said. "But as long as I can have another myself, yes, I'd be happy to get you a beer."

Eduardo nodded assent, and Claire went back into the kitchen.

"Did you know that the male flour beetle regularly engages in homosexual acts?" I asked.

"That supposed to blow my mind?"

"I just didn't know if you were aware," I said. "I just found out myself, after doing some reading on the plane."

Claire came back in with two beers.

"Of course I know flour beetles are *maricóns,*" Eduardo said, taking one of the Heinekens from Claire. He tilted the lip of the bottle toward me. "Do you know *why* they fuck each other?"

"Other than the usual reasons?" I asked.

Eduardo drank from his beer. "Turns out," he said, "that when one male beetle comes on another one, and the one that got came on goes and fucks a female, there's a chance that the female will get pregnant from the sperm of the first beetle."

"No kidding," I said.

"Whose mind's getting blown now?" he asked.

"That's brilliant, really," I said. "So having sex with other male beetles is an evolutionary strategy."

"You got it," Eduardo said. He set his beer down, shook another cigarette from the pack of Merits, and lit it. "So unless you can tell me about some faggot getting a woman pregnant by coming on some other faggot's back, flour beetles ain't got nothing to do with it."

I thought about this a moment. "Let me

193

ask you another question, then," I said. "Do you think the only purpose of sex is procreation?"

Eduardo sat back and exhaled a geyser of smoke. "So where's that rat fuck son of mine, huh?" he asked.

"He may have been delayed," I said.

"He may have chickened out," Claire said to me.

"Can you answer my question?" I asked Eduardo.

"You simple bastard," he said. "I know what Arnulfo does is wrong before God. Dance around it all you want, but you ain't gonna change my mind."

Before I could respond there came three brisk knocks at the door. In his lounger, Eduardo stiffened visibly. He lifted the cigarette to his lips, and I could see he'd pinched the filter nearly flat between his thumb and forefinger.

The oxygen tank hissed.

"Don't bother getting up," Claire said.

She went into the kitchen, threw the locks, and a moment later Arnulfo stood in the living room of his dying father's walk-up. Gone was the fantastical outfit he'd had on when we met him; now he wore faded jeans, snakeskin boots he must have purchased in the boys' department, and a T-shirt that read I WAS A GAY COWBOY BEFORE IT WAS COOL. Far from seeming afraid, Arnulfo emanated a dignity that cut through the cigarette smoke like light parsing clouds on the cover of a hymnal. He made a sort of offering of himself, arms relaxed at his sides and legs slightly apart, barely taller on his feet than I was seated. His eyes shone bright and clear, empty of any of the emotions one might expect to see from a man reunited with his tormentor.

He was beautiful.

"*Hola,* Eduardo," he said to his father.

Again, the terror of one who is slowly suffocating fled from Eduardo's face, replaced first by disbelief, then by an elemental fury. He transformed into a miniature Cronus right in front of us, sitting there with his cigarette and beer, tubing from the oxygen tank wound all around him. He would have eaten Arnulfo, if such a thing were possible. Instead he had to settle for rising from his old lounger and tottering forward one step, then glaring at his son with a bony fist cocked at his hip.

"You call me *Papi,*" the old man said, "or you don't call me anything."

Arnulfo gave a dismissive click of his tongue. "I don't think so, Eduardo. You never earned it."

"I'd rather my son call me *culo* than use my Christian name," Eduardo said.

"I'm surprised you even think of me as your son," Arnulfo said. He pointed at the lounger. "Sit down before you fall down, old man."

Eduardo took his seat again, slowly, careful not to pull the oxygen tube from his nose. I had a hunch, watching the two of them fume silently at one another, that Eduardo would not be one hundred thousand dollars richer at the conclusion of our visit. At this rate, he probably wouldn't even get to keep the balloons.

"What are you doing here?" Eduardo asked finally.

"It wasn't my idea."

Eduardo scoffed. "See, this has always been your problem, *Mijo.* Someone put you up to it? Bullshit. You decided to come here. You. It was your choice. So don't hide behind 'It wasn't my idea.' "

"Fine," Arnulfo said. "I did it because someone asked me to, and since I love him, I agreed. I don't suppose you'd know anything about that."

Eduardo glared at Arnulfo, and Arnulfo held his gaze, but calmly, still emanating that peculiar grace.

Claire jumped in. "Hey," she said to

Eduardo, "can I have one of those cigarettes?"

Eduardo continued to stare at his son, then turned to Claire finally. "You talking to me?" he asked.

"You're the only one smoking," she said.

He shook a cigarette out of the pack and handed it over. "You take that," he said, "and then you motherfuckers gotta go. This is no good. Ain't gonna end well."

"I had one other question to ask you," I said.

"No more talking," Eduardo said.

"Arnulfo told us about his cousin," I said. "Angel."

Eduardo started ever so slightly; if I hadn't been looking directly at him, I would have missed it. "Another goddamn *maricón*," he said. "This family's full of them."

"Arnulfo said that when you caught him with Angel was the first time you really gave him a beating," I said.

"His mother's rolling pin," Eduardo said. "Heavy fucker. Walnut. Clocked him in the neck before he had a chance to pull his pants up."

"But why didn't you give Angel a beating too?" I asked. "After all, he was four years older. In the contemporary view, that's statutory rape. He'd go to prison."

For a minute Eduardo didn't answer. He very carefully removed a fresh Merit from the pack and used the butt of his old one to light it. He pushed the tip of the expired cigarette into the base of the ashtray, folding the filter over to snuff the cherry. He ground that cigarette out like it owed him money, pushing so hard that it squeaked against the glass. Then he rubbed his thumb and forefinger together, and bits of ash fell, glinting in the sunlight from the smoke-smeared window behind him.

The oxygen tank hissed. Otherwise, the room was silent.

Finally Eduardo scoffed, almost under his breath. "Rape," he said, his tone dismissive of the very concept. "You can't rape the willing."

Looking back, what happened next should perhaps have been my first indication that this larger endeavor we'd set ourselves on might be a bad idea, no matter how much I wanted to help Claire after getting her fired from Total Foods. That maybe dedicating myself to repeated public refutation of people's beliefs was, as Eduardo had warned, liable to end badly. Plenty more evidence of this possibility was to come, but now Arnulfo made a sound unlike anything I'd ever heard before, unlike, perhaps, any sound that had ever issued from a human being. This sound came from Arnulfo's chest rather than his throat. It made the hair on my arms stand up, which until that moment I'd thought was just a figure of speech. I didn't know it could really happen, that one could be spooked enough that the small hairs on one's body would come to attention. I found myself preoccupied with what possible purpose this phenomenon could serve, even as it became clear that Arnulfo was about to do something bad, something perhaps irrevocable.

Either way I couldn't have stopped him, because the sound he made had paralyzed me.

In the next moment Eduardo's lounger was flipped onto its back, and Arnulfo had his father down on the carpet. The orange tabby, which had been resting on the windowsill behind Eduardo, scrambled onto the sofa and stared, its eyes wide and wild, poised to run again should further flight seem necessary. Eduardo's tubing came loose from the oxygen tank, which hissed and hissed, loosing pure O2 into the room.

Arnulfo straddled his father's chest and set about slapping him, his hands flying like the blurred combos of a very good featherweight boxer. Eduardo sputtered, squirming under his son's weight.

"K.," Claire said, "don't you think you should step in? Before he kills him?"

"What should I do?"

"I mean, not that I really mind if he kills him," Claire said.

Arnulfo began spitting in his father's face. He held Eduardo's head still with both hands and spit into his eyes, his mouth. "Did you know, *Papi*," he said, "that HIV can be transmitted through saliva? It's not just for faggots anymore!"

"Actually," I said, loud enough to be heard over the din, "HIV isn't present in saliva in large enough concentrations to be transmitted to another person."

"*K.*," Claire said. For the first time I'd ever seen, she looked genuinely alarmed.

Arnulfo gave a garbled scream as he bit down on his own tongue. He closed his mouth and sucked his cheeks in, producing, after a moment, a glistening bloody glob of mucus, which he spat directly onto his father's nose.

"You could get HIV from that, for sure," I said.

Claire took a step toward the two of them, then stopped and looked to me again. "Jesus Christ, K., do something," she said.

I got to my feet and waded into the scrum.

I'm not always the biggest guy in the room, but compared to Arnulfo I was a titan, and lifting him off his father was not unlike plucking a four-year-old away from the floor.

I handed Arnulfo off to Claire, who wrapped him in a bear hug from behind and dragged him several steps toward the kitchen.

"Oxígeno," Eduardo gasped.

"Let me clean your face first," I said, kneeling on the carpet beside him.

After a moment of looking around for a towel or throw blanket, I pulled my oxford over my head and wiped the bloody goop off Eduardo's nose and brow, sopped it away from the corners of his eyes. He continued to flail weakly, his hands making stricken little motions in the air above him, like a fussy baby fighting sleep.

"I'm going to call an ambulance," Claire said.

Eduardo shook his head several times. His mouth worked silently.

"He says no," I told her.

"Like I give a shit."

"He may have a DNR, sick as he is," I said.

Below me Eduardo nodded, his eyes closed.

"You have a DNR? He has a DNR," I said.

"DNR?" Claire asked.

"It's an acronym," Arnulfo said. "Stands for 'let the motherfucker die.'"

"More or less," I said.

"Oxígeno," Eduardo pleaded again.

"If we don't call someone we're going to be in trouble, K."

"We're probably going to be in trouble anyway," I said. "But go ahead and make the call, if you want."

While Claire directed Arnulfo into the kitchen, I reattached the plastic tubing to Eduardo's oxygen tank and slid the cannulas into his nostrils. I found a pillow on the sofa and placed it under his head. None of this seemed to do any good. His lips remained alarmingly blue, and the suffocation fear was back in his eyes, burning brighter now that the application of oxygen hadn't eased his distress.

"So you have a DNR?" I asked.

He nodded again.

"Do you want to die?" I asked.

Eduardo didn't respond. He closed his eyes for a moment, then opened them again, slowly, still able to muster some balefulness for me despite his distress.

"I'm just trying to understand what you

want," I said. "Maybe we should sit you up?"

He nodded. I slid an arm underneath his shoulders, pulling him into a sitting position against the sofa.

"Better?" I asked.

He drew a deep, shuddering breath, then nodded again.

"Ambulance is on its way," Claire called from the kitchen.

Eduardo looked at me. "You want to understand?" he said. "That's what you said, right? You want to understand."

"I'm trying to understand everything," I said.

Eduardo went into a sudden, explosive coughing fit, a dry hacking that made him list to one side like a crippled ship. When the jag released him he straightened his cannulas with trembling hands and said, "Then let me tell you, *cabrón:* you're asking the wrong question."

"What's the right question?"

He grabbed the sleeve of my undershirt and pulled my face to his. This close I could smell the sickness on him, sour and sharp. "The question," he said, "is never 'Do you want to die?' The question is, 'Do you want to keep on living?' "

"I can understand," I said, "why that

distinction might seem important."

Eduardo released my shirtsleeve and leaned back against the sofa. "Do me a favor and find my cigarettes, huh?"

I looked and saw the end table had somehow remained upright in the fracas. Eduardo's cigarettes and ashtray rested undisturbed on top of it. I retrieved them.

We sat side by side on the carpet with the ashtray between us. The oxygen tank continued to hiss. We waited: for the ambulance, for death. From time to time Eduardo went into another coughing fit. One of these was bad enough that he dropped his cigarette as though someone had slapped it from his hand. I retrieved it and waited for him to compose himself. After a few moments, Eduardo reached to take the cigarette back.

"You sure you really want this?" I asked.

"Just give it to me."

I looked at him, then handed the cigarette over. "Addiction is a fascinating thing," I said.

Eduardo took a drag. "Family, too," he said, choking back another cough as smoke surged around the cannulas in his nostrils.

11
HEROISM IS A FICTION

In this particular spot in space-time, Eduardo's fear of suffocation came to an end five days later at Hoboken University Medical Center. The official cause of death was acute respiratory failure resulting from chronic obstructive pulmonary disease. From what Arnulfo told me, it was a postcard afternoon in Hoboken. The hospital room had big westward-facing windows, and the shades were opened at Eduardo's request — his last request, it turned out. He died bathed in warm red light as the sun retreated slowly toward Allentown. A still, eerie, peaceful death. No thrashing agonal period bridging the Styx; just one last, peaceful exhalation, like in a movie, and exeunt.

"Which is too bad," Arnulfo said over the phone. "He deserved to suffer a little more."

The news came while I waited for my award ceremony to begin. Even though I

205

didn't believe Eduardo was any more dead than he had ever been, I told Arnulfo I was sorry for his loss.

Arnulfo scoffed at this. "Loss," he said. "Give me a break."

Then he started to sob.

"They're calling me to the stage," I told him. "I have to go."

The ceremony took place in an old opera house across the street from city hall. I followed an attendant from the greenroom through a series of musty, claustrophobic passageways to the edge of the stage, where we waited for my introduction to conclude. The chief of police stood at a lectern, flanked by Felicia and a pair of men who appeared to be dignitaries of some kind — city councilors, perhaps, or maybe one of them was the mayor, though I wouldn't have known our mayor from Mayor McCheese. I remained in the wings with the attendant while the chief spoke of my bravery, my selflessness, my heroic observance of the one principle that made civilization possible, to wit: our obligation to take care of one another whenever we could.

The man he was talking about didn't sound much like me, to me.

Eventually the chief ran out of superlatives, and I was introduced to exuberant applause. As I walked onstage the chief made way at the lectern, and I realized suddenly that they meant for me to speak. Not having prepared any remarks, I took my spot at the microphone and, after waiting for the audience to quiet down, said this: "I'm not sure who the chief was just talking about. That man sounds like Jesus Christ himself."

Chuckles from those assembled.

"That wasn't supposed to be funny," I said, and then, when the laughter choked off and I noticed expressions of bemusement pocking the crowd: "Though it's okay. Just because I'm not trying to be funny doesn't mean you aren't allowed to laugh."

The auditorium was quiet enough, suddenly, that I could hear people breathing. Somewhere a cell phone, muffled by pocket or purse, chimed out a snippet of the *1812 Overture.* I looked to my right, where the chief of police stood staring quizzically at me.

"I hope you understand that I don't mean to be contrarian," I said. "I often have difficulty, in recent months, making myself understood. This is a very nice thing that you're doing for me. The point I'm trying to make is, do any of you believe I'm actually the unwaveringly decent person the chief just described? Or is it more likely that

I'm a flawed, occasionally petty man thrust by chance into a situation in which he merely appears heroic?"

The chief of police cleared his throat pointedly. I looked over at the sound and saw Felicia had cast her gaze to the floor.

"I mean listen, if we're being honest, there's no such thing as a person who embodies valor," I said, turning back to the audience. "Heroism is not something you occupy day to day. It's a moment, at best. You get something right, almost by accident, and then you go back to your bumbling, myopic default setting. So I think about this — about how the vast majority of our lives are passed in a decidedly unheroic way — and I wonder, is heroism measured, then, by account balances? On the one hand, you have my acting in a way that likely saved Felicia's life. And that is not insignificant. But on the other hand, you have forty years' worth of the little injuries I've inflicted on myself and others. The casual harsh word, or else the kindness I failed to extend. The thoughtless waking hours, the willful stupidity. Garbage thrown on the roadside instead of in a trash bin. Careless lane changes, a vote cast for a man who went on to start an unjust war. The medium-rare steak that tastes like terror and desperation, when I never in this life or any other would raise the butcher's knife myself.

"And then there are the little domestic blunders we all commit. For years I hurt my wife a dozen times a day, unthinkingly, and most often without malice — these were failures of ignorance, or workaday negligence, or fatigue. The inevitable result, in other words, of what we often call the human condition. I did not want to injure my wife — I was not actively trying to injure her — and yet I did, over and over. If I cataloged for you all the ways in which I failed in my marriage, I guarantee you would lose interest in celebrating me today."

Someone coughed. Otherwise, the auditorium was silent.

"At the same time," I said, "I realize hyperbole is de rigueur at events like this. Everyone needs heroes, or at least heroic narratives. There's a reason *The Odyssey* has survived for three thousand years. But that reason isn't what we think. It's not that we hold Odysseus's deeds in high esteem, and so want to honor him by remembering them. It's that we want to *be* him. Or at least believe we could, on our best days, be like him. It's the same impulse that sends us flocking to films about decent men who reluctantly exercise their talent for violence

209

in the name of what's just. So when you get right down to it, this ceremony is more about making *you* feel good than it is about honoring me."

Crickets. I found myself, in spite of myself, growing irritated with their ongoing silence.

"And also," I said, "ceremonies like this are about confirming your belief in a just world, which you need in order to assuage a whole host of subconscious fears," I said. "Fear of existing in a universe that is completely and utterly indifferent to you, your families, whether you suffer or celebrate, live or die."

I sensed the chief of police sidling closer to the podium.

"But this notion of a just world doesn't withstand even the mildest scrutiny," I said. "A five-year-old can, and often will, tell you that existence is fundamentally unfair. For the last few months, I've been reading pretty much every spare minute when I'm not asleep, and I've learned some terrible things. Like, for example, that half of humanity lives on less than two dollars a day. That's over three billion people. Try to imagine three billion of anything. Pennies. Bottle caps. You can't do it. I'm not saying I can, either. But still. In the last twenty-four hours, enough children died of hunger to fill Fenway Park, while during that same time people actually *at* Fenway Park gorged themselves on nine-dollar hot dogs to the point of gastrointestinal distress and, in a couple of instances, probably, brief hospitalization. In the last year, people have been killed by airborne fire hydrants, runaway hay bales, and falling coconuts. Somewhere on this planet, as we speak, a man is being made to squat on a broken bottle for the entertainment of his tormentors, and a woman is being stoned to death for falling in love. Nonsmokers get lung cancer, marathoners drop dead of heart attacks. Murderers and thieves walk free, and the innocent go mad in prison cells the size of broom closets. But you want to believe in a just and orderly world, so you come here to applaud a shiny object being pinned to my lapel.

"All of which is fine, understand," I said. "I'm neither judging nor condemning. I just want to acknowledge the reality of what we're all doing here."

Murmuring now. Several people rose from their seats and departed through the large double doors at the back of the auditorium.

"I can see I've displeased you," I said, "and I apologize. Maybe I could try to explain. What would you think if I told you the thing that makes me not good with people is the same thing that made me cross the street that night?"

The chief of police drifted into my periphery and addressed the crowd without benefit of amplification. "Ladies and gentlemen, thank you. And now, with the authorization of our mayor and esteemed members of the city council, I will present the —"

"Because listen," I said, "if I were still the man I was before my wife died, I would not have crossed that street. I would have stayed in the shadows a hundred feet away, hidden and safe, under no moral obligation to help in any way, aside from placing a phone call to the police. And in that instance Felicia likely would have died, but not before horrid things, things arguably worse than death, were done to her."

The chief moved closer. "Asshole," he hissed, still facing the crowd and smiling, "shut the fuck *up.*"

"I'm being asked to keep my remarks brief," I said, "so let me conclude by saying that if you really want to honor what I did, then instead of sitting there gape mouthed you should applaud this awkwardness that we're all experiencing right now. Applaud my complete inability to adhere to the script of this ceremony. Because it's the very thing that saved Felicia's life. Thank you."

Maybe five or six people clapped, but not loud enough to obscure the sound of the *1812 Overture* going off in someone's pants again.

It took a long time for the chief to present me with my medal. Several photographers — one working for the city, a couple with local news outlets — wanted pictures of the presentation. We stood there, the chief and I, and held various poses: shaking hands and smiling, standing side by side and smiling, holding a citation from the city and smiling.

The photographers also wanted several shots of the chief actually putting the medal on me, which he did like a girl pinning a boutonniere on a prom date whom she did not like in the least. I wish I could say that the chief was merely careless, and stabbed me without actually meaning to. But I cannot say that with anything resembling certainty.

Afterward I met Claire, who'd left at the conclusion of my speech, at a bar down the street from the opera house. Her face came to life when I walked into the room, and as I approached she stood up from her drink and opened her arms to greet me.

"You were brilliant," she said, pulling my

body tightly against the hard spots and soft swells of her own, making my pierced breast ache.

12
THE SECURITY DETAIL AS A KIND OF APOLOGY

Soon after the award ceremony, Claire and I set to work on the show — now titled (over my objection and to Claire's *America, You Stoopid* great giggling delight) — in earnest. We cut seams into the map like traveling salesmen, logging thousands upon thousands of miles in the first month alone, the paradoxical effect of which was to conjure a world that seemed smaller yet ever more varied: distances were made short by air travel, but the philosophical space between people proved infinite. Yet despite the wildly disparate thoughts and opinions of those we met, I was always able to fulfill Theodore's mandate of finding disagreement, owing to what I came to think of as the Great False Binary. The dominant mode of national discourse, the Great False Binary dictated that a given thing was either entirely right and just and correct and awesome through and through, or entirely awful and evil and

215

wrongheaded and irredeemable through and through. No room existed for considering the moral and legal nuances of, say, abortion, because according to the Great False Binary, those nuances did not exist. As such, even when I agreed with the president of Planned Parenthood that abortion should be safe and legal, I still managed to upset her by suggesting that those who consider abortion to be murder perhaps have a valid point. Ditto a representative from the National Organization to Stop the Proliferation of Immigrants in Confederate States (or NOSPICS), who seemed to suffer a grand mal seizure when I noted that no matter how one felt about Mexicans, it was well-established economic fact that illegal immigrants contribute a larger portion of their income to government coffers than citizens.

These secular disagreements, however, regardless of how heated or otherwise good for television, presented no physical danger. We argued with Klansmen and New Black Panthers, radical feminists and neoliberals, without injury or threat thereof. It was only when talk veered toward that fogged-in province of burning bushes and giant obsidian cubes that we learned — mostly the hard way — that the more irrational a

216

person's belief, and the less evidence available to support it, the more likely he is to beat you up for suggesting that belief is wrongheaded.

I don't pretend to understand why this is. I'm not an anthropologist, or a neuroscientist, or a man of vestments. Despite all my experience I have no better understanding of people than I did before. I'm merely reporting the facts.

So: when our discussions turned to religion, I often, if not always, got hurt.

There was the air force chaplain who slapped me on the ear when I suggested the branch of the military responsible for our nuclear weapons stockpile should perhaps not be promoting end-times evangelicalism at its service academy.

There was the group of prominent Brooklyn Hasidim to whom I suggested it would be a great mitzvah to offer money for the construction of a mosque in Lower Manhattan (I even used the word "mitzvah," thinking that might help). They responded by smoothing their white oxford shirts carefully with the palms of their hands before kicking me around in the street like a soccer ball.

There was, most famously, the Shaolin monk who pummeled me insensate with a bamboo staff for reasons I still don't fully understand, but assume have to do with insulting his beliefs, however inadvertently.

Not a single episode of the show had aired yet, but even I knew this was the sort of television people would fall all over themselves to watch. At the same time, the worst of the assaults tended to slow production, as they forced Claire and me to retreat home, where she would drink and tend to my wounds as I convalesced.

One afternoon following the incident with the monk, Claire sat astride my lower back rubbing ointment onto slashes left by the bamboo staff. Her hands, small as mice, moved over my skin, pausing to trace each wound carefully before the sting of the ointment.

"Does that hurt?" she asked.

"There is some pain, yes," I said.

"And yet there you lie, silent as stone."

"There's not much point in making a fuss," I said.

"You're the first person I've ever seen catch a beating and not utter a sound. It's almost creepy."

"Have you witnessed a lot of beatings?" I asked.

"Witnessed, experienced," Claire said. "Sort of a rock-'em sock-'em household, growing up."

I absorbed this, considered inquiring further, then decided that if Claire wanted to be more specific, it was not my place to prompt her. "There's no doubt," I said, "that a couple of years ago I would have screamed like a scalded cat."

"I'm such a crier," Claire said. Her hands left my back for a moment as she scooped more cream onto her fingertips. "Always have been. Used to drive my mother crazy."

"Children cry," I said.

"Not like me," Claire said. "There was this cat we got when I was seven or eight. I don't really remember how he came to us. Probably a stray."

"Sometimes they just appear in your life, cats," I said.

Claire's hands returned: warm, bearing goop. "So this cat kind of hated everyone, but he was real sweet on me. He'd hide until I came home from school, then follow me around the house, everywhere I went. Slept on my head all night, like cats do. Anytime I sat down, he was in my lap. A pain in the ass, but I sort of liked it, too. He was warm and friendly and I didn't really have anything else."

Claire paused, and her hands went still, resting flat and warm against my back.

"Go on," I said, after a minute.

She cleared her throat, and her hands began moving again. "There was this old guy who lived at the end of the street. The local creep. None of us were supposed to go anywhere near him or his house. The rumor was this guy hated cats on his property, so he put out poison. And one day, our cat got into some."

Claire sat back, leaned left to reach for the bottle of beer on the nightstand. I waited, shifted my hips. She took a swig, put the bottle back, curled herself forward again. The fingers of her right hand ran slowly over a bruise on my left flank.

"I got home from school that day, and the cat didn't come running like usual, so I searched the house and found him behind the bathroom door," she said. "I'll spare you the details, but suffice it to say he was sort of liquefying on the inside, the evidence of which was pouring out of pretty much every hole. And the sounds he made, K. I still have dreams about those sounds."

"I'm sure," I said, "that any kid would have cried at that."

"I was world-class, though," Claire said. "I wailed like one of those grandmothers you see in war zones, clawing at a pile of rubble until her hands bleed. We're talking half the night. 'Why?!' I kept screaming, over and over, and finally, after a few hours of this, my mother turned and screamed right back at me: 'I don't know!' ”

We were both quiet for a minute.

"Anyway, that was the end of that," Claire said finally.

"People don't always behave the way they'd prefer, in times of stress," I told her. "Particularly when that stress is coming from their children."

Claire dismissed this with a grunt, and reached for her beer again. "Do you want kids?" she asked.

"I did, yes."

"Why?"

"That's sort of an unusual question."

"It's actually a perfectly reasonable question, K.: Why would you rip someone out of oblivion and drag them into this?"

"Biological imperative?" I ventured.

"Not good enough, Mom. Why? Why?"

I didn't respond.

"And then the answer comes," Claire said. " 'I don't know.' ”

I let the silence gather around that.

Finished with the ointment, Claire drummed her fists gently on the small of my back. "You're a mess," she declared.

"Does it worry you?" I asked. "How angry

I seem to make people?"

"A little," Claire said. "But it's going to make us famous."

"The consideration above all others," I said.

Claire reached forward and flicked my earlobe with one finger. "Besides," she said, "there's this feeling I have that, no matter how crazy things get, you're totally, utterly, completely in control."

Every time I got smacked, whacked, or bludgeoned, I could picture Theodore gleefully abrading one chubby palm with the other, visions of Emmys dancing in his head.

But then, at a café in West Hollywood in the second month of filming, Theodore surprised me by saying he had started to fear for my safety.

"Started?" I said, twirling a plastic stirrer through my Americano.

It was just the two of us. Outside, southern California hurried about its business. Chrome gleamed as cars raced by at twice the speed limit. Across the street, in buildings abutting one another, squatted a pawnshop, a sex dungeon, and a Jack in the Box. The sun baked palm fronds and pavement and people alike.

"I think back to our first conversation with

Andrea," Theodore said, "and I wonder if she wasn't right about security. If maybe I wasn't a bit cavalier. I knew, of course, that you would make people angry. What I underestimated was their eagerness to assault you when their ire is raised. This is a vicious time we live in."

"I'm not really worried about it," I said.

"Well that concerns me, too, my dear," Theodore said. "That you're not worried about it."

"I rarely worry about anything," I said.

"May I be frank?" Theodore asked.

"Of course," I said.

"It makes me wonder if you aren't mentally ill, in some way."

I thought about this. "I don't believe so," I said. "And let me add that the old notion about crazy people having no idea they're crazy isn't true. In case that's what you were thinking."

"It was, in fact."

"Though it *is* true that with certain mental illnesses, it can be difficult or impossible for the afflicted to understand that something is wrong with them. Paranoid schizophrenia, for example. But I think we can both agree that I'm not schizophrenic."

"We can."

"And even schizophrenics sometimes

understand they aren't well. They're just helpless to do anything about it."

"My dear," Theodore said, "no one is suggesting that you're schizophrenic. But may I offer an analogy?"

"I assumed you would get around to it sooner or later."

Theodore sipped from an espresso cup not much larger than a thimble. "Watching you in the raw footage," he said, "I was reminded of my enthusiasm for professional wrestling."

"It has borne some similarities, of late," I said.

"Not the glamorized, hypertheatrical version you see on television, which bores me to the point of despair," Theodore said. "I'm talking about real wrestling. Which can still be found today, but not on television. Did you watch professional wrestling as a child?"

"Not much," I said. "I remember it being a very big deal, but I had little interest. I know of Hulk Hogan and André the Giant. A gentleman with the unlikely name of Koko B. Ware also comes to mind, for some reason."

Theodore wheezed. "Koko was an entertaining character, for certain, but he was no wrestler. Not the kind of wrestler I'm talking about. So it's safe to assume, then, that you are not familiar with a man known as Abdullah the Butcher?"

"Never heard of him."

Theodore shifted forward, and the chair squealed under his bulk. "Abdullah was a practitioner of what's known in wrestling circles as the hard-core style. Baseball bats wrapped in barbed wire. Electrified ring ropes. I once saw a match in Tokyo that featured a tank of piranha. Take the most violent thing you've ever witnessed, multiply that violence by an exponent of ten, and you still won't quite understand the brutality of hard-core wrestling."

"Doesn't really seem like your kind of thing, Theodore."

"My dear," he said, "I adore violence. So long as those engaged in it are willing participants."

"What about when the willingness of the participants is in question?"

"As with?"

"Cockfighting," I said.

"Those birds are hardly forced to fight, K. They struggle to escape their handlers so they can get at each other. They stomp on the vanquished, repeatedly, until forced to quit. Beautiful, savage creatures, with their plumage and bloodlust."

"Well I'm no fighting bird," I said, "but

all the same, I am a willing participant."

"Which brings us back to Abdullah the Butcher," Theodore said. "Because he appeared to be a willing participant, as well."

"Okay," I said.

"Over the years, Abdullah became infamous not for the amount of punishment he inflicted upon his opponents — though that was considerable — but for the damage he did to himself in the ring. Do you know what the term 'blading' refers to?"

"I could make a guess," I said.

"It's when wrestlers use a broken bit of razor to cut their own foreheads. A small blood offering on the altar of entertainment that many, many have made, and quite willingly. But Abdullah bladed himself with a frequency and enthusiasm unlike any other. He slashed arteries on purpose, delighted in disfiguring himself. Eventually his bald head bore long grooves into which he would insert poker chips, as a sort of grotesque parlor trick."

"It's a strange and multifarious world we live in," I said.

"But see, K., the point is that as much as I enjoy hard-core wrestling, I gradually came to hate watching Abdullah the Butcher."

"Because he was not a willing participant."

"Correct. He merely appeared to be one, when in fact he was genuinely sick. And being compelled to do something, even if that compulsion is internal, is not the same thing as doing it of your own volition."

"So you're convinced that I'm like Abdullah the Butcher."

"Convinced? No. But after watching you bait that Shaolin monk, I began to wonder."

"I hardly baited him," I said.

"K.," Theodore said, "you challenged the deeply held beliefs of a man whose only vocation is the practice of lethal acts."

"Exactly the point I was trying to make," I said. "There has to be some dissonance when you promote a pacifist philosophy yet spend all your waking hours studying how to kick the crap out of people."

"My dear," Theodore said.

"At the very least, he exposed himself as something of a hypocrite," I said.

"Here is something life has taught me," Theodore said. "If a man carries a weapon around as a matter of course, there's a very good chance he will sooner or later find occasion to use it. No matter his espoused philosophy."

I stared out the window. Los Angeles's endless traffic continued to whiz past in either direction. A man emerged from the sex dungeon in tears, looked up and down the sidewalk as if lost, then stumbled into the Jack in the Box. The sun shone like a klieg light; even the homeless wore sunglasses.

"I thought," I said to Theodore, "that I was doing exactly what you wanted. Which is to say, the thing that I'm inclined to do."

"You are, my dear," Theodore said. "I just underestimated how dangerous it could be. I started this, and I have an obligation to protect you."

"If it's any comfort, I was doing a good job of getting beaten up and shot all on my own."

"Nevertheless," he said.

"But so what is it you're proposing?"

"That's the thing," Theodore said. "We want to preserve the environment of authenticity we've created — and let me tell you, K., there is nothing on television as honest or raw as the footage we've shot to this point — so we plan to hire a small security detail that shall remain secret, even from you. Full disclosure, we already have hired a small security detail. Two men. Ex-Spetsnaz. Dangerous fellows."

"Ex-Spetsnaz?"

"They can be trusted. Like most post-Soviet Russians, they value money over all else, and they're being paid quite well."

"Seems very serious," I said.

"We require professionals," Theodore said. "Men who are as good at blending into the background as they are at handling a sidearm. You won't meet them, unless, God forbid, something goes really wrong. But they'll always be there."

"By which you mean they're here right now."

"Well, not here, necessarily, in this coffee shop. Then again, they might be. That's the point."

"It's maybe worth thinking about how this could make things worse, rather than better," I said.

"What do you mean?"

"I'm just playing devil's advocate," I said, "but consider what these ex-Spetsnaz might have done to the Shaolin monk, for example."

"I couldn't begin to speculate," Theodore said.

"Because as much as that hurt, I don't think gunfire would have been the appropriate response."

"Ultimately that's their decision, my dear. We pay them for their judgment as much as their skill. And they're very well insured."

13
AN ANOMALY OF AERODYNAMICS

"Ex-*what*naz?" Claire said.

"Spetsnaz. Russian special forces. Possibly also formerly of the GRU. Though Theodore didn't say as much."

"So are they watching us now?" Claire asked.

"One would imagine," I said.

"They're on the plane with us right now," Claire said. This existed somewhere between statement and question.

"I have to assume. Based on what Theodore told me."

"That's just weird," Claire said. "I mean, I don't like this at all, K." She sat up and gazed around the cabin, craning her neck over the back of her seat.

"Theodore anticipated that you would feel this way," I said.

"Are they, like, *armed*?"

"Again," I said, "one presumes so. Although they probably had to check their weapons, considering that we're on a plane and all."

Claire pressed the flight attendant call button. "Wait," she said. "What do you mean, Theodore anticipated I would feel this way?"

"He said as much. At our meeting."

"You had a meeting without me?"

"He said not to bring you. For this very reason."

"What reason?"

"He believes you're too invested in being a celebrity to want to risk mucking up the show with a security team."

"That's not the problem. At all. I just don't want some creeper following me around everywhere I go, watching every move I make." She seemed to consider something for a moment, then punched me on the arm. "And what the hell? You agreed to take the meeting without me?"

"I didn't think much about it one way or the other. He said come alone, so I went alone."

"K.," Claire said, glaring at me, "there's a big difference between 'come alone' and 'don't bring Claire.' A big difference."

"That's a fair point, I suppose."

The flight attendant, all frizzy-haired impatience, appeared from the front galley.

"Can I help you?" she asked, leaning over us to switch off the call button.

"I need another vodka and soda, please."

The attendant looked at Claire for a moment. "It is my obligation to make you aware, Miss, that we have a three-drink limit on domestic flights. Company policy."

"Thank you," Claire said. "For making me aware."

"This will be your third. For the record."

"Thank you," Claire said, her eyes suddenly ablaze, "for sparing me the trouble of doing simple arithmetic."

They eyed each other a moment longer, and then the flight attendant returned to the galley.

"I think she's making up 'company policy' on the fly," a man across the aisle from Claire said. "Pardon the pun. I've had four of these already." He held up a can of beer.

"She probably just doesn't like other women," Claire said. "Catty bitches. The world's chock-full of them."

The man stared, nonplussed.

Claire turned back to me. "Is he one of them?" she whispered.

"I doubt they would be drinking."

"Maybe that's part of his cover," Claire said. "Besides, they're Russian, right? I thought they were drunk all the time. Like, as a people."

"As with most stereotypes, it has a basis in observed reality, but there are surely exceptions."

"Jesus, K., I really don't like this. It's pushing all sorts of buttons I didn't even know I had."

"I'm sorry to hear that," I said.

"Did Theodore give them access to the video feeds?"

"I don't know," I said. "We could ask."

"Because that I don't like *at all.* Watching us when we're in bed. In the bathroom. Nuh-uh."

"I guess it's hard to understand why that would bother you," I said, "when presumably thousands or maybe millions of strangers will be watching us in bed and in the bathroom."

"Totally different. Totally." Claire gave me a pointed look. "I mean, don't be an idiot."

"Forgive me for saying so, but you seem like you're more than two drinks in," I said.

"That's because I am," she said. "I bring my own shooters when I fly."

"You can get those through security?" I said.

"They're under three ounces. It's a lot cheaper than buying them for eight bucks a pop on the plane." She nodded toward the galley. "Also helps when dealing with teeto-taler flight attendants."

"Huh," I said.

"Nice job trying to change the subject," she said.

"Have you ever thought about why you drink so much?" I asked.

"K., I want to talk about this," Claire said. "I'm sort of freaking out, here, for real."

"We can talk about the ex-Spetsnaz," I said. "I just wonder if you ever ponder it. A simple question. You know I'm not judging."

The flight attendant returned, thrust a small plastic cup into Claire's hands, and walked away again without a word.

"That was sort of rude," the man across the aisle said.

Claire turned toward him. "Why do you keep talking to me?" she asked. "Who are you?"

"I'm nobody," the man said.

"Likely story," Claire said.

"You should maybe just drink your drink and try to relax," I said. "Before we get into trouble."

Claire closed her eyes, sipped vodka through a tiny red straw, and exhaled. "I'm sorry," she said. "Yes. You're right. Let's talk about something else."

"Okay. Good."

"But did you detect any trace of an accent, with this guy? I thought maybe I heard something."

"Claire."

"I drink," she said, still not opening her eyes, "because my grandmother had to hide her vodka in the toilet tank."

"I'm sorry?"

"Well obviously I drink because I'm anxious and because it makes other people more palatable, until it doesn't anymore. And also most likely because I have a genetic predisposition toward alcoholism. But it's more complicated than that. Part of that complexity is the obligation I feel to my grandmother."

"This is interesting," I said.

"This is the sort of thing that they would call rationalization, at an AA meeting. Believe me, I know."

"Still," I said.

Claire pulled the straw from the cup and set it on her tray table, leaving a gleaming parenthesis of liquid on the gray plastic. "My grandfather was a drinker. The social mores of the time permitted him to be so publicly. My grandmother, like I said, had to hide her vodka in the toilet tank. She was not allowed to be a drunk fuckup in the open."

"Times certainly have changed," I said.

"And you know what killed her? The secrecy. Not the booze."

A mild ding sounded, and the pilot came on the PA to tell us that we'd be flying through some moderate chop and he'd appreciate it if we stayed in our seats with our seat belts fastened.

"Have you ever noticed," I asked Claire, "how frequently in American culture people give orders disguised as requests?"

Claire clutched the plastic cup with both hands. "I really hate turbulence," she said.

"I mean, the pilot just said he'd 'appreciate it' if we stayed in our seats, as though we have an option not to. But if I got up right now and refused to sit back down, I would find myself on the floor of the galley, zip-tied and sedated, in short order."

The plane began to tremble, then rattled violently for several seconds. The passengers gave a collective gasp, some reaching out to steady themselves on seat backs and armrests.

"Flight attendants," the pilot said, "be seated *now.*"

"K.," Claire said, "we're going to have to talk about something a lot more interesting and a lot less obvious to distract me from what is quickly becoming freak-out-level anxiety."

"Okay," I said.

"I mean, first the Stasi, and now this."

"Spetsnaz."

"What*ever.*"

"Getting back to your grandmother," I said, "your premise is that drinking to excess in public is somehow healthier than hiding it?" I said.

"Human beings are the only animals in all of creation who try to be something other than what they fucking *are,*" Claire said. "This is the source of all our illnesses and malaise and anxiety and stupid fucking personality disorders. Mind-body connection, K. Keep secrets and your heart will reveal them, eventually, by just giving out. That's what happened to my grandmother." She raised her eyebrows at me as she paused to take a drink. "It's the contrast between what we are and what we appear to be that makes us sick. Everyone walking around pretending to be so put together, so perfect, when in fact they're more often than not one minor misfortune away from a nervous breakdown."

"Not everyone," I said. "But certainly many people, yes."

"The trick is to make your outsides match your insides," Claire said. "You can be healthy even if you're miserable — so long as you appear to be exactly the flaming eight-car pileup that you are."

Turbines sighed as the pilot decreased power. The plane suddenly began to rattle with the sort of force that if one were inclined to imagine rivets giving way and high-grade aluminum warping, one might well do so. Claire took one hand off her drink and used it to grasp my forearm. Her fingernails dug in as we swooped to the right like a Japanese Zero, whereupon a man behind us began reciting Bible verse at high volume.

"Holy fuck," Claire said.

"Turbulence is almost never dangerous," I told her.

"Shut. Up. With. Your. Facts."

The pilot came on the PA again. "Ladies and gentlemen," he said, "no doubt you've noticed this patch of rough air has turned out to be worse than we anticipated. We're going to descend a bit to find you a more comfortable ride, but in the meantime please remain seated with your seat belts securely fastened."

"You got it, champ," Claire said.

No sooner had the pilot clicked off the PA

than the plane swooped again, banking sharply enough that the sky disappeared from the starboard windows, replaced by the green and heather checkerboard of Kansan crop fields far below us. Claire's fingernails dug in deeper.

"That hurts an awful lot," I said, nodding toward her hand.

Claire looked down, and then after a second, she retracted her nails from my flesh slightly. "Gosh, I'm sorry," she said.

"It's no problem."

"Hurting people because you're scared," Claire said, "is definitely a problem. Believe me, I know."

"Can you tell me more about this philosophy of mind-body connection?"

"Well it's all bullshit, obviously," Claire said. "I'm sure you were getting around to saying that, so let me spare you the trouble."

"I may be skeptical," I said, "but I'm not at all convinced it's bullshit. If I thought it was bullshit I wouldn't be asking for elaboration."

"Oh, it's bullshit, K. Makes about as much sense as believing the center of a carrot is poisonous. The rational part of my brain knows that. But the rational part doesn't steer the ship."

"That puts you firmly in the majority," I

said. "If it's any comfort."

The plane nosed up violently. A flight attendant's arm — the rest of her, strapped into a jump seat, remained obscured behind the bulkhead — swiped at a coffeepot pinballing around the galley.

"This needs to stop," Claire said.

"It will, eventually. You were saying."

She closed her eyes. "I was saying. What was I saying? It's bullshit, but I need to believe it, because I feel beholden to my grandmother. You know that thing? We all do it, right? Convincing ourselves that somehow the dead give half a crap about how we behave?"

"It's not something I do," I said, "but certainly I've seen it in others."

"Well listen, if you want the unvarnished, totally nonsensical truth, there it is. People feel obligations to the dead all the time. 'I owe it to my father because he worked so hard.' 'I owe it to my great-grandmother because she came across the country in a covered wagon.' Whatever. So I owe it to all the women who wanted to drink themselves silly but had to take nips off a bottle in the laundry room while folding their husbands' tighty whities."

I looked at Claire. Her eyes were suddenly guileless, her face full of a pleading hope.

She needed me to accept this, even though she admitted that it made no sense, even though she knew who I was. And I almost found it in myself, bouncing around at thirty thousand feet, to give her what she needed. To say: Yes, Claire, I accept your imperfect reasoning, your flawed logic. I even opened my mouth to tell her I understood, that it made perfect sense, but then I realized that the words I wanted to say and the words I was about to say were not at all the same.

Before I had a chance to speak, though, an anomaly of aerodynamics interrupted.

Later, when I talked to the pilot, he told me this event was not nearly as dramatic as I imagined. "Passengers always say things like 'We dropped a thousand feet, just like that.' Not true. Not even close. That was more like fifty feet. Maybe. Barely registers on the instruments."

But as Peggy had said, jabbing her Winston at me like a rapier: how our minds experience things is the important part. Just as I opened my mouth to tell Claire that her reasons for drinking so heavily and publicly did not pass the smell test, the plane fell out from under us like one of those drop towers at an amusement park. This happened so suddenly that no one had the opportunity to scream, even though the instant we started to fall time became elongated, stretching out like taffy until what took perhaps three seconds seemed like a full minute or longer. As the plane plummeted and the edge of the seat belt bit into my hips, I looked up and saw a baby lift slowly into the air three rows ahead of us. The baby was calm, his parchment paper eyelids just beginning to flutter open from sleep as he rose. He wore a hoodie sweat-shirt decorated to resemble a giant panda, stark white with ebony eyes and two tufty black ears poking up from the top of the hood. He was at that early age when relative baldness and a lack of teeth sometimes conspire to make a child look paradoxically very old. Like a tiny astronaut in low Earth orbit he drifted, arms and legs weightlessly splayed and crooked at the joints, the eminently relaxed posture of snoozing infants the world over. As he continued to rise, a woman's hands, slender and long fingered and bedecked with a multitude of rings and bracelets, reached up and snagged him by both ankles, and as these hands pulled the baby down I saw, over the pha-lanx of seat backs, dozens of drinks lift into the air. Not cups, understand — drinks. Beer and water and Coca-Cola all suspended in perfect cup shapes, hovering above the people to whom they belonged as though animated by malevolent spirits. Claire's own drink had gone airborne as well. It floated directly overhead, both liquid and solid all at once, the sort of impossibility one might see in dreams on a night when the subconscious is particularly troubled. Claire watched her drink rise, all the fear gone from her face, her mouth open just enough that I could see the serrated ridge of her left incisor gleaming in the sunlight through the aft windows. Behind and below her incisor, the tip of her tongue barely announced itself. In her hand she still held the now-empty cup with the word DELTA molded into the plastic. Her other hand finally released my forearm, revealing deep half-oval indentations where her fingernails had dug in.

Relativity maintained its grip. It seemed almost as though time had ceased passing altogether, that we'd been suspended in amber like so many prehistoric insects. I began to count the cup-shaped pockets of ice and liquid in the hypnagogic mobile that hung over us. Directly in front of me, one: the jaundiced green of a Mountain Dew. To the immediate right of that, two: water, maybe, or else seltzer; something clear, in any event, that refracted the sunlight into its constituent colors like a prism, projecting a tiny rainbow onto the overhead compartment. Up another row, three: the glutinous scarlet blob of a Bloody Mary. And so on. I made it to eleven — a tan translucence, whiskey probably — before the plane leveled off, gravity reasserted itself, and the drinks assumed both an appearance and a behavior more befitting airborne liquids, breaking free, finally, of the cup molds imposed by negative Gs, aerating into drops and globules, tracing streaks across the bulkheads. This, too, happened slowly, so slowly it seemed I could reach up and pluck a bead of Claire's ice melt out of the air with my fingertips. We all watched now with a sort of comic horror, realizing as one what would happen next but helpless to do anything about it.

And then came the flood, sure and swift.

It was this rude baptism that caused time to finally contract again, returned people to their senses. As is usually the case with baptisms, there was much crying. Also a good deal of voluble if short-lived screaming. Also, here and there, some vomiting.

Most of Claire's drink had landed on her. She sat still and quiet, staring at the seat back in front of her while I picked several small bits of ice out of her hair.

"Did you see that baby?" she asked, after a while.

"I did," I said.

"I mean, my God," she said.

"Could have been a lot worse."

"That was . . . probably the scariest thing I've ever been through."

"I think everyone's alright," I said.

"Everyone, K.," Claire said, "is scarred for life. Except you, of course."

The PA dinged. "Ladies and gentlemen," the pilot said, "want to apologize for that last little bump. We think we've found some smoother air, here, but as a precaution we're going to keep the fasten seat belt sign on for the remainder of the flight, with about an hour left until we reach Boston. Flight attendants, please remain seated as well. Thank you."

Claire reached down and slowly undid her seat belt.

"Where are you going?" I asked.

"Nowhere," she said. She brushed wet strands of hair behind her ears and stood up.

"Ma'am," the frizzy-haired flight attendant said, peering out from her seat in the galley.

Claire ignored her and reached up to pop open the overhead storage bin, from which she removed her green messenger bag, from which she removed three small bottles of Swedish vodka.

"Ma'am," the flight attendant said.

"I'm sitting down, I'm sitting down," Claire said. "Christ on a pogo stick, give it a rest, will you?"

She took her seat again and, without fastening her seat belt, drank one of the bottles of vodka at a pull, then dumped the other two in the cup with the word DELTA molded into the plastic.

"Feel better?" I asked.

Claire turned and gazed at me for a long moment, looking suddenly very tired and much older than her twenty-seven years. "I love you," she said finally.

14
INTOLERANCE WILL NOT BE TOLERATED

America, You Stoopid debuted on Wednesday in Fox's ten P.M. time slot — early enough to vie for the back end of the prime time audience, late enough that children were safely in bed. Owing to a promotion, featuring the Shaolin monk beating me purple, that ran for two weeks before the premiere, our first episode did reasonably well — or at least reasonably well by the standards of broadcast television in a time of relentless competition from media of every imaginable variety. But *America, You Stoopid* was not, with a 1.9 rating in the 18-to-49 demographic, a runaway success.

"Nothing to stick your head in the oven over," Theodore assured me, though I neither felt nor had expressed any suicidal impulse. "This show will have legs. People love seeing men get beaten up."

"Just men?" I asked.

"Who else?" Theodore asked. "Toddlers?

Grandmothers? How would that be good television?"

"I thought you didn't want me to get beaten up anymore," I said.

"I don't want you to get *killed*," Theodore said. "Of course I want you to get beaten up. There's a reason *The Three Stooges* has been in syndication since Moses came down from the mount."

And he was right. *America, You Stoopid* jumped to a 2.7 rating the second week, following voluminous online chatter about the Shaolin incident, as well as a promo that featured the air force chaplain rupturing my eardrum.

The third episode concluded with me, viewed from Claire's perspective, bloodied and prone on a Crown Heights sidewalk, Hasidim scattering as police sirens caromed off of brick and concrete. The next day, with a 4.7 rating in hand and much fanfare in the trade papers, Fox ordered a second season.

Soon after, I came to learn something that I could have probably surmised: when you do well on television, television's cross-promotional symbiosis can't get enough of you, and so requests to appear on shows other than my own suddenly became more frequent than assaults.

My first such appearance occurred on something called *Crunch Time with Gil Meyer.* Meyer was a comedian whose previous show had been canceled after he said on air that transgenderism might actually be a mental illness, and that maybe we weren't all as wonderful and humane as we thought we were for applauding while sick people mutilated their bodies. Now he was on Showtime — safe, more or less, from the capriciousness of network television audiences. Meyer had three main panelists; I would come in halfway through the episode as a special guest, essentially to plug my own program, and perhaps offer a word about whatever timely subject Meyer and his guests were debating.

Just before I was to go on, I stood stage right with Claire and Theodore, who'd both insisted on attending even though I'd repeatedly told them I required no support, moral or otherwise. Claire stood directly in front of me, fussing with my necktie after deeming the Van Wijk knot I'd fashioned "ridiculous."

"And so what are we discussing?" I asked Theodore.

"I have no earthly idea," he said. "They have a loose format to accommodate whatever might come up. But surely you'll do fine, no matter the topic."

"I'm not worried about how I'll do," I said.

"Of course you're not," Theodore said. "That's why we're here to worry for you."

The stage manager, who had up to this point ignored us so completely I'd begun to wonder if he was blind, now put a hand on my shoulder. "You're on in ten," he said.

"Ten what?"

"Ten *seconds*. Make that seven."

"This tie isn't ready," Claire said. Her fingers worked like spiders' legs.

"No one gives a shit." The stage manager pushed me toward the set, laying a shoulder check on Claire in the process. "Three, two, one . . ."

I heard Meyer say my name, and emerged into a fusillade of applause and blinding stage lights; for all I could see of the audience, they might as well have been seated behind a black felt curtain. Directly in front of me, Meyer sat at a table facing his trio of guests. To his immediate left there was an unoccupied rolling chair, cheap molded plastic and pleather, like something that would come assembly required from an office supply store.

I sat down next to Meyer. He clapped me

on the back and waited for the applause to fade.

"First things first," he said. "What's up with your tie?"

The invisible audience laughed. I looked down and saw that Claire had gotten only partway through her half-Windsor; the tie was cinched loosely, wide and skinny ends hanging parallel to one another down my chest.

"We were in the middle of tying it when your stage manager pushed me out here," I said.

"Well he's fucking fired, then," Meyer said.

The audience laughed again.

"I don't think he should lose his job over it," I said.

Meyer stared at me a moment, then remembered himself and got down to business. "K., your new show on Fox is getting a lot of attention in recent weeks, not least because every episode seems to feature you getting your ass kicked at least once. So I'm curious: how did it feel to get beaten up by a Shaolin monk?"

"Well, it hurt," I told him. "Have you ever been hit with a bamboo staff?"

Meyer grinned. "I have not," he said.

"While convalescing afterward," I said, "I learned that bamboo is, by certain physical

251

measures, stronger than steel. Sort of a biological marvel."

"That's really something," Meyer said. "But if we could get back to the ass kicking."

"What's interesting is the pain doesn't end when the beating stops," I said. "It feels like you're still being pummeled hours afterward. Must be something to do with their technique. The whole thing transcends the merely physical, if you believe the Shaolin."

"But you don't believe the Shaolin," Meyer said. "Which is why that guy beat the crap out of you."

"I was skeptical about one of their central tenets," I said. "But I've always been suspicious of the 'work for peace, prepare for war' axiom, whether it comes from Reagan or Vegetius. That said, I'm perfectly open to the possibility that Shaolin practices have a supernatural element."

"After seeing what he did to you, I personally am a believer," Meyer said.

"Experience tells me you'll be much safer that way," I said.

"But I guess that brings us to my big question," Meyer said. "I mean, certainly I'm skeptical about a lot of things myself, but even I'm not stupid enough to talk shit in a situation where I could really get hurt. So why do you, over and over again? A cynic might think it's just some kind of cheap performance art."

"The quickest way to explain," I said, "though this probably won't do anything to really clarify it for you, is to say that since my wife died facts have become a tremendous comfort to me, and so I've been compelled to try and understand everything I can. This compulsion supersedes just about every other consideration. Including personal safety."

Meyer stared at me for a moment, then clapped me on the back again. "You're right," he said with a laugh, "that doesn't clarify it for me. But maybe you can give me the long version at the after party. Ladies and gentlemen, K., from the new hit reality show *America, You Stoopid.*"

The audience applauded.

"I don't care for that title, by the way," I said.

"No?" Meyer asked.

"Not at all," I said.

"Well, it's your show," Meyer said.

"If it were my show in the way you mean, the title would be different," I said.

"Okay, so perfect world, free of meddling producers and test audiences," Meyer said. "What's the title?"

"America, You're Being Kept Ignorant Through a Systematic and Decades-Long Strategy of Demonizing and Defunding Public Schools," I said. "Or something along those lines."

"Doesn't have quite the same ring, obviously," Meyer said.

"Sadly, no," I said.

"Okay, folks," Meyer said, "back to our panel. There's been a lot of talk recently about forcing companies to label foods that contain genetically modified organisms, or GMOs. Which is never going to happen for one simple reason: Corporations. Own. This country."

The panelist seated to my far left, a man dressed in all black and with a head of black hair that was almost certainly a toupee, said, "But Gil, *you* work for a corporation, don't you?"

"Sure, sure," Meyer said. "But the corporation I work for operates a bit differently than Monsanto, Dave, I think you'll allow."

Judging by his expression, Dave was not in fact willing to allow this. But he didn't respond.

"And just so you don't think I'm being partisan," Meyer continued, "this is a conspiracy of both parties. In his first presidential campaign, way back in 2007,

President Obama said that he would push for labeling of GMO foods. Here we are now, seven years later, in the middle of his second term: nothing."

The panelist on the right, a woman with spectacles and short brown hair who worked in some capacity for MSNBCBS, chimed in. "Gil, it's worth mentioning that in Europe it's already common practice to label GMO foods," she said. "In fact, they label GMO foods in China."

Meyer threw up his hands. *"China,"* he said. "A country where they put formaldehyde in baby formula. Even *they* have the good sense to slap a label on this stuff. But here? No way. And why? Because it will hurt sales. So shut up and eat your fucking mutant chili, America."

The third panelist, a mousy slip of a woman who was reportedly a novelist, stared wide-eyed into the air between me and Meyer, hands in her lap. She looked either too frightened or too snobbish to offer comment, and would in fact remain silent for the entirety of my time on the air.

Dave, evidently the panel's token conservative, spoke up in the novelist's stead. "Gil, there is absolutely no scientific evidence to indicate GMO foods are harmful to people in any way."

"But they *could* be," Meyer said.

"Well strictly speaking," I said, "you *could* be harmed by just about anything in existence. Given a long enough timeline, you *could* be eaten by a saltwater crocodile on the lam from the San Diego Zoo. Or you *could* get sucked up into a waterspout. Or you *could* bleed to death in a freak bass fishing accident. All these things are possible, in the same way that it's possible GMOs could be harmful to people. But a reasonable person would argue these aren't the sorts of possibilities we should have in mind when shaping public policy."

The bespectacled woman from MSNB-CBS jumped back in as if I hadn't spoken a word. "Here's something that never used to exist. They never used to take a gene out of a bacterium and put it in corn, so that the corn grows its own insecticide."

"Pardon me," I said, "but that's exactly the sort of scaremongering that gives people the impression that there are two valid sides to this debate."

The woman looked at me. "*Scare*mongering?" she asked, affecting a nearly comic indignation.

"The use of the word 'insecticide,'" I said. "You know quite well that when people hear 'insecticide' they picture vats of chemicals that are lethal to every known form of life. The corn you're referring to simply has a protein that is harmful to a particular insect when ingested. You make it sound like it's oozing Raid. Which inflames your leftist audience's distrust of commerce, industry, and anything not quote-unquote natural. Which gets them to tune in. Which is why you do it."

"If I may finish my point?" the woman asked.

"Of course," I said.

"It's very simple," she said, placing her palms on the table, a gesture meant to signal that a calm and well-reasoned argument was on its way. "I want to make a decision for myself about whether to ingest that genetically modified organism. If the industry believes that, as a consumer, I'm going to hysterically decide when I see that label not to buy the corn, the solution isn't to keep it a secret. The solution is to convince me that it's safe to eat."

The audience burst into the sort of enthusiastic, hooting applause one normally hears from the faithful at a sporting event. The MSNBCBS woman pretended not to notice this, pretended not to be pleased by it, pretended not to have quite deliberately angled for it with her comments.

"It is pretty simple, wouldn't you say?" Meyer asked me.

"It appears to be, but it isn't," I said. "We know, for one thing, that a majority of those in your audience cheering for their right to be informed could never, ever be convinced that GMOs are safe. No matter how compelling the evidence. No matter how irrational their fear was proven by facts to be."

Here and there, members of the audience began to low. Spurred by these evangelists, the rest joined in with rapidly blossoming gusto, until Meyer had to wave his hands to quiet them.

"That's ridiculous," the woman in the glasses said to me, once the audience had gone quiet again. She squared her shoulders and adjusted her cream blazer.

"People are capable of making rational decisions based on facts," Dave said. "That's a rather dim opinion of humanity you have there."

"I don't have opinions," I said. "I'm only concerned with what is. I don't care about being well liked, or making money, or sustaining a career in the media. So unlike you, I can tell the truth."

The audience booed again.

"I mean absolutely no disrespect, you

understand," I said to Dave.

"Oh, of course," he said.

"But to get back to your point, people are not at all capable of making rational decisions based on facts. Quite the opposite, actually. It's a phenomenon known as confirmation bias, and it's rampant and well documented."

"I'm aware of confirmation bias," the woman with the glasses said.

"Being aware of it," I told her, "doesn't make you any less susceptible. Though I understand why you want to believe it does."

The woman stared.

"Confirmation bias is what allows progressives like you to call Republicans Stone Age troglodytes for denying climate change science, while yourself denying a similar level of scientific certainty regarding GMOs."

Meyer, eyebrows raised, let loose a snort of laughter.

"To use another example, confirmation bias leads your progressives — which I'm starting to get the strong sense comprises the vast majority of the audience here — to decry the evils of fossil fuels, while standing in stout opposition to increased use of nuclear power."

"One word, fool," the woman said. "Fukushima."

"Dramatic, for sure," I said. "Also completely anomalous, much like the waterspout and the bass fishing accident. In half a century of producing exactly the emissions-free power you all claim to want so desperately, the more than one hundred nuclear plants in the United States have harmed no one. And that's including Three Mile Island."

"Fine," the woman said. "Not that I'm conceding your point at all. But tell me, what is it that makes you so much better? You're more highly evolved than the rest of us, is that it, Mr. Spock?"

"It's not a question of better or worse," I said. "But yes, unlike every other human being I've met, I am no longer subject to the irrationality of emotion. I have hardly any fear. I make decisions and reach conclusions based entirely on fact, insofar as fact can be ascertained. Whether that represents the next step in human evolution, I'm not sure. Though certainly if it did, our chances of survival as a species could only be improved. Because the brand of discourse you all engage in — which feigns interest in facts but relies entirely on emotion — cripples the mechanisms by which we might actually save ourselves."

We all stared at one another for a moment.

Then a man's voice, tight with righteousness, came to us from the audience: "Get him out of here!"

The woman with the glasses offered her approval of this sentiment, gazing at me and clapping slowly, as if applauding a successful putt at a golf tournament.

Meyer looked in the direction of the voice. "Whoever you are," he said, "go fuck yourself. This is my show, chief, not yours."

But now other voices were raised in anger, undeterred by Meyer's scolding, echoing the demand of the first man. I found myself suddenly aware of the studio's small dimensions, of how close the audience was to us despite the fact that we couldn't see them.

Meyer frowned into the darkness. "Everybody calm the fuck down," he said, "before I have you thrown out."

"Come on now, Gil," the woman with the glasses shouted over the crowd. "You're a populist, right? Well, the people are speaking. They want him gone."

Meyer looked at her. "Be careful, Raquel," he said, "or I'll toss you out with them."

The angry babble continued to intensify. Thick-necked security personnel materialized from both sides of the stage and formed a line between us and the audience. As they moved into place, an empty soda can arced down toward us like a satellite falling from orbit. It hit the desk with a hollow clink, bounced end over end, then rolled off the edge of the desk and onto the floor near my feet.

Meyer, suddenly furious, pushed his chair back and stood, straining to make out the offending party. "That's it," he said. "We're shutting it down. Get everybody out of here, now."

The house lights came up, and the audience seemed to materialize before our eyes. Most of them were on their feet, waving fists and shouting. Arms cocked back and flew forward; more objects sailed through the air and rained down around us. Dave fled backstage, and the mousy older novelist continued to sit and stare at nothing, oblivious to the din. Raquel, the woman from MSNBCBS, rose from her seat and began pulling at her boyish hair in a sudden frenzy.

"This is the moment!" she screamed. Spittle flew from her lips, and her cat-eye spectacles slanted across her face. "Rise up and stab them with whatever's handy! Ballpoint pens! Car keys! Soda straws! Be warned, neocons, libertarians, and Tea Partiers everywhere! If you think what we do to fetuses is bad, wait until you see what's in store for you! We will take your guns and execute you with them! Wrap you in American flags and light a match! If he wants to be called she, you will call him she, or your head will be stuck on a pike as a warning to others! Intolerance will not be tolerated!"

Raquel clambered up on the table and stood, waving her arms and screaming incoherently. Meanwhile, the audience followed her bidding and began to pour down the aisles toward the stage. This surge collided with the security detail like a wave hitting a seawall. Punches were thrown, chokeholds applied. Someone discharged a fire extinguisher, producing a chalky billow that for several moments completely obscured the scrum. When it came back into view, the weight and righteous ferocity of two hundred progressives had begun to push the security team back toward us. Two of the guards went down and were immediately set upon with fist and foot.

I looked over at Meyer, who had stripped off his oxford and stood now in a white undershirt tilting his head back and forth and otherwise limbering up. On the table in front of us, Raquel, by this time largely forgotten by those present, continued to curse and stomp her feet.

"Should we maybe get out of here?" I said to Meyer.

"Save yourself, friend," he told me, cracking his knuckles. "I've been waiting years for this fight."

And with that he threw himself, snarling like a badger, into the fray.

I knew both the name and the reputation of Francy Finesse when the call came to appear on her show, owing to the fact that Sarah had been a somewhat closeted fan of Finesse's true-crime program for several years before her illness, and became an unabashed devotee when the cancer rendered her housebound. It occurred to me, sitting in the studio at the Fox News headquarters in Manhattan and waiting for the segment in which I was to appear, that Sarah would likely have been excited to see me on Finesse's show, if perhaps in an ambivalent, slightly nauseated way.

For reasons no one ever explained, I'd been asked to weigh in on the case of a woman who'd recently been arrested for drunk driving. I sat to Finesse's left, trying not to choke on what seemed like mustard gas–based hairspray, as the segment began.

"And now to Watertown, Mississippi," Finesse said, glaring into the camera. "A mother of three arrested for DUI. But when she's arrested, she still has three Jell-O shots stuffed in her pockets."

The producer cut to a prerecorded video clip. Finesse and I watched a large screen mounted on the wall behind the studio camera. Still photos of the drunk-driving woman drifted slowly around the screen as a man's voice narrated.

"A Mississippi mother of three is due in court following her latest arrest for drunk driving," the man said, his voice taut with manufactured drama. "She reportedly had bloodshot eyes, slurred speech, and smelled like alcohol."

"Someone made a mistake in the text," I said, pointing at the screen. "Jell-O isn't one word. It's hyphenated. Plus it's trademarked, so you should probably have the little TM symbol there."

"Can it," Finesse hissed.

The voice-over continued. "And the mother's driver's license had been taken away, but authorities say that this time, not only was her blood alcohol well over the legal limit, but she actually had three Jell-O shots in her pockets."

In my earpiece I heard the producer. "France, back to you in three, two, one . . ."

"Megan McAdams, former director of BADD, Babes Against Drunk Driving," Finesse said. The screen behind the camera was now bisected between Finesse and a woman, presumably Megan, sitting in a studio elsewhere.

"Megan," Finesse continued, "so she still had three Jell-O shots stuffed in her pockets. Do you know what her blood alcohol was, Megan?"

"It was twice the legal limit, Francy," the woman said, her face a pinch of stern disapproval. "It was about .18."

"Obviously we're not sure how many drinks she had had, but it was a lot," Finesse said. "I know that this was a Saturday night. It was around two A.M. Allegedly, there was a babysitter with her three children. I can't confirm that. She had picked up some guy at a bar. She was driving his car. She gave the cops a fake name, gave the friend a fake name, and still had three Jell-O shots in her hoodie. I guess, what, Megan, was she just going to drink those at booking?"

Megan, evidently devoid of a sense of humor, at least when it came to drunk driving, showed no sign of appreciating Finesse's sarcasm. "Absolutely, Francy. What she was planning to do is just slingshot them as soon as she got an opportunity. And Francy, again, what happens is her blood alcohol might have been a little bit lower when they tested her the first time. But if she had actually taken those last three Jell-O shots, that would be the equivalent of another three full drinks, so her blood alcohol would have gone through the roof, given another hour."

"Would have," I said.

"How's that?" Megan asked.

"Well you keep saying she would have taken the Jell-O shots as though she did, in fact, take the Jell-O shots. But she didn't. You're just sensationalizing what was, in fact, a routine drunk-driving arrest, the kind that happens thousands of times a day all over the country."

"But this woman has children," Megan said.

"So what?" I asked.

"So what?" Megan echoed.

"Were they in the car?" I asked.

"Well, no," Megan said. "But people drive drunk with their children in the car all the time."

"But this woman did not," I said.

"Not this time."

"Then how is the fact that she has three children at all relevant?" I asked.

Under the table, Finesse's stiletto heel dug into my shin. "Dan O'Donnell, anchor joining me from WIPN," she said. "Dan, isn't it true that when she was arrested she immediately blurted out to police she already had five DUI arrests?"

On the screen behind the camera a bald man in a gray suit appeared, holding a microphone. "Yes, she did," the man said. "And a subsequent check of her record revealed that it was only three DUI arrests. But she was already —"

Finesse cut him off. "Did you just say *only* three DUI arrests? As if that's not bad enough? Okay. I guess it's all a matter of perspective, Dan O'Donnell. Go ahead."

Wilted by Finesse's scorn, Dan offered a sputtering chuckle. "Yes, I guess so, Francy. That is obviously terrible, especially when you consider that's one DUI arrest for every young child she has at home."

"Again with the children," I said.

"She was also arrested and convicted of carrying an illegal firearm about five years ago," Dan continued, "and is now charged with a couple of felonies, Francy, for this latest DUI."

Armed with this information, Finesse really hit her stride. "Okay, so Mommy has Jell-O shots stuffed down her hoodie pockets. She's blowing a .18 and she's got a concealed weapon."

"He said the firearms charge was five years ago," I said.

268

Finesse turned to me. "What," she said, "is your point?"

"Just that she wasn't carrying a gun on the night in question, the way you're trying to make it seem. Also, no one said anything about it being concealed. The words he used were 'illegal firearm.' "

Finesse stared at me.

"I'm just saying," I said.

"France?" the producer said into our earpieces.

I noticed that my hands had started to tremble. I held them up in front of my face, and without looking away from the camera Finesse reached over and shoved them back down to the table.

"So tell me, Dan," Finesse said, "a Jell-O shot. What is it?"

"Made like regular Jell-O or gelatin, Francy," Dan said. "It's very similar."

"Well, it's not 'similar,' " I said. "It is, in fact, the same."

After a pause, Dan continued. "So you take Jell-O, you take boiling water, but the difference is instead of adding ice cubes or chilled water to set the Jell-O, you use chilled liquor, normally vodka. Now, vodka doesn't have a lot of taste on its own, so when you're drinking this or swallowing it down, it tastes like a Jell-O cube. But boy,

269

are they deadly because that alcohol really sneaks up on you."

"I assume," I said, "that you're using the word 'deadly' in a figurative sense."

"Well . . . yes," Dan said. "But I suppose they could be literally deadly, too. If you ate enough of them."

"And we still seem to be ignoring the fact that this woman did not actually consume the Jell-O shots," I said.

Globules of sweat begin to sprout just above my eyebrows. The trembling worsened, accompanied now by a nauseous fluttering in my gut.

Finesse jumped in again. "Okay, so how much alcohol, Megan McAdams, is in a Jell-O shot?"

"Oh, honey, it can be ounces," Megan said, shaking her head. "And again, if you're taking it so quickly, it gets into your system immediately. It's not like nursing a drink over, you know, fifteen or twenty minutes walking around at a party. You're taking it instantly. So with those three, she would have had the equivalent of three full drinks in her within fifteen seconds."

"Except that she didn't actually *eat them,*" I said. "Please forgive me if you're tired of hearing that. But basically what we're doing here is a Wikipedia article about Jell-O shots. It's not a news item. Because we're not discussing what actually happened. I mean, while we're at it, why don't we talk about how she stole an Abrams tank from the local armory and drove it through a super Walmart? That didn't happen either, but it sure sounds interesting."

Finesse turned to me again, slowly, like a horror-film zombie, her face locked in a testes-shriveling scowl. I thought, though I could not be sure, that I heard Dan O'Donnell snicker in my earpiece.

"France," the producer said. "Let's get this under control."

Finesse seared me for a second longer with her gaze, then turned again to face the camera. "Okay, everybody," she said, "you're seeing a shot right there of Missy Ramirez, twenty-eight years old, three children. She says she has five previous DUIs."

"But it was actually —"

Finesse cut me off. "She had the Jell-O shots still stuck down her shirt when police arrested her. And Megan McAdams, for every time a DUI person is apprehended, what is the estimate of how many times they've driven drunk?"

"About thirty, Francy," Megan said. "She has driven drunk almost every time she's ever been in a car because each time she should have gotten a DUI, she just wasn't caught that day. But having five and already losing her license —"

"She had three DUIs, not five!" I hollered. I was as surprised as anyone at the outburst, but helpless, suddenly, to stop myself. "Why is that so hard to acknowledge, Megan? Why do you continue to insist on saying things that everyone, you included, knows are not true? She's been drunk almost every time she's ever been in a car? Is that what you're saying, Megan? Is that what you're trying to convince everyone of? Is that what we're all supposed to just sit here and accept without question, despite the fact that we all know it's utter nonsense?"

By now my entire body was trembling, and I felt sick on a cellular level.

"Okay so we're going to go to com*mercial,*" the producer said in my earpiece.

"Or actually," I said, "we're not supposed to merely accept it. Right? We're supposed to get good and agitated over the whole thing. Supposed to work ourselves up into a proper froth. We're supposed to say: *Five* DUIs? What an outrage! And those poor kids! What is the world coming to? We're supposed to despair and grind our teeth as though this woman is emblematic of the entire culture, a whole nation driving around gulping Jell-O shots and playing slalom on the highway with their kids unbelted in the back."

"France," the producer said, "pretty much whatever you need to do to shut him up."

"And let's not overlook the fairly obvious racist subtext here," I said. "I mean it's not an accident that of all the thousands of drunk-driving arrests in the past week, you chose to highlight one featuring a woman whose last name is Ramirez, a woman who looks very, very Hispanic in that photo you keep putting up on the screen. Your audience is probably, what, eighty percent white? Eighty-five?"

"I will throw you *directly* out of this studio, buster," Finesse said.

The discomfort in my stomach had migrated north, and now felt like someone squeezing my heart in their fist. Something hot and acrid rose into my throat, and I swallowed it back down with a full-body gulp that no doubt registered on camera.

"I mean, you've got some nerve coming on here and calling me a racist," Finesse said. "You know how many segments I've done on police brutality against blacks?"

On the screen in front of us, Megan looked as though she might start crying.

"To be clear, I'm not calling you a racist,"

I said, trying to calm myself. "I'm merely saying that there's something to be gained by providing your white audience with confirmation of their greatest fear: that America, which in their mind rightly belongs to them, is being overrun by godless subhuman mud people who speak languages other than English."

Finesse slammed both hands on the table, hard enough that I startled. "That's it," she said. "Hit the road, Jack."

"Yes, probably that's best," I said. "I'm feeling a little faint, at the moment."

She stared at me. "So get the fuck out of here, already," she said, making a shooing motion with one hand.

I stood and removed the microphone from my lapel. "You can say 'fuck'?" I asked.

"I can say whatever I goddamn please," Finesse said.

My right knee tried to buckle, and I pressed my palms against the tabletop to keep from falling. "But technically you're forbidden from using profanity, correct?" I asked Finesse. "Per FCC regulations?"

"The FCC, idiot," Finesse said, "will only levy a fine if you use words that describe sexual or excretory organs or activities. I used the word 'fuck' as an adjective in a way that could not at all be construed as a sexual reference."

"Interesting," I said. "I had no idea."

"You think I don't know my shit?"

"It would be difficult," I said, "to argue that 'shit' is anything but excretory."

Finesse stared at me once more, her gaze so steady and piercing I half expected to see hypnotic cartoon swirls form in her eyes. "Get. Off. My. Set," she said.

"I would like nothing more," I told her. "But I'm very weak, all of a sudden, and if I let go of the table I think there's a good chance I'll collapse."

I heard the producer cut in again over my earpiece, which I'd neglected to remove along with the microphone. "We really, really need to get to commercial, France," he said. "For Christ's sake, announce the next segment."

Finesse paused for a moment, took a deep breath, gave her head a brisk steadying shake, and resumed her righteous camera glare. "Coming up next," she said, "in South Carolina, a man sets his wife on fire, then claims it was all just a simple barbecuing accident."

Claire took one look at my face as I stumbled off set and said, "We're going to the hospital."

I didn't think that was necessary, but I also wasn't inclined to argue with her. She held on to my arm and guided me to the elevator. When we reached the ground floor we discovered that, not surprisingly, the car service provided by the show had demateri- alized, so I slumped against a parking sign while Claire hailed a cab, and soon enough we found ourselves in the emergency room of New York-Presbyterian.

It turns out chest pains are a very good way to circumvent the long ER waits one encounters with, say, a broken arm or scalp laceration. The moment I told the triage nurse my primary complaint, I was whisked to an examination room and given a baby aspirin, which I dutifully swallowed.

"That was fast," I said to the nurse.

"We don't play around with chest discom- fort," she told me. "Especially in men over forty."

"I'm thirty-nine," I told her.

"If you could take off your clothes, please, and put this on." She held out a thin cotton johnny with two sets of tie strings in the back.

"I'd rather not," I said. "I've always thought the only purpose of the hospital johnny was to infantilize the patient, thus making him unquestioningly compliant."

"If you could just put it on," the nurse said. "It's standard procedure."

"For cardiac events?" I asked.

"For everything," the nurse said.

"Do you anticipate, with the symptoms I'm presenting, a need for emergency access to my scrotum or anus?" I asked.

"I don't know all your symptoms yet."

"It's just the chest pain," I said. "And my hands have been shaking. There is absolutely nothing abnormal happening below my waist."

"In that case," the nurse said, "we most likely won't need emergency access to your scrotum or anus."

"Then the only reason you could want me to wear a see-through miniskirt that opens in the back is humiliation," I said. "Which is probably not good for my health, long term. There's a lot of evidence indicating negative emotions can affect the body. Even cause heart attacks."

"Suit yourself," the nurse said. "But be aware that if we do suddenly need access to your scrotum or anus, we will cut the pants right off of you. Your shirt, on the other hand, has to come off now. That's non-negotiable."

The nurse left while I unbuttoned my oxford.

"I like her," Claire said. "Sassy."

"I can't seem to help rubbing people the wrong way," I said.

"She took it well. Better than most. How are you feeling?"

"How do I look?" I asked.

Claire put a hand against my cheek. "Somewhat south of great, my love," she said. "Though not quite so pale anymore."

A few seconds later another woman came in, pushing an EKG machine before her. While she was setting up, the first nurse returned and took a blood sample with such skill that I literally felt nothing. Then the nurse helped the technician attach electrodes to my chest and back. Within a few minutes the machine was steadily scrolling out paper, as well as displaying my heart rhythm in real time on a monitor.

"Ticker tape," Claire said, watching.

The nurse snorted.

"What's funny?" I asked.

"It's a pun, dum-dum," Claire said. "Ticker tape. Get it?"

"I'm afraid I don't," I said.

Claire sighed, then turned to the technician. "How's it look?"

The technician continued to gaze at the monitor. "Hard to say, just yet," she said.

"Can I ask you a question?" I said.

"If you must," the technician said.

"Why is it abbreviated EKG, when it stands for electrocardiogram? Shouldn't it be ECG?"

"Often it's written as ECG, these days," the technician said.

"That doesn't answer my question, though," I said.

"I'm going to need you to be quiet, sir," the technician said.

"I just realized something," the nurse said.

"What's that?" I asked.

"You're that guy," she said.

"I get that a lot."

"On TV. That new show."

"Yes. In fact, I was on television just tonight when this started happening."

"What new show?" the technician asked.

"You guys mind if I have a nip?" Claire asked, pulling a pewter flask from her purse and holding it up for inspection. Both the nurse, suddenly fascinated by the presence of a bona fide television star, and the technician, absorbed in deciphering the EKG, ignored her. Claire shrugged, removed the cap, and tilted the flask to her mouth.

"That show," the nurse said to the technician. "He travels around and gets beat up. It's a reality thing."

"Well, there's more to it than that," I said.

"At least, we intend for there to be. A lot of the footage of me *not* getting beaten up is excluded from the program."

For the first time the technician looked away from the monitor. She peered at my face, squinted. "No kidding, it is you," she said after a moment.

"She's on the show, too," I said, pointing to Claire.

"Can we get an autograph when we're finished?" the nurse asked.

"You can get one now," I said.

By the time I'd signed two emesis basins, the EKG had finished eavesdropping on my heart.

"So will this be on the show?" the nurse asked.

"Hard to say," I told her. "It likely will depend on whether or not your machine indicates that I'm dying."

"Sadly, no," the technician said. "Looks pretty good to me. But the cardiologist will want to have a closer look."

"You could always just kick me, then," I said. "That pretty much guarantees footage will make the cut."

"I'm not sure my boss would like that."

Claire waggled her flask in the air in front of her. "Will it take long for the doctor to show up?" she asked. "This thing's just about empty."

"He has to stay for eight hours anyway," the nurse said. "We need to test him for cardiac enzymes, and they take a while to enter the bloodstream."

"Ah," Claire said.

"There's a bar on the corner down the block. Open all night, for hospital staff getting off third shift."

"Ah!" Claire said. She looked to me.

"You should go," I said. "I'll call you when I'm finished."

"He's okay?" Claire asked the technician.

"He's fine," she answered.

Having decided I was almost certainly not suffering a heart attack, and having decided that despite my modest celebrity I was not terribly interesting in person, the nurse and technician departed. Claire brushed her lips against my forehead and left for the bar. Over the next few hours, as the day expired and another one began, I had the room to myself. There was no television, no reading material, no amenities at all, in fact. Just the polite beep of the heart monitor as it acknowledged my continued existence every second or so. Not one to bore easily, I didn't mind just sitting there. And that's what I did, all I did — sat there on the bed, neither asleep nor, eventually, in a strict neurological sense, awake. The pain in my chest continued undiminished, but that hadn't alarmed me before, and did not alarm me now. Like most everything else in the known universe I was nothing more or less than an amalgam of carbon and hydrogen and a handful of other elements, bits of space debris, really, a state to which I would return sooner rather than later, and I experienced neither fear nor dread regarding this fact. It could happen in the next few moments — my heart, having somehow obscured its malfunction from the EKG, suddenly making a final gambit to kill me — or it could happen sixty years from now. I was indifferent to either possibility. But I wasn't actively thinking this, there in the room with the bed and the heart monitor. I wasn't thinking anything, in fact. If the doctors had attached an EEG machine to my temples it would have registered little more than the sluggish delta waves of a deep, dreamless sleep. Looking back and remembering those peculiar hours, a recollection both gauzy and distinct all at once, I find myself wondering if I'd somehow stumbled into nirvana. I have not had occasion to ask a Buddhist if this state would have qualified. But all the evidence points to it.

Then the cardiologist walked in.

"Mister . . . K., is it?" he asked, looking down at a tablet computer as he entered.

The sensation was of being yanked back into my corporeal form, not unlike the way people describe the conclusion of a near-death experience.

"It's just 'K.,' " I told him.

"Sorry, my mistake. K. How are you feeling?"

"I couldn't describe it if I tried."

He glanced up at me, his expression of professional aloofness morphing into perplexity. "Still having chest pains?"

I took brief stock of my body. "Yes," I said.

"And are you feeling distressed?"

"Not in the least," I told him.

The cardiologist looked at me again, his puzzlement compounding.

"I mean, I could tell you I'm distressed, if that's what you want," I said. "I realize it's what both your experience as a physician and plain common sense would cause you to expect, in a person with severe chest pain."

The cardiologist continued to stare. After a few seconds his expression softened. "I know you from somewhere, don't I?" he asked.

"It's not strictly accurate to say you know me," I said. "We've never met before now."

"Right, right. But I've seen your face." He snapped his fingers several times, trying to place me.

"Likely on television," I said. "I have a show."

"That's it," he said, pointing at me. "The thing with the monk!"

"Everybody loves the thing with the monk," I said.

"He really gave you a licking!" the cardiologist said.

"He certainly did," I assured him.

"Good stuff," the cardiologist said, his excitement waning now as he remembered our roles in this context. "Good stuff. So you say you're not distressed at all, but you're still having chest pains."

"That's correct."

"Well your EKG is perfectly normal. Sort of eerily normal, actually. No variations at all, and certainly no pathological variations. You might be surprised to know how rare it is to see a truly normal EKG."

"Do you have any idea why it's called an EKG and not an ECG?" I asked him.

He was reading something on the tablet computer now, and answered without looking up. "Sure," he said. "It was invented in Holland. They spell 'cardio' with a 'k.'"

"That makes sense," I said.

The cardiologist flicked at the tablet screen a few times, then brought his gaze up to mine again. "So the good news is there's absolutely nothing wrong with your heart," he said. "Under some circumstances I might suggest that you follow up with your regular doctor for more thorough testing, but I don't think that's necessary here."

"So we're done?" I asked.

"Not quite," he said. "We still have to wait a few more hours and take another blood sample, just to be sure."

"Okay," I said.

"So this new show of yours," he said. "That must be stressful. Wondering how it's going to do. Getting your butt kicked by Shaolin monks."

"I don't experience it as stressful at all," I said.

The cardiologist sat down on a rolling stool and placed his tablet on the counter next to the jars of swab sticks and tongue depressors. "Reason I ask is because by far the leading cause of ER visits for chest pain is stress. It's ten to one in terms of stress related to heart related."

"I read something to that effect recently."

"I see that your wife died not too long ago," the cardiologist said, pointing to the tablet computer.

"That depends on how you define 'not too long ago,' " I said.

"Recently enough that I suspect it might have something to do with your symptoms," he said. "Did you experience her death as stressful?"

"I did at the time," I told him. "Since then, things have changed."

"Meaning . . ."

I hesitated. "The best way for me to explain it would be to say I don't regard death in the same way most people do."

"That's pretty vague."

"I prefer not to get specific about it, anymore. It upsets people."

"I'm certain that whatever you have to say will not upset me."

"Okay," I said. "Are you familiar with general relativity?"

The cardiologist smiled. "Little known fact," he said. "I was studying to be a physicist before I made a hard left to med school."

"What happened?" I asked.

He waved a hand. "Don't worry, it's no great tragedy," he said. "I just took a close look at pay scales for college professors and decided a lucrative medical specialty was more appealing."

"So you must know of Einstein's friend Besso."

"Of course," the cardiologist said. " 'For physicists the distinction between past, present, and future is only an illusion, however persistent.' "

"How did you know that's what I was talking about?"

"Seemed likely, given the subject."

"Well so there's your explanation."

"Explanation for what?"

"Why I no longer experience my wife's being dead as stressful," I told him.

"You know," the cardiologist said, "you're the only other person I've ever met who feels that way."

"You believe death is illusory?"

He nodded. "Sure. I mean, intellectually, yes. We know without question that time is relative, that everything exists concurrently. Though death isn't illusory. It happens as surely as anything else. It's just not *conclusive,* as most people believe it to be."

"I can't tell you how long I've been waiting to have precisely this conversation with someone," I said. "Or rather, to have this conversation with someone who doesn't think I'm out of my mind."

"None of which," the cardiologist said, holding up one finger, "is to say I don't grieve. My mother passed away last year, and I cried like a baby. I'm disappointed and saddened, often, when one of my patients dies."

"As is your privilege," I told him. "Probably a good thing, given your line of work."

He chuckled. "You would think. But it's actually a professional liability. Feelings. They get in the way of clinical judgment. But now listen. Pleased as I am to meet a fellow traveler, there's just one small problem."

"What's that?" I asked.

"You're bullshitting yourself," he said, leveling a steady yet not unkind gaze at me.

"I'm afraid I don't follow."

"You're not as convinced of your wife's eternal existence as you believe you are," he said. He pointed at his chest. "Not here, where it really counts. You're still grieving, whether you realize it or not. That's why you're in my ER. Grief quite literally makes the heart hurt. This is a medical fact."

"You're not the first person," I said, "to tell me that."

"That grief can make the heart hurt?"

"No. That I'm deluding myself."

"Well whoever the others are, they're right."

I thought for a moment. "Some might

contend that, given what we know of space-time, my wife will get sick and die again, and again, and again. They could argue that this is nothing to be encouraged by. And they would be right."

"Certainly," the cardiologist said.

"If I'm being honest," I said, "that does pain me, on occasion. That particular realization."

"It's difficult, knowing the truth," the cardiologist said.

"On the other hand, she and I will meet for the first time again, and again, and again. We will spend that weekend in bed while her parents are away in Cape Cod again, and again, and again. The morning after the party at Chris McCauslin's, when I woke up and found her sleeping at my side? Her body still an almost complete mystery? The room situated, maybe even originally designed, so that you could see the blue ice on the lake without lifting your head from the pillow? The trees draped in fresh snow, and the sense that my whole life had been decided the night before in a way I felt perfectly fine with? That will all happen again and again, too."

"It will," the cardiologist said.

"So maybe everything's okay, on balance," I said.

"Maybe," the cardiologist said. "Still, you're not as okay as you think."

I took a minute to absorb this. "I am willing," I told him, "to accept the possibility that you're correct. But that doesn't change my experience of myself."

"Well I guess that's good enough for today," the cardiologist said, smiling. He stood and retrieved his tablet from the countertop. "So anyway, a couple more hours on those blood enzymes, and we should be able to get you out of here. My shift's over before then, so this'll be it for us."

"Would you like to have a drink after?" I asked him. "There's a bar down the street. You probably know about it."

He paused, looked at me, considered.

"There is nothing sexual or otherwise romantic in this proposition," I assured him.

The cardiologist shook his head. "That's not it. As a physician, it would be irresponsible for me to recommend a patient go have a drink immediately after discharge. Borderline malpractice, really."

He was smiling.

"Of course," I said, "your decision about whether or not to join me has already occurred."

"That is true," he said. "Just because we

290

don't yet know what that decision will be doesn't mean it hasn't been made."

"It was made the moment time itself came into existence."

"It's out of my hands," he agreed.

"Neither of us has any choice," I said. "Flies stuck in the amber of eternity."

"This decision," he said, "about whether I'm interested in a glass of single malt and a conversation regarding the nature of time is older than the pyramids."

"Older than the dinosaurs," I said.

"Older than the Milky Way," he said.

"But also not," I told him.

"That's true," he said. "Also not."

"It's all pretty complex," I said.

"Which complexity may require more than one glass of scotch," he said.

"There's a woman waiting for me at the bar," I said. "She's very pretty, very smart, and likely, by now, very drunk. Midtwenties. Eyes, blue. Hair, deep red. Despite her inebriation, she should make for good company until I arrive."

"My wife," the cardiologist said, "probably wouldn't dig it too much, me having a drink at three in the morning with a drunk redhead."

"Your wife's displeasure," I said, "is yet another inevitability forged at the beginning of time."

The cardiologist smiled again. "How's the chest?" he asked.

I paused for a second. "You know," I said, "it feels perfectly fine."

"Well there you go," he said. "I'll see you at the bar."

"Yes, you will," I told him. "Over and over again."

15

THE DIFFERENCE BETWEEN WANTING AND WANTING

Even with an unambiguously terminal diagnosis there were still moments of hope, cruel interludes when images of Sarah's insides, murky and meaningless to the layman's eye, indicated to the experts that the masses in her chest and femur were shrinking. Lesions reduced to the size of chickpeas, and looking every bit as benign. The doctors did their best to toss cold water on our hope, reminded us that while these developments were better than the alternative, they did not mean Sarah's long-term prognosis had changed at all. Despite their warnings, though, we were granted what felt like a two-month stay of execution, gratitude like a cramp in my heart, an optimism so sudden and buoyant it forever changed the definition of the word for me.

It was toward the end of this time that Sarah asked if I wanted a divorce.

"Do *you*?" I said, after staring at her in

silence for several moments.

" 'Want' isn't exactly the word to describe what I'm feeling," she said.

"Well it's your word, so."

"Come on, K. Don't be a jerk."

I took a breath. "Okay," I said. "Talk to me."

It was fall, the birches and elms at the height of their luminous multihued announcement of winter's approach, and because Sarah felt better than she had in a long while we'd decided to have brunch at a place up the block, across the street from the coffee shop where months later I would be shot in the trapezius. The restaurant had been a staple of our precancer marriage: close by, reliably good food, friendly servers. We'd eaten there so often the guys in the kitchen knew our names. Then Sarah took sick, and we hadn't been in since. But here we were again, against all odds, sitting on the sidewalk patio under a strong autumn sun, eating cornflake-crusted French toast and sipping coffee, and in the midst of all this splendor Sarah apparently, inexplicably, wanted a divorce.

"I don't *want* a divorce," she reiterated, pushing a sausage link around with her fork, eyes trained on the plate. "I just think it's a possibility we should talk about. Now that

294

we've got this little window where we're not totally under duress."

"Usually when someone brings up divorce, that means they *want* a divorce."

"Fine. Have it your way," she said.

"I don't necessarily think we should be discussing this on the first day we've been in public for months."

"We've been in public plenty, K.," Sarah said.

"If you call the oncology ward public," I said.

Sarah put the fork down and sat back with her arms folded across her chest. "Do you resent me for that?" she asked. There was no heat in her words, just naked inquiry. "For all the time we've spent in the hospital? For being so sick?"

"Of course not," I said. "Don't be ridiculous."

"Because it's alright if you do, K.," she said. "That would make perfect sense."

If in this conversation I had been the later version of myself, the one so dedicated to facts that he said what was true even when it almost certainly would result in him being reviled, assaulted, shouted at, spit on, I would have told Sarah that she was, of course, entirely correct: though I knew it was breathtakingly wrong, though I hated

295

myself for it, I resented her. Instead of admitting this, though, I skewered a piece of French toast and shoved it into my mouth so I could chew rather than speak.

"That's what I thought," Sarah said, watching me.

It was quiet between us for a while, save for the sullen squeak of cutlery against porcelain, and the slow approach and fade of cars passing on the street.

Finally I looked up from my plate and said, "Sarah, I love you."

I imagined, foolishly, that this would be some sort of transformative moment in the conversation.

"Well I love you, K.," Sarah said. "Jesus. Of course I love you, too. But what does that have to do with anything?"

I paused, incredulous. Then: "I don't know. Everything?"

She gave me a gently scolding look. "Let's be honest," she said. "We were heading for a divorce before. And it's not as though we've somehow *evolved* in all this. Just the opposite. We — as in *we,* the couple, the pairing, the agreement to a shared life — have been frozen. On hold, while we deal with more pressing things. Nothing has changed, K., since the day before I was diagnosed. Think about it."

I sat there stubbornly refusing to think about it.

"So if we were heading for a divorce before," Sarah continued, "why shouldn't we get divorced now? Because I'm sick and you don't want to abandon me? Because I may be getting better and we'll have another chance?"

"Sure," I said. "Both of those things. Either of them. Whichever way it ends up."

Sarah put a hand over mine on the table. "K.," she said, "we should have let each other be a long time ago. We both know that."

I pulled my hand away, lifted the napkin from my lap, and threw it over my unfinished breakfast. "I have no idea what you're talking about," I said.

"Sure you do," Sarah said.

A tour bus rolled slowly by, loaded with septuagenarian leaf peepers. I stared, and they stared back through tinted windows. I wondered how we looked to them. Did they imagine we were happy? That we both would live to be their age someday, and that when that day arrived it would find us still together in our dotage, holding hands and writing each other little notes of endearment to find around the house?

When the tour bus had passed I looked

back at Sarah and found her expression hovering between determination and regret. I couldn't bear this, so I looked away again, across the street, where a woman wrestled with her Great Dane as the dog tried to pull its leash out of her hand.

"Is this because you blame me?" I asked finally.

"Blame you?"

"Because if it is, I understand. I've been thinking about that a lot, wondering if it's my fault."

"K.," Sarah said, "what are you talking about? Blame you for what?"

"Well, for you being so sick," I said. "Obviously."

"Now you're just talking crazy."

"Listen," I said, jabbing an index finger at her over the table, surprised by the rush of my own anger, "if I have to admit I resent you for being sick, you have to admit you blame me for it in the first place."

"Well I don't," Sarah said. "And I'm not going to indulge whatever insane guilt fantasy you've created. But I appreciate you coming clean about the other thing."

We stared at each other in silence, Sarah still offering that kind, pitying look, me fuming over having been foolish enough to let slip the truth.

The waitress, a young woman with an indecipherably florid tattoo sleeve that started at her wrist and disappeared into the shoulder of her black T-shirt, came and asked if we needed more coffee, if we wanted anything else, if everything was good.

"Everything's great," I said without looking away from Sarah.

"We're fine, thank you," Sarah said, smiling, smiling.

The waitress hesitated a moment, as people will when the space they've entered is thick with anions of conflict, but then she seemed to decide that our problem did not involve her, and turned to go back inside the restaurant.

We sat in silence once more. Around us joggers jogged, bicyclists pedaled, hipster couples strolled arm in arm with their shoulders touching and their heads inclined toward the other, the solidarity which precedes a seasoned marriage's long sine wave of contempt and mellowed affection.

Or so was my thinking, in the bitter moment.

Sarah examined her hands in her lap. "Listen, I'm sorry this comes as such a shock. I guess I thought we were closer to being on the same page than we are."

"You thought," I said, "that I wanted to divorce my ailing wife."

"Is that so outrageous?" she asked. "With all the other ways our life has been upended, is that such an insane concept?"

"Yes," I said. "It is."

She raised her face to look at me, and that's when I noticed the ooze of blood issuing from her left nostril, dark lethal red flecked with black, thick as corn syrup.

"Well that's where I am, K.," she said. "I'm sorry, but I'm not going to lie to you."

The blood crept downward, hitting the little hollow directly under her nose and angling in toward the peak of her upper lip.

"Sarah," I said.

"No, K., listen to me, please. I need to say something, and if I don't say it now I may lose my nerve."

I stared at the blood. "Okay," I said.

She talked, and I let her. After a while, I reached for the napkin on my plate, found a clean corner, stood, and went to her side of the table. Sarah stopped midsentence and looked up at me, her face full of dread; maybe she thought I would try to kiss her, or some other such grand romantic gesture. Instead I slid one hand under her chin and daubed at her lip with the napkin. Not having noticed the blood herself, she had no idea what I was doing or why, but nonetheless she sat still until her face was clean. I held the napkin out to show her the crimson stain. She took the napkin from me and stared at it, then folded it twice to hide the blood. We walked home, my hand at her elbow in a show of support she neither asked for nor needed, and we never spoke of divorce again.

That night I lay in bed beside her, sleepless. My eyelids did not grow the slightest bit heavy, and I did not yawn even once. For hours I lay there listening to the sounds of our bodies: her gut gurgling and cooing, my pulse throbbing against the pillow, the bellows of her lungs sighing steadily, all our dull human clockwork blaring like a Wagner symphony in the silence. And it was during those hours, utterly awake beside my wife, when I understood for the first time why people choose to believe stories about a bearded man in the sky who loves us like a father and promises something greater and more permanent for those who are righteous.

16
A SEEMINGLY INNOCUOUS INTERLUDE

Of course one is not supposed to describe anything or anybody as "retarded" these days, but just once, for the occasion of this review, I'm going to resuscitate the word *America, You Stoopid* is and state without equivocation that retarded — but only because it reflects the inanity of our age. Come for the comic violence inflicted on the show's principle, stick around for the damning indictment of We the People, flopping around the muck of late capitalism like pigs in a sty.' "

"Pigs are actually quite intelligent," I said.

"Not according to the *New York Times*," Claire said. She pecked away at the keyboard of her laptop, peered at the screen a moment. "Here's something a little less highbrow," she said. "Vegas odds on you surviving a second season are at eight to one."

"You can bet on this sort of thing?" I asked.

"Course you can. It's Vegas. But what do the numbers mean?"

"That if you wagered a dollar on me surviving and won, you'd make eight dollars on the bet."

"So they believe, in other words, that you're going to get killed."

"Very much so, it would seem," I told her.

We sat in the living room of Claire's new condominium, an exceedingly modern two-bedroom full of stainless steel and hardwood, with a gas fireplace that resembled a television and large windows that looked out on the bay.

"You want to see what they're saying about us on Tumblr?" Claire asked, still gazing at her screen.

"Probably not," I said. Out below, where the river met the ocean, a yellow and white ferry steamed for the small coastal islands on the horizon. Squat as a tugboat, it cut the waves and turned east, and I watched it grow smaller and smaller, listening to the chatter of Claire's keyboard echo off of new drywall.

My phone rang. On the other end was Theodore, saying MSNBCBS had called.

"First, my dear," he said, "they wanted to

apologize for Raquel Haddock's mob of vegan pacifists trying to murder you with their bare hands."

"No apology necessary," I said.

"That's not what I told them," Theodore said. "And the apology was insincere besides, being as they wouldn't have issued it if not for their desire to book you on their program *The Ted Show.* They're having a discussion about guns in America. Or guns *and* America. I wasn't quite clear."

"That's what it's called?" I said. "*The Ted Show?*"

"It's hosted by a gentleman named Ted," Theodore said. "So, yes."

"Don't these political programs usually have more incendiary names?" I said. "Isn't it usually something like *Bark at the Moon with Rod Lycanthrope?*"

"Are you interested, my dear?" Theodore asked. "You're under no obligation at all. These sorts of talks can become very heated. And after that Francy Finesse fiasco."

"I'll do it," I said. "Though I don't understand why they want me instead of, say, a constitutional law professor from Yale."

"Simple," Theodore said. "Because unlike any constitutional law professors from Yale, you are the star of a new and very popular reality television program. Also, you've been shot recently."

Claire declined to come to New York, instead opting to stay in her new apartment for two straight days and consume, like Narcissus at the pool, every bit of ephemera the Internet could offer about us. I, meantime, found myself under the hot lights in the *Ted Show* studio at 30 Rockefeller Plaza, sweating through a gummy layer of pancake makeup during a commercial break. I sat at a short oval table, with the show's eponymous host to my left and, across from me at the far end of the oval, a bespectacled, jowly man who represented the NRA.

I'd been in my seat for only two minutes when the cameras' on-air lights flared to life.

"Welcome back to *The Ted Show*," Ted said. "Last week's shooting at an Illinois elementary school, in which sixteen students aged seven to nine were killed along with three of their teachers, reignited the national debate about gun control. On the left, people are calling for universal background checks and a renewed assault weapons ban; on the right, there's the usual talk about the Second Amendment, as well as threats to primary out of office any Republican bold enough to sign his name to gun control legislation. Here to discuss this issue I'm joined by executive vice president of the National Rifle Association, Dwayne La-Strange, along with the star of the new reality television series *America, You Stoopid,* who himself was recently a victim of gun violence and now is a staunch supporter of gun control, a man who goes by the name K. Thank you both for being with us tonight."

"Good to be here," LaStrange said.

"You're welcome," I said.

"Dwayne," Ted said, "let's start with you."

"If I could interject, for a moment?" I said.

"Uh, sure," Ted said. "What is it?"

"I'm not really a staunch supporter of gun control," I said. "In fact, it's not accurate to say I support gun control at all."

"Duly noted," Ted said. "But let me ask you, as a victim of gun violence, you must believe that renewing the Federal Assault Weapons Ban would be a good thing."

"I was shot with a pistol," I said.

Across the table, LaStrange smiled.

"And if we're looking at it purely from the standpoint of numbers," I added, "handguns kill a lot more people every year than what are termed assault weapons."

"Nevertheless," Ted said to me.

"As with most things," I said, "it's far more complicated than you're willing to get into on a program like this, which traffics only in hysteria and half-truths," I said.

Ted blinked at me.

"I mean absolutely no offense at all," I said.

"Well clearly," Ted said.

"Listen, of course one could make a convincing case for banning private ownership of firearms of every kind, sure," I said.

"Right," Ted said.

"One could also make an equally convincing case for having no restrictions on the ownership or use of firearms whatsoever."

"Uh-huh," Ted said, sounding somewhat less convinced.

"Other than not being allowed to kill people with them, obviously."

"Obviously," Ted said.

"But what you want is spittle, not dialogue," I said. "You want me to froth at the mouth about how everyone who owns a gun is evil and stupid and possibly an extraterrestrial reptile in human form, so that Mr. LaStrange can then froth at his own fleshy and somewhat arrogant-looking mouth about how there is only one possible interpretation of the Second Amendment, and anyone who doesn't agree with him on that point is a Marxist and a pussy."

"Oh . . . kay," Ted said.

"None of which has anything to do with either an intellectual or moral understanding of firearms," I said. "Personally, I'm much more interested in the psychology of guns than I am in the public policy aspect."

"Except that public policy is what we're here to discuss," Ted said.

"That's fine," I said, "but there's so little point. For all the effect it will have on your audience's opinion regarding gun laws, we might as well discuss homoerotic subtexts in *The Lion King,* or whether Coke Zero really has all the flavor of regular Coke."

Both Ted and LaStrange had a good chuckle at this, unaware, apparently, that I wasn't joking in the least.

"Okay," Ted said to me. "Go ahead, then. The *psychology* of guns."

LaStrange sat back and folded his arms over his chest, smilingly expectant.

"It seems to me," I said, "that neither side of the gun debate has a grasp on what gun ownership in this country is really about. The left believes psychotic libertarians are stockpiling rocket launchers and antiaircraft batteries for use in the Second Coming, and the right believes overeducated Stalinists mean to forcibly disarm them so that they — the Stalinists, I mean — can sell gun owners' children into white slavery."

Ted smirked at LaStrange. "Is that about the size of it from your perspective, Dwayne?"

"Not exactly," LaStrange said. "But we do have concerns about government overreach. That is true."

Ted turned back to me. "So if gun ownership isn't about the political divide between left and right," he asked, "then what *is* it about, in your view?"

"It's about the guns themselves, what they symbolize and the emotions those symbols conjure," I said. "For the left, guns represent a savage world that can only be tamed by force. For the right they represent God. Also, probably, penises. By which I mean large, tumescent, decidedly heterosexual penises. Whatever the opposite of a small, flaccid gay penis is — that's what guns mean to conservatives."

Ted looked to a man with a clipboard and headset standing just out of frame, and received an enthusiastic thumbs-up in response.

"Alright then," Ted said, turning to LaStrange. "Dwayne. Got anything to say about that?"

LaStrange scrunched his face. "Not really, Ted. I mean, I find it difficult to respond to someone who doesn't make any sense, and is vulgar besides."

"You consider the word 'penis' vulgar?" I asked.

"When used in combination with the word 'tumescent,' yes," LaStrange said.

" 'Tumescent' simply means swollen," I said.

"I'm aware of the definition, thank you," LaStrange said.

"If I could elaborate a bit more?" I said to Ted. "Maybe that might help."

"Please," Ted said.

"Guns, as we discuss them in this culture, are a fantasy," I said. "A fantasy that lets the left reaffirm its notion of intellectual and moral superiority, and allows the right to indulge its paranoiac daydream of oppression and resistance. Both sides are equally delusional, and whether they realize it or not, they're cooperating hand in glove to preserve one another's delusions."

"So they're working together, is what you're saying."

"Beyond that," I said. "They *need* each other for their very existence."

"This is utter nonsense," LaStrange said.

"Really, it couldn't be any more obvious," I said to LaStrange. "All of your literature, speeches, and talking points are about the left. All of their literature, speeches, and talking points are about you. If everyone who opposes the NRA's agenda were raptured tomorrow, what would remain of your organization? Merely its constituent parts, which are not armies preparing for violent insurrection, but rather men who collect firearms for precisely the same reason that little girls collect dolls."

LaStrange sat forward in his chair. "Excuse me?"

"Which part do you need explained?" I asked.

"The part about little girls and dolls," LaStrange said. "Because of all the ridiculous things you've said so far, that one truly takes the cake."

I thought a moment. "Maybe you're right," I said finally. "Maybe the better analogy would be between guns and a child's comfort object."

"A child's what, now?" LaStrange asked.

"Comfort object. Like a stuffed animal, or a swatch of the mother's clothing. Linus's blanket is probably the most famous example."

LaStrange threw his hands up in the air.

"And what we know about comfort objects is that they serve as a bridge between complete reliance on the mother and genuine independence," I said. "In other words, if a person still needs comfort objects well into adulthood, then that person, at some point, failed to separate completely and successfully from his mother."

"So if I may," Ted said, "what you're saying, in a nutshell, is that Dwayne's constituency are a bunch of mama's boys."

"That's a more concise way of putting it," I said.

Across the table, LaStrange glared.

"Probably as good a spot as any for us to take a break," Ted said.

The cameras went dark, and LaStrange removed his microphone and departed the soundstage without a word. I stood to leave as well, and Ted rose with me.

"Good luck," he said, shaking my hand.

"With what?" I asked.

"With surviving more than a week, after what you just said."

"Everyone is awfully concerned about my safety, of late," I said.

"You think I'm joking." Ted looked down and shuffled some pages on his desk. "You're lucky Dwayne didn't shoot you on air. I'm sure he's packing."

"He did seem upset. Especially toward the end."

" 'Upset' is far too mild a word," Ted said. He looked up at me again, considered. "Let me break this down in a way you can understand. There are around a hundred and twenty million U.S. citizens who own at least one firearm."

"Okay," I said.

"And in the general population, the incidence of serious mental illness is about four percent."

"I don't know those numbers," I said, "so I'll have to take your word for it."

Ted nodded. "That means there are nearly five million people in this country who both own guns and are complete loony birds."

"I can see where you're going with this," I said.

"My advice, in all sincerity?" Ted said. "Find yourself a good-quality Kevlar vest."

17

You Don't Choose Your Family, Except When You Do

A few months after the debut of *America, You Stoopid,* Peggy called out of the clear blue and asked if she could appear on the show.

We hadn't spoken since my ill-fated visit after the Einstein biography.

"Can I smoke?" Peggy wanted to know.

"You mean on the show?" I asked.

"No, I mean on Mars, K.," Peggy said. "Of course, on the show."

"I don't see why you couldn't," I said. "It's not as though we shoot in a studio or anything. We can do it outside. We can even shoot at your house, if you like."

"I'm not talking about that," Peggy said. "What I'm asking is, will they actually air footage of someone smoking? These days it seems like that would get people's panties bunched up real quick."

"I don't think it's a problem," I told her.

"I mean, it's gotten to the point where the

314

only place you can smoke outside your own home is in the middle of the street. And they only allow that because they're hoping you'll get hit by a car."

"We've had a smoker or two on the show," I said. "Arnulfo's father, for example. He smoked almost as much as you do."

"I missed that episode," Peggy said.

"You haven't been watching all along?" I asked.

"I don't really watch a lot of TV," Peggy said. "I smoke. I crochet. I flip through old *Reader's Digest*s."

"Anyway, Arnulfo's father died," I said. "Not on the show, but shortly thereafter."

"That's too bad," Peggy said. She exhaled, and I could picture her with lips pursed, a funnel of blue-gray carcinogens pouring forth like a genie. "But so the smoking won't be a problem?"

"I really doubt it. The biggest determining factor in what airs is whether or not our producer thinks it makes for interesting TV. And there's some range there. Although the surest bet seems to be assaulting me in one way or another."

"It may come to that," Peggy said.

We were quiet. I listened to Peggy smoke. Finally I said, "Can I ask you a question?"

A pause, followed by the faint pop of Peggy's lips releasing the cigarette filter. "Shoot," she said.

"Is there a reason why, after months of silence, you not only contact me but want to appear on my television show?"

"That's for me to know," Peggy said, "and you to find out."

There was, of course, no chance of getting Peggy to fly — she hadn't been on a plane since smoking had been banned on commercial flights in 1990 — so Claire and I went to her. This was a greater time commitment than it would have been previously, as Peggy had moved south to Virginia, just picked up and left everything she'd known her whole life, friends and family, the Elks club and her volunteer work at the Humane Society, most notably the house in which she'd raised her children. Claire, having never taken the train through Amtrak's northeast corridor before, and thus unaware of its being a postindustrial horror show, suggested that instead of flying we ride the rails. Thus we endured a disheartening nine-hour rumble south, through the formerly bustling manufacturing centers of New Jersey, the gutted power plants and foundries outside Philadelphia, the haunted house known as Baltimore. By the end of it, Claire, spurred by alcohol and a perhaps overdeveloped sense of empathy and/or nationalism, was in tears.

Peggy waited for us at Union Station. We loaded our bags into the cavernous trunk of her 1984 Chevy Impala and drove southwest. The sights on 28 were somewhat less dystopian than the train ride had been, and by the time we reached Peggy's new home, an old Victorian outside Bealeton with a big backyard and a shingle roof badly in need of repair, she and Claire were in the throes of a high-energy rapport unlike anything I'd ever seen before from my mother-in-law: Peggy waving her cigarette hand around, Claire laughing and swigging from her flask.

No mention had yet been made of why Peggy wanted to be on the show.

We went inside. Peggy had the windows open; their lace curtains, yellowed by nicotine, undulated in a mellow summer breeze. I arranged our bags on the entryway floor while the two of them, still gabbing, went through the dining room and into the kitchen. I heard Peggy call out, "Who wants a drink," and had a distinct sense that the question was largely a rhetorical one, since she knew by now what Claire's answer would be, and likely had little interest in mine.

By the time I arrived in the kitchen there

were three glasses on the counter, each emblazoned with an image from the original *Star Wars* movie: Darth Vader, Luke Sky-walker, and Chewbacca. Claire cracked ice from a tray and dropped cubes into the glasses while Peggy stood by, wielding a liter of Allen's coffee brandy.

"You might want to be careful with those glasses," I told Claire. "They're probably worth some money."

"Used to think the same thing myself," Peggy said, pouring coffee brandy over the ice. "I got those at Burger King in nineteen-seventy-seven. Nineteen-*seventy-seven*. Kept them wrapped in newsprint in the basement, then found them again during the move. I thought, shit, these must be worth a penny or two, thirty-five years hence. Come to find out they sell for a whopping ten bucks apiece. So I'm going to need a new retirement plan."

"No kidding," I said. "I would have thought they'd be valuable."

"There's the irony," Peggy said. "Every-one thinks that, so everyone saves them — which makes them worthless. Honey, grab that milk from the fridge, would you?"

Claire pulled out a jug of whole milk and, following instructions from Peggy, added just enough to each glass to make the

Allen's look less like molasses and more like a mud puddle.

"I thought you used two percent," I said.

"It's a special occasion," Peggy said, claiming the Darth Vader glass as her own. "Too nice to stay inside. Let's sit out in the yard and scandalize the neighbors. We'll get good and drunk."

"I'm already good and drunk," Claire told her.

"That's the spirit," Peggy said, pushing open the screen door that led onto the back porch.

We sat together at a table under an old cottonwood, the innumerable branches of which twisted high overhead like fossilized sea serpents. I hadn't been drunk since the afternoon I read the Einstein biography, but I had no particular aversion to the idea, so I matched them glass for glass. When the bottle of Allen's was emptied Peggy produced a fresh liter, and soon, weary of going back and forth to the kitchen, she brought everything out to the table. As the sun went down and the milk jug left an ever-widening stain of condensation on the tabletop, Peggy and Claire talked about me as if I weren't even there.

"I met this kid when he was in junior high," Peggy said. "Whatever you want to know. I'm practically his mother."

"Well that's a decent starting point," Claire said. "What about family? Parents? Brothers and sisters?"

Peggy looked at me, then back to Claire, taking a pointed drag on her cigarette. "He didn't tell you?"

"Tell me what?"

"Honey, when I say I'm practically his mother, it's because K. didn't have one. He grew up in foster care."

Claire turned to me now, her expression not unlike what it had been earlier on the train, when the relentless spectacle of industrial ruin had broken her down. "Oh my God, K.," she said.

"True story," I said.

"That must have been awful."

"I thought it was, at the time," I told her. "But kids always think their circumstances are awful, even when they have it good."

"Still," Claire said.

"I mean as far as being an orphan goes, it wasn't bad," I said. "I feel like when people hear the words 'foster care' they assume I was chained to a furnace and forced to sew Old Navy T-shirts for a decade. It wasn't like that."

"Well thank God," Peggy said. She snuffed out her cigarette, dumped it in a small trash can next to the table, and swabbed out the ashtray with a paper towel.

"The worst thing I can say for foster care is that it was devoid of what people think of as love," I said. "Decent foster parents keep children clean and fed and get them to school on time. In exchange, they receive a stipend from the state. It's a simple transaction, really."

"Well I guess that explains some things," Claire said.

"It sure does," Peggy told her. She rose and gathered our glasses to make another round.

"What was he like, back then?" Claire asked.

"A lot like he is now," Peggy told her. "Anal retentive. The kind of kid who'd use a calculator to split a dinner tab. That's how I would describe young Master K."

"Oh, that is *perfect,*" Claire said, laughing and clapping her hands. "That is really, really good."

"That is, in fact, completely untrue," I said. "I have never in my life used a calculator to split a check."

"Only because you can do the math in your head," Peggy said, distributing fresh drinks. "Be real, K. You were not what anyone would call easygoing. I've never met

321

another teenager who starched his shirts. You collected *stamps,* for Christ's sake."

"How is collecting stamps anal retentive?"

Peggy stared at me, then turned to Claire. When their eyes met, they burst out laughing.

"What's so funny?" I asked.

This inquiry, for some reason, only made them laugh harder, the kind of deep convulsive cackling that becomes its own source of amusement. Peggy bent over with one hand on the table for balance, and Claire gasped for breath with her eyes squeezed shut, shoulders hitching. Each time they started to gather themselves and get their wind, one would catch the other's gaze and the laughter would start anew.

It went on for two or three minutes like that. I sat and waited and sipped my drink.

Finally Peggy pulled herself together, coming around the table to take her seat between us. "So I guess I'll amend my earlier statement," she told Claire. "K. used to be like he is now. Only somewhat less so."

Claire used the heel of her hand to wipe tears from her face. "Oh, but I do love this guy," she said, suddenly serious. She looked at me, her eyes bloodshot from laughter and booze. "Despite all his borderline-autistic weirdness. In fact, *because* of all his borderline-autistic weirdness. It makes him so . . . decent."

"That so?" Peggy said, either unconvinced or unimpressed. She ashed her cigarette in the grass.

Claire nodded. "The most decent man I've ever met, anyway."

"Honey, you're young," Peggy said. She reached out a smoke-cured hand and patted Claire's forearm. "Give it time."

But Claire wasn't amused. "Look," she said. "We can be shitty and irreverent about almost everything. But not about him."

Peggy tilted her head slightly. "Okay," she said, raising her glass from the table, holding Claire's gaze over the rim.

"I've heard some of what you know about K.," Claire said. "Now let me tell you what *I* know about him. He didn't pin me down when I was a little girl and put his cock on me and say he'd kill me if I told anyone. He didn't shoot my best friend's aunt between the eyes in junior high. He didn't hit my mother with a Louisville Slugger before finally figuring out it was time for a divorce. He didn't accuse me of leading him on when I was nice, or of being frigid when I wasn't nice. He didn't respond to my opinion about abortion with a rape threat."

"Well if *that's* your standard," Peggy said,

"most men are going to look pretty good."

"I could go on," Claire said.

"I think your point's been made."

"Seriously though," Claire said. "People misunderstand him. I did too, at first. Because I thought love was about feelings."

"It's not?" Peggy asked.

"Hell no," Claire said. "Feelings have nothing to do with it. Love is an accumulation of acts, plain and simple."

"Not very sexy," Peggy said.

Claire waived this away. "Who needs sexy?" she said. "I need safe. I need sane. Most people would look at K. and think, 'How can you love someone devoid of emotion?' But emotions are the bad stuff. Emotions inspire Nicholas Sparks movies and murder-suicides. Emotions are a fucking bill of goods, if you want to know the truth."

Peggy smoked and listened, her expression an unreadable reptilian neutral.

"K. never gets upset," Claire said. "At least not with me. He never yells. He never criticizes. He never tells me I should drink less. He lets me be me, while he is, undeniably, indubitably, always him."

"That I will grant you," Peggy said. "He is always him."

■ ■ ■ ■

At dusk the mosquitoes emerged, innumerable and hungry, so we repaired to Peggy's favorite spot for socializing: the kitchen table. By now Claire was thoroughly drunk, and after wrapping Peggy in an embrace for perhaps two beats too long, she pinballed up the creaky stairs to the guest bedroom and went silent. The coffee brandy, the ice, and a fresh jug of milk sat between Peggy and me on the table.

"I like her," Peggy said, jabbing her cigarette toward the ceiling, directly above which Claire lay sleeping. "I like her a lot."

"She's a good companion," I said.

"Coming from you, that's a ringing endorsement."

I shrugged. "It's what I'm capable of. Claire seems to accept that."

"More than accept it," Peggy said. "She thinks it's your best quality."

I eyed the pack of Winstons on the table to Peggy's left. "Would you mind if I had one of those?" I asked.

Peggy lifted the pack and lighter and handed them to me. "Anyway, I'm glad you found her," she said. "Can't be anything but good. Though the age difference is maybe a little . . . what's the word?"

"Unseemly?"

Peggy pointed at me. "That's the one I was looking for," she said.

"Well, Claire is sort of an old soul," I said.

"I wonder how she'll feel when you're sixty and she's still in her thirties."

"There's not *that* much of a gap," I said. "When I'm sixty, she'll be in her late forties."

"Still."

"Besides, I don't believe either of us is thinking that far down the road," I said.

"Jesus wept," Peggy said.

"What?"

"You're just so clueless, sometimes."

I hadn't smoked regularly since college. Owing to this complete lack of practice, as well as impaired hand-eye coordination, instead of touching the lighter flame to the tobacco at the end, I lit the thing halfway down the paper tube.

Peggy reached for the lighter. "Throw that away," she said.

I stubbed the ruined cigarette in the ashtray while Peggy lit another with one deft motion and handed it to me. The first drag — experimentally shallow though it was — proved harsh. I leaned forward and hacked several gray puffs while Peggy smirked, smoke flowing from her nostrils in two silky streams.

"Try again," she said. "Or don't, maybe."

The second drag I was able to pull and exhale with only a minor hitch in my throat. The third came even easier. It wasn't long before the nicotine, combined with the liter of coffee brandy I'd ingested, were conspiring to make me a little light-headed. This was not, at first, an entirely unpleasant sensation.

"So why," I said to Peggy while considering the cigarette in my fingers, "did you suddenly decide to live in Virginia?"

"It wasn't sudden," she said.

"It seemed sudden."

"Thirty years in the making, kiddo."

"You don't say." I took another awkward drag.

"When the kids were little, Roger and I never really had the money to go on vacation," Peggy said. "But one summer . . . this must have been '82 or '83. Reagan was president, I remember that. We actually — can you believe this — we took out *a loan* to bring the kids to Virginia Beach."

"Which part is unbelievable?" I asked. "The loan, or traveling to Virginia Beach?"

"Imagine what people would think today about using a loan to go on vacation," Peggy said. She leaned back in her chair, smiling ruefully at the memory. "But that was the eighties for you."

"So you fell in love with Virginia Beach and decided you wanted to move here some-day?"

"No," Peggy said. "I hate Virginia Beach. Virginia Beach is like the McOcean. But we drove around in the country some, and that's what I fell in love with."

"What about Roger?" I asked.

"What about him?"

"I'm just wondering why you didn't make the move sooner. It's not like you had anything holding you back, with the kids grown and out of the house."

"He didn't like it. Too hot."

"It is hot," I said.

"I like to sweat," Peggy said. "Roger, he enjoyed the winter. Which was hardly the only thing we disagreed about."

"I seem to remember such," I said.

Peggy's gaze inched up to the wall behind me, her eyes soft with reverie. She brought her cigarette to her mouth. "Anyway," she said, "Roger gone ten years now, Sarah gone. Time was obviously a-wastin'. So here I am."

"Time's not a-wasting," I said.

Peggy's eyes snapped back sharply on me.

"Don't start."

"I'm just saying."

"Well, don't."

We were quiet for a minute, and I noticed that the dizziness in my head had migrated south to my stomach; it felt suddenly like I had one of those elementary school solar system models whirling in my gut. I put my cigarette out in the ashtray, half smoked.

"It's a nice place, anyway," I said, looking around the kitchen.

"And dirt cheap," Peggy said. "Anytime you've had enough of real estate prices back home, you should look into property here."

"We're making a lot of money, with the show," I said. "Speaking of which, you still haven't mentioned why you asked me to come."

"Couple reasons," Peggy said.

"Maybe start with the primary one," I suggested.

"I'll start with the fact that I wanted to meet the girl I saw you with on TV," Peggy said. "Wanted to see who had replaced my daughter."

"No one has replaced Sarah," I told her. "That's not what's happening."

"Either way, as you probably figured out by now, I approve."

My light-headedness upshifted into borderline vertigo; the room didn't spin, exactly, but it had definitely begun to tilt back and forth in a way I didn't enjoy. "And the other reason?" I asked, swallowing.

Peggy eyeballed me as she took a long drink from her Rumford Martini, holding my gaze until the glass was drained.

"I wanted to be on your show," she said, putting the empty glass down on the tabletop, "to tell you to quit doing your show."

I sat forward in my chair and put my hands on my knees.

"I think," I told Peggy, "that I need to vomit."

She pointed to the back door. "Outside," she said. "Don't you dare do it in my sink."

I took the porch steps two at a time, bent at the waist once I reached the ground, and unleashed a torrent onto Peggy's lawn. My throat and nostrils burned instantly with digestive fluids. I vomited again and felt a tingling in my face; the following morning I would awake with the freakishly rouged cheeks of a toy soldier. I gasped for breath, preparing to genuflect and silently beg whichever god would hear me to make it end. But then, just when I was about to fall to my knees, the sickness began to abate. A few more retches produced only caustic dollops of bile. By and by the world began to right itself. The ringing in my ears faded, and soon I could hear the cheerful din of bullfrogs and nocturnal insects in the bog adjacent to Peggy's property. I stood up straight, spit once, wiped at my mouth with the back of my hand. A thin sheet of ground fog, limned with silver by the quarter moon, drifted out of the trees, and I stayed outside for a few minutes, taking in the moonlight and the chirrups while a breeze wicked sweat from my forehead.

"You alright?" Peggy asked when I came back in. She was mixing herself another drink. A glass of ice water rested on my side of the table.

"Better," I said.

"Gotta know your limits," Peggy said.

I sat down in my chair. "I think it was the cigarette that got me."

"Like I said."

"It's nice out here at night," I told her.

Peggy took a seat with her fresh drink. "I like nights the most," she said. "A lot of women — hell, a lot of men, these days — would probably get spooked out here in the sticks after dark. But I love it."

My stomach, empty and offended, groaned magnificently.

"You want a bite to eat?" Peggy asked. "Some toast or something?"

I shook my head and took a sip of ice water.

"Gotta eat, if you're gonna drink," Peggy said. "The two of you didn't have dinner."

"Neither did you," I said.

"I've been drinking my dinner ever since Roger died. Can't be bothered to cook for just myself."

A sudden fatigue descended on me, oppressive and uncomfortable. I closed my eyes and let my head loll back. "If you're going to explain why you think I should quit the show, you probably ought to do it soon," I said.

"Fine," Peggy said. "Here, sit up."

I raised my head.

"You shouldn't do this show anymore," Peggy said, "because you're using it to try and hurt yourself."

"I keep hearing as much," I said.

"Then maybe you should start listening."

"That a large number of people believe something does not make that thing any more likely to be true," I said. "In fact, often it's the opposite."

"Sometimes," Peggy said, "I could just smack you."

"Again," I said, "you're not the only one who suffers the urge. Though I don't hold it against you."

"Well that's just the problem," Peggy said, tapping her index finger on the tabletop several times.

"What's the problem?"

"That you don't hold it against me," she said. "That you don't care if you get hurt."

"That's not true," I said to her. "I care. You see acceptance and misinterpret it as indifference."

"I'm going to put this as plainly as I can," Peggy said. "You're being taken advantage of, K. Whoever makes this show is using you. Using the fact that you don't care to put you in danger."

"His name is Theodore," I said. "And I have reason to believe he's concerned about my well-being."

Peggy shrugged, a gesture somewhere between acquiescence and exasperation. "You want to kill yourself, fine," she said. "Just be honest about it. Draw a warm bath and break out the straight razor. Take a bunch of pills. Have some dignity and do it in private. You're embarrassing your family, not to mention the memory of your wife."

"I don't have any family," I told her.

For the first time I'd ever seen in more than two decades of knowing her, Peggy looked wounded. "That is a hell of a thing," she said, "for you to say to me."

18
SOLIPSISM IS A SHARED FATE

In the weeks after Sarah's diagnosis we had more sex than we'd had since college, more sex than we'd had *during* college, coming together as if in an effort to make up for, or else obliterate, the time we'd spent in near total indifference to one another's bodies. Twice, three times a day, every room in the house, Sarah suddenly voracious and without qualm, caring nothing for doctors' appointments, open window shades, or any lingering mores from her Catholic childhood. Where once there had been definitive if not strict limitations on what we would do to and with one another, now almost nothing earned objection.

Except I could not, under any circumstances, touch her right breast.

This was Sarah's rule, not mine.

"It's diseased," she said by way of explanation.

"That doesn't bother me," I said.

"But it bothers me."

"Okay," I told her. "I get it."

And I did.

Except I started, slowly, over the following weeks, to obsess. As the days passed and our old routines dissolved, each time we made love my attention focused a bit more myopically on the one thing I really wanted. When Sarah said *Slap me* I slapped her, and when she said *Against the refrigerator* I obliged, but I did these things, increasingly, by rote — all my conscious attention focused on her right breast, rising and falling with our rhythm in the cup of her bra, which never, ever came off.

During my few hours of sleep each night I started to dream about reaching back and releasing the bra's hook-and-eye clasp with one flick of my fingers — a skill much discussed in the hallways and locker rooms of my adolescence, but which in real life I did not possess.

One afternoon I made the perhaps willful mistake of imagining that this new, sexually aggressive Sarah needed me to match her aggression. To be insistent.

After all, time was short.

She sat straddling my hips, and I leaned up, just as I had in dreams, and grabbed for the clasp of her bra.

She froze and looked at me. "What are you doing?" she asked.

"Taking your bra off," I said.

Sarah pushed my arm away. "We talked about this, K.," she said.

"I know," I said. "I guess I thought maybe."

She rolled off of me and pulled the covers up, resting her head against my shoulder.

"You thought maybe what?" she asked.

"That in your heart of hearts, you wanted me to," I said. "That you just needed me to be forceful."

Sarah breathed. "I've given you everything else," she said.

"That's true," I said.

"It's all for you, you know," she said.

I had not known this, having imagined, until that moment, that her passion over the past few weeks was genuine.

"So what I need in return," she said, running a hand up and down my forearm, "is for you to understand."

"I can try," I said. "I want to try."

"This *thing,*" she said, "is diseased. It wants me dead. When you touch it, it feels good. And I don't want it to feel good."

"Okay," I said.

"Can you understand that?" she asked.

It was not, in my mind, a question of

336

whether I could understand, but whether she could understand that I wanted to touch her breast not for pleasure, but by way of apology.

There was no way I could think of to explain this to her.

"Yes," I said. "Of course."

19

YOU MAY ALL GO TO HELL, AND I WILL GO TO TEXAS

To be fair, a reasonable person might have agreed with Peggy's assessment of Theodore, considering that Claire and I went to Fort Worth's Memorial Day parade at his urging. After all, he had to have known this fell on the scale of historically bad ideas somewhere between lawn darts and the Donner Party's shortcut. A large number of the people I'd called overgrown babies with semiautomatic pacifiers lived in Fort Worth, and in the evermore-shrill debate over firearms, those people had recently taken to carrying their rifles in coffee shops and chain restaurants to prove some point or another. What was more, most of them who knew me on sight, had, in fact, discharged many high-velocity rounds through images of me distributed by their gun club, Cold Dead Fingers of Denton County, in the days after my *Ted Show* appearance.

These were people, understand, for whom

the NRA was not strident enough — they'd burned their lifetime membership cards when LaStrange and Co. suggested that bringing a loaded AK-47 to Chuck E. Cheese's was perhaps not the pinnacle of either good sense or patriotism. So yes, undoubtedly, Theodore sending us to the Lone Star State for Memorial Day was at best unwise, though I continue to believe, especially given how things ended, that it was not malign. The worst that could be said about him is he was perhaps too confident in the abilities of ex-Spetsnaz to deal with any challenge, up to and including a mob of heavily armed Texans.

Claire was quiet on the flight to Dallas/Fort Worth International. She'd taken Xanax as a hedge against turbulence, and this gave her a slouched, silent contemplativeness, an almost eerie contrast to her usual liquored exuberance. She drank water, and spoke to me only once, to ask to be let out of our row so she could go to the bathroom. When we touched down and deplaned she lagged two steps behind me on the walk up the Jetway. We stopped inside the terminal and searched for an indication of where we could find a cab.

As we stood reading various signs, a gigantic man walking past did a double take, then stopped and stared. He weighed at least four hundred pounds, the sort of heft that makes one's knees look like they're buckling slowly in toward each other, like tectonic plates. He wore huge silver basketball shorts, a blue T-shirt big enough to serve as a two-man tent, and a camouflage boonie hat with the chin strap cinched tight against the fleshy bulge of his throat.

The man took one lumbering step toward us. "Hey there," he said.

"God help me," Claire said.

"Hello," I said to the man.

"You're that fella."

"It's possible that I am," I said.

"What're y'all doin' in town?"

"There's an open-carry rally after the Memorial Day parade in Fort Worth," I said. "We're going to attend."

"Y'all recordin' this raight now?" he asked. "To go on that show of yours?"

"We are recording, yes," I said.

The man looked around at people rushing this way and that through the terminal. "If you're recordin'," he said, "then where's your crew?"

"You're looking at it," Claire said.

"I don't see no cameras," the man said.

"Moore's law indicates that the number of transistors in a CPU doubles every two years," I said. "There's an inevitable minia-turization of electronics attendant to this phenomenon."

"You want to try that again in English, buddy?" the man asked.

"He means the cameras are very small and very hidden, Private Pyle," Claire said.

"Okay, whatever you say," the man said. "I just want to make sure you're tapin' this."

"Are you going to do a magic trick?" Claire asked.

"Nope," the man said. He lifted his right hand, cocked his thumb and forefinger into the universal pantomime of a handgun, and pressed the tip of his finger against my forehead.

"Pow," he said, dropping his thumb down like the hammer on a pistol.

"Is this the part where the Stasi guys come and choke him out?" Claire asked.

"I think," I said, "that he would need to have a real gun for that to happen."

"You stick around here too long, big guy," the man said, "somebody gonna do that for true. Word to the wise."

"Can I ask you a question?" I said.

"Sure." The man dropped his hand to his side again.

"This will probably seem like a non sequi-tur."

"Whatever the hell that means," he said.

"Why are fat men so fond of athletic shorts?" I asked.

The man looked down at his legs, then back up at me. "Who you calling fat, buddy?"

"The hayseed who just threatened to shoot him," Claire said. "That's who."

"For years," I said, "I've noticed that obese men often wear athletic shorts, even in winter, and I started to wonder why that was. I mean, you're clearly not setting out on a long run or getting ready to play full-court basketball."

"Now you listen up —"

"Is it because they're more comfortable?" I asked. "Is it the accommodating elastic waistband? Or the porousness of mesh? I understand that fat men tend to sweat more than the median."

The man stared, gape mouthed.

"I mean absolutely no disrespect," I said. "Though I realize it probably doesn't seem that way."

After a moment the man lumbered away, pointing at me over his shoulder and muttering. "You gonna get yours," he said. "Mark my words, buddy. You gonna get it, *big*-time."

We watched him go.

"That was fun," Claire said.

"Did you think so?"

"Sarcasm, K." Claire released the handle of her roller bag and rubbed at her eyes.

"Those sorts of threats," I said, "are almost always idle."

"In Delaware, maybe," Claire said. "This is Texas."

Idle threat or not, before leaving the airport for our hotel we encountered several other people who took no pains to obscure their dislike of me. When we asked where to find a taxi, the man behind the Terminal A information desk glowered for a moment, then used both hands to point in opposite directions. A woman at McDonald's with a tattoo of six-shooters on her wrist refused to sell me a soda, crossing her arms and staring at me in silence until I walked away. When we finally located the cab stand, the attendant looked at me, leaned through the passenger window, and told the driver to charge us double.

The driver, though, a man from Iraq named Samer, seemed to like me just fine, and charged according to the rates on the slip from the cab stand.

Given my overall unpopularity, we decided not to venture from the hotel, and ate at the restaurant on the eleventh floor. I had the thirty-ounce "Lone Star Size" porterhouse with a glass of beer, while Claire opted for the Cobb salad and, quite conspicuously, nothing but water to drink.

When she was finished, Claire pushed her plate away and put her forearms on the bar, examining the teakwood grain in silence.

"You're not drinking," I said finally.

"No, I am not," she said.

"That was my way," I said, "of asking if something's wrong."

"I'm not drinking," she said, "because I want to have a serious conversation. I don't think we should do this tomorrow, K."

"I would ask why," I said, "but I think I already know what you'll say."

"You always think you know," she said, running the tip of one finger around the rim of her water glass. "You think you know everything."

"That's not true," I said. "There is hardly anything I'm certain of."

Claire turned on her stool and gazed around the dining room. "There are exactly five other people in this restaurant right now, not counting the bartender and the waitress," she said. "Four of those people are women, and none of them looks even vaguely Russian."

"What does a Russian look like?" I asked.

"Heavy brow, predatory nose, eyes set a millimeter apart," she said. "You know, Slavic."

"I'm not sure that look is exclusive to Slavs," I said.

"The point is I think Theodore was full of crap about this security team."

"It was his idea," I said. "Besides, I thought you didn't like it in the first place."

"That was before you went on national television and called every tobacco-chomping half-wit in the country a big fat baby."

"It's possible," I said, "that you see this as more serious than it actually is."

"Have you not been paying attention today?" Claire said. "It's very, very serious. And do you know why? Because you were right. They are mama's boys, and what's more they know it, deep down in their stupid little hearts. You've challenged their most sacred delusion: the image of themselves as tough, self-reliant inheritors of the spirit of Davy Crockett, or who the fuck ever. And they'll hurt you to preserve that delusion, K. They will."

The bartender came over, lifted Claire's empty plate, and asked if I wanted another beer.

"No, I'm fine," I said.

"Thank you," Claire said as he walked away.

"He doesn't seem to have anything against me," I said.

"He's queerer than a three-dollar bill," Claire said, "and he's probably never been within a hundred yards of a gun. God knows why he lives here. He should be in Austin."

I tapped my fingers on the bar, thinking. "Can I ask you a question?" I said after a minute.

"Jesus Christ."

"It's just that once, not long ago, you were so dedicated to the notion of fame that there was nothing you wouldn't do to have it. In fact, you stated pretty clearly that celebrity was the only thing that gave life meaning, in your view."

"Sure. Back when I was considering ritual suicide in the bulk goods section at Total Foods."

"But now that you have a genuine opportunity to be famous, you're balking."

"Did someone drop you on your head when you were a baby?" Claire asked.

"Not that I'm aware of," I said.

"You didn't, like, fall off a slide at the playground and land on your noggin? Get whacked in the face with a baseball bat? Nothing?"

346

"I got a concussion in junior high," I said. "I was standing at a urinal in the boys' room, and this kid named Eddie Mayhew came up and tossed me over his hip, Judo style."

Claire swirled the ice in her glass. "That must be it," she said.

"I'm afraid I'm not following you."

"K.," she said, suddenly exasperated, "yes, I want to be famous, everyone wants to be famous, everyone thinks fame will solve all their problems and make them whole and I am no different. Yes yes yes. Okay? But I want you to be not dead more than I want to be famous. Is that clear enough for you?"

"I just don't think this will be as dangerous as you assume."

"A man you don't know walked up and mimed shooting you in the head this afternoon. A man who in all likelihood will actually *be* at that rally tomorrow. A rally the sole purpose of which is for people to parade around with loaded semiautomatic weapons."

"I understand that," I said. "But these people have an agenda. One that would not be served by hurting me, or anyone else."

Claire, in the midst of a drink of water, nearly spit up on herself. "These people," she said, reaching for a cocktail napkin to wipe her chin, "don't occupy reality, K. They live in a paranoid self-defense fantasy. Paranoid being the operative word, when one is discussing firearms."

I held a hand up to signal the bartender. He raised his eyebrows in response.

"I'm probably going to need another beer after all," I told him.

Claire put her head down until her chin nearly touched her sternum. She placed both hands down flat on the bar. "What if I told you," she said, "that if you insist on going to the rally tomorrow, you can go by yourself?"

"I'm not insisting on anything," I said. "Insisting isn't really what I do."

"But you're still planning to go."

"That's what we're here for," I said.

"Then what of it? What if I refuse?"

"That's your choice, of course," I said. "Though I have to wonder why you came here in the first place, if you feel so strongly about it."

The bartender arrived with a fresh beer. Claire and I were quiet for a few moments, each of us gazing at the mirror behind the bar. Eighties synth pop played from unseen speakers, at a volume meant merely to protect against silence rather than to entertain.

"You know, I think I'm finally starting to clue in to something," Claire said.

"What's that?" I asked.

"This has nothing to do with space-time or the Doppler effect or any of the other nonsense you go on about."

"It's hardly nonsense," I said. "It's the most important scientific theory in the history of mankind."

Claire stared at me, and beneath her stony expression a great fear roiled like magma, threatening to burst forth. "Have you checked the Vegas odds on you since the last episode aired?"

"You know I don't pay attention to those things."

"Well maybe you should start," she said. "Because as of this afternoon, they had you at twelve to one."

When I woke the next morning I found myself alone in our king bed. At first I thought perhaps Claire had slipped away and left town, but then I spotted a note, written on hotel stationery, on the night-stand.

Out buying supplies, it read. *Brb.*

I rose and threw back the curtains to an angry, imperial brightness: powder blue sky, white-hot sun, and nary a cloud to cast doubt on the preeminence of the greatest nation the world had ever seen. Seven stories below, the lampposts were draped with bunting for the holiday, and here and there stars-and-stripes streamers skittered across the pavement in a scouring wind. I walked away from the window, still squinting, and went into the bathroom. Over the leonine roar of the toilet I heard the hallway door open and latch shut again, and when I emerged I found Claire humming cheerfully as she unpacked her supplies: several old, shriveled limes, a bottle of añejo tequila, and a shot glass it would turn out she'd borrowed from the bar downstairs.

The alarm clock read seven minutes after seven.

Claire bounded over to the bathroom doorway and pecked me on the cheek. "Let's get this party started," she said.

I rubbed my eyes with the heels of my hands. "Do you maybe want some breakfast first?" I asked. "Or else a cup of coffee?"

"That would no doubt be wise," she said. "But I figure if it's going to be Colossally Stupid Day, we might as well get started with the stupid bright and early."

"This probably qualifies," I said, looking again at the booze and accoutrements.

Claire gazed around the room. "I need a

knife for the limes," she said. She looked at me. "Knife?"

"Haven't seen one," I said. "I doubt there's anything suitable just lying around in here."

Claire opened drawers and closets until she found a letter opener in the desk near the window.

"You sure you're not hungry?" I asked.

"Order room service, if you want," she said, stabbing the tip of the letter opener into a lime. "I might pick at it."

By the time my eggs Chesapeake arrived under a fingerprint-smeared aluminum lid, Claire had just thrown back her fourth shot.

"When do we have to be down there?" she asked, prodding the eggs with a fork as though they might suddenly spring to life.

"Anytime, really," I said. "The parade's at eleven, and the rally follows immediately afterward. So as long as we're there by noon."

"Maybe we should go early," Claire said. "Scope it out. Get you some breakfast that's actually edible."

"Last night you didn't want to go at all," I said, "and now you want to go early."

"A lady," she said, "reserves the right to change her mind."

After I dressed and Claire secreted the

tequila in her purse, we walked ten blocks to the Fort Worth Water Gardens, a large public park near Interstate 30 where Cold Dead Fingers and allied parties planned to hold their gathering after the parade. Presumably they'd chosen the Water Gardens because its western border, Houston Street, was also part of the parade route, making reconvening after the festivities easy.

It was on Houston that we found a place called Diner's Delight, directly across from the Water Gardens. We lingered in a window booth — I had the impression from the rapidly souring mood of our waitress that the coffee refills I continued to order were not, in her mind, sufficient to justify our continued presence — and watched as the streets outside began to fill with parade-goers.

If you've never been to Texas, or any other place where the purchase, use, upkeep, and discussion of firearms is considered divine mandate rather than mere lifestyle, it will be difficult, probably, to understand what we bore witness to that bright and terrible morning. Nearly everyone on Houston Street had a gun of some kind. A plurality carried rifles — AR 15s and AK-47s, of course, but also MP10s and the CT9 (which 'ked like some piece of advanced alien weaponry from a science fiction film), a handful of World War II–vintage M1 carbines, and at least two Barrett M82s, a sniper rifle capable of blowing a man's leg clean off at a range of over one mile. Accessories, some of them purely cosmetic and perhaps even coming at the expense of the gun's performance, were clearly an enthusiastic priority. One gentleman with a placard proclaiming his weapon the "FrankenRifle" carried what had started as a humble AR15, but now bristled with a one-hundred-round ammo drum as well as four additional thirty-round clips, a bayonet, two laser scopes, three red dot sights, a holographic sight with magnifier, three flashlights, a contour camera, and a bipod. This determined feat of customization drew fawning attention in much the same way that a puppy might at a parade in, say, New Hampshire.

Clothing and regalia suggested a patriotism as facile as it was rabid. Lots of red, white, and blue in an endless variety of presentations, from the common (T-shirts and hats), to the somewhat less expected (bikinis, chenille skirts), to the downright bizarre (one man of indeterminate but likely young age wore a second skin bodysuit of red and white stripes, capped off by a blue codpiece festooned with stars). And then there were the flags. Every third person seemed to carry one. We saw plenty of standard-issue Old Glorys, to be sure, but these were outnumbered roughly three to one by the Betsy Ross variant, with a circle of thirteen stars in the upper left quadrant (inside this circle the manufacturer had helpfully printed the number "76," lest anyone miss the blisteringly obvious reference to the Revolutionary War and, by extension, the Founding Fathers these people fetishized and misunderstood in equal measure). There were plenty of Gadsden flags, as well, with its banana-yellow background and rattlesnake, coiled petulantly and looking more like it's about to sneeze than strike. A banner with the image of a cannon and the words COME AND TAKE IT was also popular, being as it was a reference to Texas's revolution against and independence from Mexico. And finally, mixed in with all the other flags was the standard of the Cold Dead Fingers gun club, a pair of M16s crossed at the barrels against an off-white background, with the letters CDF centered above.

Half an hour after police blocked Houston Street to traffic the crowd had already swelled five and six deep on the sidewalks.

Within our range of sight from the window booth there were at least three hundred firearms visible. Black plastic and custom chrome finishes gleamed under a biblical sun. People sweated and smiled and craned their necks to see if anything resembling a parade was yet approaching. They waved to friends. They fondled and massaged their weapons. They hoisted children onto their shoulders and handed them tiny flags to wave as the sound of marching bands and fire truck Klaxons gathered in the distance.

"I hate them," Claire said. She stared through the window, her eyebrows raised in the perpetually surprised expression of the deeply inebriated. "The things they care about are so stupid. And they're so proud of them. Their stupid guns. Their stupid fat kids. Their stupid hot-as-fuck bumpkin state."

We didn't realize the waitress was standing there until we heard her speak. "They probably ain't all that fond of you, either, sweetheart," she said.

Both Claire and I turned to face the waitress. She gazed down at us, her expression even more openly disdainful than it had been in our interactions to that point.

"I think it's time for you two to settle up and come with me," the waitress said.

Claire turned in the booth to face the waitress. "I think," she said, "that you can just keep slinging coffee. We'll decide when we're ready to leave, thanks very much."

I leaned forward and pulled my wallet from my back pocket. "If we could just get the check," I said.

The waitress ignored me. She squared up to Claire and planted her hands on her hips. "Who exactly," she asked, "do you think you're talking to?"

"Forty ought to do it, yes?" I asked. I placed two twenties on the cracked Formica tabletop. "Here you are. That ought to be more than enough, I think, to cover one egg special and several coffees. That's an extremely good tip, right there."

Claire got to her feet. Her hips pushed the table several inches over to my side, pinning me in the booth. "I'm talking," she said, "to the cracker-ass hag standing right. In front. Of me." She punctuated these last words with three firm jabs of her index finger into the waitress's sternum.

Claire was, as always, impressive in her anger, but the waitress, a Texan through and through, turned out to be no shrinking violet herself. In an instant the two of them were on the floor, flailing at one another and spitting like angry cobras. Neither asked quarter, and neither gave any, but donations did include a swatch of hair, several tea-spoons of blood, the crown from someone's molar, a gold nugget glinting on the carpet among several pieces of flatware, and the shards of a broken coffee mug.

The match was, at first, quite even, but then the waitress tired, began to huff instead of hiss, her movements suddenly in slow motion, and Claire achieved what wrestlers call a full mount: sitting on the woman's chest, knees on the floor to either side. She rained down punches, her fists landing with dull thuds against the waitress's face. Two men in soiled aprons arrived from the kitchen just as it was about to get truly bad for their colleague, peeling Claire off and tossing her to the floor.

One of the cooks, older and significantly more corpulent than his partner, pointed to Claire, then to me. "Both y'all stay where you are. Robbie, go call the police."

"No," the waitress said. She pulled herself into a sitting position on the floor, brushed her hair back with both hands, and felt at a spot below her left eye, where a welt was already starting to rise. "No cops."

"Raylene," the fat cook said. "Wait until you see your face. You'll call them yourself."

Robbie, tall and wide-eyed and likely afflicted by some mental blight, stood frozen between Raylene and the fat cook, two poles of equal influence in his world.

Raylene got slowly to her feet and glared at Claire, who now stood beside me. "Look at them," she said to the fat cook.

He did as instructed. "So?" he said.

"No, really look at them."

Scowling in confusion, the fat cook turned his gaze to us again. After a few moments, recognition dawned.

"No shit," he said.

"Yep," Raylene said.

"Robbie, call the cops on his Yankee ass," the fat cook said.

I pointed to the crown on the floor. "Does anyone know who that belongs to?"

"It's mine, asshole," the waitress said. "Shut your mouth. Robbie, you ain't calling no one."

Robbie, who'd taken several tentative steps toward the kitchen, froze once more.

"I don't get this, Raylene," the fat cook said.

But Raylene ignored him, instead focusing her attention on me. "What the hell are you thinking, coming down here?" she asked. "You got a death wish or something?"

To my left, Claire, investigating a cut on her lip with the tip of her tongue, nodded vigorously.

"There is growing consensus," I told Raylene, "that that is the case."

"Well that must in actual fact be the case," Raylene said. "Because there's no way you're getting through that crowd without someone taking a shot at you."

Raylene led us back to the kitchen.

"Now what?" the fat cook asked, arms folded over his pony-keg belly.

"I don't know," Raylene said. "Have 'em organize dry storage or something. Just keep 'em back here until the parade's over."

"Isn't this, like, kidnappin'?" Robbie asked.

"I don't like this at all, Raylene," the fat cook said. "They want to come down here and shoot their little show, have fun with all the rednecks? Let 'em take their chances."

"They may be too stupid to know what's best for them," Raylene said, "but that doesn't mean I have to pretend I am, too."

Just then, my phone vibrated in my hip pocket. I pulled it out and saw Theodore was calling.

"I should probably take this," I said to Raylene.

She dismissed me with a brusque wave.

I walked over to the dishwashing station. "Hello," I said.

"My dear, are you alright?" Theodore asked.

"We're fine," I said. "Well, Claire has a cut on her lip. But we're fine otherwise."

"Because the Russians just called and told me you've disappeared. As in vanished. Whereupon I reminded them that I was paying an obscene amount of money to prevent exactly that sort of thing from happening."

"Tell them we've been taken into the kitchen of the Diner's Delight."

"What?"

"For our safety," I assured him.

"Yes, well," Theodore said, "it sounds as though you're in the middle of a war zone, according to the Russians."

"There are a lot of people carrying weapons," I said. "But it's peaceful."

"They have also informed me that current circumstances in Fort Worth are such that it constitutes breach of contract on my part, and their final and terminating obligation under said contract was to inform me the two of you had been sitting in a restaurant, and then disappeared."

"I have to wonder just how good these men are at their job," I said, "if moving from the dining room to the kitchen constitutes 'disappeared' in their book."

"So I want you to inform me the precise moment you leave this *Diner's Delight,*" Theodore said. "Which sounds horrid, by the way."

"The coffee's quite good," I told him.

"And I want you to go straight from there to the airport. Where we will get you on the very next flight to anywhere, and you will never set foot in Fort Worth again."

"I think Claire would be pleased with that," I said.

"Undoubtedly," Theodore said. "Listen, K.: the precise moment."

"I'll be in touch," I said.

Up until that point, my only acquaintance with the life of food service professionals came from television programs like *Steely Chef* and *America's Next Basting Star,* shows that portrayed working kitchens as an environment only slightly less exciting and dangerous than the battlefield. By contrast, washing dishes at Diner's Delight turned out to be a dull, sweaty, hand-scalding affair. Within minutes Claire and I were drenched sternum to shin, bits of congealed oatmeal clinging to our forearms, smears of egg yolk and pork grease on our clothes. As she loaded the dish machine, a stainless steel behemoth more than loud enough to warrant hearing protection, Claire plotted aloud the vengeance she would take upon me, Theodore, the whole of Texas. With the parade on, Diner's Delight had no customers, and given the lack of newly soiled dishes Raylene moved us to dry storage, a dark and malodorous space that, owing to near-total sensory deprivation, turned out to be even more mind numbing than the dish area. We rotated and replenished stocks of flour and sugar, gallon jars of mayonnaise and hot sauce, innumerable canned fruits and vegetables, and bag upon single-serving bag of pork rinds.

"How often do you have to do this?" I asked Robbie, who'd been assigned to direct our work.

"Get a shipment twice a week," Robbie said. "I only do it once, though, 'cause I have Fridays off."

"My goodness," I said. "You must feel lobotomized when you go home."

"I don't know what that means," Robbie said.

"That'd be a 'yes,'" Claire said, hoisting a massive tub of Crisco onto the top shelf.

"Was this what working at Total Foods was like?" I asked her.

She looked at me. "Didn't you ever have a shitty job? McDonald's in high school? Anything?"

"Not really," I said. "I had a work-study in college as an attendant at the campus bowling alley."

"How exactly was that work-study?"

"I wondered the same thing, at the time," I said.

"Anyway," Claire said. "Certainly when you're stocking shelves, Total Foods is a lot like this. But it's not the donkey work that gets to you."

"What gets to you?"

"It's the sense — the certainty, really — that most of your life is spent doing something that doesn't matter one goddamn bit. To anyone. At all."

Robbie, absorbed in picking at a callus on his right hand, nodded without looking up. "That's true," he said.

"But Robbie, you cook people's breakfasts, help them get started with their day," I said. "And Claire, you know better than I do that Total Foods customers count on the shelves being well stocked with wholesome, organic, cruelty-free, sustainably sourced foods. And also on cheerful, knowledgeable staff who can help find what they're looking for."

"Total Foods customers are idiotic yupsters who think they're saving the world because they vote Democratic and buy fair trade coffee," Claire said. "There's no satisfaction in serving the desires of people you loathe."

"What's a yupster?" I asked.

"Yuppie-hipster hybrid," Claire said. "Close taxonomic relative of the trustafarian."

"I don't know what that is, either," I said.

"Never mind."

"I probably should have told you this before," Robbie said to Claire, "but the Crisco goes down there. You know, with the rest of the oils."

"For Pete's sake," Claire said, looking up at the dozen tubs of lard she'd already hoisted to the top shelf.

Robbie rose from the stack of soda syrup boxes he'd been sitting on. "It's my fault," he said. "I'll take them down."

"Sounds fair," Claire said. "And while you're doing that, I need to find some more mother's little helper. Is there a liquor store nearby?"

"I don't drink," Robbie said, lifting a tub of Crisco in each hand and moving them to the bottom shelf on the opposite wall.

"That doesn't answer my question," Claire said.

"I don't think Raylene wants you to leave," Robbie said.

Claire put her hands on her hips. "I'll be fine. Where's the liquor store, Robbie?"

After a moment's deliberation, Robbie decided his fear of a present Claire trumped his fear of an absent Raylene. "Go out the service door. Fifty-four feet, take a left. Six hundred thirty-two feet, take a right. Three hundred eighteen feet, there's a Sigel's at the four-way stop."

"How the heck am I supposed to count out feet?" Claire said.

Robbie looked her up and down. "You're five feet one, and your legs are five eighths of your body length. Which means your stride should be about 24.1 inches. Round down, if you like, to make it simple. Two feet per step."

"How do you know all that just from looking at her?" I asked.

"I can measure distances with my brain," Robbie said. "It's how I get around."

"Really," I said.

"Really," Robbie said.

"And you've always been able to do this?"

"Long as anyone can remember," Robbie said.

"Were you ever diagnosed with any autism spectrum disorder?" I asked. "Asperger's, maybe?"

"Nope," Robbie said.

"You boys carry on," Claire said. "I'm going to find this liquor store."

With Claire gone and Robbie and me trying to determine what neurodevelopmental tic enabled him to accurately measure distances by eye, work in dry storage came to a halt. Empty boxes lay strewn about, waiting to be broken down and deposited in the recycling Dumpster; still others sat unopened on the tile floor. This disarray, however, was not what upset Raylene when she came back to check on our progress.

"Where did she go?" Raylene asked.

"To the liquor store on Twelfth Street," Robbie told her.

"Jesus Christ, Robbie," Raylene said.

"She told me she'd be okay."

"She'll likely go unnoticed," I concurred. "I'm the one people are angry with."

Raylene rubbed her temples with the thumb and forefinger of one hand. "I hope you're right," she said.

"I have to say," I told Raylene, "I'm surprised, given everything, that you're at all concerned with our safety."

Raylene peered at me. "You really don't understand what they would do to you if they had the chance, do you?"

"I guess not," I said.

"I mean, don't get sentimental, mister,"

Raylene said. "I'm not your friend. But I'm not a monster, either. I don't need to see you hanging from an oak tree."

"They still hang people down here?" I asked.

"Not often. But they keep the rope handy for special occasions." Raylene gazed around at the mess we'd made of the dry storage room. "How long she been gone, anyway?" she asked.

"Half an hour, give or take," I said.

"Thirty-eight minutes," Robbie said.

"That's a ten-minute walk," Raylene said. "Even with the crowd, she should be back by now."

"You can do that with time, too?" I asked Robbie.

"Yep," Robbie said.

"I'm going to look for her," Raylene said. "You two finish with the shipment and clean up in here."

"Okay," Robbie said.

"Okay," I said.

In my pocket, my phone began to vibrate again. I pulled it out.

"Wait one minute," I said to Raylene.

She turned. "What is it?" she asked.

"Claire's calling."

I put the phone to my ear. "Raylene is worried," I said. "She's getting ready to come looking for you."

"No need," Claire said. "I'm at the service door. Back entrance. Whatever you call it."

"She's apparently right out there," I said to Raylene, pointing at the door across the hallway from the dry storage area.

"Thank goodness," Raylene said. She went to the door and pushed the handle, whereupon we discovered that Claire had neglected to mention that she wasn't alone. She stood flanked by three men with a decided uniformity about them — ratty Van Dykes, skin the color of boiled ham, short-sleeved plaid shirts. Together they formed a sort of East Texan Cerberus. For her part, Claire appeared too drunk and irritable to be frightened.

"You," one of the men said, pointing at me. "Let's go."

"What happened?" I asked Claire.

"I said let's go," the man repeated.

Raylene pulled a phone from her pocket, dialed a very short number, and put the phone to her ear.

"What are you doing?" the same man, evidently the leader of the trio, asked her.

"Calling the police," she said.

"Hang up the phone," the man ordered.

"Shoot me." Raylene turned away and stuck a finger in her free ear to block out noise from the parade at the end of the alley.

Apparently our abductors were unwilling to go so far as to call Raylene's bluff. Instead, they grabbed me by the upper arms, one to a side, and repeated that it was time for us to leave.

I was not inclined to resist, so off we went, walking briskly up the alley toward the crowds. I looked back once and saw Robbie watching us from the doorway. He raised a hand. I returned his wave, receiving a jab in the back from the barrel of an AR15 for my trouble. Then we turned the corner, and Robbie and Raylene and the Diner's Delight were gone.

We headed north on Houston. I could feel now, out in the midst of the celebration instead of merely observing it through plate glass like a visitor to the zoo, that the crowd had entered a collective fugue state, a trance of patriotism, regionalism, and tribalism, fidelities like nesting dolls. These people were Americans, they were Texans, they were free men prepared to defend their perceived liberty with violence, and they had gathered today to celebrate these three things they held in common. For them, Memorial Day meant something other than just extra time off from work — which was, frankly, more than one could say for most of the liberals in the East Coast's urban centers, Claire's yupsters, who were waking up in tents on mountain ridges that morning, too engaged with conspicuous consumption to attend their local parade and spend an hour actually memorializing on Memorial Day. I knew this because Sarah and I lived among the yupsters, there in our grossly overpriced house on the hill, and when we attended the Memorial Day parade — which we did every year except the one in which she died — we saw very few of our neighbors among the crowd. The people who did attend the parades at home looked a lot like the people surrounding us there in Fort Worth — minus the guns. And it was this fact, rather than a lack of patriotism, that ultimately explained my neighbors' absence. They didn't go to parades for the same reason they didn't go to monster truck rallies or state fairs: because those events were filthy with people beneath their caste, people they did not understand, people they feared and disdained in equal measure.

Though being good progressives they'd sooner eat fifty boiled eggs than admit this, even to themselves.

In any event, despite my personal circumstances at the moment, I found beauty in the fellowship of those gathered for the parade and the rally to follow, even though this fellowship was precisely the same psychosocial phenomenon that inspired the Holocaust, radical Islam, and unwavering devotion to Apple products.

Claire, for her part, didn't seem to be discovering anything of beauty in our surroundings, but this likely had to do with her displeasure over being kidnapped at gunpoint, about which she was far less sanguine than I.

"Where are you assholes taking us?" she asked the men.

"Someone needs to teach you some manners, lady," their leader told her.

"I'm pretty sure," Claire said, "that when a man says someone should teach a woman manners, what he actually means is someone should kick her ass and rape her."

"Don't give me any ideas," the man said.

"I'll ask again: where are we going?"

"That's for us to know."

"Fine," Claire said. She came to a dead stop on the sidewalk. "I'm going to start screaming bloody murder. What'll you do then?"

"Murder you," the man said, matter-of-fact.

"The hell," Claire said.

"Look around, lady," he said. "There are a hundred people who could put two in your chest and one in your head right now. You happen to end up shot, no one's going to know who did it."

"He's got a point," I said to Claire.

"Now get moving," the man said. He poked Claire in the spine with his rifle barrel.

We trudged through the heat and noise. After some time we reached the end of the parade route, and the crowd gave way. Old vets, marching band members, and little girls in dance leotards milled about the street, directionless now that their portion of the parade had come to an end. We weaved our way through the dissipating mass until we arrived at a Honda CR-V parked a block farther north. A man not at all dissimilar in appearance to the three men who'd kidnapped us sat at the wheel.

"That's your getaway vehicle?" I asked.

"What about it?" the leader of the group said.

"Well," I said, "for starters, it's a Honda."

"What's wrong with Hondas?" he asked.

"Nothing's wrong with Hondas," I said. "I just would have expected a cargo van, or a pickup truck. Something made in the U.S.A., in any event."

"Don't stereotype," the man said. "Gas is just as expensive down here as it is up in Priusland, smart guy."

Perhaps coincidentally, perhaps not, this was when they slipped a hood over my head.

"Kidnapped," I repeated into my phone.

"How's that, now?" Theodore asked. "This connection is terrible, my dear. Where on Earth are you?"

"I don't know," I told him. "They put hoods on us so we couldn't see where we were going. Actually, my hood turned out to be an empty family-size potato chip bag."

"What are you talking about, my dear?" Theodore asked. "Why would someone put a potato chip bag over your head?"

"Well I think they would have used a proper hood, except they weren't planning to kidnap anyone," I told him. "They seemed fairly ill-prepared. Aside from the guns."

There was a pause on Theodore's end. "Did you say 'kidnap'?" he asked finally.

"Yes," I said. "That's what I'm trying to tell you. We've been kidnapped."

"You and Claire both," Theodore said.

"Correct."

He absorbed this for a moment, then began to sputter and hack. "People warned me: Don't hire Russians, they said. Unreliable, immoral creatures, they said. But I didn't listen. And now this! Those cowardly fucks!"

"It's alright," I said. "We all have to learn the hard way, sometimes."

"But how are you calling me?" Theodore asked. "Did you escape? Did you keister your phone so you could use it in a stolen moment?"

"Keister?" I asked.

"It's a technique used by drug mules and convicts to hide contraband, my dear."

"You mean did I put the phone in my rectum," I said.

"Yes."

"I did not put the phone in my rectum," I told him. "They wanted me to call."

"You're breaking up again," Theodore said, employing that slow, loud diction people use when speaking to foreigners or the deaf, despite the fact that it does nothing to help foreigners or the deaf understand any better.

"I said they wanted me to call," I told him again.

"Who are 'they,' exactly?"

"Cold Dead Fingers Texas."

"I believe," Theodore said, "that part of the problem we're having is a bad connection, and the other part is that when I *can* hear you, I have no earthly clue what you're talking about."

" 'You can have my gun when you pry it from my cold, dead fingers'?" I said.

"I thought it was 'cold, dead hands,' " Theodore said.

"So did I," I told him. "The gentlemen here explained that misinterpretation is due to Charlton Heston mangling the source quote when he was president of the NRA. The original phrasing is 'cold, dead fingers,' I am assured."

"So what are we dealing with? A Southern fried Weather Underground?"

"They're a gun club," I said. "With ambitions to be much more, evidently. There may be a martyrdom reflex at work. I think they see themselves as the Branch Davidians of the gun rights movement."

"Goodness."

"Although given how heavily they were armed, one could say the Branch Davidians were the Branch Davidians of the gun rights movement."

"I see," said Theodore. "So these Cold Dead Fingers fellows are interested in making a name for themselves outside the provincial backwater that spawned them."

"It would appear so."

"And they intend to use us to achieve that end."

"Again, appears to be the case," I said.

Theodore sighed. "What are they asking for?"

"Nothing, actually. Except that you contact the federal authorities and let them know what's happening."

"The federal authorities?"

"They were explicit about that," I said. "Actually, they asked to convey a very specific message to some very specific people. They want you to tell the FBI that they're in possession of more than three hundred weapons that have either been illegally obtained, or modified in a manner that makes them illegal to possess."

"Let me write this down," Theodore said.

"And they said to let the FBI know that this is both a statement of fact, and a warning."

After a minute or so Theodore read what he'd written back to me. I confirmed that he had it verbatim.

We were quiet for a moment. Then Theodore spoke. "God in heaven," he said. "These fellows are spoiling for a Second Amendment showdown."

"Second Amendment," I said. "States' rights. Probably some border control frus-

tration wrapped up in vague white suprem-
acist notions, for good measure."

"My dear," Theodore said, "we have to
get you out of there."

"That's what Claire keeps saying. But I
think getting word to the FBI is probably
the first priority."

"Well yes," Theodore said, "but we need
to have some sort of *plan,* do we not?"

"I'm not sure what plan we can come up
with that won't include law enforcement," I
said. "It's hard to know for certain, but
they've got probably a hundred armed men
here, Theodore."

"Sweet and sour Jesus."

"Also, they said if they don't hear from
federal officials within an hour of this phone
call, they're going to shoot one of us."

"Do you think they mean it?"

"I'm not sure if they know whether they
mean it," I said. "They don't seem to be the
best-organized bunch, and it's clear this
whole situation is spontaneous and thus sort
of volatile. I mean, consider the fact that
they put hoods on us so we couldn't see
where we were going, but pretty much the
moment we got here they wanted to call the
feds and give them the latitude and longi-
tude."

"Also that the hood was actually an empty

potato chip bag," Theodore said.

"So probably best to just do what they're asking, for now. Unless you can find a lot more Russians to hire in a very short time frame."

"Please, my dear," Theodore said, "don't joke about that. I feel awful enough as it is."

"I wasn't joking," I said.

The guard who'd been assigned to me came back into the room, rifle slung across his chest, eyebrows raised.

"Just about finished," I said to him.

He twirled an index finger through the air in front of him: *Wrap it up.*

"Theodore, I have to go," I said.

"Is everything alright?"

"It's fine," I said. "I'm just being told it's time to end the call."

"When will I talk to you next?"

"I'm not sure," I said. "I doubt they'll be giving me my phone again anytime soon, now that I've done what they wanted."

"Well I'm coming down there, my dear," Theodore said.

"You can if you like. Though I'm not sure what it will avail anyone."

"Oh, it will avail," Theodore said. "I'll walk right in the front door if I have to."

"Theodore," I said.

"Yes," he said.

"This is, without question, a bad situation," I told him. "I'm not sure it would be improved if they had three hostages instead of two."

There was a pause.

"I mean, just logically speaking," I added.

"My dear," Theodore said, "I will be there soon."

He hung up. I held the phone out to the guard, and he took it with a swipe of his hand. "Let's go," he said. "Got someone wants to see you."

20

The Inheritor of the Spirit of Davy Crockett, or Who the Fuck Ever

I probably shouldn't have been surprised, given Cold Dead Fingers' raison d'être, but for a property that was otherwise a crumbling frontier-era ranch, they had a remarkably large and very modern indoor gun range, complete with a dozen shooting booths, adjustable-speed target carriage systems, light fixtures capable of simulating any time of day or weather condition, and remarkably effective central air-conditioning.

"Crowdfunded," I was told by Abraham Trumbull, the man who'd wanted to see me. "This is a two-million-dollar facility. Raised the money in less than a month."

"That's impressive?" I asked. "I confess I don't know much about crowdfunding."

Trumbull stood six and a half feet tall, his chest and shoulders I-beam thick, a fact evident even through the brown duster he wore in the meat-locker cold of the firing

380

range. The Desert Eagle he held, one of those large-caliber pistols sometimes referred to colloquially as a hand cannon, looked no bigger than a derringer in his grip. He loaded a fresh magazine into the weapon and motioned to a set of olive drab earmuffs resting on the shelf in front of us. "You're going to want to put those on," he said. "This thing goes boom, for real."

As I fiddled with the earmuffs, trying to find a comfortable fit, Trumbull explained the larger context of crowdfunding. "There've been projects that raised a couple million in just a day," he said. "Movies and video games, usually. But two million for a private firing range? Yes, that is impressive. Then again, this *is* Texas."

I finished adjusting the earmuffs and put my hands in my pockets.

"You ready?" Trumbull asked. He chambered a round.

"I think I'm all set, yes," I told him.

Trumbull checked the safety and turned the gun around so the butt faced me. "There you go," he said.

"I thought you were practicing, or whatever those knowledgeable in such things call it," I said.

"Usually just 'shooting,' " Trumbull said, still holding the Desert Eagle out to me.

"You want me to fire that?" I asked.

"Sure," he said.

"How do you know I won't use it on you?" I asked.

Trumbull smiled. "I'm pretty good at reading people," he said. "Besides, if you even started turning the barrel in my direction, I'd break your hand so fast you'd forget to say 'ouch.' "

I took the pistol. It was precisely as heavy as it appeared.

Trumbull stepped to the side of the shooting booth. "That's a fifty cal. Six in the clip, one in the chamber. It's accurate to about one hundred fifty meters, but we'll start you at twenty. Try not to point that anywhere but downrange, please. Unless you want to shoot your foot clean off. In which case, keep doing what you're doing now."

I didn't realize I'd let the gun drop to my side. Now I lifted it and, as instructed, pointed it down the alley toward the target.

"Never fired a gun before, I take it," Trumbull said.

"Is it that obvious?" I asked.

Trumbull stepped in and adjusted my hands, using one foot to widen my stance. "Safety off," he said. "Keep your finger outside the trigger guard until you're ready to shoot. Line up the front and back sights on your target. Try to avoid closing your eyes when you fire."

"Sort of a dizzying amount of instructions," I said.

"We're not just popping off rounds," Trumbull said. "This is an art."

"Okay," I said. It felt like I was holding a bowling ball at arm's length. The muscles in my shoulders began to sing.

"It's impossible to focus on both the sights and the target at the same time," Trumbull said. "So you want to keep the sights sharp in your vision, and let the target go a little fuzzy."

"Got it," I said.

Trumbull stepped away. "Keep the wrist on your strong hand locked. Otherwise you'll end up with a broken nose."

"And my strong hand is my right hand," I said.

"Correct."

"Okay," I said, not at all certain that my wrist was locked in the way Trumbull wanted.

"Here's the important part," Trumbull said. "Make damn sure you're ready to kill whatever you're aiming at."

"I have to do that with a paper target?" I asked.

"It's a good idea to practice the mind-set."

As instructed, I let the target — a life-size cartoon of a police officer in blue patrol uniform — go fuzzy. I lined up the front and back sights repeatedly, but the weight of the pistol made keeping them aligned near impossible; it didn't take long to realize that if I waited for my aim to become and remain perfectly true, I would never fire a round. So, thinking of Peggy's fondness for the phrase "Can't see it from my house" whenever she'd decided something could not or need not be flawless, I let my finger slide in against the trigger and fired.

The barrel of the gun flipped up like a gymnast performing a back handspring, the front sight slicing my cheek as cleanly as a razor. I tumbled backward out of the shooting booth. A few seconds later, having recovered my senses, I was surprised to realize that I'd somehow managed to hold on to the gun.

Trumbull leaned out of the booth and looked down at me, the corners of his mouth twitching, like an improv actor trying not to break character. "Congratulations," he said. "You just scored a kill shot on the ceiling."

"That was unexpected," I said.

Trumbull extended a hand. "You want to try again?" he asked.

"I guess so," I said, rising to my feet with his help.

After using a handkerchief proffered by Trumbull to clean my cheek, I hoisted the Desert Eagle again, this time with a much clearer sense of what Trumbull meant by a locked wrist. I emptied all seven rounds in the clip and managed to hit the cartoon police officer twice without concussing myself in the process.

"How's that feel?" Trumbull asked. He took the pistol from me, removed the clip, and gave the slide a brisk pull.

"Interesting," I told him. "Also physically invigorating in a way I never would have anticipated."

Trumbull smiled, which turned out to be a low-wattage affair despite his large, square, and freakishly white teeth. "Well especially with the Desert Eagle. It's a workout just holding that piece, let alone firing it. But you realize what you're feeling, right? The reason you're flushed and out of breath? Pupils dilated? Maybe a slight, tingly stirring in the groin?"

"I'm not feeling anything in my groin," I said.

"All the same," Trumbull said.

"I didn't realize there was going to be a quiz afterward," I said.

"It's because for the first time in your life, you've satisfied one of man's most primeval needs," Trumbull said.

"That being."

"To hold the power to kill in your hands."

I looked downrange at the paper policeman. "Okay," I said.

Trumbull plugged fresh rounds into the clip with his thumb. "Among the most essential experiences a human being can have," he said. "On a level with sex."

"Okay," I said.

"I can see you're skeptical," Trumbull said. He hit a switch on the wall, and the target slid toward us with the spooky smoothness of a mechanical rabbit at a dog track. "Let me explain it to you this way. You know how people on your end of the political spectrum are always extolling the virtues of Native Americans?"

"I don't have an end of the political spectrum," I said.

"In any event, liberals and progressives," Trumbull went on. "They view Natives as some kind of saintly race. Appropriate their cultural and spiritual practices, while the people themselves are left to rot on the shittiest tracts of land in the country."

"That's probably a fair assessment," I said.

"Do you know what a scalp lock is?"

"I'm afraid not."

Trumbull slapped the magazine into the Desert Eagle and chambered a round. "Actually, you probably know what a scalp lock is, but just haven't heard the term. Any number of traditional Native haircuts qualify. The Mohawk, for example, is a scalp lock. As is a top knot."

"Well sure," I said. "I know what those are."

Trumbull placed the pistol on a counter and loaded a fresh target into the holder. He hit the switch again, and watched as the target slid downrange.

"Some people would tell you that the purpose of the scalp lock, as its name implies, was to make scalping the wearer more difficult," Trumbull said, keeping his eyes on the retreating target as he spoke. "But talk to some true elders, if you can find them, and they'll tell you what they told me: if you wore a scalp lock, it was to make scalping you *easier.*"

"It's hard to understand why one would want to do that," I said.

By now the target had reached the end of the range — fifty meters distant, according to the digital display on the wall next to the switch.

"That seems a lot farther than fifty meters," I said.

Trumbull squared up and raised the pistol. "That's because you're used to just looking at things," he said. "Not trying to shoot them."

The Desert Eagle erupted, thunderous reports coming in startlingly quick succession, seven rounds in less than three seconds. When Trumbull had finished, he secured the weapon and placed his earmuffs on the counter, hitting the switch to bring the target back to us.

"Whatever the purpose of the scalp lock," he said, "its very existence indicates that Natives — those saintly people — believed violence was natural and inevitable. They expected it. They prepared for it. They sought it out."

"Sure," I said. "That's fairly well documented."

"And willfully ignored," Trumbull said. "Because for liberals to acknowledge this inconvenient fact would be to admit that the people they revere and the people they revile are not all that different."

"Just so I'm clear," I said, "the people they revile are people like you?"

"Correct."

The target finished its journey back, and in the absence of the carriage's whirring the firing range swelled with a peculiar hollow silence. Trumbull reached out with one hand and ripped the target down to inspect it. He was, not surprisingly, an exceptional shot: at half the length of a football field, he'd put three rounds through the policeman's hat and four in his chest.

"Something I meant to ask," I said to him.

"Go ahead," he said, still admiring his marksmanship.

"Why do your targets feature policemen instead of the more traditional 'generic armed bad guy' motif?"

Trumbull let the target fall to his side and fixed me with a gaze. "Now who ever told you the police were the good guys?" he asked.

The entrance to the firing range opened, nearly blinding me with a column of sunlight, though I was able to make out the silhouette of a man as he stepped into the doorway.

"Frank just showed up," this man told Trumbull.

Trumbull stared silently for a moment, then said, "So send him in."

■ ■ ■ ■

Frank, it turned out, was a police officer. Despite this, he was considered one of the good guys, for two reasons: first, because Trumbull believed county sheriffs were the only legitimate law enforcement in the country, and second, because in addition to being sheriff, Frank was also a member in good standing of Cold Dead Fingers. This latter fact was at the moment something of a problem, however, since Frank, being a sworn officer of the law, was understandably upset that an organization to which he'd paid dues for twenty years had committed a double kidnapping.

"For Christ's sake, Abe," Frank said, pacing around the back of the firing range and gesticulating wildly as he talked, "do you know what we're talking about here? We're talking Alcohol, Tobacco, and Firearms, man. We're talking the ever-loving Eff. Bee. Eye."

"That's the whole idea, Frank," Trumbull said.

"I can't do *nothing* about this," Frank said. "This is federal all the way."

"You can do something," Trumbull told him. "You can stand with us and wait for them to show up."

"I mean, what were you even thinking?" Frank asked.

"Or you could arrest me and save your bacon," Trumbull suggested. "I recognize your authority to do so, as sheriff. Though of course as a human being, and a free man, I would lose respect for you entirely."

"No one's arresting you, Abe, Chrissake," Frank said. He removed his cap and mopped at his pate with a yellowed handkerchief, then pointed at me. "This him?"

Trumbull nodded.

"And the two of you are just hanging out here in the gun range," Frank said. He put his cap back on and adjusted it with shaky hands. "Real casual like."

"He's an agreeable sort," Trumbull said.

"Shit, if he's so agreeable, why not give him a gun, let him take some target practice, while you're at it?"

"Already did," Trumbull said.

Frank looked at me, incredulous. I nodded with what I hoped was an apologetic expression.

"You listen to me, Abe," Frank said. He turned back to Trumbull and reached up to put a hand on his shoulder, more supplication than demand. "There is no way to completely unfuck this situation. They're coming, and they know you have the guns. But you can still half-unfuck it."

"Let's say for sake of argument that I had an interest in, to use your quite colorful term, *unfucking* the situation," Trumbull said. "How would you suggest I do that?"

"Simple," Frank said. "Let him and the girl go. Now. Before anyone gets hurt."

Trumbull shook his head.

"Abe, I'm telling you," Frank said. "You think you're in control of this. But you're not. It will get out of control very quickly. Like, *Waco* out of control."

"You know," I said, "I made more or less the same analogy. Though it's sort of an obvious one, really. Texas. Guns. Fervent adherence to an ideology the rest of society considers borderline insane."

"Shut up," Frank said, pointing a finger at me. "You, buddy, are seen and not fucking heard, right at the moment."

"Frank," Trumbull said, "please don't be rude to my guest."

Frank looked at him. "Your guest?" he said. "Your *guest*?"

"That's what I said."

"Don't be rude to him? Oh, please forgive me." Frank started up again with the pacing. "You know what else might be considered *rude,* Abe? Kidnapping someone. A sensible man might think that's somewhat *rude*, too."

"Except I didn't kidnap him," Trumbull said. "That was a spur-of-the-moment act committed by others in the organization."

Frank held his hands out to his sides, palms up. "All the more reason to let them go, then," he said.

Trumbull sighed, leaned back against an ammunition shelf, and made a show of excavating something from under one of his fingernails. "You know, Frank," he said, "for years we've satisfied ourselves with refusing to file tax returns, and not much else. You've been firing rounds and running your mouth along with the rest of us. Now it's time. Now we'll see if you meant what you said. If you did, then stay here. If you didn't — if you are in fact a cheese-eating rat fuck coward — then get back out there and play lawman."

Frank stared, his expression caught somewhere between terror and impotent rage.

"Your choice," Trumbull said, still picking at his fingernail. "Make it now."

"Okay," Frank said. "Okay, so let's say I do stay here with you. What do you think is going to happen?"

"War," Trumbull said.

"War." Frank snorted. "Seems a little . . .

what's the word?"

"Grandiose?" I offered.

"That's it," Frank said.

"Frank, there are over one hundred people in this compound," Trumbull said, "all of whom qualify as expert marksmen. They're well armed, dug in, motivated. When those government boys show up they're going to see the size of the problem they're dealing with and realize they'll need an infantry battalion to clear us out of here. That's a fight they're not going to want."

"Exactly," said Frank.

"If it were just the guns, they'd try to figure a way to avoid that fight," Trumbull continued. "With two hostages, they won't have any choice but to come in sooner or later."

"And they'll kill all of you," Frank said.

"No matter," Trumbull told him. "Did you know, Frank, that as we speak there are more than half a million militiamen and sovereign citizens in this country?"

"So?"

"So that's a very big army, by any standard," Trumbull said. "As big, in fact, as the army of these United States. We die on CNN, and that army is suddenly mobilized."

Frank looked at Trumbull, then to me,

then back to Trumbull.

"You're out of your goddamn mind," he said.

Not surprisingly, Frank decided against standing with Trumbull and his men, opting instead to sit outside the compound in the air-conditioned comfort of his patrol car, flanked by half a dozen deputies, to give federal officials the impression that he was a man dedicated to the letter of the law.

And surely Frank must have thought he'd made the correct choice when, several hours later, the federal officials arrived with a scale of force I had never seen except in news footage from far-off battlefields. As this was prairie country, the compound's main building enjoyed an unobstructed view of both the driveway and the main road that led to it. This allowed us — by which I mean Trumbull, Claire, and me, standing at the window of an upstairs room that served as Trumbull's study — to see the entirety of the FBI convoy as it arrived: forty or so Humvees and Bradley Fighting Vehicles, a quarter-mile-long column led by two Black Hawk helicopters that shot ahead and began buzzing Trumbull's ranch the moment they came into sight.

Diesel engines growled and roared as the

convoy turned right onto the long dirt driveway. Reddish-brown plumes of dust rose from knobby tires, coalescing into a cloud thick enough to blunt the remarkable fury of the Texas sun. Nearly every Humvee was capped with a turret, from which protruded the gleaming snouts of machine guns and grenade launchers. The Bradleys, armored behemoths seething with chain guns and antitank missiles, chewed up gravel in their heavy tracks. As the vehicles drew nearer, the floor under our feet began to tremble, minutely but unmistakably, as if at the approach of some movie monster. The overall effect, as the convoy reached the terminus of the driveway and deployed around the property, was decidedly apocalyptic — and no one had yet fired a shot.

Claire's hand found mine and clutched it. "Jesus Christ," she said. "I am way too sober for this."

"Perhaps if you asked them nicely," I said, "our hosts might be willing to give you a drink."

"I don't see why we couldn't," Trumbull said, still gazing out the window. Even he sounded a bit awed.

"If these people are here to save us," Claire asked, "why do I feel a lot more scared than I did a few minutes ago?"

"Because you're starting to understand who the real terrorists are," Trumbull said.

"I mean, for God's sake," Claire said. "It looks like Fallujah out there."

"In fairness," I said to Trumbull, "you did inform them that you're in possession of an arsenal."

Trumbull raised his eyebrows and tilted his head slightly to the side, half an assent. "Valid point," he said. "But their response, as you see, is always to increase force twentyfold. It's been unofficial policy since Sherman torched Atlanta."

Below, Frank got out of his car and shook the hand of a tall man wearing a business suit and a Kevlar vest marked "FBI."

"That's right, Frank," Trumbull said. "Kiss the ring, old pal."

We watched as Frank and the agent conferred amidst the choreographed chaos of armored vehicles taking up tactical positions.

"So now what?" Claire asked.

"Now I'm hungry," Trumbull said. He checked his wristwatch. "Anybody else hungry?"

"Um," Claire said.

Trumbull moved toward the door. "Got a nice fatty brisket going," he said. "Come on."

Claire looked at me. "This is by far the strangest kidnapping I've ever been a part of," she said.

"You've been kidnapped before?" I asked.

"It was a college thing," she said. "Sort of consensual."

Trumbull stopped in the doorway and looked back at us. "A good brisket takes twenty-two hours to cook. Nothing gets in the way of dinnertime when it's finally ready."

On our way down the stairs we were met by one of Trumbull's men, a wide-eyed and breathless fellow whose state of distress was hardly surprising, given the circumstances.

"Guys are talkin' about leavin'," the man said. He bent at the waist with his hands on his knees, trying to catch his wind.

"Already?" Trumbull asked.

"You did see what's out there, Abe?" the man said.

"Sure. What's out there is exactly what I expected. And what you and everyone else should have expected, too."

The man stood up straight and brushed a sweaty strand of hair away from his face. "Abe, you know I'm with you. But these other fellas. Tracy. Bob C. Ray Ray. The Childress boys."

"All six of them?" Trumbull asked.

"All six of them," the man confirmed.

"I knew his brothers were useless, but I thought Al would stay the course," Trumbull said. He crossed his arms over his chest and thought a moment. "Let them go," he said finally. "Anyone who doesn't have the stomach for this is dead weight anyway."

"So we're just going to watch them walk out the front door?"

"What else can we do?" Trumbull asked.

The man considered, stared at Trumbull for a second, and shrugged.

"Tell whoever wants to leave that they're free to go," Trumbull said. "Tell the rest that I'm having a bite, then we'll discuss the plan one more time."

"You've got a plan?"

Trumbull put a hand on the man's shoulder and spoke to him as a father to a son. "Listen to me. Nothing has changed," he said. "This is exactly what we wanted. So take a breath."

The man set his jaw. "Okay," he said.

"Good. G'on now."

The man turned and began descending the stairs two at a time.

"Oh, and Gus," Trumbull said.

"Yeah?"

"No one talks to them," Trumbull said. "The phones are going to ring off the hook, and they'll get the loudspeaker out presently. But no one talks. No matter what."

21
THE DETAILS OF THE PLAN

"I want to be perfectly forthright with you," Trumbull said over plates of brisket and potato salad. "Because I think of you as guests, not hostages."

"You mentioned that earlier," I said. "Quite gracious, considering."

"Guests," Claire said, "can come and go as they please."

The compound's dining room, a dark and dusty affair, sat in the center of the main building and was, as a consequence, windowless. Decorations consisted of taxidermy of varying quality — elk heads mounted on walls and over doorways, prairie dogs perched on shelves, a coyote, one front paw cocked, next to the doorway to the kitchen. The light fixture, hanging above the oak table at which we sat, was constructed from red deer antlers, their gnarled spread resembling the root system of a tree.

Outside, the concussive slap of helicopter

rotors waxed and waned, waxed and waned.

"This is exquisite," I said through a mouthful of beef.

Trumbull smiled and leaned back in his chair. "Come to Jesus," he said. "Prepped, cooked, and sliced by yours truly. My granddaddy's rub recipe." He turned to Claire. "Sure you don't want any? You have no idea what you're missing."

Claire eyeballed Trumbull wearily. "I'm fine, thanks," she said.

"Suit yourself." Trumbull cut through a piece of beef with one swipe of his knife, a pearl-handled bowie he'd produced from the weathered sheath on his hip. "Want to know an interesting fact about brisket?" he asked me.

"I always want to know facts," I told him.

"Brisket is a very tough cut of meat," Trumbull said. "Basically it's a steer's pectoral muscle. Gets a lot of work over the course of its life. So anything you can do to minimize the toughness is critical. Especially if you cook in competitions, which both my daddy and granddaddy did."

Trumbull popped a piece of meat into his mouth, closed his eyes, and chewed exultantly. The helicopters buzzed and buzzed.

After a moment Trumbull swallowed and opened his eyes again. "My granddaddy was a wildcatter," he said, "so he spent a lot of time outdoors with herds. One day he was eating lunch and watching a bunch of steer, and it dawned on him: they almost always lie down on their right sides. Which means every time they get up, their right leg has to work a little bit harder to get them standing. The way he figured it, that meant the right brisket would usually be tougher than the left. From that day on, he never cooked a right brisket again."

"Fascinating stuff," Claire said.

"Was he correct?" I asked.

Trumbull thrust his fork in my direction. "Excellent question," he said, "and there's two ways to answer it. The first is to tell you that over the next eighteen years my granddaddy won the Lone Star State Finals four times, and never placed lower than sixth. We're talking a couple hundred of the best brisket cooks in Texas."

"Anecdotal," I said, "but still pretty impressive."

"And that leads to the second answer, if empirical evidence is what you're after: the next time you come across a herd, have a look for yourself. I guarantee all but a few will be lying on their right sides."

"It seems doubtful," Claire said, "that we're ever going to have a chance to observe cows at rest again."

Trumbull looked over at her. "You want a beer?" he asked. "I'm gonna get myself one."

"I told you I was fine," Claire said, her tone flat as fettuccine.

Trumbull rose and went into the kitchen.

"I don't think I've ever seen you turn down a drink," I said to Claire.

She was staring up at the macabre spectacle of the deer antler chandelier, and responded without looking at me. "As my mother liked to say," she said, "miracles never cease."

Trumbull returned with a Corona almost completely obscured in his massive fist. "When this is over you will have a chance to observe bovine behavior again," he said as he took his seat. "You will have a chance to eat Thai takeout and go to the movies and do the twist and anything else you like."

"None of that's going to happen," Claire said. "Here's what is going to happen: we are going to die some serious Old Testament deaths. And that will be that."

Trumbull forked brisket into his mouth. "Maybe," he said. "Maybe not."

"I saw what's out there," Claire said, "and I see that you are out of your mind."

" 'Conviction is worthless,' " Trumbull said, " 'unless converted into conduct.' "

"Who is that?" I asked.

"Thomas Carlyle," Trumbull said. "A man, like me, of Highland Scot stock."

" 'I would never die for my beliefs, because they might be wrong,' " Claire said. "That's Bertrand motherfucking Russell."

Trumbull squinted at her across the table, his expression taut and dangerous. Then his face opened up, and he chuckled. "I never much cared for Russell," he said. "A little too prim."

"Philosophers can be that way," Claire said.

"Let me ask you something," Trumbull said. "Do you think the 9/11 hijackers were crazy?"

"Is this a trick question?" Claire said.

"Not in the least."

"Okay then," Claire said. "I think 'crazy' doesn't begin to describe the batshit depravity of flying a jetliner into a building full of people."

Trumbull turned to me. "What about you?" he asked.

"I'm not very useful with that kind of value judgment."

"Ah. A *true* philosopher, this one," Trumbull said. He forked more brisket into his mouth and looked back and forth between us as he chewed. "Well? Aren't you going to ask what I think?"

"No," Claire said.

"What do you think?" I asked.

"I think," Trumbull said, "the 9/11 hijackers displayed a brand of courage so alien to our culture that we don't know what to call it, except 'crazy.' "

"They also murdered a whole bunch of people," Claire said.

"Don't misunderstand me," Trumbull said. "I hate everything they stood for. They served a misguided, juvenile faith in desperate need of reformation. But they were courageous, and they were sane. When I saw what they'd done, I knew I wanted to be just like them. To see with clear eyes, to act without flinching. That's how I ended up on three all-expenses-paid tours of Iraq."

"Please," Claire said. "You just wanted to shoot brown people and blow things up. Ideology had nothing to do with it. Don't try to put lipstick on that pig."

"When in your entire life have you displayed even a fraction of their courage?" Trumbull asked.

"Every day I showed up for work at Total Foods."

The two of them stared at each other. Claire folded her arms over her chest. It was clear she meant to go without blinking for however long she had to.

One of the helicopters swooped low above us. The deer antler chandelier trembled, and shadows waved across the walls. In the kitchen, plates and glasses chattered against one another in their cabinets.

Claire and Trumbull went on staring for several more moments despite the racket. Then, finally, Trumbull looked away. Claire rose from her seat and walked toward the kitchen.

"Is there something I can get for you?" Trumbull asked.

"I'm perfectly capable of fetching myself a glass of water," Claire said without looking back. She disappeared through the threshold.

Trumbull took a deep breath and tilted his head sharply to one side and then the other, making the vertebrae snap. At that moment a booming but garbled voice, like God talking around a mouthful of jawbreakers, spoke to us through the walls of the main building.

"Abraham Trumbull," the voice said. "This is special agent Roy Pinto with the FBI. We're trying to establish contact with you. Please answer the telephone."

Trumbull looked at me. "So it begins," he said.

From the kitchen came the sound of cupboards opening and closing.

Trumbull leaned back and turned his head toward the doorway. "Everything alright in there?" he asked.

"Fine," Claire called out.

Trumbull wiggled his eyebrows and hooked a thumb toward the kitchen, as if inviting me to share in a private joke. "Claire," he said, "I'm going to give you five seconds to rejoin us at the table."

The sounds of rummaging stopped abruptly. "Or else what?" Claire asked after a pause.

"Or else," Trumbull said, "you are going to learn the limits of my hospitality."

Silence from the kitchen.

"Why don't you come back in here, now," Trumbull said.

Claire drifted into the doorway like an apparition. She studied the back of Trumbull's head for a moment, then made her way slowly to her seat.

"For future reference, we keep the knives in the top drawer to the right of the refrigerator," Trumbull told her as she sat down again.

"I was looking for a glass," Claire said.

"You think you're the first woman ever wanted to slit my throat?" Trumbull asked

408

her. "You think I don't know what that looks like?"

Claire folded her arms again. "I have no idea," she said, "what you're talking about."

"Course you don't, darling," Trumbull said. "Course you don't."

"I'm going to need you to take off the glasses for this," Trumbull said to me after Claire had, at his request, left the dining room with an unsmiling escort.

"I think the battery died awhile ago," I told him.

"Even still," Trumbull said. He motioned with two fingers for me to hand them over.

I did as he asked. By this point I'd grown so accustomed to wearing the glasses every waking moment that I felt suddenly incomplete without them, as though I'd realized, in a most public place, that I'd forgotten to put on pants.

Trumbull turned the glasses over a few times, then took a lens in each hand and twisted, snapping the frames in two.

"Don't worry," he said. He placed the broken glasses on the table next to his empty plate. "The networks will record the important parts from here on out."

"I'm not worried," I told him.

"That's good," Trumbull said. He stood,

lifted both our plates from the table, and walked toward the kitchen. "I'm going to have a beer. You want one?"

"I guess so," I said.

A few moments later he returned with a pair of Coronas and set them down where our plates had been.

"Tell me," he said as he took his seat, "how do you want all this to turn out?"

I gripped the bottle and pulled it to me. "I'm not wedded to any particular outcome," I said.

"But you'd prefer to live through it, yes?"

"I don't think of life and death as mutually exclusive," I told him.

Trumbull's eyebrows bunched together. Outside, the FBI agent on the public address system promised that if Trumbull and his men came out they would be treated fairly.

"Are you going to talk with them?" I asked.

"Eventually," Trumbull said.

We looked at each other.

"I'm sorry," I said. "Maybe if you told me what you have planned, I could be more helpful."

Trumbull leaned forward with his elbows on the table. "Okay then," he said. "For a few days we're going to let the FBI cool their heels, so they understand that I'm in charge. Then we arrange a meeting."

"A meeting," I said.

"Which by then they'll be only too eager to agree on. They'll think they're getting somewhere, making progress toward a peaceable outcome."

"Okay," I said.

They're going to play this by the book," Trumbull said. "Quid pro quo all the way. So I'll ask for something — pizza delivery, lose the helicopters, whatever — and tell them if I get what I want, we'll hand you over."

"Right," I said.

"Except that when we meet for the exchange, instead of going with them, you're going to kill my good buddy Frank."

"The sheriff?"

"Correct."

"Kill him," I said.

"Well, you're going to shoot him," Trumbull said. "Of course I would prefer that, in doing so, you also kill him. But there's only so much we can control in this life. And you're not exactly a crack shot."

"Forgive me if this seems like a stupid question," I said, "but why would I shoot Frank?"

"Because he's a coward and a traitor,"

Frank said. "Also because if you don't, I'm going to kill Claire."

I was silent.

"This is happening," Trumbull said. "You should say something."

"You want to make a murderer of me," I said.

"I understand," Trumbull said, "that it's an upsetting prospect."

"I can tell you," I said, "that this is as close as I've been to what you would call 'upset' in a long time."

"Regrettable," Trumbull said, "but sadly, it can't be helped."

"I do have a couple of questions."

"Ask away."

"Why not shoot Frank yourself? You're much better with a gun than I am."

"A fact none would dispute," Trumbull said.

"Also, I have nothing against Frank, whereas you seem to harbor a great deal of animosity toward him."

Trumbull nodded. "It is true that I'd like nothing more than to usher him directly into the next life with my own hand."

"So why don't you?" I said.

"I can't."

"Why not?"

"Well for starters, he's my brother-in-law,"

Trumbull said. "A man doesn't just go around shooting family. Much as he might want to."

"Actually, a large percentage of murders are committed by people related to the victim," I said. "At least in America."

"This isn't America. This is Texas."

"So Frank is married to your sister?" I asked.

"That's correct," Trumbull said. "And though I don't much care for her either, she's still my blood."

"I guess I'll defer to you on this subject, seeing as how I never had a family."

"No?"

"I'm an orphan."

"I would say that's too bad, but the truth is in some ways you're probably better off. Family's a gigantic pain in the ass." Trumbull seemed to ponder this for a moment, then drained his beer at a pull and rose to go to the kitchen again. "You good?" he said over his shoulder.

I'd barely touched my Corona. "All set," I said.

A minute later Trumbull came back with a fresh beer for himself. "Talk about family," he said as he sat down. "My daddy installed a flagpole in our front yard the moment he got back from Vietnam. This was seven, eight years before I was born. Big thirty-footer, custom job. Bronzed aluminum. Put a hundred pounds of concrete in the ground to hold it in place. That pole stood up to a Cat four hurricane."

"He must have been quite patriotic," I said.

"Oh yes," Trumbull said. "Great patriot, my daddy. For thirty years he flew the Stars and Stripes over the POW/MIA banner. Every day. I could still recite for you United States Code, Title Four, Chapter One. Floodlights at night. Lanyard goes up the pole briskly, comes down slow and solemn. If the flag touches the ground, burn it and put up a new one. And I learned the hard way that when you fly a flag half-mast, you don't just run her halfway up and call it good. You run it all the way to the top, then bring it back down."

"Rules are rules," I said.

"You got that right, at least where my daddy was concerned," Trumbull said. "So anyway, I come home from my third tour of the sandbox, and I'm not feeling real chatty. My hitch is over, and I'm planning to just keep my head down for a few months, figure out what's next. He wants to talk, though. What's it like over there, he wants to know. I think he imagined it would be a way for us to bond, or some such. I'd talk about my war, he'd talk about his, we'd find some deep manly love for each other. But he was about twenty years late on the draw, as far as father-son bonding was concerned. And after a while I got tired of him asking. So one day I went out to the garage, grabbed the Skilsaw, ran an extension cord out to the front yard, and cut that flagpole down like a dead elm while my daddy watched.

" 'You wanna know what it was like,' " I said to him. 'That's what it was like.' "

"And how did your daddy react to that?" I asked.

Trumbull smiled. "Ten years earlier he would've given me a beating," he said. "Anyway, that's family for you."

I thought for a minute. "If I shoot Frank," I said, "won't the FBI become much less interested in a peaceable solution, as you put it?"

"I would certainly think so," Trumbull said.

"So the whole thing is tantamount to suicide," I said.

"No," Trumbull said, leaning forward in his chair. "Suicide's only aim is death. We don't have a word for what this is. Hindus refer to it as 'saka.' The Japanese, as you probably know, call it 'kamikaze.' "

"I'm sorry to quibble," I said, "but unless I completely misunderstand what you're asking me to do — and what is likely to happen pretty much right after I do it — this sounds a lot like suicide. I mean, for me at least."

"You seem less concerned about dying than about semantics."

"That should be obvious to anyone who's seen me on television," I said.

"Well listen, you'll be the only person out there without a sniper's reticle trained on your forehead. You'll have three, four seconds before anyone draws down on you. Which might be enough time for you to beat feet back to the building."

"Might be," I said.

"No guarantees," Trumbull said. "Twenty, thirty percent chance, probably."

"Again, I don't mean to be a noodge," I said, "but most people would think doing something that would result in your death eight out of ten times qualifies as suicidal."

Trumbull stared at me. "Fine," he said. "Since like most people you have faith in nothing, believe in nothing, and aspire to nothing besides the satisfaction of your own base desires, this will be suicide. For you. If you're killed."

"Okay," I said.

"Better?" Trumbull asked.

"Not really," I said. "Still grappling with the murder part."

"Take all the time you need," Trumbull said. He lifted his bottle, tapped it against mine, and drained it with three big swallows.

"You understand," I said to Claire, "the either/or nature of the situation."

"Considering that it's my life on the line, yeah, I get it, thanks."

We lay side by side in bed, both of us on our backs, staring up as floodlight beams played across the ceiling. Trumbull had arranged for us to occupy a room on the third floor of the main building. The upside of this was relative privacy, with two guards on the other side of the door in the hallway. The drawback was that we couldn't have been any closer to the thunderous rhythm of the helicopters. Each time they passed overhead the floor shook and the wrought iron bed frame squeaked beneath us. We listened to the Bradleys rumble around the perimeter, tilling prairie grass and spewing diesel smoke, while the agent on the public address system continued to promise a fair and impartial consideration of all grievances and demands.

"I guess I don't really know what to say to

you about this," I told Claire.

"Say you won't do it."

"Okay," I said. "I won't do it."

"Jesus Christ." Claire popped up out of bed. She stomped across the room in her stocking feet, threw open the door, and demanded a glass of water.

"You want something?" she asked me.

"I can't think of anything," I said, "that I might want."

Claire sent the guard on his way and closed the door again.

"I have to confess," I said, "that I don't understand why saying what you asked me to say is so upsetting."

"Because it doesn't mean anything," Claire said. She came back, sat on the edge of the mattress, and gazed out the window. "They're just words to you. I ask you to say them, and you say them."

"That's not true," I said. "I meant what I said. I won't do it."

Claire ignored this. "Also because if you had just listened to me — if anyone had just listened to me — this wouldn't be happening."

"Listened to you?"

"When I suggested it was maybe not a terrific idea to come to the goddamn Memorial Day parade in goddamn Fort Worth."

"Ah, that," I said.

"But you and Theodore were all gung ho. Didn't want to hear it."

"I don't know if 'gung ho' is really the way to describe my state of mind, at the time."

"Whatever. Theodore, then," Claire said. "And where is that fat bastard now? Sitting somewhere counting his money. Sipping one of those fruity drinks he likes so much."

"He told me," I said, "that he was on his way here."

"Likely story."

"I'm sorry," I said. "I'm sure Theodore is sorry as well. For what it's worth."

"It's not worth a whole lot right at the moment, K."

The bedroom door opened again, and the guard came in, placed a glass of water on the dresser, and left without a word.

Claire was quiet for a moment, still watching the FBI through the window. "What are we going to do?" she asked finally.

"We've only got a couple of options," I said.

"That was pretty much the definition of a rhetorical question," Claire said. She rose, went to the dresser, and came back with the water. "You can't shoot that cop, K. There's your one option: don't kill anybody."

"I'm surprised," I said, "that you're so concerned about the life of someone you've never met. Especially over your own."

"I'm not worried about his life. I'm worried about my soul."

"Meaning."

"Meaning what will happen to it if a bunch of people die because I couldn't go two hours without a drink."

I thought about this. "So you actually blame yourself. Not me or Theodore."

"Ding ding ding!" Claire said. "Bob, tell him what he's won! A luxurious all-inclusive stay at the Cold Dead Fingers resort and spa in East Bumfuck, Texas!"

"There's no need to be nasty," I said.

Claire sighed. "Oh, there's every need, my love," she said sadly.

22
THE REPETITIVE, REDUNDANT, MONOTONOUS SPLENDOR

Who knew armed insurrection could be so dull? Perhaps the defenders of the Alamo, who spent two cramped, sweaty weeks in the mission waiting for Santa Anna to make his move. But certainly not Trumbull's men — no students of history — who must have envisioned an immediate, cinematic clash with the FBI, both sides hurtling toward one another across a wide panorama, teeth bared and bayonets fixed. They envisioned, in other words, a movie, or a Revolutionary War reenactment — a fantasy at the conclusion of which they would rise and wash the fake blood off their clothes and return to the agreeable tedium of life in twenty-first-century America, the jobs selling lumber and balancing tires, the homes with the leaky rain gutters and hostile children, the eventual real deaths, ever distant, from the usual base indignities like stroke and heart failure.

It didn't take long, there in Trumbull's compound, for the lesson to sink in that it's one thing to imagine fighting for a cause, another thing entirely to endure terminal boredom for it. Ill behavior abounded. Sentries slept at their posts, and people took more food than they were rationed, munching furtively in bedrooms and closets. Toilets clogged, then overflowed. The hallways echoed with the sounds of bickering nearly around the clock, and two fistfights — one involving the loss of several teeth — occurred on the same afternoon.

Then the electricity was turned off.

The next four days passed according to Trumbull's plan, which is to say uneventfully. Helicopters circled, cell phones chirped, and the negotiator with the loudspeaker issued one overture after another. On day three the FBI parked a flatbed stacked with amplifiers just outside the main building, and at dusk began blasting Norwegian death metal, music that sounded not unlike a Cyclops screaming at the top of its lungs while operating a jackhammer.

The men of Cold Dead Fingers occupied their posts in twelve-hour shifts. Despite rapidly waning morale, Trumbull continued to ignore the FBI, instead conducting phone interviews with every major media outlet, save NPR, whose requests he shunned at least twice. When not occupied giving interviews he spent nearly all his time watching them as they replayed endlessly, the television powered by a small generator. On the cable news networks our kidnapping and the resultant standoff remained the top item for days, beating out stories about live nuclear weapons being accidentally flown over the United States, as well as the emergence of a virulent new illness dubbed "equine flu" even though it appeared neither to be influenza nor to have anything to do with horses.

It's worth noting, probably, the gulf between the histrionics of the television coverage, with its frantic string arrangements and breathless commentary, and the crushing ennui inside the compound as we sat around waiting for something to actually happen. We draped ourselves over furniture, shifting a little from time to time as the parts of us in contact with leather and upholstery grew sore. We ate sardines in mustard sauce straight from the can. We read Trumbull's library of *Field & Stream* back issues. All of us grew steadily more rank, until a sort of ambient funk hung in the air of the compound's interiors, much like what I imagine a medieval castle would have smelled like.

It may be true that there was a time in America when journalists sought clarity of circumstance and certainty of fact, but now, as I listened to speculation after speculation, each one more baseless than the last, I realized that the bread and butter of the modern newsman was opacity. When one has an endless succession of twenty-four-hour news cycles to fill, the fewer known facts, the better.

And oh, the scenarios they concocted. Every hour Trumbull had a new favorite, beginning with the civil rights lawyer who claimed that contrary to the popular image of militias as white Christian organizations, many in fact had satanic underpinnings, with all the dark beliefs and rituals that implied, and from what he knew it seemed likely that Cold Dead Fingers was one of these groups who worshipped Beelzebub. Others suggested that the men of Cold Dead Fingers were required to lend their wives to Trumbull for sexual favors whenever he desired (Trumbull's reaction, scoffing as he threw his bowie knife into the wall behind the TV: "Now, why didn't *I* think of that?"). A retired hostage negotiator worried that since no proof of life had been offered, it was possible that Claire and I had already been executed, and now Trumbull was stalling while, lacking any real leverage, he tried to figure out his next move.

Trumbull, for his part, did nothing to either encourage or dispel any of these notions. When it was suggested that he might be heading a satanic cult, Trumbull responded that Cold Dead Fingers was simply a fraternal gun club whose members believed in the primacy of individual rights — but he did not explicitly deny the Satanism charge. When asked about serial cuckoldry with his men's wives, Trumbull sidestepped and said he did not understand why the FBI had lain siege to his home with a mechanized army, except that perhaps in a time when the majority of Americans had surrendered their liberties for a modicum of security, even talking about reclaiming those liberties was too great an offense for a power-drunk government to let pass.

"And this is hardly the first time the federal government has overstepped its legal bounds," Trumbull said during a prime-time talk on CNN with Rolf Kibitzer. "This is the important thing for your viewers to remember: the government has actual limits on its authority. Now everybody hears that and says, 'Well yes, of course.' But they don't really believe it, deep down. Their relationship to the government is the same as the relationship of a child to his father. In the child's eyes, the father has limitless power — genuine omnipotence — and it could not be otherwise. But this of course is not the reality. In reality, the father's power is more or less the same as any other man's, and the limits on the father's power are set by nature. They are codified and inflexible. So it is with our government."

"That's all fine and well, Mr. Trumbull," Kibitzer said. "But the FBI insists that a call was made from your compound with the telephone of one of your hostages, the reality television star K. And that during this call, you claimed to have kidnapped K. and his costar, and also claimed to be in possession of hundreds of illegal weapons."

"As I've said repeatedly, Rolf, we're hoping for a peaceable solution to all this," Trumbull said. "Frankly, we're terrified by what we see outside our windows. But we also believe that the world needs to be shown how the United States government deals with dissent, which was written into our Constitution as a patriotic duty. Look at the army assembled on my property, and you'll see what the government thinks of dissent now."

Claire, Trumbull, and I sat in front of the

small television in an upstairs room, watching the rebroadcast of the Kibitzer interview. Trumbull and I dined on cold beans and rice, while Claire continued to subsist on water and little else.

"Not for nothing," I said to Trumbull, "but you don't seem terrified."

"I'm not," he said.

"I don't understand why you'd say you were terrified," I told him, "if you aren't."

"He's setting them up," Claire said.

Trumbull looked at Claire and touched a finger to the tip of his nose. "What she said. You think they're smart enough to figure that out?"

"If you mean do they know you're full of shit with this 'peaceable solution' nonsense," Claire said, "the answer is yes."

"You may be giving them too much credit," Trumbull said.

"Can someone explain this to me?" I asked.

"A setup, K.," Claire said as Trumbull flipped the television to MSNBCBS, where the Muppets sang maniacally about the virtues of the Toyota Highlander during a commercial break. "Our boy here tells the FBI that he's got a stockpile of illegal weapons, as well as a couple of hostages. Then he spends the next week telling any-

427

one who will listen that he's the victim of an overbearing police state. Meanwhile, people are being treated to nonstop images of government storm troopers plowing around in deathmobiles just waiting to spill some blood. When the FBI is finally forced to blow the place up, the libertarian shitstorm will ensue."

"More or less the size of it," Trumbull said, stirring his food with a spoon.

"Have to hand it to you, it's actually quite elegant," Claire said.

"A few rough spots," Trumbull said. "But it'll do."

MSNBCBS came back from commercial and, after an in-studio lede, suddenly the screen was filled with the incongruity of Theodore's mass. He stood outside the compound in the Texas twilight, dressed in full safari gear, looking like a morbidly obese Crocodile Dundee. Beside him stood MSNBCBS's man on the scene.

"Turn this up," I said.

"What is he *wearing*?" Claire said, snatching the remote control from Trumbull and mashing the volume button.

". . . to get in there one way or another and do whatever I must to secure the release of my colleagues," Theodore said into the microphone proffered by the reporter.

"You have to know," the reporter said, "that the authorities are not going to allow you to enter."

"The authorities are doing absolutely nothing," Theodore said. "I repeat: one way or another. I will fly a hot air balloon in there, if I have to. I will build a trebuchet and fling myself into that compound."

"Sure you will," Claire said. She sat forward. "Whatever, Theodore, you pork chop."

"Who is this man, now?" Trumbull asked.

"Our producer," I told him.

"You don't say."

"There are people who have suggested," the MSNBCBS reporter said, "that this situation is nothing but an elaborate publicity stunt for you and your show. How do you respond to that?"

"With absolute indignation," Theodore said. "This is the very definition of life and death, for people about whom I care a great deal. I am not a violent man, but if I were I might be inclined to punch you in the nose for repeating such baseless slander, my dear."

Behind Theodore it was now almost full dark, the time when the FBI usually began its lullaby of Norwegian death metal. But tonight there would be no Norwegian death metal. And now the first hint of why took form: glittering sequins on the horizon, like earthbound stars. These lights grew steadily larger and brighter, multiplying and drawing closer as Theodore spoke. Headlamps, it became evident. One set followed another off the main road, until there were forty or fifty lined up in the long driveway.

"What is that?" Claire asked.

Trumbull set his bowl on the floor next to his chair and went to the window.

"Looks like cars," I said. "Lots of them. Or maybe mostly pickup trucks, actually."

"Hey, why not," Claire said. "More the merrier."

"Let's assume that you were able to get inside," the reporter said to Theodore on the television. "What would you do then, unarmed and outnumbered a hundred to one?"

"I am a businessman," Theodore said. "Businessmen negotiate."

FBI tactical teams in full combat gear ran past Theodore and the reporter, setting up positions at the mouth of the driveway. Spotlights and gun turrets were hastily rotated away from the compound and pointed at the approaching vehicles. Through both the television and the walls of the building we heard the man on the PA bellowing at the new arrivals to halt their advance.

Which they did, twenty feet or so from the end of the driveway.

At the window, Trumbull shoved his hands into his pants pockets and took in the scene. "Right on time," he said. "More or less."

23
THE PRINCIPAL DIFFERENCE BETWEEN DOG AND MAN

The next morning Trumbull requested my presence again in the shooting range.

When I entered, escorted by a guard, the range reeked of burned sulfur. Emergency lighting produced a gray twilight, and with the air-conditioning off for nearly five days the atmosphere resembled a dim corner of hell. Trumbull waited outside the first booth, clad in his brown duster despite the heat. We barely spoke for the first fifteen minutes or so. I was at first reluctant to even handle the Desert Eagle, let alone aim it at a representation of a human being. But as I'd been given little choice, I concentrated on sights, target, locked wrist — efforts that yielded middling results at best.

After three clips I was trembling, damp of both armpit and forehead, weak-legged from the heat. Trumbull called for a break.

"So if you didn't have a family," he said as he secured the pistol, "I assume you didn't have a dog, growing up?"

"A couple of my foster families had dogs," I told him. "But they didn't seem like mine, any more than the people did. In fact, one of the dogs actively disliked me. Richard. A little Lhasa apso mix, named after the Shakespeare character, and aptly so. Sometimes he'd get me cornered somewhere and wouldn't let me escape. This went on for months, until the family was forced to make a choice between me and the dog."

"And which choice did they make?"

"Richard had tenure. Whereas I did not."

Trumbull shook his head. "Now see," he said, "that leads quite nicely to the reason why I brought up the subject in the first place. Down here, not only would Richard have been the one on the outs, but it's likely someone would have taken him in the field and plugged him with a twenty-two."

"This couple were humanities professors," I said. "They were not in the habit of shooting their problems, I don't think."

Outside the sound of helicopters circling was still audible, though barely so through the concrete walls of the gun range.

"How you kill the dog is not the point," Trumbull said. "The willingness to do so — especially when the choice is between a dog and a human being, an orphaned boy no

433

less — is the point."

"For what it's worth," I said, "I hardly resented them for going with Richard."

Trumbull placed the Desert Eagle on the stainless steel counter and crossed his arms over his chest. "I had a bunch of dogs, as a kid," he said. "First one was the best, though. German shorthaired pointer by the name of Bentley. He started as my daddy's, but became mine as soon as I got old enough to hunt. Bentley was an outstanding gun dog. Swam four hundred yards in whitecap chop to retrieve a snow goose. Four hundred yards."

"That's impressive?" I asked.

Trumbull raised his eyebrows. "Average mutt, you're lucky to get him to go half that distance. And Bentley was nine, ten years old at that point."

"Fairly aged, for a dog," I said.

"Especially a gun dog," Trumbull said. "In fact, the very next year I took Bentley on his last hunt. He'd gotten old fast. Cancer, probably. So that day, instead of birds, we hunted for a place to bury him. When he found a spot he liked and lay down, I measured him with the shovel and dug a hole while he sunbathed. Then I took out my Walther and put one behind his ear. And that was it for old Bentley."

I didn't know what to say, so I said nothing.

"What do you think about that?" Trumbull asked.

"I think," I said after a moment, "that that must have been hard for you."

"And you'd be wrong," Trumbull said. "It was easy as rolling out of bed in the morning."

"How old were you?" I asked.

"Twelve."

Again, I was silent.

"What was there to be sad about?" Trumbull asked. "Bentley never spent a second of his life on a leash. Sure, he got hit by two cars and had more porcupine quills yanked out of his muzzle than you could count. But that's just the cost of doing business. He had as good a life as a dog could hope for. Better than those city dogs you all claim to love so well, who spend most of their lives cooped up in an apartment. Wearing ridiculous costumes. Shitting on sidewalks, for God's sake."

"I don't claim to love any dogs," I said. "I own a cat."

Trumbull lifted the empty magazine and began loading bullets into it one by one. "Today if I did Bentley the favor of putting him out of his misery, I'd be looking at two

435

years in prison. Now tell me, what kind of country do we live in where a man can't shoot his own dog?"

"A civilized one?" I asked, not very hopeful that this was the answer Trumbull sought.

"Funny you should use that word," he said. " 'Civilized.' Because that's really what this is about. For a hundred and fifty years you bluecoats have been trying hook or crook to civilize us. Animal cruelty laws are just the latest gambit. It's class warfare, and it's snobbery of the first order."

"Again, I'm not sure I figure into this one way or the other."

"Do you eat meat?" Trumbull asked.

"I do," I said.

"Then you figure into it," he said. "Out here, we don't have the luxury of softheartedness. We slaughter ten million cattle a year to keep you Yankees in steak dinners and clean consciences. Some things die on their own, other things need to be killed, and that's just the way it is."

Having finished loading the magazine, Trumbull slid it carefully into the butt of the pistol and pulled the slide to chamber a round.

"Speaking of which," he said, holding the weapon out to me once more.

24
GUILT IS NEVER
TO BE DOUBTED

Sarah and I hadn't been getting along well for the better part of a year. Less fighting than just feeling as though we weren't quite sure what the other person was doing in our house.

This was before she got sick.

Actually, it's more accurate to say she was sick, but we just didn't know it yet.

What we did know, both of us, without question, was that we hadn't had sex in over six months. Eventually I got frustrated enough to backtrack and pinpoint the date we'd last made love, the better to stoke my resentment with an exact count of days. I'd also mounted a petty campaign of civil disobedience, engaging in small domestic misdeeds that I knew drove Sarah crazy: not closing the shower curtain after bathing, for example, or putting dirty dishes in the kitchen sink with food still on them.

Childish, I know. And not likely to help

break our cold snap. Also more than a bit regrettable, given everything that was about to happen.

Then one day, Sarah came home from her office, and I came home from a different office. I went into the kitchen and found her at the sink, rinsing the breakfast plate and coffee cup I'd left behind that morning. Both of us taller than average for our respective demographics, with nice teeth, nice hair, nice bodies kept slender and taut by treadmill and barbell. Both of us dressed in tasteful wool suits designed to leave absolutely no impression on anyone, both of us the very picture of white middle-class kayaking-on-the-weekends success, and both of us carrying a bale of misery in our guts like we'd bundled up a length of barbed wire and swallowed it. Meowser perched on top of the refrigerator behind Sarah, watching us with his cold cat eyes, passing silent judgment on us as individuals and as a couple. We gazed at one another, Sarah and I, across the counter that separated the food prep area from the dining area, and although for many weeks we had traded the sort of look one gives to a bare acquaintance for whom one feels little other than disdain, tonight, instead, in her eyes shone familiarity. Affection, even.

It pierced me. I stood there like a deaf-mute for a few moments while dueling impulses of *Yes please* and *Fuck that* duked it out in my frontal lobe.

"What do you think," Sarah asked, "about getting a cocktail?"

"On a Tuesday?" I asked.

"Don't be a stick-in-the-mud," she said, the affection flickering. "It's not like we've got three kids or anything."

Thank Christ for that, I thought.

She picked the place, a small gastropub on the edge of downtown called North Point. With its brick interior and exposed ductwork, a cramped bar where the liquor bottles huddled together like refugees, and those dim Edison bulbs that suddenly seemed like they were everywhere, North Point was more Sarah's style than mine. I preferred clean lines, bright splashes of track lighting, gray sheetrock walls hung with unobtrusive bits of contemporary art. But I hardly intended to complain. The barroom was warm, the martinis were dry, and Sarah was smiling, then laughing. I laughed with her as the vodka set my earlobes afire and made my eyes well in a pleasant way.

We sat facing one another on adjacent bar stools. Near the end of her second drink Sarah draped an arm over my shoulder and

said, "What exactly is our problem, anyway?"

"I'm not sure," I told her. "If I knew, I'd
do something about it."

"Would you?"

"I'm not enjoying this any more than you
are, Sarah."

"You know what my mom says?"

"You've been talking to Peggy about this?"
I asked.

Sarah shrugged. "She's a tough old bird,
but every once in a while she's able to cut
through the bullshit in a way that's enlight-
ening."

"Did she this time?"

"Hardly. 'Have more sex,' she said."

I fished an olive out of my martini. "That
was it?"

"The entirety of her wisdom on the subject of marriage. Yes."

"As far as relationship advice goes," I said,
"that's not the worst I've ever heard."

Sarah offered a mock-suspicious squint.

"I'm just saying, I can only think of maybe
two scenarios in which 'have more sex' is a
bad relationship strategy. And one of those
scenarios involves a prolapsed rectum."

"But I mean what are you thinking?" she
asked. "Are you thinking what I'm thinking? That marriage is marriage and we're in

a trough and given enough time we'll hit an upslope again?"

"More or less," I said. "We've hit troughs before. Not quite like this, but."

She looked at me. "You're not fucking around, are you?"

It was, suddenly, like being interrogated by a cop: even if you tell the truth, you feel like you're lying. "No," I said, barely convincing myself though I was being honest.

"Are you thinking about it?"

"No," I said, and this was the truth, too.

"Because if you were thinking about it I could hardly blame you. After, what, five months or so."

"Six months."

She smirked. "Not that you're keeping track."

"Anyway," I said, "I'm not fucking around, and I'm not thinking about it, either."

She removed her arm from my shoulder and lifted her martini glass. "Well to hell with it, anyway," she said. "Tomorrow we can get back to whatever mysterious ailment is crippling our marriage."

"And tonight?"

She shrugged, tilting her head from side to side. "Tonight," she said, "I want to get good and drunk. After that, we'll leave it to the Fates."

The Fates, it turned out, were conspiring to land Sarah and me in bed several hours later. Half a year's worth of pent up carnal impulses, along with most of a bottle of Ketel One, had us pawing at each other with good enthusiasm, heading toward what would have been, in all likelihood, satisfying coitus. But then I put a hand on Sarah's right breast, and froze.

She picked her head up off the pillow and looked at me. "Why are you stopping?" she groaned. "What's wrong?"

"I felt something," I told her.

"You felt nothing, K."

"I'm serious," I said.

Sarah sighed magnificently and pushed herself into a sitting position against the headboard. "You felt what. Where."

"In your breast," I said. "Something lump-like."

"What? Show me."

I took her hand and guided it to the spot. "There. You feel it?"

"Maybe."

"It's in there pretty deep," I said.

"Oh," she said, and, like mine, her hand came to a halt. "Yeah. Yeah, that's something. For sure."

"You've had it checked out?"

"I hadn't noticed it. But it's probably just

a cyst. Women of a certain age, you know. Everything starts falling apart." She shoved a loose swatch of hair behind her ear. "Jesus, are we actually having this conversation right now? Because up until about thirty seconds ago, I thought we were going to have sex."

"Not feeling it anymore?" I asked.

"It was pretty tenuous to begin with, K." She grabbed the covers and disappeared, bunching the top of the comforter in a ball under her chin.

"I guess it was," I said.

After the nine days Sarah procrastinated on the gynecologist appointment, after the two days we waited for the needle biopsy and the four days we waited for the results, after the three days we waited for a CT scan and the two days we waited for those results, after nights of staring into the dark as the reality of what was happening first closed around us like a vise and then, slowly, cleaved us into the two discrete states of existence known as well and sick, after we sat in the examination room while the same doctor who, two weeks earlier, had palpated Sarah's breast and tried to obscure a growing dismay at what he felt finally told us why he'd been so dismayed, after Sarah had gone from golemlike silence to uncontrolled tears and the doctor lamely offered a box of tissues and I lamely took a few and pressed them into Sarah's hand, after she excused herself and went to the hallway bathroom to be by herself for however long it took to regain her composure, I found myself alone with the doctor.

We didn't say anything for a minute. He cleared his throat once, then again, more forcefully this time. I let my head hang and rubbed the back of my neck slowly with one hand.

Between his fingers the doctor held a designer fountain pen, gold, with his initials engraved on the barrel in florid cursive. He tapped the pen in a steady rhythm against Sarah's file folder, which rested on his lap.

Finally, the doctor said, "Are there any questions I can answer for you? While we're waiting?"

"I don't think so," I said. I felt alternately as if I might vomit or burst into tears myself, and did not desire a witness to either. "In fact, if you have other patients, feel free to go tend to them. I'll just wait for Sarah."

"I don't mind at all," the doctor said. "And really, listen, with this type of diagnosis, in many ways I'm *your* doctor, too.

Sarah may be the one who's ill, but there's a lot of weight about to come down on your shoulders. So please, ask anything you want."

I had a question to ask, but I wasn't sure I wanted to know the answer.

"Really," the doctor said again.

"Okay," I said. "We mentioned that I noticed the lump in her breast, I think."

"Yes. Oftentimes intimate partners are the first to discover malignancies. It's quite common."

I swallowed. "Would it have made any difference in her prognosis," I asked, "if I had noticed it sooner?"

The doctor looked down at the file on his lap. "I'm sorry," he said. "I know I said ask anything you want, but I don't like to engage in that sort of speculation. I don't deal in what-ifs or should-haves. This is where we are now."

"Right," I said.

"Besides," he said, "usually a partner will notice a mass pretty much the moment it becomes palpable. So if you didn't feel it before now, it must have been because it couldn't be felt."

"Yeah," I said. "Must have been."

The doctor looked at me. "What?"

"What if I told you," I said, "that we

hadn't had sex in six months? Sarah and me?"

The doctor stared for several beats, then snapped back to himself. "I'd say, again, that speculation is pointless."

"Except I saw something cross your face, just now," I said.

"How's that?"

"Something that said, quite clearly, that if I'd touched my wife six months ago she might not be dying today."

"Which doesn't change the fact that speculation is pointless."

Now the tears came.

The doctor leaned forward in his chair. "Listen to me," he said. "As a physician I can't say for certain that it would or would not have made a difference. But my advice, as a human being who has watched many people go through what you're about to go through, is to spend as little time as possible thinking about it."

The doctor and I sat there for another three or four minutes, trying to avoid one another's gaze, and by the time Sarah came back with her eyes nearly swollen shut from crying I was more than ready to go, and said so, and I left that place as though fleeing the scene of a crime.

25
JOIN, AND DIE

With the arrival of the ragtag militia, television headlines came fast and shrill. REBELLION IN EAST TEXAS read one. LONE STAR SHOWDOWN read another. Still others, either more coy or democratic-minded, framed the story with rhetorical queries and let the viewer decide for herself if she thought the SECOND CIVIL WAR? had begun.

Typical bug-eyed overstatement from the news-industrial complex? Perhaps. But consider the concentric circles: Claire and I in the center, surrounded by Trumbull and his men. Trumbull and his men, surrounded by the FBI. And the FBI, now themselves surrounded by two hundred or so angry people from all over the country, neo-Nazis and disillusioned ex-military and Second Amendment warriors who shared in common precisely two things: a great and consuming hatred of government, and a uniform whiteness.

Consider, further, that two of the newly arrived revolutionaries, a man and woman from Michigan's Upper Peninsula, had peeled off from the main group and, after dressing themselves rather foppishly as villains from the Batman universe, executed a pair of police officers on their lunch break at a pizzeria in Plano. Simultaneous point-blank shots to the side of the cops' skulls, bone shards and gray matter sprayed all over their thin crust like some macabre Expressionist painting, a Gadsden flag draped carefully atop the whole mess while terrified diners hid under tables and ran screaming into the street. Real violence had now been committed, real blood spilled in the name of armed insurrection, and given that, one might be slightly less inclined to view the media's revolution narrative as hyperbole.

Certainly, the networks no longer needed to manufacture tension for their audience. If previously a fight had seemed possible, now a sense of inevitability presided, and that sense came through on the television without any embellishment from newscasters. The abject stillness of the air seemed both portent and grim promise. Images of the FBI and revolutionaries with rifles trained on one another, perched in truck beds and kneeling behind open car doors, were such that one could almost smell the blood to come. Tactically, this display of aggression on the part of the revolutionaries was beyond foolish; the Bradley chain guns could have ripped up all the Bondo'd F-150s and dusty Astro vans in less time than it takes to scramble an egg. But psychologically their posture made sense, as a clear willingness to die will always give one's enemy pause — in particular if that enemy has reason to worry about public relations.

That afternoon the agent on the public address system went quiet for the first time in five days, and I surmised that Trumbull had finally broken his silence and contacted the FBI. This supposition proved correct when Trumbull came to us that evening in the third-story bedroom where we'd spent the entire day, passing the hours with endless hands of gin rummy, the general strategy of which had been altered considerably by the fact that the deck of cards was short two sevens and the queen of clubs.

"Tomorrow morning," Trumbull said. "Ten o'clock."

Claire leapt from her seat, spitting and cursing, and threw herself at Trumbull. She swung on him repeatedly, and he backed up half a step as her fists pelted his chest and shoulders like raindrops hitting a rock. He could have broken her in two, but did nothing to restrain or repulse her, instead turning his face to avoid an unlikely but still possible blow to the virile arch of his nose. Claire kept this up for an impressive amount of time, but did eventually tire, as we all must, whereupon she stood with her fist still cocked at her side, panting, yet more furious in her impotence.

"He knows what he has to do," Trumbull said, and left.

In the dream I performed psychic surgery on my wife, folding my hands into her wasted body, pulling out pieces of tumor like raw stew meat and depositing them in a blood-streaked steel bowl at her bedside.

Everyone we'd ever known stood gathered in the room, looking on.

Sarah lay awake and aware on the bed. Each time I pushed my hands into her she arched her back and sighed. I worked carefully, seeking out every last malignant bit in her chest and brain and femur until, satisfied that none remained, I wiped my hands on a white towel and told Sarah she was healed. All those assembled clapped and cheered, and Sarah, still lying flat, turned her head toward me and waited for the applause to die down, then smiled and whispered: *"That doesn't matter."*

I snapped awake next to Claire, gasping as sweat ran in rivulets down my rib cage and across my thighs, my mind spinning with thoughts of Einstein at Auschwitz, dressed in rough striped wool, his head shaved clean and a Star of David sewn to his tattered shirt, Einstein on corpse detail, carrying nude bodies to be stacked and burned endlessly like cordwood, Einstein scribbling formulae by moonlight with a nub of pencil stolen from the crematorium, Einstein running each afternoon to the canteen, where he is given just two minutes to eat a watery soup served boiling hot so that his mouth and throat seethe with blisters, Einstein loading and unloading the ovens and sweeping up ashes, Einstein twisting the head of a corpse and yanking on pliers with both hands until a gold bicuspid pops loose, Einstein telling prisoners about to be gassed that they are going to receive a nice, hot shower, Einstein exhorting his partner in crematorium work, who has just found his brother among the dead, to cease weeping lest he anger the guards, Einstein too weak to run to the canteen any longer, arriving with only enough time to eat half his meager scalding ration of soup before a bayonet tip prods him back outside, Einstein rummaging through refuse bins behind the kitchen, wolfing potatoes and cabbage that drip with rot, Einstein, naked from the waist down, his legs white fleshless sticks, squatting over a ditch beside the barracks, brown water issuing from his rear end, Einstein devouring a paper upon which he'd scrawled equations as though it were a medium-rare fillet in red wine jus, Einstein reduced by starvation and beatings and the relentless abrasive force of sun and rain to a spiritless creature beyond fear, beyond caring, a creature to whom *that doesn't matter,* and *that doesn't matter,* and *that doesn't matter,* Einstein muttering nonsense as he wanders the camp with only one boot on, Einstein, now useless to his captors, shot dead with utter lack of ceremony, Einstein in a cart under a pile of other corpses, Einstein stripped naked and relieved of his own gold teeth by a fellow Jude, Einstein, limbs stiff and belly concave, loaded into an oven, Einstein removed after several hours and swept into a bin, Einstein dumped into eddies on the Sola river, Einstein whisked downstream and dissipated by the current.

Beside me, Claire stirred and put a hand on my chest, and when she felt the cacophony inside she propped herself up on one elbow and searched my face, her eyes wide with alarm.

"Hey," she said. "Hey, what's going on?"

I gasped for breath. "I'm scared," I told her, awed by both the fact and the feeling.

26
ALL THE DEVILS ARE HERE

Fear abided, carrying me sleepless through the rest of the night and into the most dreadful dawn I've ever witnessed, the sun a bloody disk peeking over the horizon while below us men and women checked their weapons, boiled coffee on camp stoves, eyed one another with wary hatred.

"Tell me you won't shoot that cop," Claire said as we sat at the bedroom window looking down on the scene. "No matter what happens."

For the first time in as long as I could remember, I had both the impulse and the ability to lie. "I won't shoot him," I told her.

The heat, more than anything, is what I remember. Stepping out as Gus, Trumbull's lieutenant, held open the reinforced steel door, sunlight like a blast furnace, the air inert, thick, nearly unbreathable. Nothing and no one moved. The prairie grass on

Trumbull's property, tall and proud only a few days before, lay wilted against the chalky earth. Perspiration sprang up on my forehead so quickly that it caused pinpricks of pain, as though my sweat glands were cramping. I could feel hundreds of eyes on me as I strode with Trumbull to meet Frank and an FBI agent, who waited for us with an oversized Radio Flyer stacked high with pizza boxes.

Trumbull greeted them.

"Appreciate you brokering the deal, Frank," he said, extending a hand. "The men are anxious for some hot chow."

Frank looked at him like he knew very well Trumbull had no real interest in pizza. He put his own hand out, and it quavered into Trumbull's enveloping mitt.

I stood there in the sun, sick and trembling myself, chilled despite the astonishing heat, knowing it was mine to decide: both whether to shoot Frank, and when. There would come no signal, and there was no agreed-upon moment. The opening salvo in Trumbull's war belonged either to me or to the man holding Claire at gunpoint somewhere inside the compound, and as I was unsure how long I would be able to keep my feet I reached for the Desert Eagle that very moment and shot Frank, there in front of the federal agents and sovereign citizens and television cameras circling in distant choppers, I shot Frank for audiences in Madrid and Beijing, Ottawa and Oklahoma City, I shot Frank for the purposes of Trumbull's agenda, for the entertainment of millions, but I shot Frank, ultimately, for the sake of Claire's life, for this dear strange young woman whose existence I wanted to preserve badly enough that I was willing, if not eager, to become a murderer.

I shot Frank in the thigh. It was the best I could do, even at close range.

Trumbull pulled two pistols from his waistband and began firing while I scrambled back toward the main building. As I ran, I turned my head and saw Trumbull draw himself up to his full, impressive height. Here was his moment, august in its visuals yet pathetic in its futility — which, I suppose, could be said of most acts of principle. Were his eyes clear? Did he do what he believed needed to be done, without flinching? It appeared so then, and remains so in my memory. In that regard, he stayed true to his vision and purpose. He fired on his enemies. He bared his teeth under that amazing sun, bellowing like Attila. He had his two, perhaps three seconds of glory. And then the first couple of bullets slammed into his chest, sending twin red parabolas arcing through the air. His blood hit the dirt like tobacco spit. His shoulders snapped forward and his back bowed. His sneer became a grimace. He pitched sideways, and another round ripped through his left arm as he went down. And that was that.

It's not possible, I have decided, to understand the distinction between a noble death and a pointless one.

For what it's worth, mine was not the bullet that killed Frank. That slug arrived in the moments after I fired, as Frank sat in the dirt and the world around us became a study in terminal ballistics. The autopsy in Frank's case would prove imprecise, and all that was known, after the killing had finished and nothing remained but to catalog it, was that the bullet found in his skull had come from a rifle. Whether that rifle belonged to an FBI agent or a Son of Liberty, whether the round it fired was paid for by taxpayers or Tea Partiers, we will never in this life know. Here's what I do know, and what I told investigators: Frank seemed oblivious to the swarm of projectiles cutting the air and kicking up dust around him. His entire attention was taken with the wound he'd already sustained, not the thousand others he might. He struggled to a seated position, clutching at his thigh as blood burbled up through the hole in his trousers like a drinking fountain. Seeing this, I stopped and turned back, seized for a moment by the instinct to help Frank in some way. His mouth hung open and his eyes flashed with horror. His hat had flown off when he fell, and his bald pate gleamed with sweat. For perhaps the first time in his life, and certainly for the last, he was completely unselfconscious. If he hadn't been so focused on the fact that I'd shot him, he might have had the presence of mind to not sit up in the middle of a shooting gallery, and in that case he might have lived. Because if he'd remained prone, the bullet that hit him in the side of the neck and ricocheted up through his brain stem as I watched would have otherwise sailed harmlessly through the air above him.

There is, in all our lives, the innumerable ways things might have happened, and the one way in which they did.

The Radio Flyer, having taken multiple hits of its own (though somewhat more stoically than Frank), capsized and strewed its stack of pizzas on the ground. I looked up and saw the FBI agent who had accompanied Frank, crouched beside the monstrous tracks of a Bradley, draw down on me with his sidearm while pizza boxes exploded nearby as though filled with strings of firecrackers. The agent took aim with calm deliberateness, as if he were alone on a practice range rather than in the middle of the largest gunfight in U.S. law enforcement history. He might have been the only person actually aiming at a target, instead of just spraying rounds in the general direction of those with whom they had quarrel. Later he would tell me that all he cared about, all that was on his mind in that moment, was making certain that he shot me, preferably center mass. What he'd perceived as my deception could not be allowed to go unanswered, no matter what else happened. So he took his time, costing himself the opportunity to kill me in the process.

Because while the FBI agent aimed, I noticed at the periphery of my vision a shape, roughly the same mass and velocity as a meteor, hurtling in my direction. I caught a glimpse of flashing khaki before the object was upon me, plowing into my chest and driving me backward. We tumbled through the doorway, and Gus slammed the steel door shut after us.

We lay on the floor, gasping and writhing, while bullets continued to chip at the cinder-block walls and ping off the door, leaving pimples of varying caliber in the steel.

"My dear," said the object that had crashed into me. "Could you check my back? I believe I may have been shot."

I looked and saw the khaki-clad celestial object on the floor next to me was, of course, Theodore. Whether he'd been shot by the FBI agent — whether, in other words, he'd taken a bullet for me — was unclear, but in any event he'd certainly been shot, a fact I did not need to check his back to confirm, since an exit wound, in his upper right abdomen, was evident from where I lay.

I pointed this out to him.

"Oh my," he said, looking down at himself and pawing at the fabric of his safari shirt. "That does not look very good at all."

It didn't. A peculiar black blood pumped from the wound, thick as crude oil.

"I think," I said, "that maybe it hit your liver."

"Sweet Mongolian Barbecue," Theodore said. He laid his head against the floor. "Where is Claire, my dear?" he asked.

"I don't know," I said. I pointed to Gus. "He might."

Gus was crouched against the wall, arms enveloping his head, AR15 forgotten on the floor beside him.

"What the fuck was that?" he said, peering at me through his forearms.

"What the fuck was what?" I asked.

"You fucking shot Frank!" Gus said. "You're supposed to be a *hostage.*"

Outside something exploded, a concussive wallop followed by several rumbling waves like the approach of a thunderstorm.

"I didn't have any choice," I said. "It was Trumbull's idea."

"What?" Gus said.

"He didn't tell you?" I asked.

Gus dropped his arms and stared. "No, he didn't fucking tell me," he said. "Because I would have said he was out of his goddamn mind. We're just making a *point* here. Nobody's supposed to get *killed.*"

If Gus didn't know, I realized, then no one knew. Light dawned: Trumbull's threat to kill Claire had been a bluff. We'd all — me, the FBI, and Trumbull's men — been victims of the same con.

"My dears," Theodore said, still clutching at his belly, "where is Claire?"

"The girl?" Gus asked.

"Of course, the girl," Theodore said.

"Fucked if I know," Gus said. "Upstairs in the bedroom. Full of fucking holes, probably."

"I'm not sure I'll be able to climb any stairs," Theodore said to me.

"Forget her," Gus said. "We have to get to the bunker."

Outside, the Bradley chain guns roared to sudden life, a sound like God panfrying the universe, signaling with spectacular, Fourth-of-July finality that the FBI had taken stock of the situation and decided their only immediate concern was surviving: public relations were no longer a consideration and so none would be spared.

"There's a bunker?" I yelled at Gus over the sizzling of the guns.

Theodore coughed up a smear of blood. "My dear," he gasped, "what kind of self-respecting survivalists would not have a bunker?"

"I thought they'd gone out of fashion," I said. "More of a Cold War thing."

"If you assholes are done?" Gus said. "It's under the shooting range. Let's go. Now."

Gus and I each grabbed one of Theodore's hands and, with no small effort, pulled him to his feet.

"For Christ's sake, who is this guy, even?" Gus asked.

"I'm his friend," Theodore said.

Either this was sufficient explanation for Gus, or, more likely, he didn't care enough about the details of my relationship with Theodore to inquire further. Without another word he led us into the dark, cramped network of hallways on the main building's first floor, bent at the waist to make himself as small a target as possible. Men hurried in every direction, seemingly without any real purpose, their faces wild with rage and terror as they pushed past us. The more hardy members of Cold Dead Fingers held positions and attempted to fight back, poking their weapons through shattered windows and firing blindly at the FBI. Here and there we encountered men who lay prone and bloodied. Some cried out for help — from God, from their companions, from their mothers. Some sat dying silently, white with shock, eyes fixed in blind stares, no longer concerned in the least with the proper interpretation of the Second Amendment or the offense of federal overreach. Still others breathed no more, their bodies already beginning to attract flies, which swirled down into pools of blood and drank at their leisure, undisturbed by the tumult.

We picked our way through the gruesome scene as quickly as we could with a wounded and corpulent Theodore in tow, eventually reaching the door that led to the interior courtyard and, beyond, the firing range.

Gus placed a hand on the doorknob. "We ready?" he asked.

"You go," I said. "I have to find Claire."

"She's dead," Gus said. "But suit yourself."

"Be careful, my dear," Theodore said. "I'd accompany you, but I'm afraid I would, in my current state, be a liability."

"That's probably true," I said.

"I want you to know," Theodore said, "how very sorry I am about all this."

"It's alright, Theodore," I said.

"The fuck it is," Gus said. "Let's *go.*"

They fled into the daylight. I retraced our steps back into the main building, ducking bullets and stumbling over bodies as smoke began to fill the hallways, noting the sequence of turns so that I'd be able to find my way to the courtyard again. A growing number of Cold Dead Fingers members, particularly in the rooms with windows, had entered the state their club name referred to, though mostly their ARs and AKs rested on the floor rather than in their stiffening hands. Deeper into the building the smoke thickened into great billowing clouds that poured down the hallways like a black liquid, closing my throat and stinging my eyes. It smelled like gasoline and burning plastic and also, faintly, the sickening sweetness of charred flesh. By now not only was it difficult to breathe, but I could barely see more than a foot or two in front of me, which was why, when we finally met by complete and utter accident, Claire and I literally ran into each other.

The collision sent her careening into a wall. She ricocheted but somehow managed to keep her feet. We stared at each other for a few seconds. She was coated in blood, hair tangled into wet dreadlocks, face streaked crimson, shirt hanging heavy and wet.

When our surprise melted away she called me several nasty names and pounded on my chest with her fists. I tried to grip her upper arms, but my hands slid around in all that gore.

"Are you hurt?" I asked.

"It isn't mine," she said, still hitting me.

"Are you sure?"

"I think so," she said.

"Okay," I said.

"What are we going to do?" she asked.

"First let's get down on the floor," I said. "Then follow me."

We dropped to the pinewood boards, which by now were strewn with broken glass and shell casings. "You should be aware," I said, "that you're going to see some things. You will likely have to crawl over bodies."

Booted feet passed us at a run, barely missing my hand.

"K.," Claire said.

"Yes?" I said.

"Look at me. There won't be anything worse than what I've already seen."

We made our way back to the courtyard exit, Claire following with one hand on my ankle so as not to lose me in the smoke. When we reached the door I stood, turned the handle, and peered out to see the roof of the firing range in flames.

"That's not good," I said

"What's not good?" Claire asked.

I closed the door again. "The building where we're supposed to take shelter," I told her, "is on fire."

"Remind me why we're supposed to take shelter there?" Claire said.

"It would be impossible to remind you, given that I haven't told you yet," I said.

"K."

"Apparently there's a bunker," I said.

Claire absorbed this for a moment. "Correct me if I'm wrong," she said, "but bunkers are usually made from fireproof material, right?"

"I'm no expert," I said, "but one would imagine so, yes."

"So that leaves us with two options. One,

466

we can stay here and burn to death. Or two, we can take our chances with a reinforced concrete bunker that was probably designed to withstand a direct hit from a nuclear bomb."

"That's almost certainly overstating its functionality," I said.

Claire pushed past me and opened the door again. "For God's sake," she said, running out into the bullets and sunlight, a streak of red against the bleached-out beige of the prairie.

27
THE SOLUTION TO
ALL PROBLEMS

"*Pimp House,*" Theodore said. He sat on the floor of the bunker with his legs splayed and blood pooling on the concrete underneath him. "We'd been in Miami for about four months. That's when I met Arnulfo, so I will always have a fondness for the show, and the city. But my dear. What monsters we were. I mean, the next summer I'm onstage at the Shrine Auditorium, and I'm saying thank you, thank you all so much, but what I'm thinking is, if you people saw everything we shot you wouldn't be giving me an Emmy, you'd be throwing me in prison for life."

He paused, gulped air, wiped his pallid brow with one hand.

"It was our second season," he said, "so by this point we'd seen plenty of not-safe-for-prime-time behavior. Everyone was guilty of it sooner or later. The hos, the johns, but of course, as you might imagine, primarily the pimps. They all engaged in violence nearly every day. They smacked the hos when the hos got out of line. They punched and stomped johns who failed to pay for services rendered. Derrick did all this, the same as the rest. It wasn't as though he'd shown any special acumen for cruelty, relative to the other pimps in the house.

"But then one night he called and asked me to meet him, saying he wanted to talk," Theodore said.

The heat was almost literally unbelievable. Beyond the dome of white light cast by the camping lantern at our feet, the bunker's steel bulkhead door glowed red-hot. Not only was the air uncomfortable to breathe, but I'd begun to suspect that the oxygen content was falling as the inferno outside burned. Claire's head rested heavy against my shoulder.

"Maybe it was the sudden celebrity from season one, gone to his head," Theodore said. "Or maybe he'd just been hiding the fact that he was a demon from an altogether different circle of hell, as genuine psychopaths are said to do."

Theodore paused, caught his breath, glanced toward the corner to his left, where Gus's body lay in shadows, torn by bullet wounds sustained crossing the courtyard.

"I thought my humanity had completely expired," he said. "I thought I didn't care about suffering. Or rather, that I did care about suffering, but only insofar as it could be used as entertainment. Derrick proved I was wrong about myself.

"He had the girl — whose name I never learned, by the way, I'd never seen her before that night, though as savagely as he beat her they must have had some sort of professional relationship — facedown on the floor in front of me. He held an aluminum baseball bat over his shoulder. Other instruments were arrayed on the table beside him. A length of electrical cord. A straight razor. A nail file. A butane lighter. Half of a broken pool cue.

"He'd planted one of his big alligator-skin boots — which we'd bought for him before season one, so he more closely resembled the white suburban notion of what a pimp looks like — squarely on the girl's behind, so she couldn't rise from the floor. When I entered the room she was making this sound, over and over. The Germans probably have a word for it. The anticipation of certain agony, and the terrible uncertainty of how long one will have to endure it. Do you know that sound?"

I shook my head, slowly.

Theodore went on. "I asked Derrick what he wanted to talk about, and he told me he had no interest in talking. He just wanted me to see what he was going to do to this girl. He never said why he wanted me to witness this. Perhaps it was habitual for him to seek an audience for his cruelty. Or perhaps he thought if he demonstrated something that set him apart from the other four pimps, I might make him the centerpiece of the second season."

Theodore stared at the bunker's concrete floor. He slapped the side of his head, once, as if trying to jar the memory loose from his head.

" 'Just sit there and watch and keep your fucking mouth shut,' Derrick told me. One of his eyes was bigger than the other and it was staring right at me. The other eye had wandered off to the side. I've never seen anything like it. My skin almost literally crawled."

I looked down. Claire's eyes were closed. With my right hand I searched for and found the pulse in her neck. It throbbed steadily.

"You know, my dear," Theodore said, "maybe he just wanted me to be afraid of him. Maybe that was his only aim. If so, he certainly succeeded."

Theodore took a deep breath and let it out again, his chest and belly expanding and contracting like a massive bellows. He coughed several times, and when he drew the back of his hand across his mouth it came away black with blood.

We were quiet for a while. Theodore let his head hang; he might have passed out briefly, though it was impossible to know for certain. Outside the volume of gunfire increased suddenly, like the moment when popcorn reaches its flash point, and I surmised, listening to the cacophony, that the flames must have ignited a cache of ammunition somewhere in the shooting range. This would prove to have been the case, later on, after the ashes were sifted through by both hand and bucket loader, the charred bones inventoried, the shell casings discovered and their calibers identified.

Theodore lifted his head and coughed again. "Now," he said. "Where was I? Young, evil Derrick. He was about to commence torturing the prostitute. Although you know, now that I really think on it, the fact is we're assuming she was a prostitute. It's more likely she was a former prostitute, trying to get out of the life, as they call it, and this was the reason Derrick treated her so viciously."

Claire stirred against my shoulder. She murmured a bit, almost conversationally. Wherever she'd gone in her dreams, it was not, apparently, too unpleasant a locale.

"Derrick hit the girl two or three times with the bat, then stopped suddenly and said he wanted me to film what was about to happen. He wanted something to show the other hos and keep them from getting any ideas about how much leeway they had in their dealings with him. By now, my dear, the girl was most definitely crying. She would cry so much, eventually, that she ran out of tears. I wanted to leave, but I was too frightened to do anything other than what he told me. So I got out my cell, as we called them back then, and recorded him beating her with the baseball bat, and then recorded everything he did after."

Outside the bunker the exploding ammunition cache began to exhaust itself. Theodore paused and looked down at his khaki shirt and enormous cargo shorts, which were sopped with blood.

He drew another long breath. "I am going to be dead soon, my dear."

I nodded.

"Anyway," Theodore said, "Derrick beat and cut and burned that girl until she wished to die, and said so out loud. Eventually, Derrick granted this wish. When he was finished I handed him my phone so he could show the video to his hos whenever he felt the need, and then I walked out and went to Mango's."

Claire caught her breath for a moment, then exhaled and adjusted her head against my shoulder without waking.

"Mango's pays pretty girls to dance almost naked at all hours of the day and night," Theodore said. "I wanted, quite desperately, to see them smiling in their samba costumes. So I went to the bar and ordered a margarita and watched them dance. I sat through two shift changes. I drank until the barroom started to twirl like a religious ecstatic. Eventually, Arnulfo rescued me. The next morning I came to with the air conditioner blowing so hard I had goose bumps even with the blankets pulled over my head. And for the first three or four seconds I was awake, I forgot all about Derrick and the girl, and I believed the worst thing I would have to deal with that day was my hangover, which was formidable enough. Then it all came back."

A rivulet of blood spilled suddenly from the center of Theodore's mouth and trickled down over his chin. I nudged Claire a bit, shook her shoulder gently, thinking she might want to say good-bye to him. But she remained asleep.

"Here's the thing, my dear," Theodore said. "Yes, I felt awful, and I regretted that this girl had died so horribly. But what is it worth, to simply feel bad? I still finished filming the show, and if Derrick wasn't a stand-out cast member, he at least figured prominently in the story line. I let that be so. I pretended my fear justified inaction. I built a firewall between what I'd seen him do and what he could do for me. I paid for the discreet disposal of the girl's body, and season two of *Pimp House* aired to dream-like ratings. We made millions on merchandising alone. There were action figures, my dear. A one-to-ten scale model of Derrick, ivory cigarette holder between his teeth, holding up his pimp hand in preparation to slap someone."

Theodore paused and sighed, causing a reddish bubble to form and pop on his lips. "We collected our money and our Emmys. End of story. Everyone wins — except for her, of course."

Outside the bunker, very faintly, I heard shouting, then several bursts of gunfire, then more shouting.

"Flash forward to several months ago,"

Theodore said. "I weigh four hundred pounds and haven't made a decent episode of television in a decade. I will pass the rest of my days sitting by one pool or another under one cloudless sky or another, slurping cock and cocktails, watching as my own personal field of gravity continues to grow without limit. Then you appear, goose and golden egg in one, and suddenly I rediscover my conscience, which prior to that had last been seen outside the entrance to a bathhouse in Providence, Rhode Island, my junior year of undergraduate studies."

Theodore looked down at himself again, pushed his hands into the blood on his shirt, and held them up, dripping thickly, for me to see. "The next thing, I'm gut shot and bleeding out in some hillbilly's basement, and you are now only the fourth person who knows what happened that night in Miami.

"And so I suppose that's it."

Thus unburdened after a decade, Theodore gave in to the exhaustion of blood loss and leaned his head back against the wall.

"I wish I could tell you I wouldn't change anything," he said. "But I would, my dear. One or two things, at least."

A few minutes later, Theodore died there in the bunker. I didn't need to check to make sure he was dead, because my wife had died with her eyes open, too.

And I cried — for Theodore, yes, but for Frank and Abraham Trumbull and their companions as well, and for the FBI casualties sure to be lying twisted and torn beyond the walls of the bunker. I cried for Peggy's husband, Roger, and Arnulfo's father, Eduardo. I cried for the anonymous prostitute, and I cried for another unnamed and unknown woman: my mother, she without face or form. I cried for all the dead across time, for every soul plucked from oblivion and forced into the torment of consciousness. I cried for the victims of jet crashes and siege machines, burst appendixes and Black Plague, starvation and snakebite and ritual sacrifice, but most of all I cried for Sarah, my Sarah, whom I had loved but did not know, just as she had loved but did not know me. I cried glorious cascades of tears, until it seemed I must die from it. I cried while several more hours passed and the air in the room began to cool and the voices outside drew ever so gradually nearer. I was still crying when by and by the bulkhead door opened, and as I emerged at gunpoint into the charred dawn my first thought was that Trumbull had gotten his wish, because war had to be the only thing that could look and smell and taste like that.

28
Now

It's been four years. A short enough time that we're not old yet, a long enough time that people have forgotten, or nearly forgotten, why they once cared who we were.

We live in Toledo, of all places.

"Toledo," Claire says, sometimes, upon returning home in the evening. She'll stand on the back steps, gaze at the downtown skyline as it strains upward toward relevance, and either shake her head or shrug her shoulders. Sometimes she seems more or less content; other times she seems like she's wondering how, exactly, time's undulations managed to deposit her here.

I have no such moments of bafflement, but I understand the reasons she does.

Thanks to both the United States Witness Security Program and our own discretion, we exist anonymously. This was all Claire wanted, once we crawled out of the bunker and rinsed the ash and blood off ourselves and explained, to the eventual grudging satisfaction of the FBI, why I'd thought I had no choice but to shoot Frank in the leg. "Nondescript" has become the watchword. Our house features taupe vinyl siding, and is of an appraised value that many American couples could easily afford. In our driveway sit a used Dodge minivan and a used Ford Fiesta. There is a picket fence, and a durable, low-maintenance carpet of zoysia grass front and back. Last summer we installed an aboveground pool, oval, twenty-eight by twelve feet, less because we like to swim, and more because ours was the last house in the cul-de-sac without a pool.

I work doing what I did before Sarah passed away, a job so inconsequential to humanity that it hardly bears mentioning, though it is, ultimately, the only vocation for which I am qualified. I wear unremarkable wool suits to this job, just as before. During winter — which in northern Ohio, on the lake, is a merciless horror — I wear unremarkable wool overcoats. I fold myself into the Fiesta, merge with traffic on 280, cross the river, and descend onto surface streets, the names of which — Manhattan Boulevard, New York Avenue — broadcast Toledo's inferiority complex. I park in a municipal lot with prorated fees for monthly pass holders, of which I am one. I sit for between seven and ten hours in a ground-level office, at a particleboard desk, under fluorescent tubes that allegedly produce a soft white light. I spend time conversing with people, some via telephone or video chat, some in person. I engage in work on a computer. I eat, I use the restroom, I idly consume trivialities on the Internet. When 100 percent of any given day is used up, I go to the parking garage, get into the Fit once more, and drive back across the river. Most often the river roils brown; on occasion, when the air is still and the sky clear, it flows a tranquil dark blue. The trees are green; the trees burn yellow and red and orange; the trees, gray and skeletal, huddle against the cold. The sun shines, or else doesn't. Between Thanksgiving and Valentine's Day, I drive to work in the dark, and return home in the dark. During summer, by contrast, I often go to bed when it's still light out, while Claire sits on the front steps drinking cranberry juice and club soda, watching that skyline about which she can't seem to decide how she feels.

For the last three years, Claire has been employed at a nearby Tim's Club. Each morning she puts on one of several electric blue Tim's Club vests in her possession and drives the Dodge van six miles to work. Her areas of responsibility are the books and clothing sections. One day it's soft-core-porn novels and celebrity memoirs; the next, great stacks of denim, mounds of irregular T-shirts, Everests of tube sock multi-packs. Sometimes, to ward off boredom and repetitive motion injury, she dons a hair net and electric blue apron and offers passing customers bits of Heluva Good cheese or Poppies mini cream puffs. As she has no interest in ascending the Tim's Club career ladder, she has turned down multiple offers of commission as a shift leader. She packs a lunch each day, the centerpiece of which is always a tuna salad sandwich. On occasion she drives a forklift, though doing so is not part of her job duties. In the afternoon, she, like I, drives back across the river, weaves her way through the civil engineer's nightmare known as suburban Toledo, and parks under our carport.

From time to time it occurs to me to wonder aloud if Claire really is happy living such an unremarkable existence, when just a few short years ago she was of the rigid belief that it was better to be dead than anonymous.

She always responds the same way.

"Adventure? Excitement?" she says. "A

Jedi craves not these things."

Though her words indicate humor, her eyes indicate otherwise. And I am left with no clearer sense of whether, in her heart of hearts, perhaps in a place hidden even from herself, she wants more than the taupe house, the blue vests, the late summer sunsets over Toledo.

I suppose this life, dull though it may be, provides Claire some consolations. She rarely rises with a headache anymore, and when she does can take comfort in the fact that she's blameless in the matter. We do the Saturday crossword together. We sit side by side in darkened theaters and take in films with our forearms touching on the armrest, our hands mingling in the popcorn tub. We have plenty of money, owing to residuals from the first and only season of our television show, which continues to do remarkably well in overseas markets where both disposable income and television ownership are on the rise. Claire has also, in her sobriety, taken up smoking, which seems to have mitigated the loss of alcohol somewhat.

She has been guided in this new habit by the steady and nicotine-yellowed hand of my mother-in-law, Peggy, whom Claire visits four or five times per annum.

I am rarely invited on these trips. I stay behind, most often, and take care of the cat.

Though in reality of course the cat requires very little actual care.

I read recently that most domestic cats have at least two households in which people believe they own the cat exclusively. The cats oscillate between these households like philandering husbands. So presumably if one of those households were suddenly unoccupied, the cat would simply get everything it needed from the other. Or else just wander onto another porch at random, pretending to be a stray, and get taken in by yet another family eager to be duped into the illusion of cat ownership.

So yes, Claire and I, in our government-shielded domesticity, are now co-owners of not just a nondescript house, two used vehicles, and a new swimming pool, but also of Meowser, the cat I used to own with Sarah, the cat that has grown quite old by cat standards, the cat whose real name is seemingly forevermore lost to me.

Of course, it's not the cat's name that is lost to me, but rather that the me who knows the cat's name is lost to me.

In the same way that my first wife is not dead, so much as *unavailable.*

Perhaps it is for the better that I can't

remember the name Sarah gave the cat.

Perhaps it is, all of it, for the better.

Who am I to say? What do I know?

Five things, give or take. None of which sheds any light on the issue of the cat's real name, what it means to know it, what it means not to.

If there's anything I can be said to have learned in all this, the wisdom in limiting idle thought is probably it.

And also that Claire was correct when she said that certainty is a myth only children and Republicans ever truly believe in.

I guide the Fiesta home one crystalline and jungle-hot early evening in July to find the Dodge van in the carport, even though as far as I knew Claire took on evening forklift work beyond her regular shift, and so is not supposed to be home for another two hours.

Experience has taught us that only one of our vehicles can really fit in the carport at a given time. The left side of the Fiesta and the right side of the van bear testament to this fact, in the form of numerous dings and slashes of gray paint from the carport's front support poles. So I park in the driveway and get out, briefcase in hand, jacket draped over my shoulder, the armpits of my oxford dark with sweat. I am curious about Claire's presence, but not alarmed, so instead of rushing inside I pause at the back of the Fiesta to watch the McAleer boy, Larry, who lives directly across the street, as he pilots a large RC plane back and forth over the neighborhood like an attack aircraft on strafing runs.

The plane dips and rises, following the contours of the gable rooftops, then performs a crisp barrel roll as it streaks overhead. The wings flash in the sun, and Larry and I pivot on our heels and follow the plane's trajectory out toward the high-tension wires that run parallel to 280.

Even though I'm standing right next to him, I'm not sure Larry has yet registered my presence.

"You want to fly planes when you grow up?" I ask.

He answers without looking at me. "I fly planes now," he says. "As you can see."

"What I mean is, do you want to be a pilot?" I say. "As in, actually get into a plane? Slip the surly bonds? Feel the weightlessness of negative Gs, and the extraterrestrial crush of multiple Gs? Perhaps be responsible for the lives of hundreds on a daily basis as a commercial airline captain?"

Larry continues to peer out to where his plane traces a long, menacing turn back in our direction. "No," he says.

"So this is just a hobby, then," I say.

"A hobby is something people do for fun," Larry says. "This is not fun. I don't enjoy standing in the middle of this stupid cul-de-sac. I don't enjoy living in this stupid cul-de-sac. I disapprove of the existence of this stupid cul-de-sac."

"I'm a little confused, I guess," I tell Larry.

He heaves a sigh loud enough to be heard three doors down. "I'm going to fly drones," he says.

"Drones?" I ask.

The plane cruises overhead again — a mammoth dragonfly from either the distant past or the distant future — and resumes faux-strafing the rooftops.

"Drones," Larry says. "I've been preparing for it my whole life. I play video games for hours in my bedroom with the lights off, killing people all over the world. What do you think the difference is between that and a climate-controlled booth in Nevada, where you sit for hours in a flight suit shooting Hellfire missiles at people on a screen?"

"I would think the principal difference, in the latter scenario, is that the figures on the screen are actual people."

"Wrong," Larry says. "The difference is, right now I don't have a flight suit."

The plane buzzes us again, and again we rotate to watch it streak away.

"I got my first recruitment letter when I was ten," Larry says.

"They recruit for this sort of thing now?" I ask.

"Sure. It's bigger than college football. Chat rooms and gaming tournaments are filthy with military talent scouts."

"I see. And so they take the best gamers and turn them into drone pilots?"

"Not pilots. We're called *drivers*," Larry says. "And no, not just the best gamers. There's a lot more to it. All kinds of tests, psychological profiles. Joystick skills can be taught. A certain moral flexibility, on the other hand . . . well, either you've got it, or you don't."

"And you've got it?"

"I'm a blue chip," Larry says. "Guaranteed commission as a second lieutenant, right out of high school. Sky's the limit. Pardon the pun."

"How does your father feel about this?"

"My father's job is to fuck people over on a daily basis," Larry says. "He's cool with it."

Larry's father, if I remember correctly, is an investment banker.

The plane cruises overhead again, executes

487

a smart left turn, and speeds straight for the steeple of the U.U. church, an alabaster spike half a mile due north of where we stand.

"Good talking to you, Larry," I say.

Larry flashes a peace sign over one shoulder. I turn and walk toward the taupe house.

There's no sign of Claire inside, so I drop my things on the kitchen table and go to the back porch, where I find her sitting on the steps. In the distance, Toledo's skyline is like a game of Tetris that ended almost before it began. A Miller High Life gathers condensation beside Claire's left hip.

"No forklift work after all?" I ask, trying to sound casual despite the presence of the beer and all it could imply.

"I put a Clearly Canadian in the fridge," she says without turning to face me. "Should be cold by now."

I hesitate, think a moment, check my mental calendar. "It's not Sarah's birthday," I say.

"No. It is, however, a special occasion." She holds the beer up. "As you can see."

I go back into the kitchen and find the bottle of Clearly Canadian in the refrigerator. On the counter there's a lime-green beer koozie that reads THE BEST PARTY IS A WEDDING PARTY! MIKE AND SARAH, SAR-

ATOGA SPRINGS, 2002. I have no idea who Mike and Sarah are, and no idea whether I'm supposed to. I slip the koozie over the bottle and return to the porch, where Claire has stretched her legs across the top step with her back resting against the railing. A cigarette burns between the index and middle fingers of her right hand.

"Mind if I sit?" I ask.

"Of course not."

I step over her and sit down. She drapes her free hand over my shoulder.

"So you're home early," I say.

"There's something I've been wanting to get off my chest," Claire says.

"Okay," I say.

"I didn't get fired from Total Foods because of you," she says.

"Okay," I say.

Larry's plane appears above us, performs a Split-S with airshow precision over the backyard, then disappears again in the direction from which it came.

"What the hell was that?" Claire says.

"The McAleer boy, across the street," I tell her.

"The creepy little ginger with the pet snake?"

"That's the one," I say. "He wants to fly

489

drones for the government when he gets older."

"Perfect job for him."

"Apparently the government agrees," I say.

Claire drags on her cigarette. "Aren't you even a little bit curious why I actually got fired from Total Foods?"

"I am," I tell her. "Just figured I'd let you come out with it in your own time."

"You can probably guess," she says.

"You know I don't like to speculate anymore."

"They fired me because I was drunk half the time, and hung-over the other half."

"Stands to reason."

There's a pause.

"You're not upset?"

I think for a moment. "It's not exactly a surprise," I say. "My only concern is the possibility that this might not be all you've lied to me about."

"It is," Claire says. "Scout's honor."

"I'm glad to hear that," I say. "I guess what I'm really wondering is why you're drinking now."

"Bad day at work," she says.

"What happened?"

"You wouldn't believe me if I told you."

"I'd believe anything you told me," I say.

"Even though you know I lied before?"

"You lied," I say, "because you wanted an excuse to get close to me. That's about as bleached white as lies come, I guess."

It's a simple enough statement, but in its wake I sense the air around us ionize, charged with the sudden expulsion of long-pent shame. Claire sniffles, kneads the muscle between my shoulder and neck with her hand.

"Customer got crushed to death," she says after she composes herself. "A pallet fell on him. Eight hundred pounds of OxiClean. One of the forklift guys fucked up big."

This is not what I expected to hear. I have no idea what to say about it, so I take a drink of Clearly Canadian Orchard Peach. It tastes like peach in the same way Pine-Sol smells like pine.

"I didn't see it happen," Claire says. "But I saw after."

"I'm really sorry, Claire."

She drinks from her beer, grimaces. "This stuff is shit," she says. "I can't believe there was ever a time when I liked it so much."

"It's not great when it gets warm," I say.

"It's not great, period," Claire says.

We're quiet for a few moments. Larry's plane buzzes in the distance. Two squirrels bound across the lawn, pause to cock their heads, flick their tails, sniff the wind for threats.

"There's a darkness on me, K.," Claire says. "I realize that sounds silly, but I don't know how else to put it. It's like I've been wearing a black sash for the last four years."

"I understand," I say.

"Do you?"

"I think so," I say.

"I'm not sure how much more I can take," Claire says.

"What can I do?" I ask.

She is silent.

"Do you need to talk to someone?" I ask.

"This will not yield to therapy, K.," Claire says. "I am sick to my soul, here."

"Tell me what to do," I say, "and I will do it."

"The guy was a smear on the concrete," Claire says. "All that was left when they hauled the pallet off him was a stain. A *stain*, K."

"That's terrible," I say.

"People went right on shopping. Barely missed a beat," she says. "At first I was appalled. But now I think maybe that's the only reasonable reaction to something like this. Just keep on taking advantage of those exceptional wholesale values. Grab an extra twenty-pound bag of wing dings, just in case."

"Just in case what?"

"The next pallet has your name on it."

Larry's plane appears overhead once again. At the same time, a cloud glides across the sun. The squirrels, clucking and squawking, scrabble up and over the fence into the neighboring yard. A chill rams through me, head to sole, despite the heat. I know what's coming next, though neither of us has ever once mentioned or even alluded to it before now.

"We, K. — you and me — are responsible for two hundred and forty-eight deaths," Claire says. "Three people will spend the rest of their lives in a vegetative state because of us. Another thirteen are maimed, some of them so badly that they hardly resemble human beings anymore."

I could, of course, argue the fine points. I could rightly argue that responsibility for all that death and dismemberment belongs to a much wider swath of humanity than is present on our back porch at the moment. Our abductors, for example. Or Sheriff Frank, who allowed an apocalyptic malignancy to fester under his watch. Every last member of Cold Dead Fingers, wholly complicit even if they lacked understanding of how they were being used, or for what purpose. The FBI, with their Operation Overlord response. Trumbull, of course, who conjured all that destruction, planned it for years, tended death like a farmer in his field, patient and deliberate, happy to wait for the bumper crop. And then, further expanding the sphere of responsibility beyond those on the ground: politicians and talking heads, entertainers masquerading as newsmen, charlatans and outrage profiteers everywhere. All of them, and others, bought shares in the carnage of that day.

I could cite these guilty parties, spread the blame thin as parchment. But that would completely miss the point.

"Yes," I say to Claire. "We are responsible."

The rogue cloud slides away, and the sun flares so bright against the grass that I squint involuntarily. Claire shakes a fresh cigarette out of her pack.

"The question," I say, "is can you live with it?"

"Can you?"

"I have yet to find a circumstance that I can't ultimately live with," I say. "I imagine if it were going to happen, it would have by now."

"I'm sure that's true," Claire says quietly.

"I hope you can find a way to not resent me for that," I say.

Claire blows jets of smoke from her nostrils. "It's not resentment," she says. "It's envy. With a dash of awe."

"I'm not sure awe is indicated, either."

"It's also why I'm leaving," Claire says.

As we've established, time is relative. This is true in both a strict physical sense, and also, as anyone can tell you, in the way that we perceive the passage of time, particularly during traumatic or dangerous events. The texting driver looks up to see he's crossed the center line and is about to collide head-on with a pickup truck; though the vehicles are only fifty feet apart and traveling at a combined speed of 140 miles per hour, it seems, to the driver's mind, to take at least seven or eight seconds for the impact to occur, a span during which he has all too much opportunity for regret, terror, even self-recrimination. Or: a woman is cutting zucchini at her kitchen counter. She is a practiced knife wielder, having worked in professional kitchens her entire adult life, and experience has made her careless. As the knife rises and falls in rapid staccato, the tip of her left thumb slides underneath it; she notices this too late to avert the accident, as the blade is already coming down again, but she has plenty of opportunity for her eyes to go wide with horror, for her mind to anticipate the slice, the blood, the pink nub of flesh that will remain on the countertop when she rushes to the bathroom, right hand clutching left wrist, to find the first aid kit.

This same phenomenon is often mimicked in film, when lazy or untalented directors use slow motion as shorthand for the sense, in the moments preceding disaster, that time has stretched out like a strand of bubble gum.

And this is this phenomenon that enables me, in the second or two after Claire voices her intention to leave, to ruminate about car crashes, severed digits, and rote film-making.

That goddamn plane again, cheerfully showing off overhead: barrel roll into a steep, sun-glinting climb.

"I don't know what to say," I tell Claire.

"Say you understand," Claire says.

"But I don't."

"Say it anyway."

"I'd be lying."

"So lie to me."

"This could very quickly make me crazy," I say.

"Then you'll know how I feel."

"What, exactly, is making you crazy?" I ask.

"Every day that I wake up next to you," Claire says, "I smell burned blood. It's like a pork roast left in the oven too long. I get in the shower with the smell in my nostrils. I smell it in my coffee cup. I smell it in the van, in the break room at work. It drifts up as I fold the shirts and jeans. And let me tell you, I can't go anywhere near the meat counter."

"So maybe a new job is the thing," I say.

She gives me a scolding look, though she must know I'm not joking in the least. "Have you ever wondered," she asks, "why I eat a tuna sandwich for lunch every single day?"

I shake my head.

"Because it doesn't matter what I eat. Everything tastes the way everything smells."

I say nothing.

Claire stubs the cigarette out in the ashtray and gets to her feet. I follow her into the kitchen, down the hallway, and up the staircase to our bedroom, where her two-piece luggage set — one wheeled upright, one wheeled duffel — is packed to bursting on the floor in front of the dresser.

"I can take the van, or the Fiesta," she

says. "Which would you prefer?"

"You usually drive the van," I say.

"Which has never made sense," she says. "You're six-three and pack yourself into that tiny car every day, and I'm five-two and almost need to sit on a phone book to see over the van's dash."

"So this is more about your preference, then," I say.

She gazes at me. "It's about what's logical, K.," she says.

"But what if I say I want to keep the Fiesta?"

"I'd say that seems more like bitterness than preference."

"Regardless."

Claire grabs the handles of her luggage. "Please don't make this harder than it has to be," she says, wheeling the bags around me and out into the hallway.

"Let me help you with those, at least," I say.

She stops at the landing, glances back over her shoulder, and steps aside to let me hoist the larger of the two bags. We clomp down the stairs and out the front door into the driveway. Larry still stands in the middle of the cul-de-sac, peering skyward.

I pop the hatchback on the Fiesta, push aside a snow brush and half a jug of windshield wiper fluid, and swing Claire's duffel into the cargo space.

"Where will you go?" I ask her.

"Peggy's, for starters," she says. "After that, I don't yet know."

I hoist the upright roller and place it on top of the duffel. "You really think this will make you feel better?"

Claire jams her hands in the pockets of her jeans and looks off over the rooftops toward the western horizon. "I have no idea, K.," she says. "I just know if I stay here with you I'm not going to make it."

"Well if you're certain of that," I say.

"I am," she says.

We're quiet for a moment, listening to the drone of Larry's plane.

"This is so strange," I say. "Fifteen minutes ago I was thinking about what we might do for dinner."

"It's all so strange," Claire says. She holds her hand out. "From the first breath to the last. Can I get those keys?"

The skin beneath her bottom lip bunches. Her eyes implore me to hurry.

I hand the key ring over. Claire gets in the Fiesta, backs out of the driveway, and takes off at a much higher rate of speed than the neighborhood association–mandated twenty miles per hour.

"She going on a trip?" Larry calls across the cul-de-sac.

"Mind your own business, Larry," I say, and go back inside.

It is quite late, and I am required, by both contract and custom, to drive across the river by dawn's early light, park in the municipal lot, sit down at my particleboard desk under the soft fluorescents, and dedicate a certain percentage of my day to this, a different percentage to that, until all of the day is used up.

Instead of retiring to bed, though, I am sitting in my lounge chair rereading the Einstein biography given to me by my physicist friend. And I am taking in things about Einstein that I did not, in my excitement over relativity, notice or remember from the first time I read the book.

For instance: Einstein had two wives, Mileva and Elsa, both of whom he outlived.

There is evidence that he was not particularly kind to either of them, or really anyone in his family.

Consider, for example, the strong possibility that Einstein forced Mileva to surrender their first child, a baby girl, for adoption.

Or that later, when their marriage had curdled, Einstein wrote Mileva a list of conditions upon which he would agree to stay with her, including a stern insistence that she not ask for or expect intimacy of any kind.

Or that Einstein's elder son, Hans, said, in reference to his father's renowned dedication to his work, "Probably the only project he ever gave up on was me."

Even I am shocked by the cruelty. I sit here stunned, as if ambushed by a custard pie to the face. And like someone who has been ambushed with a custard pie to the face, I feel my shock give way to a rapidly rising swell of anger.

I set the Einstein biography aside, rise from my chair, and go about the house, room to room, smashing things like a poltergeist.

Dishware, plant pots, Mason jars, picture frames, electronic devices both high- and low-tech — everything is reduced to bits. The less-sturdy furniture I rend with my hands. For the hardier items — bed frame, dressers, china cabinet — I employ the ax we keep in the basement for splitting firewood. When everything in a given room is broken, I take the ax to the walls, cleaving plaster, gypsum board, wood paneling. I swing and sweat and curse. I put the ax aside for a moment and break a floor lamp over my knee, which in seconds develops a contusion like a waterskin. I hoist the ax again and limp into the bedroom and catch a glimpse of myself in the full-length mirror: wild-eyed, impotent, confused beyond language. Not caring for what I see, I smash my forehead into the mirror. The glass spiderwebs but remains intact. I step back and look at the kaleidoscope I've created, a dozen bent and misshapen versions of me, each with a fresh rose of blood unfurling above his eyes. I stare at myselves, shoulders rising and falling as I breathe. Then I hoist the ax, spin twice on my heels, and swing the poll as hard as I can into the mirror, which disintegrates as the ax head lodges deep in the wall behind it.

I stop to catch my breath and call Claire. While the phone rings I realize if she has driven without pause she should just be crossing the state line between the Virginias. The phone rings and rings, and eventually I get the familiar recording of Claire's voice, offering the option to leave a message and telling me she may or may not care if I do so.

The possibilities: One, she is driving and did not notice her phone ring. Two, she noticed her phone ring but chose not to answer. Three, she crashed into a ditch on the side of some country highway and is sitting there bloodied and unconscious, while the Fiesta's hazards strobe an inky Appalachian night.

I dial Peggy's number. She picks up before the second ring, as though she's been expecting a call.

"Where are you?" she asks without greeting or preamble.

"I'm home, in Toledo," I tell her.

"K.," she says.

"Yes," I say. "Obviously Claire hasn't arrived yet."

"Not yet," Peggy says. I hear her drag on a Winston, exhale magnificently.

"Do you know if she's alright?"

"I haven't heard from her since she left," Peggy says. "But I'm sure she's fine."

"Why is she doing this? What has she told you?"

"Probably nothing she hasn't already told you," Peggy says.

"Send her home, Peggy," I say. "When she gets there, tell her to come home. She'll listen to you."

"Honey, you didn't listen to me," Peggy says. "So what makes you think she would?"

I drop the phone on the floor and stomp it, over and over, ignoring the pain in my injured knee until what used to be a state-of-the-art pocket computer is in a condition that could best be described as minced.

Then I hoist the ax again.

If I had the skills and the equipment I would break everything down into quarks, and not in the detached systematic manner of a laboratory, but with the violence of a nuclear weapon or particle collider. A cliché of masculinity, I know. Build and destroy. The two imperatives printed on my Y chromosome. But I am only as God made me, so I rage and rage, though I'm smart enough, this time, to keep my anger from spilling into the yard and inviting the attention and censure of our neighborhood watch program.

When the doorbell rings I have little idea what time it is and no way to find out, having broken all the clocks in the house.

I open the front door and find Larry standing there, dressed in the same paint-flecked cargo shorts and orange polo he wore earlier. He gazes at me plainly, as though he either doesn't notice the ax in my hand, or doesn't find it alarming in the least. A mosquito hovers between us, glowing like a faerie in the light from the bulb overhead.

"Looks like you're having a time in there," Larry says.

"You've been watching me?" I ask.

"Last twenty minutes or so," he says.

The mosquito drifts and drifts.

"You may want to step back a minute," I say.

"Why?"

I grip the ax and thrust it straight up at the porch light. Both the bulb and the fixture explode, baptizing us in glass shards and argon.

"Come on in, Larry," I say, turning to go back inside.

There's no furniture left intact, so we stand in the remains of the kitchen. Milk and cranberry juice mingle in a puddle on the tile. The refrigerator door rests on a jumble of kindling that was, until recently, the dining table. The air smells like sweat and miso and citrus. I set the ax on its head and lean the handle against the wall.

"I'd offer you something to drink," I say. "But."

"Why'd she leave?" Larry asks, brushing bits of glass from his hair.

"I can't really talk about that," I say.

"Because it's none of my business?"

"Because I'm not supposed to mention the past," I say. "You aren't the only one who has dealings with the government."

Larry looks around, taking in the devastation. "Everyone knows who you are," he says. "They just don't talk about it."

"Why not?" I ask.

"Because they're polite cul-de-sac people."

I nudge a ceramic olive oil cruet, somehow spared in my rampage, off the countertop. It hits the floor but does not break. "Then tell me, Larry," I say, "do you think I'm responsible for what happened in Texas?"

"I was, like, eleven when it went down," Larry says. "I barely remember."

I lift the ax with one hand and drop the head on the cruet. It cracks into several large pieces and disgorges its contents in thick, creeping rivulets. "Even still," I say.

Larry thinks for a moment. "We all court our own fate," he says finally.

"By which you mean?"

"Well look. If I see someone planting a roadside bomb, I'm going to blow him away. But I'm not responsible for his death. He is."

"Go on," I say.

"I didn't put him in a ditch with a hot-wired artillery shell in his hand. He made that choice."

"That's valid. Simplistic, but valid."

"How is it simplistic?"

"There are a lot of theoretical influences on our theoretical bomber. Poverty. Lack of education. Religious dogma. The lingering effects of colonialism."

Larry stares at me. "You people always make things more complicated than they are. It's like some weird mental illness."

"Which people?" I ask.

"Liberals," he says.

"I'm not a liberal."

"Let me simplify it for you," Larry says. "Man trying to kill you. Kill man first, if you can. The end."

"But that's his exact perspective, too."

"And around and around we go."

"Nice that you've got it all figured out," I say.

"Listen," Larry says, "with regard to your particular question: FBI tactical teams implicitly accept the possibility of dying that comes with the job. Right-wing loons implicitly accept that poking the bear comes with better-than-even odds the bear will poke back."

"Claire would disagree with you. She thinks it's all on us."

"She doesn't think that," Larry says. "She feels that. There's a difference."

"Okay," I say. "But what can I do about it?"

"Intergender relations are not my forte."

"You've never had a girlfriend."

"I'm gay."

"So you've never had a girlfriend."

He smirks.

I crouch in front of the doorless refrigerator and dig around in Parmesan cheese and smashed cantaloupe until I find two bottles of High Life. I rinse these under the tap and hand one to Larry.

"You know I'm only fifteen?" he asks.

"You're a mature fifteen," I say.

"That's what Humbert said about Lolita."

"She was twelve. And don't flatter yourself, Larry."

He shrugs and twists the cap.

I slide down and sit on the floor among the juices and honey and shattered things, letting my injured leg stretch out in front of me. Larry swigs from his beer and makes a face. That scrunched-up look of distaste may presage a lifelong abhorrence of alcohol, or it may indicate, paradoxically, that this is the thing his amygdala has been waiting for unawares, the biochemical puzzle piece that fits just so with his neurological reward system. He may end up a vehement teetotaler, or he may be found dead at thirty-five with more booze than blood in his veins. It's impossible to know.

For a while we observe an agreeable silence.

"The other day," I say eventually, "I went to Market on the Mount. You know the place?"

"The hippie food store. On Riley Hill."

"That's the one," I said. "So I park the car and walk up to the entrance. It's a set of double doors. And the door on the right has a sign that reads PLEASE USE OTHER DOOR TEMPORARILY."

I look up at Larry. He meets my gaze, holds it for a moment, then raises his eyebrows as though he knows I'm fishing for a response but has no idea what I expect him to say.

"How on Earth do you use a door temporarily?" I ask. "Tell me, Larry. Help me out here. I need to know."

"Well there's what the sign says, and then there's what it actually means. It's not that tough to understand. They just made a syntactical goof."

I hoist my beer and toss it across the kitchen. It smashes against the far wall, leaving a Rorschach of fluid and foam on the plasterboard.

"Everything is an utter mystery," I say. "Listen, I studied Kant in college, passed with a solid B-plus. This morning everything was fine. Now my wife is gone. And I don't understand why."

Larry takes another drink of beer. "She'll be back," he says.

"How do you know that?"

"Because what she's trying to get away from can't be outrun. In twelve-step programs they call it a geographic cure. Never works."

"It's not exactly a comfort to me," I say, "to know that she'll always be tormented."

"Well, anyway."

"Should I ask where your knowledge of twelve-step programs comes from?"

"My father's been sober four years."

"Good for him."

"Not really," Larry says. "It made him nasty. He's got nothing to help him relax now, except treating people poorly."

"Well, I guess I'm sorry about that, too."

"Hardly your fault," Larry says. He leans over and holds his half-finished beer out to me. "You want this one? I'm not really developing a taste for it."

I take the bottle from his hand and toss it against the wall. More glass, more suds, more dribbles of beer flowing floorward. The eggshell paint begins to bubble in spots.

"So what are you going to do once everything's broken?" Larry asks.

"Haven't really thought that far ahead," I say.

"Do you know where she went?"

"Yes."

"Then go get her."

"It doesn't really work that way among adults, Larry."

"Then how does it work? Among adults?"

"Well, one adult expresses a desire to be left alone, and the other adult honors that desire. Or gets slapped with a restraining order."

Larry thinks about this. "Okay," he says, "since you don't understand anything, I'm going to go ahead and explain something for you."

"Alright."

"You've destroyed your house."

"To an extent."

"Made it unlivable."

"By most people's standards, certainly."

"In other words, you've given yourself no choice but to leave."

"One could argue."

"That is not an accident," Larry says. "The question is, why can't you just be honest with yourself, pack a bag, and follow her wherever she's gone?"

From where I'm sitting I have a view of the sky outside the kitchen window, just beginning to brighten from black to slate.

"The way I see it," Larry says, "there are

very few things that we can't do anything about. My mother's dead. Nothing to be done there. But your wife . . . what's her name?"

"Claire."

"Claire is not dead."

"No."

"You should remember that."

Claire is not dead, and yet unless she returns there will be no release from this grief. I will never leave this place. The one thing I have learned is I have learned nothing. The moment I pulled the Desert Eagle from my waistband, and every moment that preceded it, are indelible, everlasting, and so too, therefore, is Claire's sorrow. These are all notions that Larry, precocious as he is, cannot grasp. So I don't try to articulate them. Instead, I begin to cry for the first time since the bunker in Texas. Great seismic sobs, a display for which Larry seems ill-equipped. His eyes go wide, then are dragged to the floor by the gravity of embarrassment. He nearly pants with relief when I compose myself enough to tell him I have to prepare for work, that the very first light is the time when I bathe and put on my unremarkable wool suit and drink coffee and drive across the river and do my job, and that being the case, it's been nice talking to him but he should probably head home.

The shower door rests in hundreds of jagged pebbles on the floor of the bathtub, as hostile to my feet as a bed of razor clams. I lay a towel over the shards, step in gingerly, and lather myself under the spray. I'm forced to shave blind, owing to the fact that I destroyed the medicine cabinet mirror. I dress by twilight, and later, downstairs in the kitchen, as I try to make instant coffee with hot water from the tap, the room brightens enough for me to realize I've put on a jacket from a gray suit, pants from a blue one.

Outside it's already midday-warm. The van groans to life and blows hot air through the vents even though the air conditioner is on. I back out of the carport and drive through mostly empty suburban streets with the windows down. When I stop at intersections the engine bogs and hacks, threatening to stall, and I reflect that Claire failed to tell me the van no longer runs that great. This omission seems significant, but as usual I can only speculate as to what that significance is.

I park the van in the municipal lot. I cross the street and enter the office with the warm fluorescents. People sit at identical desks with identical cardboard coffee cups. People stare into computer screens. People rub their eyes, pick at breakfast pastries. People talk into headsets.

Ours is a thoroughly modern life, so despite the fact that I've destroyed my phone there are ways for Claire to get in touch. She has my office number. She has my email addresses, both personal and business. There are no fewer than five social media websites through which she could contact me.

Colleagues drift in and out of my office throughout the day, and I address them with a steel-belted formality. "I've been meaning to consult with you regarding this matter," I tell them. "I'm afraid that issue has already been decided," I say. This stately diction is unusual even for me, but no one seems to notice. They nod their heads and scribble notes. They promise to get back to me, to check the numbers, to arrange a conference call. Nobody asks why I look so haggard. No one inquires about my limp, or mentions that I'm wearing a mismatched suit. In fact, when I'm not engaged in work-related conversation, it's as if I've suddenly been rendered invisible. I pass people in the hallway and they keep their eyes trained on their electronic devices. I have energy only to finish the coffee but not to start a new pot, yet no one complains.

I have ceased displacing air. I am a ghost.

And then, when the schoolhouse-style analog clock on the wall strikes five, I find out why. My coworkers burst into the office as one mass, bearing balloons, kazoos, party favors. They wear pointed hats and wide smiles. Two of them carry a massive cake impregnated with so many candles it's like a scale-model forest fire. Someone puts one of the pointed hats on my head, pulling the elastic-band strap under my chin. Others clear paperwork from my desk and replace it with the cake. Tiny paper plates and a clutch of plastic forks are deployed. Under the candles the cake bears a message, written in green frosting that is quickly becoming adulterated with hot wax: HAPPY 45TH, K!

I had forgotten it was my birthday, in part because of the trauma of Claire's departure, and in part because it's not really my birthday. This date was chosen, years ago, by some anonymous bureaucrat when I entered the foster care system as an infant. I needed a date of birth to be a full and legal person, at least as far as the state was concerned. It's been a useful marker for everything from job applications to the purchase of age-restricted goods, but it has certainly never held any celebratory significance for me. Claire and I never marked it, and neither did Sarah and I. The only reason my colleagues know is because the information can be found in my personnel file.

Everyone in my office sings "Happy Birthday," almost on key. I look into their faces; I can put names with roughly half of them. They seem to genuinely wish me well, these people. They must be so happy in their own lives, it strikes me, to be able to call up such generosity of spirit on demand.

The whole thing is very nearly unbearable, and I have to look down at the cake before I start crying again.

Make a wish, they tell me. They say this jokingly — after all, they are adults, rational members of a rational culture, and they have not believed wishing for something can make it so since they cut their last permanent teeth.

But I am game. I believe. I compose a wish, and hold the thought in my head long enough that it can be transmitted to whatever force is the arbiter in such matters. I am, in this moment, as deeply, hopefully irrational as any person has ever been. I believe in voodoo and black magic, mojo and cooties. I believe in luck, jinxes, angels, good and bad karma, the influence of planetary alignment on the minutiae of everyday human business. I believe the slaughter of goats and/or virgins is a useful tool for achieving one's goals. I believe in the power of my mind to manipulate the physical world, to turn the Fit around and bring Claire back to Ohio, to Toledo, to the cul-de-sac, to our home.

I inhale deeply and purse my lips.

Remember, my colleagues tell me as I lean forward in my chair: you have to blow them all out, or else your wish will never come true.

ABOUT THE AUTHOR

Ron Currie, Jr. was born and raised in Waterville, Maine, where he still lives. His first book, *God is Dead,* won the Young Lions Fiction Award from the New York Public Library and the Addison M. Metcalf Award from the American Academy of Arts and Letters. His debut novel, *Everything Matters!,* will be translated into a dozen languages, and is a July Indie Next Pick and Amazon Best of June 2009 selection.

His short fiction has appeared in many magazines and anthologies, including *Alaska Quarterly Review, The Sun, Ninth Letter, Swink, The Southeast Review, Glimmer Train, Willow Springs, The Cincinnati Review, Harpur Palate,* and *New Sudden Fiction* (W.W. Norton, 2007).

The employees of Thorndike Press hope you have enjoyed this Large Print book. All our Thorndike, Wheeler, and Kennebec Large Print titles are designed for easy reading, and all our books are made to last. Other Thorndike Press Large Print books are available at your library, through selected bookstores, or directly from us.

For information about titles, please call:
  (800) 223-1244

or visit our website at:
  gale.com/thorndike

To share your comments, please write:
  Publisher
  Thorndike Press
  10 Water St., Suite 310
  Waterville, ME 04901